PRAISE FOR MEL

'Meticulously plotted and UTTER
you want from a contem
Paula Hawk

'McGrath excels in creating believably flawed characters,
and her masterful control of suspense and pacing make for
a psychological thriller that is both perceptive and disturbing'
Guardian

'Absorbing . . . McGrath asks: should it be a crime
to witness a violent event, and say nothing?'
The Times

'This well-crafted, chilling tale of guilt and
innocence has a compelling moral anchor'
Woman

'This roller-coaster read will have you hooked'
Closer

'Chilling, fiendishly plotted and surprising, this
stayed with me long after reading'
Woman & Home

'McGrath tackles hard-hitting issues in a thought-provoking
way . . . an interesting crossover between page-turning
thrillers and a book club novel ripe for discussion'
Adele Parks, *PLATINUM*

'Lots of twists and turns in this toxic thriller'
HELLO!

'A dextrously written thriller and examination of guilt and
innocence . . . [McGrath is] a diamond-hard talent'
Financial Times

'Clever, compassionate and completely compelling'
Erin Kelly

'I loved the claustrophobia . . . and seriously twisted characters'
Sarah Vaughan

Mel McGrath is an Essex girl, co-founder of the Killer Women writing collective, and an award-winning writer of fiction and non-fiction.

As M. J. McGrath she writes the acclaimed Edie Kiglatuk series of Arctic mysteries, which have been optioned for TV, were twice longlisted for the CWA Gold Dagger, and were *Times* and *Financial Times* thrillers of the year. As Melanie McGrath she wrote the critically acclaimed, bestselling memoir *Silvertown*. As Mel McGrath she is the author of the bestselling psychological thrillers *Give Me the Child*, *The Guilty Party* and *Two Wrongs*.

Also by Mel McGrath

Two Wrongs
The Guilty Party
Give Me the Child

TELL ME YOUR SECRETS

MEL McGRATH

HQ
An imprint of HarperCollins*Publishers* Ltd
1 London Bridge Street
London SE1 9GF

www.harpercollins.co.uk

HarperCollins*Publishers*
Macken House, 39/40 Mayor Street Upper,
Dublin 1, D01 C9W8, Ireland

This edition 2024

1
First published in Great Britain by
HQ, an imprint of HarperCollins*Publishers* Ltd 2023

ISBN: 9780008336929

This one's for Claire, Gemma and Kate, my beloved friends and fellow travellers on the long, rewarding and occasionally painful road to becoming proper psychotherapists.

I cannot grow
I have no shadow
To run away from
I only play . . .

('HYMN TO ST CECILIA' BY W. H. AUDEN)

PROLOGUE

She did not see what was coming. None of them did, not the little boy with the balloon, or his mother, nor even the girl herself. If she had spotted the blue vehicle bowling around the corner too fast, she might have had time to run back to her mother, she might have thrown herself to the ground and avoided it or waved at the driver or propelled herself forwards to the far side. Any of those things might have saved her. But the fact was that she did not see it because in that split second her attention and her mother's attention and the attention of the little boy and his mother was elsewhere. And perhaps the driver's attention was elsewhere too, though that will never be known by anyone but the person who was driving; no one on the ground was afterwards able to give a good description of either car or driver, the shock and horror of what they witnessed having shattered their recollections into sharp shards floating in a foggy dust. What *is* known is that in the split second before the impact, the driver must have been aware of what – or who – was in the road in front of them because they braked, hard, sending the car into a small skid before it came to a stop. Even now the girl's mother sometimes dreams of the puff of black smoke that rose from the tyres as they spun against the asphalt, and the fierce, raw stench of rubber. The last thought in her head before everything crackled and split continues to repeat itself in an endless loop: *please let that be me and not her.* A useless thought, as it turned out, since even as it came to mind, the girl's body was being tossed into the air as if she were a rag doll thrown by a toddler in a fit of temper. The mother did not remember that part. But it was described this way by a bystander, a retired teacher who happened to be on her way to a yoga class in the park that afternoon and was one of the witnesses called at the coroner's inquest. A rag doll, the woman observed about the girl, as if saying this in front of the girl's mother would somehow be of use or comfort when of course she was anything but a rag doll, a flesh and blood girl, a beloved daughter who had lost her life at the hands of the anonymous driver who probably wasn't paying attention.

In her terror, the blind panic, of getting to her daughter, the mother did not for one second imagine that she would never discover anything about this driver or their car; that the vehicle would roll on for a few metres before jerking forward and disappearing at speed around the bend, just as it did not occur to her that no one at the scene, not the boy or the boy's mother or the handful of others who witnessed the accident, would ever be able to come up with a consistent memory of the event when the questioning began later. Some said the car was light blue, others that it was silver, that the driver was a white middle-aged woman, a young man. The police said that the chances of being able to identify the man or woman or even the car were diminished by this, and by the fact that the accident had happened on one of the few stretches of road in the capital with poor CCTV coverage.

What the mother *does* remember is running, running. She remembers the look of fear on the face of the little boy and his mother who were clasped together in a frozen embrace on the other side of the road. She recalls thinking, *Take me, not her.* At last she remembers the girl's body, her darling daughter Lily, in the deep, silent privacy of her death.

ONE

More than anything they needed a new beginning. And so, on a cool day in September, they moved into the cottage on the edge of an ancient forest that stretched as far as the chalk escarpment of the Weald of Kent. There had been a house on the site overlooking Covert Wood since the time of the Domesday Book; first a wattle and daub shepherd's hut, then a timber-framed medieval yeoman's hall and followed, sometime in the 1710s, by a Queen Anne flint lodge. Each had burned down and the site was returning to nature when, not long after the agricultural riots of 1830, a local farmer, undeterred by the area's reputation for anarchy, put up the modest red brick farmhouse which Marc and Meg were about to call their home.

They would not have been able to afford Covert Cottage were it not for the fact that Jimmy had left it to Marc in his will. As a matter of fairness, Marc had planned to sell the place and split the proceeds with his sister, but Helen was keen that it remain in the family. She was in no hurry for the money, which, in any case, was only morally but not legally hers, so they'd agreed that Marc and Meg would spend a year or two doing it up, then, maybe, extend the mortgage or take in a lodger. As it was, the place was only just habitable, having lain empty in the months since Jimmy's death, and, despite the heat of the summer, succumbed to must and black mould.

Marc parked the couple's old Fiesta in the gravel driveway. They got out and filled their nostrils with the unfamiliar scents of moss and drying bracken, taking it all in, this ancient place, the solemn sense of embarking on a new journey, free to make fresh discoveries and to dream new dreams. She turned to him and they exchanged a smile.

Holding a cupped hand to his ear, Marc said, 'No traffic, no sirens, no planes.'

'Isn't it brilliant?' Meg replied.

With a chin flick towards the oak front door, Marc said, 'I'd offer to lift you over the threshold…'

'Oh God, please don't,' Meg said, amused. In the early days of their courtship, an acquaintance at a party had told them that a man should always carry his lover into their new home because this would protect them both from evil spirits. When they'd first moved into their scrappy East London rental flat, they'd joked about it and Marc had ironically lifted Meg over the threshold and promptly slipped a disc. They'd spent the rest of the day in casualty waiting to be seen by a doctor.

Now, they laughed at the memory. Meg reached into the back seat and handing over a couple of boxes, said, 'Carry these in and try not to end up in A&E.'

As she was busying herself unpacking the boot, a silver Peugeot slowed down in the lane beside the gate and a young woman with a tight bun leaned out and waved.

'Hi. I'm Lisa, I work in the shop.' She flicked her head in the direction of the village green. 'Welcome to Coldwater. Need any help?'

Meg smiled back. 'Thanks so much but we can't really do anything until the removals lorry arrives.'

'Oh, all right then. Be seeing you.' And with that Lisa waved and drove away.

Marc came up beside her. 'Who was that?'

'One of the villagers wanting to know if she could help with the move. I guess news travels fast in a place this size.' Something Meg was going to have to get used to.

They went in and while waiting for the removals lorry to arrive, Meg unpacked a few kitchen things while Marc built a fire in the living room from the empty cardboard boxes to chase the damp away. In the flicker of the flames, they sat cross-legged on the wide old oak floorboards and drank from the bottle of champagne they'd picked up at a motorway service station on the drive down from London, toasting new beginnings, until the crunch of gravel in the driveway alerted them to the arrival of the lorry.

At Meg's insistence, the removals men brought in the willow trunk before anything else. To leave it in the lorry for a moment longer than necessary felt unbearable. She had wanted to bring it with them in the car but it wouldn't fit in the boot and they couldn't manoeuvre it onto the back seat without blocking the rear window. Now she directed them to carry it carefully up the rickety staircase onto the upstairs landing while she went to fetch everyone a cup of tea.

A few chipped mugs left over from Jimmy's day sat in one of the cupboards in the kitchen and a furred kettle perched on the countertop beside an ancient microwave. In their rush to buy champagne at the service station, they'd forgotten to get any milk. Or biscuits for that matter. Meg could hear the male voices laughing. She picked up her purse and an old shopping bag wedged between the microwave and the wall and went outside. Marc was standing in the driveway beside the removals van, hands on hips, watching the men unload their bed.

'I'll get us some pasta for later.'

Marc, smiling, planted a kiss on her forehead and she took off across the gravel, turning left at the gate into The Lane, glad to have some time to herself. A short distance from the house, the road began to run alongside a narrow skein of fast-moving water. In the trees, birds called. This was how life would be from now on, the quiet calm of the scene so complete that it was difficult to imagine that fifty miles to the northwest lay a capital city of nine million whose streets teemed. All that was behind them now. Lily was behind them. The sense of that brought on a dizzy spell and she had to stop and take a deep breath. Janette, their therapist, had always counselled her not to dwell on what could have been, not to ruminate or refuse to live in the present and close her eyes to the future. *Keep facing forward.* And so she went on, one step in front of the other, until she was past the overhanging canopy of trees, rusty with autumn, to where the vista opened out to fields. At the side of the road lay a dead rabbit, the mouth open, yellow teeth caked in blood, the one visible eye staring blankly up. A neat, blackened bullet hole in its flank where a shotgun pellet had penetrated the flesh. In Meg's mind the blue car appeared then everything went red and for a moment she thought she might be sick. Janette's voice came into her head again and she raised her hands to her chest and began gently to tap her collar bones, crossed her elbows and rubbed her upper arms until the colours in her mind gradually faded away. Havening, Janette called it, one of the techniques that helped to dispel the memories. It was just a rabbit. It was sad to see it dead but they shot rabbits in the countryside and she'd better get used to it.

Proceeding along The Lane she crossed over the bridge and came to what passed for Coldwater's village green, once a common but now diminished to a patch of grass with a bench on one side and a war memorial on the other, below which sat a stone watering trough. This was home now. The medieval church at the end of a gated pathway would be the place they went for Christmas carols. If they ever had another child, he or she might be christened here. On a whim Meg pushed open the gate and going up the path and through the heavy oak door found herself in the cool quiet of the flint and stone interior. There was a noticeboard with a reminder about a movie night and the next parish council meeting.

Beside the nave a woman was removing dead flowers from a vase. She did not turn to see who had entered. Meg stepped backwards, intending not to intrude any further, and as she did so her eye was drawn to a mural of skeletons and naked human bodies. There was something bullying about it, as if the painter had been under some compulsion to broadcast his view of life as brutal and pointless to the captive audience of the congregation.

A voice said, 'The Last Judgement. Fifteenth century.'

Meg swung round. The woman who had been dealing with the flowers was smiling directly at her.

'They call them Doom paintings.'

'Oh.' Meg felt herself taking a step backwards and then another, keen not to offend but anxious to get back out into the light.

The woman, sensing this, said, 'Not to everyone's taste. But do come back any time.'

Outside, she had to take a deep breath to quell the drumming of her heart. The creepiness of the mural, the way the woman volunteered detail that she, Meg, hadn't asked for and then invited her to return. For what? *No thanks.*

The wind had picked up, blowing the first of the season's dead leaves along the paving towards the large yew at the gate. There was an old yew, too, in the garden at Covert Cottage. Symbols of death, but also, she reminded herself, of resurrection. This was why they had come to Coldwater after all. To be born again into a new life.

In any case, they were likely to spend more time in the village pub than the church. The Palterer's Arms sat on the common, overlooking the war memorial. It, too, bore the marks of age but was handsome where the church was merely impressive. This would be their local, the place they came when they wanted to be in easy company or didn't fancy cooking. The village store was a couple of doors down from the pub, a red letterbox inset into its brickwork, a dull green sign hanging outside. An old-fashioned bell rang as she stepped inside. Behind the counter stood the young woman who had been driving the silver Peugeot.

'Lisa! You were kind enough to stop and offer to help us move in. I'm Meg.'

The young woman looked at her blankly at first then with growing recognition.

'Oh of course. In a world of my own for a minute there. Can do that to you, working in this place.'

Smiling in lieu of a response, Meg swept an eye around the shop, keen to get the food and leave. There would be time for conversation another day.

'You must be busy,' Lisa said. 'They say Jimmy left the place in a bit of a mess.'

'A bit.' She had no idea who 'they' were but it didn't seem to matter. In London you could live next door to someone for decades and know almost nothing about them. But here, she imagined, nothing would remain private for long.

'The daughter used to come in here quite a bit. Helen, is it?' Lisa went on. 'I don't remember seeing your husband much, but I've only worked here a couple of years, so...'

Meg met Lisa's tone with an apologetic smile. 'Well, I'm pleased to say you'll be seeing a lot more of us both.'

She finished her shopping and walked back along The Lane. The rabbit was gone now and the unsettling atmosphere of the church had left her. As she turned into the driveway to the cottage her eye fell on a single pale pink rose lying beside the gate. She picked it up and took in the heavy perfume. A welcome gift? And if so, who from? The removals men were standing beside the lorry taking a break and as she approached ceased their chatter. She asked if Marc was inside and was told that he was. They hadn't seen anyone drop off any flower. Going directly to the kitchen, she filled a glass of water for the bloom, then filled the kettle and while waiting for it to boil, unpacked her shopping and dropped a tea bag in each of the mugs. She was spooning in the sugar when she heard a voice raised in anger, and recognising it immediately as Marc's, she abandoned her tea-making, went out into the hallway and stood for a moment, trying to locate the sound. Peering up the stairs she saw Marc standing on the first-floor landing with his arms crossed and a thunderous expression on his face. Beside him stood a pale, lanky man she didn't know. Marc glanced at her but said nothing, his body stiff as a brush, spittle gathered at the corners of his lips.

As she made her way upstairs she saw the upturned willow trunk, a couple of children's books, Lily's pink cardigan, her Mini Me doll and a card that Marc and Meg had given her on her last ever birthday strewn across the dusty floorboards.

'What happened?'

'I was only trying to help.' The pale man raised his palms in a defensive gesture. At this Marc seemed to rise up. For a moment Meg thought he might be about to punch the guy. When she reached out for him, he started and stepped back, his eyes fixed on the ceiling, a ball of shame. He'd been like this since Lily died. Unpredictable, subject to flare-ups.

Addressing the pale man she introduced herself. 'I know this stuff doesn't look like much, but it's...' She wanted to say *it's all we have left of our daughter.* '...it's of sentimental value.' She bent down to pick up the tiny pink cardigan from the mess on the floor. 'We're both a bit stressed.'

The man softened. His name was Steve Savage, used to do odd jobs 'for the old man', by which, Meg assumed, he meant Jimmy. He'd dropped by to see if he could be useful and now he wished he hadn't bothered.

They stood in awkward silence for a moment, Steve's eyes fixed on Marc.

'I apologise,' Meg said, irritated by Marc's intransigence.

Steve nodded but did not leave. There wasn't time for this. Why couldn't Marc just say sorry so they could all move on? It occurred to her then that Steve was expecting to be paid. She fished in her pocket and drew the four twenty-pound notes she'd kept as a tip for the removals men.

'I hope that's enough for your trouble,' Meg said. Marc glared at her. Eighty pounds was far too much for the botched job but a small price to pay to keep the peace. Steve reached out his right hand, took the cash and began counting. *Twenty, forty, sixty, eighty.*

'The old man told me about your little girl. I'm sorry about that but it don't give no one the right to have a go at me,' Steve said, pocketing the money.

Meg repeated her apology.

'I'll be going then,' Steve said, finally.

She waited until he'd gone. To Marc: 'What the hell was that?' She dropped to her knees and began scooping up the spilled contents of the trunk.

'I was trying to put the trunk in the attic while you were out so you wouldn't have to see it. Mr Fuckery appeared out of nowhere and took over.'

'So I wouldn't have to *see* it?' Grief, Janette once said, is a country with a population of one. Not even Marc got it. They were together in their sadness, and alone – he with his helpless rages, she clinging hopelessly to scraps, he with his drinking, her with her pills. She drew the pink cardigan to her face and breathed in what once smelled of Lily and was now only unused wool. 'Never mind. I'll get this tidied up.'

Marc, relieved, said, 'It's going to be all right, Meggie.'

Once he'd left, she sat on the floorboards and wept. Beside her the trunk seemed to shimmer and creak like something coming up to the surface after a long sleep. She folded the cardigan, put it back in its place and closed the lid.

Downstairs, the hubbub of men moving boxes. A voice said, 'The fire's gone out in the living room, want me to chuck on some more cardboard?'

Marc's voice, from the hallway. 'No, mate. Let it die.'

TWO

Days went by in a blur. Marc returned to work, most days catching a later afternoon train in time to take his place in the orchestra pit at the Phoenix Theatre in the West End for the evening's performance. On matinee days, he'd head in earlier, abandoning Meg to the deep solitude of the cottage and returning after she had gone to bed. She passed her days unpacking and cleaning, gradually accustoming herself to the still, grey light of the rooms, the deepness of the silence punctuated by occasional sighs and creaks. Though she was alone she had the odd sense of being accompanied. That must be how it was with old houses, occupied, if not with spirits exactly, then with the atmosphere of previous lives. And that seemed fitting for she, too, was inhabited by the past and she, too, understood how it was to be in the world right now whilst at the same time occupying some other, more distant ground.

On one of these afternoons she found a small, battered photograph at the back of one of the cupboards. Two girls, one very young, about six, wearing a pair of dungarees and brown sandals with sweet pink polka dot socks, the other older, with a serious expression on her face. From the girls' hair and clothes, Meg thought most likely sometime in the mid-Nineties.

The next morning she showed Marc the picture over breakfast but he did not recognize them and they concluded that the picture must have been left by a previous owner. It felt too sad to bin it, somehow. Instead, Meg stashed it in her bedside drawer and pretty soon forgot about it.

On the fourth morning she was in the attic, cleaning, when the doorbell rang. Making her way gingerly down the ladder she headed down the stairs, opening the front door to a tall woman she recognized immediately from the church. She was casually dressed in jeans and a shirt and crew-neck sweater over which peeped a dog collar, and had an expectant look on her face. In one hand was a Tupperware box containing what looked like brownies.

'Oh good, you *are* here!' The woman smiled warmly and thrust out an unusually large hand. Meg took it and noticed that the palm had the unworn texture of someone who didn't do much physical work though the grip was astonishing.

'We met, briefly, last week. I was about to introduce myself but you'd gone. Anyway, we're here now.' The woman introduced herself as Sandy Griffin, the vicar for Coldwater and a couple of the other parishes around. 'There was no car in the drive so I thought I might have missed you.'

'I don't drive.' Which version of herself did she want to be now that she could be anyone? She went on, 'My husband Marc takes himself to the station in the mornings. He works in London.'

'Ah, right,' Sandy said, simply. It was a relief to Meg not to have to explain.

'Would you like to come in?'

Sandy smiled. 'If I'm not disturbing you?'

'Not at all. Glad of the company.' Relieved to have someone else in the house, she led the way through the front door with its great brass knocker and iron latch and through the hallway to the kitchen at the back, apologising for the mess. Meg had kept her loneliness at bay and now, in the presence of company, she felt it all the more forcefully. She was anxious too, and rather more than anxious. Afraid?

She invited Sandy to sit at Jimmy's old kitchen table, moving a pile of papers and setting down a vase containing the rose she'd found a few days before. It was past its best now but it had kept its smell, a rich, honeyed scent which reminded her of summer picnics in the park. She went over to the counter to make tea.

'I got to know Helen better in Jimmy's last months. Our visits often seemed to coincide.'

'It was good of you to come and see him. He could be a tricky old so-and-so,' Meg said. She was wondering if Sandy knew about Lily and hoped not. The moment people knew something like that about you, assumptions were made. It was enough that Jimmy had told Steve.

'How did you and Marc meet?' Sandy asked, changing the subject.

Meg closed her eyes for a moment and allowed herself the luxury of going back to the before time. 'I went to see a musical and I just noticed this guy in the orchestra pit. I don't know what it was about him but sometimes you just know. After the performance I waited for him at the artists' entrance and asked if he'd like to come for a drink. Marc always says I stalked him.'

The two women laughed and Meg poured more tea. Sandy, pointing to the rose, said, 'Is that from the garden?'

'Actually no. I found it by the gate the day we moved in.

Someone must have dropped it. The petals are looking a bit sad but it still smells gorgeous.' Meg picked up the vase and made a show of taking in the scent. Sandy watched her but made no effort to join in.

'Are you churchgoers?' Sandy asked.

'No,' Meg said emphatically, and hoping she hadn't caused offence, added, 'Well, you know, Christmas, Easter. The typical hypocritical English thing.'

They each took a brownie.

'I was curious about the building. Doom paintings are a new one on me.' Meg took a bite out of her brownie and made appreciative sounds.

'Most were painted over in the Reformation so you don't see them very often. Apparently there was a wall panel obscuring the one in St Joseph's which is why it survived.'

The dead rabbit came into Meg's mind.

Putting down her cake, Sandy said, 'This is such a wonderful house.'

'We're very lucky to have it. We'd never have been able to afford anything remotely like this if Jimmy hadn't left it to Marc in his will.' Meg was eager to convey that they were not spoiled people, the way you might imagine the son and daughter-in-law of a rock star to be. To be sure, Jimmy had enjoyed his fifteen minutes in the limelight – two top-ten hits in the mid-Eighties – but they had been followed by a long slide downhill and at the turn of the millennium, short of ready cash, he'd got suckered into selling the publishing rights. At the time of his death the cottage was his only possession of any real value. She wondered if it was worth telling Sandy that Marc had done the decent thing and offered to sell the place and split the money with

Helen and that it was Helen who'd wanted her brother to keep it. Sandy should know that they were good people. Did she, Meg, still believe that? Oh, it was all so complicated!

She said, 'There's loads to do and we can't afford to pay anyone so I'm going to have to brush up on my god-awful DIY skills,' immediately regretting the blasphemy, though there was no sign that Sandy had taken offence. Just the opposite.

Laughing, Sandy said, 'They can't be worse than mine. I'd love a tour if you're not too busy. You can tell me your plans.'

Meg led them through the hallway and up the stairs to the first floor.

'Oh gosh, *black*,' Sandy said as she entered the master bedroom.

'That's Jimmy. Once a rocker, always a rocker.' Meg smiled. She'd been fond of Jimmy, felt freer to enjoy him than Marc ever had. He'd been a crappy father but he'd loved his children. Not as much as he'd loved their mother, Astrid, but as much as he knew how.

They left the black bedroom and moved across the landing to the spare room which offered a view of Covert Wood but Sandy seemed less interested in the outlook than in a moth-eaten teddy bear that Meg had found in the attic and propped up on the mantelpiece, and that she hadn't quite been able to bring herself to throw away in case it had belonged to either of the two girls in the photograph.

'Not ours. But it seemed too sad to bin it somehow.'

'I could take it? Might come in handy for the church jumble sale. Only if you really don't want it, though,' Sandy said.

Meg handed her the bear. 'I'm sure we'll have some other bits and pieces too. Kitchen stuff mostly.'

'People do like the toys,' Sandy said, which Meg took to be a polite thanks but no thanks.

They poked their noses briefly into the bathroom and the room at the side which Marc had already designated as his study. On the landing on their way back down, Sandy stopped at the trunk and hesitated for a moment but she waited until they were on the stairs before she said, 'I heard that Marc got off to a bit of a rocky start with Steve.'

So this was why she'd come. A peace mission. This confirmed how it was going to be from now on: everyone knowing everyone else's business.

'Yes. We were all just a bit stressed.'

'Of course I understand. Steve can be an acquired taste. Rather like the Doom paintings.' She flashed Meg a smile. 'He's a complicated soul but he's part of the fabric of the village. Your late father-in-law used to put quite a bit of work his way, I believe.'

'So Steve said.' Meg had never heard Jimmy mention him, but then neither she nor Marc really knew much about Jimmy's daily life. They made the duty calls, came to see him during holidays, but once Jimmy left London he didn't want to come up again. He rarely called or messaged. Helen had always been closer to him, which was why it was odd that he'd chosen to leave the cottage to his son. Garden variety chauvinism, perhaps, or a misguided attempt to try to recompense for the loss of Lily.

They were downstairs now in the hallway. Meg led Sandy into the living room, intending to show her the view of Covert Wood from the French windows and get back to the kitchen, but to her surprise Sandy took a seat on the Ikea sofa they'd brought down from the flat. Following her lead Meg settled herself in the armchair on the other side of the coffee table.

'It's a wonderful view, isn't it? I do so love Covert Wood. I'm sure you will too.'

Meg nodded. She hadn't ventured into the wood which seemed a bit gloomy and intimidating. Besides which, the back gate was stuck and they hadn't yet got round to fixing it.

From somewhere outside a crow cawed and the atmosphere in the room grew awkward. At last Sandy said, 'Meg, this is a little delicate, but it's important that you know that Steve may have had expectations when Jimmy died. I don't know the details but I do know he was hoping to be recognized in your father-in-law's will.'

At least this explained Steve's eagerness to take their eighty pounds. The visit was turning out to be *much* less casual than Meg had at first imagined.

'Jimmy was terrible with money. Apart from the cottage he didn't really leave anything so I'm not sure where Steve would have got the idea that he was entitled.'

Sandy smiled, embarrassed. 'I'm not suggesting you give Steve any money, only that it would be kind to put some work his way.'

Silence fell once more and was broken by Meg. 'I'll see if I can find some small jobs for him.'

'Thank you,' Sandy said simply.

Outside, the clouds had gone and a pale blue sky was visible through the windows and Meg, keen to steer the conversation into less tricky territory, asked Sandy if she would like to see the garden. They left by the French doors and had only taken a few steps onto the patio when Sandy spotted the climbing rose and letting out an 'ahh' went over to smell the cascade of late season creamy blooms.

'I came here for Christmas one year and they were still blooming,' Meg said, lifting a flower to her nose. The petals smelled only faintly sweet and there was a bitter, woody note. 'It's different from the one indoors, less fragrant.'

'That one's a St Cecilia, I believe,' Sandy said. 'They're very popular in the village.' Sandy shut her eyes. When she opened them again she had become a slightly different version of herself. Older, maybe, or more sombre. 'This one's more to my liking, though.'

They made their way along the brick path lined on either side with beds full of fading delphiniums and flagging wallflowers towards a brick shed then followed the path round into an area of raised beds now populated with tall grasses but designed, long ago, to be a kitchen garden.

'You must be familiar with most of the houses in Coldwater,' Meg went on.

'I suppose so. I have a soft spot for Covert Cottage though. No one else has this view over the wood.'

'Where does the name Covert come from? I never thought to ask Jimmy.'

'If I'm not mistaken it's a place of refuge for game.'

A refuge. Meg liked that idea. As they walked on, the clouds dispersed and sunshine began to pour onto the garden. Sandy reached for a blade of grass and ran it slowly between her fingers. Where the light fell on her cheeks a pulse flickered. At that moment a bird with a huge wingspan flapped overhead, heading in the direction of the wood. They followed the animal's flight for a moment.

'Buzzards usually come out when something's died. A deer maybe or a rabbit.'

They'd come to an iron archway flanked on one side by the large yew tree which led to the back part of the garden.

'I haven't been this far down the garden for years. Is this arch new?' Sandy said.

'I don't think so.' The arch had been a feature of the garden as long as Meg had known Marc, just shy of a decade now. The happiness of those first years, especially after Lily's arrival. Neither of them had ever felt so full of possibility. She let herself float along on the gentle waters of remembrance until Sandy's voice fetched her back into a present that somehow seemed less real.

'I think I would have remembered it.'

'If it's been that long then you might not have seen the studio.'

They went through the arch and past the yew to the back of the property where Jimmy had built the modest, brick single-storey block in the expectation of a life that had never materialized. Long after his performing days were over, he'd hoped to revive his songwriting career, penning songs in the studio with its view across the field to the wood beyond. Before long he'd given up. He'd still come down to the studio to smoke weed, surrounded by his memorabilia, listening to tracks that reminded him of the good old days, but he said that, without Astrid, he couldn't write.

'You're right, this is new to me,' Sandy said.

'I'd show you inside but it's a mess. Jimmy developed a bit of a hoarding habit. Helen put most of the stuff in bags when she and Marc came to clear out the place but I guess she didn't want to throw anything away until Marc had a chance to go through it.' Meg gently unhitched a cobweb from the front door. 'We're thinking of doing it up a bit, maybe renting it as a holiday place eventually. It would be nice to have someone staying there from time to time. It's very quiet here when Marc's at work.'

As she said this, Meg realized, suddenly, how much she missed her weekly sessions with Janette. Time went by so slowly here and she was alone for so much of it. They walked back, chattering about her plans for the garden. At the climbing rose Meg turned to Sandy and said, 'I've been very rude, yacking away about me.' She cocked her head to one side. 'Tell me about you.'

Sandy snorted. 'Oh, I'm not very interesting.'

Meg expected something to follow, an anecdote or a quip, perhaps, but when it didn't, she went on, 'I'll bet you know everything there is to know about Coldwater. All the secrets.'

'One or two.' Another laugh. In the air above them the buzzard began a plaintive cry then banked off on the thermals towards the woods. Sandy shook her head as if to say that whatever she knew wasn't really worth telling, then checked her watch. 'Well this has been lovely.' She thumbed back to where they'd just come from and said, 'You mind if I leave by the back gate? It's so much quicker across the fields.'

'It's sunk on its hinges. We might have to lift it a bit.'

They made their way towards the back entrance and heaved open the gate.

'Steve could fix that for you in a jiffy. He can turn his hand to almost anything.' She got out her phone and said, 'I'll text you his number just in case.'

'Thanks,' Meg said.

On the edge of the path sat a single pink rose, almost identical to the first. Meg bent and picked it up. 'How odd!'

Sandy sighed and in a quiet voice, said, 'I thought perhaps you knew. That's why I didn't say anything.'

'Knew what?'

'About Cecily.' Sandy went on to explain that a girl went missing from somewhere near the cottage nearly thirty years ago. Her family had been staying with relatives in the village and they'd left her in their care for a few days while they went back to wherever they'd come from.

Meg cast her eyes across the dark fringe of trees. She felt hollow and sick suddenly.

'How old was she?'

'About six?'

Six. Such a sweet, tender age, full of unwarranted certainties and a fierce, fragile independence. In her mind Meg could hear Lily's six-year-old voice, swinging between quest and conviction, unaware that the world would never be as knowable as she imagined it must be.

Mummy, tell me now! Do crocodiles have kidneys?

People who are mean to animals should be told to stop and then they will.

If God exists why don't they just stop hiding and then it would be easier to believe in them?

'Was she ever found?' Meg said.

Sandy looked pained, a little jig playing at the edges of her mouth. 'There were all sorts of rumours. She'd been abducted or got lost in the woods and died of exposure, or maybe something had happened at the cottage, an accident, and the people who were living there at the time covered it up. People said they'd seen her here, there and everywhere. The usual carnival of psychics and opportunists turned up apparently. But no one ever found her.'

'That's awful. Her poor parents.'

'Yes. As you can imagine, in a tiny place like this, the police interviewed almost everyone, all the men anyway. No one was ever arrested. After a couple of years everything died down.'

'And the roses…?'

'It's always like this in the run-up to a big anniversary. A way of keeping her memory alive without actually having to talk about it. No one wants to do that.' Sandy looked away, eyes on the path ahead, then checked her watch. 'Oh gosh, I absolutely should be off. Parish meeting.'

'The Tupperware,' Meg said, just remembering.

'I'll pick it up some other time.' Sandy extended her outsized hand, something sorrowful in her smile. For a few moments Meg watched her stride determinedly across the field, the long length of her back lurching to the rhythm of her legs. Alone once more, Meg turned and made her way back up the path to the cottage. At the back doorstep she took off her sandals and padded into the kitchen. She put the dirty crockery in the dishwasher and washed her hands in the sink, hoping that might make her feel better. When it didn't, she made her way upstairs to the bathroom and took one of her pills then came back down to the kitchen, took a seat at the kitchen table, beside the still-open Tupperware box, pulled out her phone and called Steve.

THREE

On the tenth anniversary of their first date, Meg woke early and crept from the bed. It was a Sunday, Marc's day off, and they planned to spend the day unpacking and doing things around the house before having dinner at the pub.

Meg had always been the early riser in the family. In the before time, she would get up and ready herself for the day before Lily and Marc were up. She'd drop Lily off at nursery before going to her own job as a teaching assistant at Hawthorn Primary. Marc would usually do the afternoon pick-up and the three of them would have an early tea before Marc had to leave for work in the West End. When Lily graduated to Victoria Park Primary, the arrangement changed, since Hawthorn and Vicky Park lay in opposite directions, but together they made it work. Life had a busy, complicated but satisfying fullness to it. Sometimes exhausting, sure, but young parents everywhere felt that. She missed the daily churn, especially here in the country where a particular kind of stillness hung in the air. There was no longer any need to get up early but to stay in bed would be too much like closing the book on family life, which would feel unbearable.

She went out onto the landing and laying her hand on the

trunk, whispered a greeting to Lily, before going downstairs to make coffee. The night had passed fitfully and she was mightily in need of a jolt of caffeine. In part it was the bittersweetness of the occasion, but there was something else too. A couple of days after they moved in, Meg had begun to experience an odd night-time thrumming, a subtle but unmistakeable sensation, like a change in pressure. Sighs leaked from the walls and the floorboards creaked, as if trodden by some unseen feet. Lying awake at night she experienced a kind of tension in the black bedroom, as if the walls themselves had absorbed enough and now wanted to be left alone. Marc slept through the sounds and in the mornings laughed off her complaints. He insisted that all old houses had the same repertoire of ancient plumbing, wooden floors and night creatures running across the roof. Meg would have to get used to it. Meg, sure that the sounds emerging from the brickwork were something more than air moving over old pipes, nonetheless stopped reporting them to Marc and developed her own theory. Though she wasn't religious in the usual understanding of the term, it seemed clear to her that the years and decades and centuries had animated the cottage with the energy of the countless people who had made it their home. Their work, their dreams, their lovemaking, their arguments, their illnesses and sorrows, these were the mortar that held the place together. And if the walls were steeped in life it stood to reason that they would also be drenched in death. There was no one without the other. Covert Cottage had been a witness to it all; even, possibly, to murder. A six-year-old girl disappeared on her way to see a friend… Was it any wonder the walls could not be silent?

And so the desire began in Meg's mind to investigate. She

had plenty of time alone and so she began to spend the lonely evenings online, searching for snippets of information about Cecily's disappearance and for the most part drawing blanks. This was hardly surprising. Thirty years ago the internet was in its infancy. Finally, after many hours of fruitless searching she found a reference to a short piece in the local paper on the tenth anniversary, after the local nursery had donated the St Cecilia rose bushes. A further search brought up a recap of the case in the local press on one of the more recent anniversaries. But there was nothing more substantial than she had already gleaned from Sandy. And this, too, was not surprising. If no body had been found and there were no suspects and no new information, what was there to say?

What did catch her attention – and played in her mind over the hours and days – were the stories of St Cecilia herself, the way they seemed to have echoes in Meg's own life. Not that Meg was saintly, or even a believer, it was more subtle than that and more meaningful somehow. She hadn't known anything much about the lives of any saints before this and it came as a surprise to discover that St Cecilia was the patron saint of music and musicians, so there was a connection through Marc. When she looked more deeply into the saint's life she was startled to discover that an angel had appeared to Cecilia and lain a wreath of roses and lilies on her head. Roses and lilies. Cecily and Lily. It felt like a call somehow.

She began to wonder what guiding hand had brought her here. Not God, exactly, but destiny or the fates or the spirits of the house. Was any of that possible? What if Lily was speaking to her from some unreachable place? What if some higher power existed, some common unconscious or universal energy that had its own intelligence, that spoke its own truths? What if some things really did happen for a reason and the universe wasn't the fluxing chaos that scientists seemed to think? As senseless as it seemed, just suppose Lily's death was part of some bigger plan or pattern that had yet to reveal itself? Why else would Sandy have told her the story of the missing girl unless it was for some good reason that Sandy herself did not fully understand? Why else would the walls be speaking to her?

What if she, Meg, had some greater purpose to being here than simply to begin her life again? To make a new meaning for her life, do something that would make sense of all the senselessness. Wouldn't that provide some crumb of comfort? She allowed herself to imagine, just for a moment, being able to relay to Cecily's parents that after thirty years, what happened to their daughter in her final hours was no longer a mystery. To discover where her body lay even. What a gift it would be to allow them, finally, to lay their darling girl to rest; to grieve and let go.

Let go.

She drank her coffee and ate her yoghurt and muesli alone at the kitchen table, put the crockery and cutlery into the dishwasher and went to the back door. A rainstorm was approaching, dark clouds scudding over a blue sky. The great yew at the bottom of the garden beside the studio swayed wildly to and fro like a drowning man signalling to the shore and beyond it, the tips of the trees in Covert Wood seethed and gave the fleeting impression that the whole wood was marching forward towards the house. Meg turned away, reminding herself that it was okay to feel unanchored here, to miss the cosy urbanity of her London life. There was something wilder in this place which was calling her. She had not been able to muster the courage to face it yet but she knew it would not stop until she answered its call.

Willing herself back to the present moment – the *only* moment, Janette had said, that would make living rather than simply surviving possible – she went to fetch the anniversary present she'd bought for Marc, a vintage walnut Maelzel metronome, from the cellar where she'd left it already wrapped on a shelf just inside the door. The device hadn't been wildly expensive, but it had taken her a long time to source it from the internet and she wanted to send him the strong message that, however distracted she'd been in the last months, there was a place deep inside her that was devoted only to him. As she cracked open the door, faint scuttling sounds came from below. She felt around for the light and stood at the top of the steps, reluctant to go down, thoughts turning to Cecily. To the possibility of secret panels or rooms behind thick old walls where it would be possible to keep a small girl imprisoned. You read about such cases in the press every now and then. Horror stories of girls (it was almost always girls) imprisoned by their captors for years before being killed or abandoned and left to die. If something like that had happened to Cecily, she would be long gone. What if the truth was down there, in the basement, with the rats?

She took a breath and waited for her pulse to slow before beginning her descent. The cellar was large, running under most of the footprint of the house, and lined with small, handmade bricks. Jimmy had never used it which explained why it smelled of dead air and rodent piss. Her eyes swept across the floor looking for signs of disturbance but she saw only what looked like mice droppings. She made a mental note to call a pest control service. The light was dim and there was something about the atmosphere of the place that made her want to get out quick, but she also recognized in herself a strong urge to stay. It was terrifically unlikely that she would find any clue to Cecily's fate but something in her wanted to be sure. To rest more easily. How would she forgive herself if at some point in the future Cecily's remains were discovered on the property and she had done nothing to look for her?

Gathering her courage, she made her way slowly along the cellar walls, checking the brickwork for any sign of disturbance or repair and in the corner farthest from the light, she came upon something that made her heart take a turn and begin to pound. At a height of three feet, carved into the brickwork, there was a tiny heart. The shape was clear and defined, as though it had been scraped out in the not-too-distant past and the height seemed significant. There was only one way to make that mark if you were an adult, and that was on your knees. She peered at it, then, with her pulse ticking in her temples, turned her attentions to the area around it, looking for some other mark or carving, some fissure in the brickwork which might hint at a space behind. After what seemed like an age, with nothing to show for it, she gave up and returned to the kitchen carrying the metronome. Leaving it on the kitchen table along with a note for Marc to find when he came down – which if past experience was anything to go by, was unlikely to be before ten – she decided to take herself off for a walk to the village, hoping to bump into Lisa or Sandy so she could ask them if there was anything else they might know about the circumstances surrounding Cecily's disappearance and, in any case, to book a table at the pub for their anniversary dinner.

Going out into the blustery day and taking the longer route along The Lane, she passed the place where the road ran parallel to the Sour Water, went over the bridge and on past the ancient stone-hewn horse trough and the war memorial towards the village shop. It was growing chillier now and she noted, not for the first time, a kind of deadness in the air, as if it had been drained of all its oxygen. As she walked across the green she spotted the figure of a man hurrying round the back of the church as though eager not to be seen. Was that Steve? She had made an appointment for him to come round to widen the hatch into the attic, clear out the studio and take a look at the back gate. Had he seen her? Was he trying to avoid an encounter?

She wandered the few steps to the pub, heaved open the door with its iron hinge and was hit by the spicy smell of wood soaked in centuries of bitter hops and alcohol. A middle-aged man stood behind the bar polishing glasses. He said the pub was closed but when she asked to make a reservation he took out his book, his eyebrows moving upwards when she gave the name Mair and repeating it to himself as he made a note of her contact details.

'Are you the owner?' Meg asked.

The man nodded but did not introduce himself.

To make conversation she asked him for the meaning of the word 'palterer'. He said it was an old Kentish word for a con man or a fence. He went on to say that grifters of all sorts were common around this part of Kent. Smugglers had operated in the county more or less with impunity for centuries. The story went on. It seemed she'd inadvertently hit on the owner's particular obsession. At last, when there was absolutely nothing more to say about the history of paltering, the man finished polishing the glasses and stood looking at her with his hands on his hips. 'Okay, then, see you later.'

Glad to have been dismissed finally, she made for the door. It was bright now and she had to stop for a moment to allow her eyes to adjust. She was tired and wired from too much coffee. Maybe the night sounds bothered her more than she was willing to admit. She took off across the green and was stopped in her tracks by a familiar sight. A dark figure in silhouette who darted behind the war memorial. For an instant Meg was too astonished to speak, then she cried, 'Janette?'

There was a moment's pause before the woman stepped out from behind the memorial. For a fraction of a second her face seemed unresolved, as if it were scattered mercury in the process of collecting itself. Then there she was, unmistakeable, the familiar long, elegant face, eyes even from this distance as bright as glass.

'What are you doing here?'

Meg went towards her, with each step some new memory coming tumbling back. For almost a year they'd seen Janette in London Fields for therapy every week, usually together, and once, separately, and they had left their final session in the expectation that they would be unlikely ever to see their former therapist again.

Janette waited for her approach. 'Meg, dear, what an extraordinary coincidence. I saw you a moment before you spotted me. I wasn't sure if you'd welcome me saying hello. Confidentiality and all that. You must think I've gone mad hiding like that.'

'Not at all, it's...it's great to see you. It's just a bit... unexpected.' An understatement. They'd told Janette they were moving into Marc's late father's cottage but Meg couldn't recall now if they'd ever mentioned the name of the village. It seemed likely that they had, but Meg had no memory of it.

Meg returned Janette's smile. Janette held her gaze. It had always unnerved her that look, friendly but searching.

'And how wonderful to see you again.'

'Didn't we tell you we were coming to Coldwater?' Meg said, immediately regretting her forceful tone. The shock.

'Well, no, I don't think so. You said you were moving to the countryside,' Janette said, looking slightly confused and a little hurt. 'Is there a problem?'

'Absolutely not. *Of course* not. It's just...' Meg tailed off, feeling bad at having sounded so unwelcoming.

'Oh, you're wondering why I'm here? You must be, naturally.' Janette was all smiles once more. 'I've been looking for a weekend cottage somewhere around here for a few months now.' She listed a few other villages around Ashford, none of which had turned out to be suitable. 'Obviously I had no idea I'd run into you.'

'Well, here we are.'

Janette's smile faded and she rubbed her hands together. 'It's really turned rather chilly.'

Meg checked her watch. Marc would almost certainly be up by now. 'Are you in a hurry?'

'Absolutely not,' Janette said. 'I can take a train back to London any time. No plans.'

'In that case, would you like to come back to the cottage for a coffee? We're only a few minutes' walk away and I'm sure Marc would be delighted to see you. We can give you a lift to wherever you'd like to go afterwards.' As soon as she said this, Meg felt settled about it, though she wasn't really sure whether Marc would welcome the visit or not. It had been his idea to finish their sessions with Janette. Meg had wanted to carry on but Marc insisted, saying they were just 'going over old ground' and needed to cut their ties to the past and face towards their future. Meg sensed that there was something more to it but she'd never worked out what and it didn't seem to matter now. Besides which, as Marc pointed out, therapy was expensive, and they were strapped for cash. Meg hadn't been able to face going back to work after the accident. She was curious to see what Janette would make of the house and its magnificent view, and something in her wanted Janette to know that they were both fine and settling into their new life.

They walked back along The Lane, not the shortest route, but Janette wasn't wearing footwear for tromping across the fields. They arrived at the cottage to find Marc dressed and in the kitchen making coffee.

'Look who I bumped into!' Meg said.

'Oh, Janette! How amazing!' Marc's eyes flared and something flickered at their edges but he came towards them with a smile plastered on his face and his hand outstretched.

'Lovely to see you too, Marc,' Janette said effusively and ignoring the hand, went in for a peck on each cheek.

Marc made more coffee while Meg related the story of how she and Janette had run into one another.

'A weekend place?' Marc said, bringing the cafetière over to the kitchen table.

'Yes, you know, to get out of London. I'm thinking of scaling down my practice, maybe going online only or perhaps even retiring completely. I might move down more permanently eventually. I haven't really thought it all through yet.' She took in the kitchen. 'What a wonderful, atmospheric home.'

Marc poured some milk into a jug and brought it over. 'Thank you. It's not without its problems. Dad...'

'...was quite the character!'

Marc was momentarily startled until he remembered that Janette knew this about his father. What he'd actually been about to say was that Jimmy had left them with a terrible damp problem. 'And the roof is going to need doing at some point.'

'I think we may have mice in the cellar too,' Meg said. 'I went down there this morning and there were droppings.' Thoughts of the missing girl bubbled up again, and she pushed them down.

'The plan is to do the cottage up ourselves and either sell it or find a way to buy my sister out of her share,' Marc said.

'Helen's been very good about it all,' Meg went on.

'Yes, I remember,' Janette said.

At this Marc smiled. 'You know all about us. Which is funny, really, since we don't know anything about you.' Meg saw something in his eyes that she didn't recognize, an embarrassment, perhaps, almost as if he'd run into an old lover or someone he'd once crushed on and wanted to forget.

'I'm wondering now if you *did* mention Coldwater to me and I'd just forgotten,' Janette said. She was watching a robin on the kitchen windowsill peck at a handful of cereal Meg had left out. Whichever, it seemed to Meg that fate had intervened to bring Janette back into their lives and as they drank their coffee and caught up on news, Meg wondered if it might be rather wonderful to have their former therapist nearby.

'Would you like to see the garden?' Meg said, once they'd finished their drinks.

They strolled through the garden and past the great yew to the studio and as they went, Meg began to imagine a life where she and Janette might share a cosy supper on a Saturday night. How pleasant it would be not to have to spend so much of every weekend alone while Marc was up in London. By the time they were walking back up the garden a new vision for her life in Coldwater had begun to crystalise. It would be a life containing the very particular kind of regard that Meg had only ever experienced with Janette. Unerringly positive, affirming, steady. Exactly what she needed.

'If you let us know what kind of weekend place you're after, we can keep an eye out,' Meg said.

'I wouldn't want to put you to any trouble.'

'Not at all,' Meg said. 'It would be lovely to have you nearby.'

'In that case, if you happen to hear of somewhere, you have my phone number. My needs are really very modest. A little place like the studio at the bottom of your garden would do me perfectly well.'

They went back into the house. Soon it began to rain and Janette decided to return to London earlier than planned.

Marc insisted on giving her a lift. In the hallway, putting on her coat, Janette suddenly stopped, her hands clasped to her chest, and said, 'Oh! I've just remembered the date – and my manners. Those beautiful pink roses in the house. Of course! It's your wedding anniversary! How lovely of you to make time for me!'

SESSION 1, LONDON FIELDS

SEVENTEEN MONTHS AGO

An elegant woman in her sixties, expensively dressed and with immaculate silver hair stylishly bobbed, met them at the door to her consulting room and waved them in. Marc waited for Meg to enter then followed. She invited them to sit on a small white leather sofa in one corner of the room and settled herself into a leather Barcelona chair in the other. The room, one of a dozen situated in a large Victorian villa just off London Fields, was decorated in tasteful neutrals and there were photographs of famous people, musicians mostly, on the walls.

'So,' Janette said.

A fortnight earlier Meg had been sitting on a park bench in London Fields for what seemed like hours, weeping, passers-by staring or craning their necks as they went by to catch a glimpse, the odd stranger asking if she was okay and accepting her nod before moving along. One man had laughed and told her to smile because it couldn't be all that bad, not seeing or caring that it *was* all that bad, that it was worse, the worst thing that could ever happen. It had been the eight-week anniversary of Lily's death and Meg had been inconsolable, suicidal even, unable to speak, unable to go on, unable even to stand and make her way back home, when a graceful-looking woman had sat beside her and taking her hand, said, 'Tell me all about it.'

Janette had saved her, Janette with her kindness and with the softness of her voice and with the simple gesture of coming to sit with her amid her anguish. She'd gone home that day and when Marc got back from the theatre, she'd told him that they needed to get help and she'd met just the woman.

'So, I'm not sure why I'm here,' Marc said, once they'd settled themselves.

'No?' Janette said evenly.

'Please don't take this the wrong way but I don't see what good it can do, raking things over with a complete stranger.'

Meg sighed.

'Would it help if you knew a bit more about me?' Janette volunteered.

'I suppose,' Marc said. Meg saw him tilt his head as if he were trying to read something upside down.

'You've noticed my tattoo,' Janette said, holding out her long arm for inspection. They both craned forward. She was wearing a dress with bracelet sleeves revealing a tattoo on her wrist that read *Stat sua cuique dies*.

'Everyone has their day,' Janette said, settling herself back in the chair. 'I had it done when I lived in Australia.' She smiled. 'Moment of madness, perhaps. But it seemed like a good idea at the time.'

'Cool,' Marc said. Meg observed him clock the photographs of musicians. He seemed to be warming to this stranger who had come into their lives in such a propitious way.

'We checked out your website like you said,' Meg added hastily. 'All that experience. The amazing testimonials.'

Janette flicked back her bob and said, 'People can sometimes be anxious coming into therapy. I try to do what I can to put clients at ease.'

There was another silence but it didn't feel awkward. Meg supposed this was part of it. She and Marc were both a bit clueless. All they knew about therapy was what they'd seen on TV.

'So what brought you back from Australia?' Marc said.

'You don't have to answer that,' Meg said. Already she felt the need to protect Janette. It was her idea that they come here and she was keen that the first session went well.

Janette pushed at a silver ring on the index finger of her right hand. 'The heart wants what the heart wants,' she said enigmatically, then slapping both hands on her knees she went on, 'But we're not here to talk about me, are we?'

FOUR

On his return to the cottage Marc found Meg in the patch of raised beds they were hoping to revive as a kitchen garden. She was focusing on something on her phone and didn't hear him approach.

'There you are.' He planted a kiss on her fine wavy brown hair. 'Anything interesting?'

'A text, nothing important.' Meg shoved the phone hastily into her pocket and turning to him, more brightly this time, said, 'Janette get her train?'

Marc, noting the change of subject, said, 'Yup. Funny bumping into the old oracle.' He'd decided on the nickname early on in their sessions in order to poke gentle fun at a woman who had actually been an enormous force for good in their lives. To lessen her importance to him, perhaps, so that he could mitigate – in his mind at least – the discomfort he'd at first felt in the whole process. He hadn't wanted to be one of those men who dug their heels in and refused to talk about things and were then surprised when their partners left them but it didn't come naturally to him to delve deeply into his feelings. Pretty soon into the process, though, he'd found himself relaxing into it. It had been a relief to have someone to talk to. From the first session he'd decided he liked Janette. He thought she was cool, too, the way older women could sometimes be. Self-possessed. He enjoyed thinking about the celebrities she might have treated. As their sessions grew more intense, more urgent somehow, and the trust built, his scepticism faded so completely that there was a part of him that had found it hard to let go of her. Not that he'd ever wanted to start an affair with Janette or anything like that, only that he had developed feelings for her which he found confronting and hard to entangle. He'd never admitted as much to Meg but seeing her now had made those feelings come rushing back.

'I didn't get a chance to thank you for the metronome,' he said now, pulling her into him. 'It's amazing. Thank you.' A robin was picking around in the newly forked soil looking for grubs and worms. 'I suppose it's too late to pretend those roses were from me? I didn't know what to get you.'

Meg smiled in a way that made him feel sad because it was a sad smile. All her smiles were sad now. She told him about finding the blooms, how the vicar had said that they were tributes to some girl who had gone missing a long time ago. He listened with half an ear, enjoying the closeness of their bodies. The robin flew away. He gazed off into the middle distance. From somewhere deep in Covert Wood a group of crows began to squabble.

'I called Steve to come round and fix the back gate, get rid of Jimmy's stuff in the studio.'

He felt a flash of irritation and pulled away from her. '*That* guy, really?'

'You know anyone better?' Meg asked. He didn't, and Meg knew it. She'd already told him what Sandy had said about

Steve being popular in the village but he didn't care about that. He didn't like the man.

'Point taken. Ask him to fix the hatch in the attic and put the trunk up there while he's at it.' He felt an obscure need to reassert himself. He knew that Meg was in no hurry to move the trunk, that she viewed putting it up in the attic to be another little step on the painful path away from Lily, towards a future that was as yet completely undefined. He wasn't unsympathetic. He'd lost Lily too, but he longed to draw a line under the past and was impatient for whatever the future held.

On their way back to the house together, Meg raised the topic of the studio. 'Was that a hint I detected from Janette?'

'I'd say so,' Marc said. 'She said something about it in the car on the way to the station too.'

'Maybe it would be *fun* to have her stay in the studio? Just till she finds somewhere more permanent. Everything's there. A shower room, a little kitchenette. All it really needs is a clear-out, a lick of a paint and a bit of sprucing.'

This thought had also occurred to Marc, though he didn't want Meg to think he was keen in case she read something into it; his feelings towards Janette were still a source of confusion in him. 'Let me have a think about it,' he said, simply.

Meg hung up her fleece on the pegs in the utility room while he pulled off his boots using the step up into the utility room as a jack. Meg went up to shower away the garden grime and dress for dinner. At seven they took off down The Lane. Above them the sky seemed to throb as though it were alive and breathing. An owl sounded. From time to time they held hands and they crossed over the bridge and across the green until they were standing on the steps of the Palterer's Arms where, in a sweeping gesture of gallantry that was only half ironic, Marc held the door and bowed Meg into the fuggy warmth of the saloon bar. In the grate a log fire burned, though it wasn't quite cold enough for it. Meg took a seat and they decided what they wanted to eat from the menu before Marc went off to the bar to order. He came back bearing a bottle of champagne and they raised a toast to their anniversary.

'And to meeting Janette again,' Meg said.

'And to the future,' Marc added.

The barman came over with cutlery and a tray of condiments and smiled at Meg. Maybe it was the champagne or maybe it was the fact that Meg had bought him such a thoughtful present but in that moment, Marc felt hopeful about them, here, together, embarking on a new chapter. They'd struggled to be together like this with each other since Lily died. If not happy, then settled and comfortable. And then as quickly as his optimism had arrived, Janette came to mind, and a knot appeared in his stomach.

'I've been thinking, it might be a bit weird having Janette staying in the studio,' Marc said, putting down his glass.

Meg took a sip of her drink but he caught her disappointment and felt his stomach hollow. Seconds ago everything had been perfect and he'd managed to ruin it. He wanted to row back but didn't know how. He refilled his glass and topped up Meg's but already the glittery sheen of the moment before was gone.

'It would only be weekends,' she said but as he was formulating a response, Meg sat upright and smiled awkwardly at something out of his view and when he turned he saw Steve heading their way. *That* clown. As he drew near it was obvious he'd been drinking. His face had that stupefied look of a man who'd been doing so all day.

'Please, Marc, be nice,' muttered Meg.

Okay, then. Rise above. He wasn't going to let some arse wreck their anniversary dinner. To Meg's surprise he stood up and swivelling around to face Steve, held out a hand.

'Celebration, is it?'

He didn't want Steve Savage anywhere near what he and Meg had had going only moments before but this was an opportunity to show Meg that he meant to become part of village life. So he gathered himself and summoning a smile, he said, 'Look, mate, we got off to a bad start and I'd like to start over. Can I buy you a drink?'

Steve's eyebrows went up, impressed by the gesture. 'All right. Me and your old man always drank Highland Park 18. They kept a bottle here just for us. I'll ask Terri to put it on your tab if you like? Save you the trouble of getting up.'

He remembered Jimmy's taste for expensive Scotch. Marc had even bought him a bottle or two of Highland Park for birthdays and such. But Highland Park 18. If he remembered rightly that was over a hundred quid a bottle. The fucking arse had got the better of him. Worse, he, Marc, had more or less served himself up to be rinsed. But there was no way back without causing a ruckus.

'Right,' Marc said. He watched Steve turn and wander back to the bar. For a while he and Meg sat enjoying the warmth of the fire. The food arrived. Neither raised the possibility of Janette's staying at the studio again and the intensity of the moment when they first opened the champagne had gone, but they ate and were quietly content in one another's company.

Just before ten o'clock, exhaustion creeping over them, they rose. Meg went to the ladies while Marc paid the bill. They met in the porch. In the light above the pub sign gnats bustled and churned.

'Note to self, never buy Steve another drink,' Marc said wearily, and immediately regretted it. Should have kept his mouth shut. He had so wanted tonight to be only about the two of them, walking into their future together.

'How much?'

'My weekly commuting bill.'

Meg blew air from her cheeks. She took his arm and they began the short walk home. A full moon and a clear night, star speckles guiding their way. An owl hooted and something else they didn't recognize. Country sounds as yet unfamiliar.

After a short while Marc, unhitching his arm and slinging it around Meg's shoulder, drew her in closer. From behind them came the distant purr of a car engine. They walked on a way, the headlights of the vehicle coming closer now. After the *incident* Marc had got straight back behind the wheel. The only way to have a future was to protect it from the past. But Meg had sworn off driving. Traffic meant the potential for accidents. He felt her stiffen and he reached out and grabbed her hand.

'Darling, it's fine.' He gave her a reassuring squeeze.

The vehicle, a blue van, had slowed and drawn up close. It came to a stop beside them. A head leaned out.

'Get in, I'll take you home.' Steve. Blind drunk and slurring his words. Marc felt himself tense.

Meg reached out for his arm and said hastily, 'We're fine. Enjoying the walk actually.'

'Don't say I ain't neighbourly.'

Steve's head disappeared back inside the van as it lurched forward, heading for the middle of the road.

'Fucking idiot,' muttered Marc.

The van swerved and came to a halt again a few metres up ahead. Marc's heart began to pound. He felt for the phone in his pocket and remembered that there was a signal drop-out where the road dipped down right about here.

The window opened and one arm appeared, Steve's nasal twang cutting through the night sounds.

'Word to the wise, townies. You go out at night, bring a torch. This ain't London. Someone could run you over, easy as.'

At that Marc stiffened and Meg, sensing this, threaded an arm around his waist and said, quietly, so that Steve couldn't hear, 'Don't. He doesn't realize what he's saying or who he's saying it to.'

FIVE

It was a Tuesday morning, about a month after they'd moved into Covert Cottage, and Meg was in the kitchen making scrambled eggs. It had been a disturbed night – one of many – and she was hoping that a hot breakfast might perk her up. Over the past week or so the cottage, which could be so still, so thickly silent during the day, had seemed to come alive at night. It was almost as if whatever had been living in the basement had made its way up into the attic. Marc, who had always been a deep sleeper, sinking into unconsciousness moments after hitting the pillow, remained oblivious to the nightly crackling and shuffling. When she brought it up he had brushed the whole thing off, saying if it wasn't animals running over the roof it was the plumbing and if not that then an old building settling down for the night. Nonetheless, it often seemed to Meg that the noises were coming from *inside* the roof space. There was an echoey quality to them and they often went on for an hour or more. There was no plumbing in the attic and only a single light bulb. She hadn't fancied going up there in the dark but she'd taken a good look around for signs of animal habitation during the daytime and found nothing. To be on the safe side she'd bought several humane traps in various sizes from the internet and checked them every day for a week but they remained empty and there were no tell-tale droppings as there had been in the basement. It was unsettling.

Marc was upstairs getting dressed, intending to head into London earlier than usual to have lunch with his sister. When the eggs were ready she brought the bowl to the table and called up to Marc who appeared a few moments later and pulled up a chair. Eyeing the food he said quietly, 'I wish you'd stop doing this.'

'Doing what?' She was exhausted and her head thrummed.

'Cooking for three.'

The words hit Meg like a punch. She could feel herself becoming unanchored, floating away from her body, and suddenly had the impression that she was looking down at the table from a great height. She saw her hands reach out for the bowl as if they were someone else's hands and followed them as they seemed to hover across to the kitchen counter, then open the cabinet under the sink and slide the contents of the bowl, silently, into the bin. The eggs landed with a soft plop. She stood frozen, returning to her body and shocked by what she'd just done but mostly so pained, so wounded by Marc that she could hardly breathe. It still felt as if they were in some limbo place, the past stretched out behind them like a sleeping monster, the future still misty and unformed.

'How *could* you?' she said.

Marc shrugged. 'I don't know what to say to you when you're like this.' There was a weariness in his voice which made her wonder if he was tired of her and the burden of her grief, her unwillingness simply to let go. He pushed back his chair and went over to the toaster. She watched him fling in a couple of slices of bread and had never felt quite so alone. She wanted so much for this new life to be fully theirs, for them to build it together.

'I'm sorry, okay? I just lost it. I'm lonely, Marc. It's difficult here on my own. Couldn't you get your orchestra fixer to find a dep so you can take a week or two off? It would just be so lovely to have you around for a bit.'

But Marc seemed impervious to her, reminding her that he'd taken a month off for compassionate leave after Jimmy's death back in January. He didn't want to risk losing his chair in the pit. He added, casually, 'Someone's got to bring in regular income.' There was a pause. Another barb.

'Why are you being so cruel to me this morning?'

He rolled his eyes. 'Why are you being so needy? If you're feeling lonely, go and find a job locally? We'd be under less financial pressure and it would be a good way to meet people.'

She noted the resentment in his voice. How reasonable all this sounded. But she wasn't like him, couldn't compartmentalise, didn't *want* to, had said as much in their therapy sessions together. The mere thought of being near a school made her break out into a panicky sweat.

'I'd have to drive.'

'Meg, you have to get back in the driver's seat eventually. We're living in the middle of a field for fuck's sake. I don't know why you're just being so difficult about it.'

She put the egg bowl in the sink and turned on the tap. There was a gurgling sound and a plume of rusty-coloured water shot out. She supposed she'd have to call a plumber which would give Marc the excuse to moan about the cost.

'I'm doing my best. Not your best, *my* best.'

'If you don't try to get over what happened we won't survive this,' Marc said. There was an edge to his voice now and he seemed to have forgotten the toaster. A smell of burning bread reached her nostrils.

She wanted to strangle him. His condescension, his cruelty. They were never like this to each other in the before time. And now, what? Was this what she could look forward to? Being shut away on her own here to moulder, like some latter-day Mrs Rochester, while he essentially had the same life as before? What about this was any good at all? It was brutal of him to focus on her fragility, her anxiousness. What about his irrational storms, his hair-trigger temper?

She knew that in her own quiet way she was going in for the kill but she couldn't stop herself. She took a breath and in a calm voice she said, 'It's so easy to make it all about me, isn't it? What about you? You're so angry all the time.'

The atmosphere in the room changed immediately. She felt his rage stampede towards her. He turned on his heels and strode to the door, slamming it behind him.

She sat at the kitchen table for a long time, shaking from adrenaline, then went out into the garden and busied herself pulling moss from the patio flags. She wished she smoked or drank to excess. The relief to be had, albeit of a temporary kind, in giving yourself up to self-loathing. It wouldn't fix anything but if you weren't able to protect your own daughter, if you actively contributed to putting her in harm's way, then was there anything left to fix?

She pulled up a wad of moss and ran the soft outer edge across her cheek then slid it into her mouth and made herself chew down. The inner edge crunched grittily between her teeth. The taste was earthy and bitter, unpleasant. The robin appeared and watched her doing this crazy thing. How much simpler to be an animal. None of the guilt, the sense of failure, the necessity for pretence. The task of an animal was to feed and breed. And then to die.

The front door slammed and moments later the sound of the car engine being revved and gravel crunching in the driveway signalled Marc's departure. She stopped what she was doing and went inside. A note lay on the table reading, simply, '*Sorry.*'

They were both sorry. They were stuck in their respective silos of sorriness. It was no way to make a future, a life. She made herself some coffee, drank two cups, then scrolled down her phone for Janette's number. When the call went to voicemail she waited for the tone and said, 'Hi, Janette, it's me, Meg... We really need some help. I think Marc might be about to go off the rails.'

SIX

That morning Meg was in the garden digging the flower beds, hoping to be able to plant in some shrubs before Steve arrived to fix the gate and do the work in the studio and the cottage. The row with Marc had left her shaken and the hard physical labour of moving soil occupied her enough so that she was able to stop obsessing about checking her phone in case Janette had returned her call. From where she worked she could just smell the roses on the climber by the patio. It was an unseasonably warm day which was bad, obviously, with global warming, but less of a worry to her than it once would have been. The future was strictly limited now. There wouldn't be another child. She hadn't kept her firstborn safe and that was a risk she never wanted to take again.

There were a hundred and one other jobs in the house that she'd been avoiding. Over the past few days she had become aware of an anxious, watchful thrum. Whenever she was alone, she felt as if she were being observed, not by ghosts exactly – Meg didn't believe in those – but by some invisible energy which wanted to make itself known. There was no point in telling Marc. His response to the attic sounds told her he was likely to say it was all in her head.

The robin sat expectantly on the wall beside her. She stopped, wiped a gloved hand across her brow on which tiny beads of sweat had gathered and checked her watch. It was nearly eleven and she had been working since eight. Her stomach churned and she realized that she hadn't eaten anything or stopped for coffee. Steve was expected any minute. *I should take a break or I'll crash.*

'Wait there a bit, I'll be back,' she said to the bird and leaving a fork in the hard clay, turned back towards the house. Inside, she made a cheese sandwich to eat with her cup of tea and watched while a gusty wind rose up and wrapped itself tight around the house and made it creak and sigh. She went upstairs anyway and on an impulse, opened the trunk. Everything sat in the same place as it had when she'd repacked it on moving day. The pink cardigan, the pair of striped dungarees, the Mini Me doll, a pile of books and photograph albums. She went downstairs, finished her sandwich and took down a package of bird food from the pantry and padded back out into the now still air. The robin had disappeared. She poured a handful of seeds on the wall where the bird had been then resumed her digging.

In that moment the sound of snapping twigs reached her. Beyond the kitchen garden the great yew was violently swaying. She took off down the garden to investigate. The swaying had stopped by the time she reached the tree but through the branches there was an unmistakeable flash of something large and green. Gathering her courage and in as deep and authoritative voice as she could muster, she said, 'Who's there?'

There was a rustle. She repeated herself and to her astonishment, Steve emerged from behind the yew. He was wearing an old camo jacket and khaki cargoes and in his hand was a rifle. Her pulse was pounding in her temples but she kept her cool. 'What are you doing in the garden with a gun?'

Steve shrugged and in a voice which already contained a hint of resentment said, 'Been rabbiting over at the Salisbury's. Jimmy never minded me coming in the back. Thought I'd have a quick look to see what needs doing then bring back the tools in my van. Only take me a few minutes to walk the back way.'

His smile displayed a set of even teeth discoloured by tobacco.

As they walked back down to the gate at the bottom of the garden Steve chattered in his thin, nasal voice about Jimmy and Jimmy's prog rock band, Cascade, and the work he'd done on the property over what he called the 'Jimmy years'. The black bedroom? According to Steve that had been his idea. The laminate flooring in the bathroom? All Steve. He and Jimmy 'were like mates'.

'I never saw your other half around much,' he said as they made their way through the kitchen garden. 'Ask me, the sister deserved the place more than your old man.'

'You don't know anything about it,' she said. He'd rattled her and she wondered if this had been his intention.

They were at the gate now. Steve gave the lock a cursory inspection. When he lifted his arm to reposition his baseball cap, she noticed then that there was a hole under the arm of his jacket. He gave the gateposts a cursory inspection. The gate had been playing up for years, he said, and he didn't see how it could be mended. They'd have to buy an entirely new lock and, very likely, a new gate.

'It's not worth it, to be honest. Cost you a couple of grand for nothing. I'd have to get a new gate custom-made. Could take months and cost you a pretty penny. Don't even know if they could do it to be honest with you. Everyone knows everyone around here. No one gonna nick anything.'

'I'd like to do it, though. Better safe than sorry.'

Steve put his hands on his hips and shot her an amused look. 'You Londoners crack me up.'

They left the gate and walked to the studio. She unlocked the door and showed him the mess inside, then they went up to the house and climbed the stairs to the landing to inspect the attic hatch.

'Just need to take a saw to it,' Steve said. 'Then we'll get that trunk up no problem. Jimmy got me to put some things up there one time. I never liked going up there much, tell you the truth.'

Meg's stomach tightened. 'Why not?'

Steve wiped a hand across his face. 'Well, you know, it don't feel right up there. Something off, like. It's like something's watching you. Or someone maybe. Ain't nothing you can see, more like a feeling.'

Silence fell and for a moment Meg felt too tense to break it. She took a deep breath and said, 'Sandy told me about the missing girl.'

Steve's eyes darted over to her then away. He bit his lip. 'Nothing to do with the girl. Or maybe it is. All I know, there's been houses on this site since the Domesday Book and they've all burnt down. Every single one. I used to say to Jimmy, the flames of hell are under them foundations. They've come up before and they'll come up again.'

'That's just silly. No such thing as hell,' Meg said.

He gave her a quizzical look, as if she were a child and had just said something hopelessly naive. 'Right, well, I'll get me van and be back in half an hour.'

She felt unsettled for a while after he left then made herself some tea and did her best to shrug it off. It was an hour before he returned in the blue van and rang the doorbell.

'I'll start with the studio before it gets dark, that all right with you?'

She said it was and watched him open the side gate and go down the garden then went back into the kitchen for more tea. What a strange man, all that talk of hell, full of his own demons.

From the kitchen she watched him going back and forth through the side gate. An hour and a half later he rang the doorbell again.

'It's all in the van.' Holding up a vinyl disc for Meg to look at, he said, 'Mind if I keep this?'

'I don't see why not,' Meg said obligingly. Helen had already removed anything of value, including most of Jimmy's old vinyl collection and the two gold discs Cascade won for 'Twilight' and 'Dirty Blonde'. Neither Helen nor Marc was interested in Jimmy's studio equipment. Helen didn't have room for it in her one bed in Peckham and Marc said it was outdated now that everything was digital. Marc had put the lot up on eBay and sent Helen a cheque for the proceeds – one hundred and twenty-seven pounds – which Helen had never cashed. As for the rest? Old copies of music magazines, now hopelessly damp, technical manuals Jimmy must have used when he was renovating the Spider and a pile of absolute junk.

Steve nodded his thanks.

'You want to do the attic now?'

Steve agreed, picked up his toolbox and took a step forward. He was in her personal space now, though it didn't appear to bother him. Wiping the back of his hand across his brow, he said, 'Thirsty weather. A cold beer would be good.'

There was no beer – Meg and Marc usually only drank wine – but she went into the kitchen anyway and fetched him a tall glass of cold water. By the time she went back out into the hallway Steve was already upstairs. Leaving the glass on the bottom step she called up to him then retreated to the kitchen. While banging and sawing sounds were going on upstairs, she busied herself unpacking the last of the boxes. Then they stopped and she smelled cigarette smoke. She went upstairs and found Steve was standing beside the ladder, a rollie clamped between his lips. A crude square had been cut around the existing attic hatch which was now a gaping hole leading into the dim space above.

'That beer never turned up,' Steve said, blowing smoke. He leaned on the ladder, folded his arms across his chest and took the water from her. 'I'll just put me tools away then I might need your help moving the trunk.'

She nodded and stepped into the spare room while he busied himself, humming the guitar solo from Cascade's 1982 hit, 'Twilight'. Before her eyes, the sun sliced across the floorboards, which glowed like a new blade. She and Marc had had the conversation about the trunk a million times but he was right and she knew it. At some point she needed to let go and now was as good a time as any. A voice crashed through her thoughts. 'I passed out in this room once, after a sesh with old Jimbo.' Steve was standing just inside the threshold.

He put the glass of water to his lips. She watched his Adam's apple moving up and down and the thought came to her that there was something frightening about him.

'Right, let's do this,' he said, wiping the back of his hand across his mouth. She followed him out onto the landing. He went over to the trunk, grasping both handles and trying out the weight.

'What you got in here?'

'The same as before.'

'Feels heavier, like a dead body.' She watched him slide the trunk along the floorboards. 'I'll pull it up the steps if you just support the other end,' he said.

She did as he suggested, watching the trunk inching further towards the gaping hole of the hatchway. At last, a shout came from the attic.

'You can let go now; I've got it.'

As the trunk disappeared into the dark space above her, an image flashed through her mind of the curtains at the crematorium closing around the tiny basketweave coffin. Then Steve re-emerged and she suddenly longed for him to leave so that she could be alone again. They went downstairs and he packed his things into the van and returned holding the small shoebox she'd seen him with before. She thanked him, handing over the agreed sum in cash.

'What did you mean earlier when you said something's off and it might or might not be about Cecily?'

He gazed at her with a deliberately blank look. 'Nothing. I didn't mean nothing.'

'You meant *something*.'

'I shouldn't have said anything.' And with that he turned

and walked back to the van, got in and stuck out an arm from the open window and waved. She watched him drive away and as his van turned and disappeared down The Lane it seemed to her that Steve Savage knew more than he was letting on.

She went back into the house and saw there was a missed called from Janette on her phone. She pressed call back and waited.

SEVEN

Marc sat in a branch of Pret near King's Cross drinking coffee and licking his wounds. The argument with Meg had knocked him back. He'd been needlessly mean and now he felt angry with himself. What was wrong with him? Why couldn't he rise above and be a better man? Meg's stuckness, her insistence on clinging to the past kept him there too and with every new day that became a little more unbearable. The only person who knew what he'd done, the part he'd played in his daughter's death, was Janette. Every day it threatened to eat him alive, not least because he could never say it out loud, could never confess and receive absolution from the one person he most wanted it from, his beloved Meg. An abyss of silence separated them. There had to be some escape, some bridge that could connect them back to one another, a portal into a more spacious future. It was the only way either of them had any hope of making a decent life. It was the only way they stood a chance of survival.

He got up and throwing his paper cup in the recycling, made his way to the station and onto the Victoria line. He got out at Oxford Circus and walked the five minutes to the chain pizza place on the fringes of Soho where he and Helen had arranged to meet for lunch. It was Helen who had suggested the lunch and booked the table. Marc would never have chosen a chain place. It somehow offended his sense of being creative, an individualist, above being seduced by clever branding and the promise of predictability. Whereas the mad instability of their childhoods had engendered in Helen a need for orderliness, it had given Marc a comfortable familiarity with chaos. They knew each other's quirks and for the most part tolerated, even appreciated, them. It was for this reason that he didn't feel the need to apologize to Helen for being five minutes late. His sister had already been shown to a table and was sitting beside a glass of what looked like sparkling water, examining her phone. The siblings hadn't seen each other since the move to Coldwater.

'Hey, sis, how's tricks?' he said now.

Helen looked up and smiled. 'Sparky Marky!'

'You're looking…' he searched for a word that was both flattering and ironic, '…spiffy.' He took a seat.

Helen patted her hair. 'New "do".'

'They're obviously paying you well over the odds at…' He momentarily forgot the name of the place where Helen worked as an arts administrator.

Helen laughed. 'Broke Arts? I wish. They're threatening redundancies.'

He wondered if she was expecting a particular response from him. His sister waved and a waiter approached. 'Do you know what you want?' When Marc did not immediately respond she turned her head to the waiter and said, 'Fiorentina for me. He'll have a Giardiniera – no mushrooms, he's allergic – and a beer.'

'No mushrooms,' the waiter said, pretending to write that down.

'You look tired,' Helen said, once the waiter had gone.

'I've been working so...' He immediately thought that sounded rather negative. He was tired not so much from work but from the burden of so much grief. He longed to be done with it, this sack of stones he carried always on his back.

'The commute can't be fun,' Helen said.

The waiter approached with his beer. He took a long, cold draught and felt instantly better.

'It's okay. I just listen to music.'

Helen finished her glass of water and ordered another. Marc called for a second beer.

'Off the sauce?' he said.

'Ages ago,' she said. 'Gone veggie too. Have you only just noticed?'

'I've been a bit preoccupied.'

She gave a nod and looked at her hands for a moment which made Marc feel bad. Her father had died too and though it was true that Helen hadn't lost her daughter, she'd always said she wanted kids and had never met anyone she felt able to have them with, so there was that.

Helen pointed at the beer glass which he'd already, somehow, managed to drain.

'Having a liquid lunch today?'

'Nah, it's...' he searched around desperately for something to say to change the subject and landed on, 'Meg and I had a bit of a row this morning.'

'Moving is a shitshow.'

He acknowledged this and went on, 'She could do with

someone to talk to. She's a bit lonely down there all by herself.'

'She'll make friends in the village before too long.'

'The local vicar came by apparently and suggested she join some church group.'

'I thought Sandy might pay a visit,' Helen said. Reading the confusion on her brother's face, she added, 'The vicar. She was lovely to Dad, even when he kept trying to get a rise by going on about being an atheist. She was always popping in with cakes. We've got quite close over the years.' She gave Marc an intense look that he could not read.

'I don't think I ever met her.'

'No, well, you were hardly there. But let's not go over all that again,' Helen said.

Marc agreed, relieved. One day, when he'd left the orchestra pit and was a successful songwriter – he'd already written a song in his head for Beyoncé – he would buy Helen her own house. But he wasn't going to tell her that in case she scoffed or, worse, laughed.

The awkwardness between them passed and they were soon swapping tales of growing up as unwitting participants in the Jimmy and Astrid show. The booze, the dope, the house constantly alive with people, skittering over the bitter truth that, by the time Helen, the eldest, came along, Jimmy's performing career had already peaked and he was heading in a slow downward spiral that would take the rest of his family with him. 'It was lucky in a way that Astrid died before Dad,' Marc said as the waiter approached carrying their pizzas.

As the waiter put down their plates, Helen gave her brother

a beady look and said, 'Why? So you could be sure of getting the cottage? You were always Dad's favourite.' Marc noticed the waiter flinch a little before beating a hasty retreat. Marc felt winded by the barb. Seeing this, Helen leaned forward and in a teasing voice said, 'It was a *joke*, Sparky.'

'Oh, a *joke*,' Marc said, though they both knew it hadn't been. He had actually meant that Astrid would not have dealt well with Jimmy's declining fortunes. 'Did you ask me to lunch so you could have a go?'

Helen rolled her eyes and recovering her composure, said, 'I want to put Dad's stuff up for auction. The guy who took those early pics of Cascade, you know, the ones before Dad started looking like a wino, he's collected in his own right apparently. The valuer seemed to think they could fetch thirty grand. You won't mind, will you? I could do with the cash to tide me over till...' She popped a piece of pizza in her mouth.

'Fine by me.' She meant until such time as Marc was able to give her a percentage of the value of Covert Cottage.

Helen finished chewing and looking directly at her brother said, 'Tell the truth, I was hoping you'd come along to the sale for some moral support. It's next month.'

'Right, why not?' Marc said, making a mental note of the time and venue. They ate in silence for a while.

'Sooo...tell me about country life. It is bliss?' Helen said, finishing up her pizza.

Marc went back to the morning's row. 'I guess Meg's feeling a bit overwhelmed by how much there is to do. And she's not used to the countryside. She gets spooked by the sounds of creatures skittering on the roof.'

'I hope we can find a way for you to keep the place. I always loved Covert Cottage.'

'Really? You used to say it was dark and depressing.'

'I never said that,' Helen said dismissively. 'Dad ran it into the ground. I'd have *killed* to live there.'

He reached out and patted her hand. 'You've been so understanding about all that, Helen. I don't know why Jimmy chose to be so shitty. I had no idea before he died or I would have told him it was unacceptable. You believe that, don't you?'

Helen nodded and took a deep breath in to chase away the tears. 'He never forgave me for not being Astrid,' she said, in a resigned voice.

Doing his best to change the sombre mood, Marc said, 'One day I'll write a smash hit and buy us each a house.'

Helen raised her glass to that, then called the waiter over and ordered two coffees.

'Are you still seeing someone for...what happened?' she said, helping herself to sugar. She'd been very supportive at the time of the accident but referred only to it obliquely now, which Marc didn't mind.

'No, why?'

Helen shrugged. 'Maybe you should.'

The lunch ended and Marc went out into the street. He wasn't due at the theatre for another four hours and had planned on looking up some musician chums and putting out feelers to see if there was any session work in the offing. He made a few calls but no one was available. Time to kill. Sit in one of the parks and hope for some songwriting inspiration? As he was crossing Trafalgar Square it began to pour so he ducked into the National Gallery and found himself at an exhibition of eighteenth-century British painting which he had no particular feeling for but none against either. He wandered idly around the vast gallery halls until one canvas caught his eye. The painting, by Henry Fuseli, depicted a clothed woman swooning on a bed with what seemed to be a monkey sitting on her chest. Intrigued, he approached and was shocked to see that the monkey was in fact a demon and that peeking from behind the bedcurtains was another figure which could only be described as a sinister-looking horse. The painting, he saw now that he was close enough to read the label, was called *The Nightmare*.

He drew back, feeling the need to get away suddenly. In the café he ordered himself a cup of English breakfast tea, found a spare table, sat down and, to his surprise, found himself dialling Janette's number.

'Marc!' That glorious voice, the reassuring tone. 'It was so lovely to see you the other day.'

'Yes, it was...good,' he said. He opened his mouth and found himself stumped for something else to say. He'd never rung her like this but he realized now that he still needed help and that Meg was in no condition to offer it to him. Or was it Meg who needed the help? Yes, it was Meg, not him.

'You sound as if perhaps you've had a shock?' The painting came back to him in all its awfulness and he felt wretched and scared.

He hadn't thought that he sounded shocked, but Janette was right. She was always so absolutely spot on. 'I'm fine, it's just...' He tailed off, secure in the knowledge that he wouldn't have to come out with it in all its incoherence and fearfulness, that Janette would draw it out of him in a way that was manageable and safe. 'I just saw a painting by Fuseli and...' He stopped, unable to complete the sentence. To have been so spooked by a painting!

'*The Nightmare*? The one with the demon sitting on the woman's sleeping body?'

'Yes,' he said. It was uncanny the way she could read him.

'Some say it represents the unconscious.' It was always the same with her, the feeling of being unpeeled, seen in all his rawness. His dark, nightmarish, most secret self. The rotten heart of a man who could never forgive himself because he did not deserve it. Someone brushed past his table and he once more became aware of Janette's voice. 'Did you call me about the painting?' she went on.

The question pulled Marc back into the reality of his current situation. He felt silly suddenly. 'I wanted to talk to you about Meg. She's not herself at all.'

'Can you tell me a bit more?' Janette said in such a reasonable way that Marc found himself doing just that. He spoke about Meg's insomnia and her obsession first with mice in the basement and then with animals on the roof. How the vicar had tactlessly let slip a story about a little girl going missing in the woods near the house thirty years ago and Meg had somehow conflated the sounds and the missing girl in her mind, how he'd come home to find her on her phone searching for information about the girl's fate, how he'd recently gone into the bathroom cabinet and seen a foil of pills that he thought she'd long since stopped taking, how they'd rowed that morning because she'd made breakfast for three.

Janette listened, occasionally saying 'ah' to indicate that he was being heard.

'You won't tell her I called, will you?' he said, as they were finishing up.

There was a pause before she spoke and when she did there was a smile in her voice. 'Keeping secrets is my *job*.'

SESSION 4, LONDON FIELDS

'She died at the scene,' Marc said. 'The force of the steering wheel hitting her chest. It was an old car, a classic, so there were no airbags or anything.' He had no idea how Janette had managed to get him to speak about Astrid's death. When it happened he was away at uni. He'd come back for the funeral but not the inquest and had hardly spoken about it since.

'That must have been awful,' Janette said.

'Yes,' he said simply. He remembered the sense of numbness after the college dean had found him in the library and escorted him to the deanery to call Jimmy. This was before most people had mobile phones. Seeing himself walking along the corridor as though hovering over his own head. 'She'd been drinking,' he said. He didn't know why he'd brought this up. It didn't make it any easier.

'Was that something she did often?'

'Yes,' he said again. 'She and Jimmy always drank a bit, smoked dope, you know, they were a rock couple, it was part of the deal. The last few years of her life, though, the drinking had got out of hand.'

'So it sounds as if perhaps she couldn't be the mother you wanted?'

'Not really. I mean, she was loving but sort of permanently distracted if you know what I mean. Looking over her shoulder all the time.'

'And the accident?'

'Hard to say. She ploughed into the back of a lorry. It happened on the M20 on her way down to Coldwater to look at the cottage with a view to buying.'

Janette shook her head sympathetically.

Marc was in full flow now. How had that happened? Something almost alchemical about the way Janette teased the details out of him without seeming at all intrusive. 'The inquest was inconclusive. The coroner thought that maybe there had been something wrong with the brakes but she was pissed so there was that too. Jimmy – Dad – has never really accepted either of those explanations.'

'Because?'

'I'm not sure. He never spoke about it, but if I had to guess I'd say he wouldn't be able to bear the guilt. The Spider was the first present he bought my mother from the proceeds of "Twilight", his biggest hit, which he also wrote for her. And he's never accepted that my mother had a drinking problem despite all the evidence.'

'Some people prefer to live in denial. It's more comfortable,' Janette said.

Marc looked over at her, struck by the intensity of her tone, watching for a twitch or a flexing of the jaw that might give something away, but her face remained cool and expressionless. He caught himself wondering if she was married. An odd thought. His eyes moved to her hands, a silver band on her ring finger of her right hand, another on the index finger of the left. What beautiful hands she had. Long and sleek, the nails left natural and exquisite somehow.

'Astrid was Dad's one and only.'

'Has he ever mentioned anyone else?' Janette said.

'There were women before Astrid, obviously, and in his rock star days he got a lot of unwanted attention. Astrid's death got into the papers and I think he was approached by women who found the rock thing irresistible or maybe wanted to mother him.'

'From what you've said, your father may well have reason to feel guilty,' Janette said.

This seemed harsh and Marc wondered whether this was true.

'What happened to Astrid wasn't Dad's fault,' Marc said, preparing to come to his father's defence. Beside him, Meg laid her hand on his.

'Janette didn't mean it like that, darling,' Meg said. She was *his* great love and he was struck suddenly by a terrible fear that losing Lily would deprive him of Meg too. They had drifted apart since their daughter's death, pulled by diverging currents, Marc into his music, Meg into her misery, until each had beached on a different shore.

'No, of course not,' Marc said, feeling guilty himself now. 'I'm sorry. It feels like a lot, dredging all of this up.'

Janette made a sympathetic face. 'I want you to know, Marc, that in this room you can say whatever's on you mind. Your darkest, most secret thoughts and feelings are welcome here.'

Marc sat back. It felt like a great weight had been taken from his shoulders. He liked Janette, he decided. This thing, counselling, it was good for him. Janette was good for him.

EIGHT

A few days later Meg and Marc were eating a late breakfast of yoghurt and muesli together. Meg hadn't made eggs since their row nor had they spoken about it, instead carrying on as if nothing had happened. On the surface, at least, their days had been peaceful and ordinary, Marc heading off to London to work, returning late and exhausted, Meg setting herself to tasks around the cottage as if there were nothing more going on. Meg had made no more mention of the night-time sounds though they had continued and had, if anything, grown more frantic and more regular since the trunk had gone up in the attic. She had begun to think of them as whispers from the realm of the dead, at first faint, then louder and more insistent until her mind had become almost wholly taken up with what they might be trying to say. It seemed clear to her that they had something to do with Lily and with Cecily, the two girls having become not exactly interchangeable but somehow a part of one another in her mind. When she thought about her daughter, Cecily popped up and when her mind turned to Cecily, Lily was never far behind. In life they had been strangers but now, in death, it was as if they had morphed into ghostly twins who called out nightly for their voices to be heard, for wrongs to be righted.

With Lily that felt impossible. There were as many descriptions of the hit-and-run driver as there were witnesses. Everyone seemed to think the culprit was wearing a red baseball hat but on every other detail their recollections varied. No one had been able to recall a single letter or digit of the number plate and one witness even went so far as to say that the plate been removed, leaving only a blank. It was bad luck that only a single CCTV camera pointed to the part of the road where the incident took place. It belonged to a corner shop and had been disabled and the whole incident had happened so quickly and had been so clearly catastrophic that the only passers-by to have had the presence of mind to take out their phones had used them to call for an ambulance rather than record the car as it disappeared around a corner. There was no doubting what had happened, no particular mystery to it. Lily had taken off after a red balloon that a toddler had let go of and was screaming for, stepping into the road to retrieve it just as a car had come too fast around the corner. Later, at the inquest, the coroner had said that, though tragic, Lily's death had been just one of 28,000 hit-and-run accidents that year, only about 8 per cent of which would ever be resolved.

Cecily's disappearance and presumed death was materially different, it seemed to Meg. From what Sandy had said, no one really knew what had happened. The mystery remained alive even though the girl probably did not, and that meant that there were memories to plumb, details to uncover, witnesses to find, secrets people had kept to themselves all these years. Perhaps in finding out what happened to Cecily she could help bring justice to Cecily's family, even as she understood that it was likely that there would never be any for her, for Marc and most of all, for Lily. Perhaps that was what the sounds were trying to tell her, that there might be something to be gained from Lily's death if only justice for another dead girl.

As she cleared away the breakfast things she decided it would be best not to say any of this to Marc. He wouldn't approve. Things had grown more relaxed between them after they'd decided that they would invite Janette to use the studio. Meg had expected Marc to put up more of a fuss, what with his mantra of never looking back, but to her surprise he seemed open to the idea now. They'd been getting on much better since she'd stopped mentioning the nightly symphony of creaks and groans which continued to interrupt her sleep. She'd also been careful to let him know that she was coming to love the cottage and could see a future for them there. He even brought home a bunch of flowers for the first time since before their daughter's death, with a gap where Meg supposed he'd removed a lily, because she'd seen him doing it once before, and it was a gesture she found so tenderly moving that it made her love him all the more. They'd agreed among themselves that it would be a temporary arrangement until Janette could find somewhere more permanent. It had resolved something unspoken between them and Meg didn't want to jeopardize that by bringing up her growing investment in solving the Cecily case.

They kissed goodbye in the porch, Marc heading off early so he could accompany Helen to the sale of Jimmy's photography collection at Barham's in Bloomsbury. She waited till he'd driven away before going into the mudroom and pulling on her wellingtons for the trip to the village. Rain was forecast and in lieu of her waterproof, which seemed to have gone for a walk all on its own, she grabbed Marc's beanie and took off along the path over the fields by Covert Wood. It was a soft, dappled morning and a pair of buzzards were surfing the thermals. The path narrowed at the end of the fields and snaked along the backs of gardens and past a couple of semi-detached farm workers' cottages and the vicarage and coming out alongside the church. Steve lived in one of the semis, which together were the only council properties in the village. Meg knew this because Steve had launched into a very detailed account of all the improvements he'd made to his cottage when he'd come over to fix the gate and sort out the attic hatch and the mess in the studio.

The place precisely matched his description and the presence of his blue van outside confirmed it. A large plastic gnome sat in the front garden beside a concrete tortoise with yellow eyes. Meg opened the gate with caution – he hadn't mentioned a dog but you never knew – and hearing no barking, approached the front door and rang the bell. Big Ben chimes. Barking from next door. She leaned into the frosted glass panelling and made a frame with her hands. Nothing moved and when there was no sound she pressed the bell again. This time a side gate opened and Steve appeared. The expression of mild surprise gave way quickly to a smile, displaying those tobacco-stained teeth.

'To what do I owe the honour?' he said in an excruciating imitation of poshness.

'Can I come in?' she said.

He shrugged. 'If you don't mind me carrying on with what I was doing...' – the posh voice again. He tipped his chin to indicate the side gate.

A path of broken ballast led to a backyard laid with concrete slabs peppered with what looked like chicken bones. Steve's jeaned backside poked out from a shed at the side. There was a strong yeast smell. Stepping inside Meg was not surprised to see brewing paraphernalia; along one side a crude counter on which sat various buckets and flagons attached to tubes, along the other a series of shelves housing a number of bottles of homebrew. A dead rabbit hung on a hook in the corner, offering up a sweet smell of decay.

'Take a seat,' Steve said, moving a box in the corner nearest the door to reveal an old rusted garden chair, which he wiped with a filthy hand. 'Fancy a beer?'

Meg pushed the beanie from her head and hung it on the chair, declining as politely as she knew how but Steve took no notice and grabbing one of the bottles from the shelf, he twisted the screw cap and handed it to her. His eyes were the unsettling blue of an iceberg. When she hesitated, he said, 'Go on then.'

She tried to take a sip without her lips touching the rim of the bottle. The liquid ran down her throat in a thin sour stream that made her want to retch.

'Top brew,' Steve said.

'Uh huh.'

An awkward silence fell. They both knew this wasn't a social call.

'I've come about the girl who went missing.'

Steve looked up from under hooded eyelids. 'I told you I don't know anything about that.'

'You said she was in Covert Wood.'

'That was the cops, not me. What I said was I didn't want to talk about it.' A deep line settled on his forehead.

It had been a bad idea to come alone after all. Her eyes alighted on a hammer hanging from a hook in the corner of the shed. In her mind's eye she could see the weapon flying. How easy it would be for him to grab it. Or to grab her. She would have no chance. He turned suddenly, the unearthly eyes on her. She wanted to run then but stopped herself. What if he ran after her? And if he didn't, what then?

'It just seems so awful not to know what happened to her.'

She told him about the St Cecilia roses left at the front and back of the cottage. He listened impatiently then he said, 'If you've half a wit about you, you'll leave it alone. Nabblin' 'bout that girl's the fastest way to make enemies in this place.' He crossed his arms as if he'd won an argument. 'I got to be getting on.'

She bade him goodbye and left the property by the side passage, walking down the path to the church. Sandy was inside tidying up piles of hymn books. At the tap of Meg's shoes on the flags she turned and exclaimed, 'Meg! How lovely to see you.'

'Do you have a moment?' Meg said.

Sandy checked her watch. 'My barista skills aren't up to much but I can do you a half decent cappuccino in the vicarage if you like?'

Meg thanked her and waited for her to finish her task before the two women left the church, crossed the track opposite the side entrance to the churchyard and walked up the little garden path leading to the dreary modern box that served as the vicarage.

'Come in,' Sandy said, pushing at the unlocked front door. 'It's not much to look at but it's cosy.'

They took off their boots and went into a kitchen that had long passed its sell-by date. Sandy invited Meg to sit. While she made the coffee, Sandy explained that the church had decided that the old vicarage was just too expensive to maintain and had sold it off some years previously to a couple from London, the Falconers.

'Have you met them?'

'No, I've hardly met anyone,' Meg said. She was on speaking terms with Lisa now, and on nodding terms with the staff at the Palterer's. And there was Steve of course. But that was about it. This would have been more painful were it not for the fact that Janette was arriving at the weekend to stay in the studio until such time as she could find somewhere to buy.

'Oh, well, we must remedy that,' Sandy said, bustling about in the fridge for the milk. 'Everyone's very friendly.'

Sandy brought over two sorry-looking cappuccinos and pushed one towards Meg. 'Best I can do, I'm afraid.'

Meg thanked her and took a sip. The coffee was barely hot but strong at least. 'I was thinking about those roses,' she said.

She watched Sandy struggle to recall. Then her face softened and she said, 'Oh yes, I think that must have been for her birthday rather than the anniversary of her disappearance which is in November if I remember rightly.'

'Twenty-second November,' Meg said.

'You've done your homework.'

'It's the feast day of St Cecilia.'

She caught the look of surprise on Sandy's face. They sipped their drinks. Meg was the first to break the silence. 'Did Helen ever mention that the police never found the person who killed my daughter?'

Sandy nodded. A solemn look came over her face, but she said nothing.

'It eats at you, the not knowing; like a chronic infection or a cancer.'

'I can only imagine,' Sandy said quietly.

'But at least I know what happened to Lily because I was there, I saw it, I was there with her when she died. Cecily's parents don't even have that small consolation. All they have is an absence.'

'No, I suppose... It *was* a long time ago though.'

'For those who love her I'll bet it feels like yesterday.' She stopped to catch her breath. 'I'm going to be frank with you, Sandy. I want to find out who took Cecily.'

Sandy clasped her hands around her coffee cup. 'What makes you think you can succeed where everyone else failed? Only God knows what happened to Cecily. Sometimes we have to accept there aren't any easy answers.'

Meg reached out then and placing her hand on top of Sandy's, she said, 'Everyone needs a witness, if not to their life, then to their death at least. Please, tell me whatever you know.'

Sandy closed her eyes and bit her lip and Meg had the sense that she had been anticipating this moment, had been waiting for it. As she began to tell the story it was almost as if it had played in her head so many times it was no longer something that had happened but rather a fairy tale, the contours of which existed outside time. Cecily's family often came to stay with one of Cecily's mother's sisters who lived with her husband in the village. Sandy couldn't remember their names now and in any case they had left Coldwater not long after Cecily's disappearance. Cecily's parents had gone back home, leaving their daughter in the care of her uncle and aunt for a couple of days. They needed to go to some family thing on the father's side so they were going to do that and pick up Cecily on their way back. On the day she disappeared the aunt and uncle had taken her for lunch at the pub. They had a table at the front of the pub beside a window from where they could see the kids playing on the green. When she finished eating Cecily asked to go out and play with the others. At some point she came back saying she wanted to go and see a friend's pet rabbit. They tried to persuade her out of it but she was insistent. The aunt, not wanting to interrupt her lunch, went outside and spoke to the children on the green, offering a few coins to whoever would escort Cecily, suggesting they go the back route across the fields, which were pasture land then, since it was safer than walking along the road. They agreed that she would be back by 4 p.m., which was when it began to get dark. Cecily and her companion set off up the lane by the church. And that was the last time her aunt and uncle saw her.

'What happened when they didn't return?'

'They waited till just after 4 p.m. then the aunt went to the house while the uncle and a friend of his went out looking for them in the fields and on The Lane and finally in Covert Wood. The police were called but by then it was pretty dark.'

'And the kid who was supposed to be accompanying her?'

'They found him hiding in the shed at the bottom of the garden in his house. He'd gone with Cecily across the fields but abandoned her. The police couldn't get anything out of him. No one could. Elective muteness they call it. Went on for years. Even after he recovered his speech he said he couldn't remember anything and he's stuck to that even now.'

'Is he still in Coldwater?'

'Yes.'

'I'd like to speak to him.'

Sandy took her eyes from her cup of coffee and looked directly at Meg. 'You already have.' Meg held her breath and waited for Sandy to go on.

'It was Steve. So far as we know, he was the last person to see Cecily alive.'

NINE

The weekend came and with it, Janette. Marc waited at the station for her, arriving stupidly early. As the minutes went on his pulse quickened as if anticipating the arrival of a lover, though there was nothing explicitly sexual about his feelings towards her, which was strange and disconcerting – she was somewhere between a beloved sister, a friend he'd fancied long ago but no longer did and a mother. She had a certain mesmerising power over him. He found himself longing for her in the same way he had when they saw each other in sessions. Back then this had been partly why he'd insisted to Meg that they stop the therapy. There was something Janette would call erotic transfer, he supposed, some hangover from another relationship, perhaps with Astrid, which was playing itself out in their interactions, but whatever, it excited him. Meg, too, was looking forward to Janette's arrival with enthusiasm, if for different reasons. Neither of them had really had a mother, or not one who gave off that warming, soothing maternal energy. Astrid had never been very maternal and Meg's mother, Pamela, had always been too lofty and aloof for Meg to have been able to sustain a warm and loving bond. Things had come to a head at Lily's funeral, when Pamela had made an off-the-cuff remark about Meg failing to protect Lily which had been so wounding that Meg felt she had no choice but to cut off contact.

Once they'd decided to invite Janette to stay in the studio, things had grown less tense between them. His mind switched to a recent mid-morning episode of lovemaking with Meg, which had been as long and intense as the early days. He'd dressed quickly and while Meg was blow-drying her hair, he'd gone down to the studio and called Janette with the news.

Janette asked him how he thought Meg was doing.

'A bit lonely perhaps but much better in the last couple of days. Something seems to have shifted. She's stopped going on about hearing things in the house and she's talking about helping our local vicar with some festival or other.'

Janette gave a little hum in which there was buried a question mark. He knew her verbal expressions. This one signified a gentle scepticism. After Lily died Meg had got some comfort not from religion exactly but from her own blend of spirituality. Not Marc. Would loving God bring Lily back? Then what was the point?

Janette said, 'Perhaps you and I are too invested in reality to have much space for religion.'

'Perhaps,' he said, flattered by the suggestion. 'Whether she goes to church or not is up to her, obviously. I'm just glad she isn't going on about weird sounds and atmospheres and the spirit of some missing girl or whatever.'

'Aha,' Janette said in a thoughtful tone that suggested further exploration before adding, 'When someone senses that their thoughts or feelings aren't acceptable to another person or to society, they tend to take them back inside. What Freud called suppression. The unacceptable thing gets pushed out of awareness so that it doesn't have to trouble the person on a conscious level. The problem is that suppressing it doesn't make it go away. It just retreats further into the psyche and lays down deeper roots.'

'I'm not sure what you're saying exactly.'

'Only that Meg might appear to be feeling better about things but that doesn't mean she is. *Reculer pour mieux sauter.*' He'd heard Janette use this phrase before. Withdraw in order better to advance. 'What I'm saying is, we're not out of the woods yet.'

He felt a stab of anxiety. Janette had such an unerring knack of getting to the heart of things by the most direct route. He repeated the offer for her to come and use the studio, adding that it would be so helpful to him if she could keep a professional eye on Meg.

'Well, dear Marc, I'll come if you think I can be useful. You know how much I care about you.' He felt a flush of heat. Was it possible that she knew he loved her and that she too loved him? Not like a lover but in a pure way, a way he'd always longed to be loved. Like Astrid might have loved him if she'd been less preoccupied with Jimmy, with herself. Afraid too, uncertain as to whether he could trust it. Trust her. Most of all, trust himself.

Some of these thoughts continued to skitter through his head as Janette's train drew into Coldwater station. He leapt from the car to meet it. After what seemed like forever Janette emerged pulling a large wheelie case. He ran along the platform and grabbed it from her.

'Oh Marc, how lovely,' she said. Reaching out a hand, she touched him on the face and it was all he could do not to push back the tears. She would fix them, she would do whatever was necessary to help them find a future together.

'Welcome,' he said, thinking that he had never said that word with more feeling than he did now.

On the journey over, Janette caught up with his news and in no time they were turning into the gravel drive just as Meg emerged from the front door, beaming. He brought the vehicle round and pulled on the handbrake. The passenger door opened and Janette got out. A stab of envy as the two women embraced, then turned their backs to him and walked arm in arm towards the front door, leaving him to heave Janette's bag from the car. He felt a familiar sense of having been sidelined, the way he had sometimes felt in sessions, that as the mother she, Meg, had more of a right to Janette's support than he, a mere father.

He followed them inside, bringing up the rear, setting the bag down in the hallway. All three made their way to the kitchen before Meg and Janette set off down the garden path to the studio. Before long they returned, smiling and chattering, bringing with them the tail end of some joke that Marc was not privy to.

Meg came in first.

'Oh Marc, darling, there you are. I don't suppose you've put the kettle on?'

Janette, following on, said, 'The studio is wonderful how you and Meg have fixed it up. And what a view from the gate. I do so love a wood, don't you?'

'I do,' Marc said, though he did, in fact, have rather mixed feelings about Covert Wood, preferring to look on it from afar. The stillness, the deep matt of the light among the trees had always spooked him, even when he came on short visits to see his father.

'I'll make the tea while you give Janette a tour of the house,' Meg said obligingly. 'We hadn't really unpacked last time, but I've spent ages cleaning and sorting things.'

'Let's go then, shall we?' Marc said, leading Janette out into the hallway. At the bottom of the stairs, out of earshot of the kitchen, he turned. 'I haven't said anything to Meg about our arrangement.'

'Understood.' A hand patted his arm.

When they reached the landing, he stopped and pointing to the hole in the ceiling, which had yet to be topped with a properly fitting hatch lid, said in a low voice so that Meg couldn't hear, 'I finally won the battle of the trunk. It lives up there now.'

Janette's lips moved upwards in an unreadable Mona Lisa smile.

'Come and see my workroom.' She followed him past the bathroom to the end of the corridor. On his days off Marc had given the walls a couple of coats of white paint and put up some shelves. His keyboard stood in one corner beside a mixing desk. On the opposite corner he'd put the grey daybed on which he lay when he composed – even though most of what he composed these days was library muzak – and under the window, another desk on which sat his laptop.

'This is where I'm going to write the song that will make us rich,' he said.

Janette laughed, the lines around her eyes fanning out like

the tail feathers of a bird, and he felt himself expand, the blood rushing to his fingers.

'Oh, but isn't this...' Her eyes fell on the photograph of Jimmy at the keyboard in the early days before Cascade, wearing a sweatband to keep his long hair out of his face. '...your father?' she went on, going in for a closer look.

'Yup, Dad in his pomp.'

'And beside him, is that...?'

'Marc Bolan. They met through Astrid. I think my mother may have had a fling with him before she got together with Jimmy, but they stayed on good terms. I'm named after him.'

She tilted her head in his direction. 'Hmm. And that woman there?' She was pointing to the picture of Astrid he kept on his desk, his mother at her most flamboyantly beautiful, tall, lithe and with a kind of rangy sexiness particular to young women certain of their allure. She was wearing a witchy goth outfit which set off a mane of white-blonde hair that made her look like a Scandinavian Stevie Nicks.

'My mother. Gorgeous, wasn't she? Jimmy was a lot older, obviously. Poor Astrid. She died so young.'

Janette picked up the photograph and gazed at it for a moment, then placed it back down on the desk.

'You spoke about her in one of our early sessions. I remember the newspaper reports of the accident. I wouldn't have told you that when we were in therapy, but now that we're not...'

This news came as a surprise. When Astrid's Spider had veered off the road, her death had made a two-line mention in the papers. 'It' girl of the early Eighties in smash horror. Hints that there was more to it than an accident. Then the world moved on. It seemed quite a random thing for someone who didn't know her to recall nearly twenty years after the event. Her sports car, the 1979 Spider, still sat in the garage. After Astrid's death Jimmy had insisted on getting the crumpled remains of the vehicle towed back to their house in Chelsea. He spent the next decade restoring it.

'I don't think I ever told you this but I met your father a few times, before he knew your mother. Before he was famous even.'

This knocked Marc off his stride. He'd had no idea. It struck him how little he really knew about her.

'You never said anything.'

'Self-disclosure by the therapist is discouraged,' she said evenly. 'It can lead to all sorts of unhelpful fantasies. Besides, there isn't much to say. We knew a few of the same people. It was all such a long time ago.' In the soft light Marc suddenly saw an echo of the young woman she had once been. 'I was only ever on the edge of that scene. If I'm honest it all felt a bit shallow, even then. Not really my cup of tea.'

'I wish I still had the original photographs. That picture with Marc Bolan is a photocopy. Dad sold off most of the memorabilia from the early days to pay his debts. By the time he died there were some band photographs and old concert programmes. Helen inherited all those and put them into auction, but they didn't fetch as much as she was hoping.' He'd gone to the sale to support her as she'd requested. Afterwards they'd had a gloomy lunch and he'd bought her flowers in the hope of cheering her up. Broke Arts looked like it was about to go to the wall, propelling her into the gig economy, and she didn't know how long she could last.

He was suddenly beset by the possibility that Janette might

be expecting to be paid. They hadn't talked about that when they'd spoken about their arrangement. He realized now that he'd simply assumed that Janette would keep an eye on Meg in exchange for using the studio. 'We're not in great shape financially,' he said. 'I hope we won't have to sell the cottage in a hurry, but it might come to that.'

Janette was staring through the window as though she hadn't heard. When she turned back there was an expression on her face that Marc couldn't read. 'Does Meg know?'

'Not as such.'

She flashed him a smile which may have been intended to reassure. He felt a hand on his head, stroking his hair, not seductively, but in a wonderful, comforting, maternal way. When she took her hand away, he wished she hadn't. He felt embarrassed then, humiliated by his vulnerability. He turned on his heels and left the room. She caught up with him on the landing.

'I wouldn't tell Meg about the financial thing. She needs a period of stability. She's more fragile than perhaps you realize. And she likes it here. All the plans she's making.'

Marc pictured Meg coming up the garden path, her face all smiles. He loved his sister but after everything that had happened, how could he take that from Meg?

TEN

After lunch – Janette was vegetarian, one of the many things Meg hadn't known about her – the two women returned to the studio to unpack and get Janette settled in.

As they wandered down the path together, Janette stopped at the raised beds. Meg had been planning to turn them back into a vegetable garden, digging them over and pushing in a few rows of bamboo stakes to support her autumn planting.

'I always think a flower garden says so much about a person,' Janette said.

'Broad beans are more practical,' Meg said, feeling just a little offended.

'Who wants broad beans when they can have roses?'

Perhaps Janette was right. After all, you could buy broad beans in the frozen food section of any supermarket. It was a strange thing to feel funny about, her choice to plant vegetables rather than flowers, and yet she now doubted herself.

'Oh, but I'm going to make a rose garden too. Along one side of the garden by the patio with lilies on the other side. I've sent off for the bulbs and I've chosen St Cecilia for the roses,' Meg said, wanting so much to redeem herself.

'Lilies. What a beautiful tribute.' Janette smiled and went

on, quoting from the Bible, '"They toil not, neither do they spin." But you're working very hard I see.'

'It helps to have something to look forward to.'

'That's true, but in all of this activity don't forget Marc, will you?'

'What do you mean?' Meg said, suddenly alarmed. Had she somehow found out how preoccupied Meg was by the missing girl? How not a day went by when she didn't think about her? She hushed herself. Of course not, Janette knew more about her than anyone but even Janette couldn't read her mind.

Janette, ever serene, said, 'Only that Marc's more fragile than perhaps you realize.'

They passed the yew tree and came once more to the sheltered little plot where the studio stood.

'I *do* realize that,' she said, more defensively than she'd intended. 'It's why I called you.'

'Yes,' she said. 'Though Marc doesn't need to know that.' She waited for Meg to open the door then swept in before her and looking about at the newly whitewashed walls, she said, 'I wonder what it might look like in a pale, almost ghostly yellow?'

Meg wondered if the word 'ghost' was significant. Had Marc been talking about her to Janette? Did she know something about the attic sounds? She let it slide. Right now Janette seemed more interested in the space than she was in Meg.

'It's the strangest thing, but after we finished our work together I always sensed we'd meet again. If I were a believer in destiny—'

'But you're not?' Meg said, standing with her back to the door.

'We therapists say that each individual creates their own destiny.'

Meg had risen early to bake cookies and gather fresh flowers from the garden to place on the little table beside the sofa bed and now wondered if it was overkill.

What a large case she'd brought! Expensive, Meg noticed, its contents no less so. They turned to the task of unpacking, Janette handing Meg a pile of clothes to hang on the rail. She'd noticed the quality of Janette's clothes before, their precise cut, the shimmering density of the fabric. For a woman using the place as a weekend bolthole she'd brought a lot of outfits, many of them better designed for city wear. Well, never mind. She'd soon be resorting to cosy fleeces and practical, waterproof jackets.

'I suppose you didn't have much use for warm country clothes in Australia,' Meg said.

Janette stopped what she was doing. 'So I told you about that.'

'Yes, the first session, don't you remember? You didn't go into any detail though. What took you there?'

'Oh, the reason most people leave the place they call home.'

'Opportunity?'

Janette gave a tinkly laugh in which there was sorrow as well as wry amusement. 'A broken heart.'

'I hope you didn't think I was prying.'

Janette shook her head and smiled broadly. 'I'm an open book. And a wounded healer.'

'Wounded...?'

'Carl Jung said that only those who are wounded can heal others. You know the myth perhaps? Chiron, the immortal centaur, who was wounded by one of Heracles's arrows which had been dipped in the poisonous blood of the Hydra. Neither able to recover from the wound nor to die, he was fated to wander the earth healing others. At least, that's one version of the myth.' She went and sat on the sofa bed and sensing, correctly, that Meg's mood had grown melancholy with all this talk of wounding, changed the subject. 'I'm so grateful, dear Meg. You've made the place delightfully cosy.'

Meg, suddenly anxious that cosy might be code for cramped, said, 'Obviously, you're more than welcome to have your meals with us but it's fine if not...' She tailed off, not liking the way she sounded flustered and silly.

'The odd supper would be lovely. I don't want to take you over though.' With that she got up and walked over to where Marc had deposited her shoulder bag then unzipped the front compartment and began to unpack its contents.

'You'd be welcome to stay longer if you liked, not just at weekends.' The words spilled out of Meg. She hadn't discussed this with Marc at all. She was thinking how good it would be to have Janette's company in the week when Marc was away so much. She felt embarrassed by her neediness and went on, 'But obviously it's only a tiny place and you've got your clients in London, so...'

Janette had taken out a pile of clothes and was shaking them out and putting them on hangers. 'That's kind of you. The funny thing is that I was thinking it was about time I retired when I bumped into you in the village. My last client left this week, in fact, and I haven't decided whether to take on any others.' She put the shirt she was holding down roughly as if she didn't care much about it and swept the remainder of the pile to one side, then taking a seat on the sofa bed, she said, 'Come and talk to me for a moment. I've been wanting to ask. How *is* everything between you two?'

'Okay,' Meg replied then caught herself and swallowed the word back in. Janette hated words like 'okay' and 'fine' and always said they were strategies for avoiding feelings or saying anything real. 'Marc hasn't had another of his rages, so that's hopeful. And things have been easier over the past few days, but I...'

Janette stretched out her legs before crossing them in a comfy position and patting the cushion beside her. 'Come and sit on the sofa with me.'

After Meg did as she asked, Janette shifted in her seat so her knees were close. They were solemn now, Janette's attentions focused on Meg in a way that Meg found comforting and a little intense.

'I'm sensing there's something I need to know.'

I've never been able to get anything past Janette, Meg thought, not that I've tried very hard. She confessed now to hearing the sounds in the attic and feeling that she was being called, somehow, that she couldn't let go of the nagging sense that somewhere in the damp earth beneath the leaf mould Cecily was crying out to be found. 'I've stopped talking to Marc about it because he gets impatient with me. He says it's animals or else I'm imagining things and I need to move forward. But the past feels more real to me somehow. You don't think I'm mad, do you?'

Janette patted Meg's arm and said, 'Grief takes many forms.'

They lapsed into a comfortable silence, then Janette said,

'And how does it feel now that I'm here to keep an eye on Marc's moods, his anger?'

At that moment a robin flew by, narrowly missing the window and catching both women by surprise. Meg felt her breath leave her. The thought of the bird hitting the glass. A sudden panic rose. Janette's hand gripped her arm and brought her back.

'It's okay,' Janette whispered.

Her face was hot. 'Sometimes I feel that I might be going mad.'

She felt Janette's hand on her chin, gently pushing her face towards her so that their eyes met. 'Listen,' she said in the same whisper, only more urgent now, 'I'm more worried about Marc than I am about you.' She let go of Meg's face. 'I can see the rage dancing at the surface,' Janette went on darkly.

Meg thought about the encounters with Steve where Marc seemed almost to boil over. She was alarmed too, enough to have asked for Janette's help. She felt helpless and a little afraid, not of Marc himself so much as what he might do.

'What can we do?'

'For now, keep quiet and be vigilant. If Marc thought we had planned this or even spoken about it, it's quite possible that he would act out, do something unpredictable. He might even hurt you.'

'No way! Marc can get out of control sometimes, but it's *never* been directed towards me,' Meg exclaimed, Janette's words trembling in her belly even as she understood the truth in them. Even though he had never laid a hand on her, she could sense what Marc was capable of because she knew men, could feel the darkness in them which was neither bigger nor deeper than women's but of a different, more chaotic order. It was not that women were innocent, helpless victims of the marauding invaders they invited into their hearts and their beds, but the female capacity for violence was more precise somehow, more psychological. You never heard of a woman who went into a pub for a drink and emerged a half hour later blinking in bewilderment with her hands covered in someone else's blood. When women killed they did so meticulously, as a final act at the end of a long and well-mapped plan. And this was why, on the basis of no evidence, she knew that it had to be a man who had taken Cecily from the path across the fields, just as it had to have been a man who had driven over Lily and then away.

Janette had got up from the sofa and gone over to the window. 'Have I shocked you?' she said, turning her head to Meg.

'Yes, no. I suppose...' Meg was torn between not wanting to believe Marc capable of violence and knowing that he was, '...it's just that Marc would hate to think of himself that way.'

'Of course. That's why it's important to keep this...' she gestured between them, '...to ourselves.'

Turning back to the window, Jeanette said, 'This is even lovelier than when I first saw it.'

Meg, following her gaze, saw that the shrubs were beginning to brown and beyond them, the branches of the old yew seemed to slump towards the ground, as if burdened by the years.

'Have you been to the woods yet?' Janette asked.

'Not much.'

She told Janette about the missing girl, how, even after the official search, the police hadn't ruled out the possibility that the body lay somewhere among the trees.

Janette turned her head and stared at Meg as if she could see past the skin and flesh directly to her tenderest, most vulnerable place. 'You want answers.'

'To know what happened to her would at least bring some closure to her parents. Maybe even help find whoever took her.'

The robin flew past the window once more. Janette followed it for a moment then turned and with her back to the window, she said, 'Forgive me, but if neither the police nor the locals have managed to find her in last thirty years, how likely are you to be successful? In any case, finding her won't bring Lily back, even if she were yours to find, which she isn't. My advice is to let the whole thing go.'

In her tone Meg detected a hint of impatience, as if Janette would rather not have the subject broached again.

'I suppose,' Meg said, unconvinced.

Janette smiled. Leaving the window, she came over with one hand outstretched, saying, 'Now, let's go for a walk in the woods and forget about everything else for a while.' Meg took her proffered hand and felt a pull with such force that she had to steady herself on the back of the sofa.

Janette, laughing, said, 'You see how strong I am. Strong enough for the both of us.' She flashed Meg a conspiratorial smile and in a tone that sounded a little too bright to be real, she said, 'So, I've had an *idea*. When we get back from the woods, why don't we plan a housewarming party? Bring a bit of big city glamour to the back of beyond. What do you think?'

Meg put on her game smile but in her gut, some more troubled feeling stirred.

ELEVEN

After they returned from their walk and had had tea, Janette retired to the studio, saying she had some work to catch up with. They ate a simple supper of soup and cheese together and Meg went to bed early, taking two of her pills and waking early on Monday morning feeling groggy but rested. Leaving Marc sleeping, she threw on some joggers and a sweatshirt and crept onto the landing to make coffee. At the top of the stairs she froze. There was a strange change in pressure. She felt as if some force was dragging her backwards. Without turning she took a step back. Immediately the sensation grew stronger. She repeated the step until she found herself directly under the hatch into the attic. It was almost as if something – or someone – was drawing her upwards, as if she were being swept up into a vortex. She stood her ground now, braced for whatever was to come, but moments later, just as suddenly as it had arrived, the sensation left her body. Feeling cold and shivery, she went downstairs, switched on the heating and made a pot of hot coffee.

Later, she boiled eggs for breakfast and exchanged pleasantries with Janette and Marc, feeling preoccupied by yesterday's conversation in the living room, the experience on the landing and the missing girl and longing to be alone once more. She did not have to wait long. Just before ten o'clock Janette and Marc left to catch the train to London and Meg spent what remained of the morning unpacking while planning her next move. At lunchtime she set off down The Lane towards the village shop.

The trip had another purpose besides the shopping. She reached the bridge over the Sour and crossed it. Evidently it had blown a gale in the night and leaves and small branches were scattered across the asphalt. Arriving at the village green just as Lisa was opening the shop after her lunch break, she smiled a greeting, stepped inside and busied herself, scanning the shelves until Lisa had finished opening the till. A litre of semi-skimmed and a loaf in hand, she went to the counter and while paying brought up the forthcoming housewarming party and declared her intention to order everything bar alcohol – which the shop wasn't licenced to sell – from Lisa. Delighted by this news, Lisa went to fetch the order book and together they made a list. Lisa would deliver everything in person on Friday.

'Mind if I bring someone to the party?' Lisa asked, tentatively.

Meg did not mind. In fact, she insisted on it and the two women parted in high spirits with Meg going back out into the world feeling she'd made an ally and that this might serve her well some time in the future.

Outside the Palterer's, the manager, Terri, was sweeping up leaves. She figured that Terri was somewhere in her early fifties and might remember Cecily's disappearance. She went over and introduced herself, being careful to drop in the fact that she and Marc had eaten at the pub and were looking forward to becoming regulars, which seemed to please Terri no end. They continued to make small talk about the village before Meg, sensing the moment was ripe, steered the conversation around to the St Cecilia roses still blooming in the small, neat flower bed in front of the saloon side of the pub.

'You're a keen gardener, I see.' Flattery came easily to Meg. She genuinely liked people, felt relaxed in company for the most part and enjoyed putting others at ease, but it seemed that she had touched on something raw because she saw Terri stiffen. The publican stopped sweeping and an energy fizzed behind her eyes. Anger, fear or maybe something more nebulous? She said, tersely, 'My mother's project. Remembrance roses.'

Meg, surprised at her tenaciousness when everything in Terri's demeanour suggested that this line of enquiry was unwelcome, pressed on. 'For Cecily, I suppose?'

Terri frowned and shifted her weight between her feet. At last, she said, irritably, 'Why did you ask me if you already knew?'

'I was hoping you would be able to tell me something about her.'

At this, the older woman seemed to soften and leaning her broom against the porch she said wearily, 'She was a little girl, that's all I've got to say. She played on the green sometimes with the rest of the village kids. My son was about the same age so they used to be on the swings together. There are no swings now, the council took them down. Kids are on their screens these days anyway.'

'Maybe your son remembers something?' Meg said.

'He was six.' Terri snatched up her broom and began to sweep, this time more vigorously and Meg sensed that to press any further would prove unproductive. Instead, she extended an invitation to the housewarming and bidding the older woman a good day, crossed over the green and went up the path beside the church. The old yew beside the churchyard had lost a branch in last night's gale. The broken branch lay beside it, white-raw and frayed where it had been ripped from the tree. She thought how sad and fragile it seemed then and tears began to prick her eyes. She felt rather weak, as if her legs no longer belonged to her. At that moment a hand landed on her arm and a voice said, 'Are you all right?'

When she turned there was Sandy's face looking at her with concern. Both women glanced at the broken branch for a moment, then stooping to pick it up, Sandy said, 'Would you like to come in for tea? I was just opening the church but that's done now.' Sandy rolled herself up to her full height.

'I was...' Meg held up the shopping bag. And then she said, 'Thank you, I'd love that.'

From the cheerful chaos inside the vicarage Meg got the idea that Sandy spent her time on more spiritual matters. As tea was being made, Meg mentioned the housewarming party, saying she was hoping as many locals as possible would come.

'So please feel free to mention it around.'

'That's generous of you. And I will.'

She waited for Sandy to sit down with the tea. They sat in silence for a moment while Meg considered how best to raise the topic of Cecily. Finally, she said, 'Terri was telling me there used to be swings on the green.'

'That's right, there was a little playground there, I believe. People stopped using it and the council eventually took it away.'

'So I suppose there must have been a school at one point,' Meg said. Since the encounter with Terri an idea had begun to take root. School archives would surely contain a list of names of kids who would have been around the same age as Cecily at the time of her disappearance. With a bit of luck one or two of them might still be living in Coldwater.

Sandy drank her tea before going on, 'Yes, a primary school called St Joseph's, same as the church, but after the business with the missing girl a lot of parents moved away, and enrolment fell to unsustainable levels. It closed about twenty-five years ago. The building's still here; a red-brick Victorian on the other side of the green. It's a private residence now. Why do you ask?'

'Passing interest in local history,' Meg said, casually.

The two women chatted inconsequentially for a bit before Meg rose and thanking Sandy for the hospitality, walked back down the path and across the green. The old red-brick building had so obviously once been a school that it was surprising Meg hadn't clocked it before, particularly since the front garden was densely planted with St Cecilia roses, on which, just like those outside the Palterer's, a few bedraggled blooms still clung even as November approached. She went up the path and knocked on the door. A woman in her early thirties answered, holding back a large buff-coloured dog. Too young, most likely, to remember Cecily.

Meg stretched out a hand and introduced herself. She mentioned the housewarming party. The woman, whose name was Lucy, gratefully accepted. She and her husband, Nat, had recently come down from London to escape the rat race. They'd thought about holding a housewarming but hadn't got round to it.

'Everything's still a mess. I mean, look at the front garden for a start.'

Seizing the moment, Meg said, 'Really? I was just thinking how gorgeous your roses are still.'

'The bushes are a bit raggedy but the flowers are lovely,' Lucy said. She'd noticed the village was full of very similar roses and presumed locals had taken cuttings from a single, original bush because it gave such beautiful blooms. She didn't know their name. Meg, sensing that Lucy had no idea about a missing girl, finished up the conversation and waving her goodbyes, crossed over the green and returned to the cottage. Putting away the shopping, she made herself some coffee and sat with it at the kitchen table, realising only then that, in the couple of hours she'd been away from home, she had not once given thought to Marc or to the conversation in the living room. What a relief that was. Some things were best forgotten.

She passed the rest of the afternoon unpacking. About four, as the light began to dim, she found herself on the upstairs landing when there began the same strange stirring she'd felt that morning. A rise in pressure and...not sounds exactly but the impression of sounds. The closer she moved towards the attic hatch the stronger the sense of being drawn upwards. Part of her wanted to dash down the stairs to the safety of the kitchen but another, more curious and, perhaps, braver part felt compelled to investigate. There was no question in her mind that the disturbance was emanating from the attic so, pulling down the ladder she climbed up into the space and reached for the light switch. In the dim grey illumination of the single bulb it seemed that all was quiet, nothing disturbed. Yet there it was, a pulsing or quivering: an expectancy. Yes, that was a better word. An expectancy, almost as if the room were waiting for her to bring it something. Or someone.

Clambering back down the steps she dimly recalled an article she'd read on a popular science website some years ago about infrasound, ultra-low frequency disturbances caused by earthquakes and certain weather conditions, which could only be very faintly detected by humans. As she reached into her memory more details presented themselves. She remembered the article saying that the phenomenon often showed up as a feeling of uneasiness or a sense of destabilisation, like the whump of a distant helicopter and that it was sometimes mistaken for supernatural or extraterrestrial events. If it went on for a long time an infrasound could create nausea, dizziness and disorientation but it was otherwise harmless save for the unsettling psychological feeling of menace. She remembered the article's title now. The Fear Frequency. But if that's what it was, why was the feeling so much more powerful in the attic? Why did it seem to throb and pulse more strongly at night? And why, if it was called the fear frequency, was she so drawn to it?

She headed down the stairs into the kitchen and made herself a steadying cup of camomile tea. She didn't believe in ghosts, exactly, but there were things, communications, perhaps, from some unseen dimension of consciousness, which she'd been picking up ever since Lily's death that she could not shake off. She'd never mentioned any of this to Marc or even to Janette. They were private and special somehow. She had the sense that she had over the months picked up the frequency of the dead but it was not till she'd arrived here, at Covert Cottage, that she'd begun to understand that they were speaking to *her*. The communication still felt too diffuse and foggy to make out any message, but each time she sensed it, the signal appeared to grow a little louder, a little clearer.

TWELVE

When Marc got back on Tuesday night, Meg was asleep in bed. Unusual of her not to wait up for him. He'd noticed that she was back on the pills. Perhaps that was it. He slept well, got up earlyish since it was a matinee day, dressed and was in the kitchen having his breakfast when Meg emerged, still in her pyjamas.

'Hey. You're up early.'

She sat down, yawned, rubbed her eyes and poured some coffee.

'I've got that audition, remember?' He'd told her this.

'Oh, right,' she said.

'Which, you know, could be a big break.'

'Right.'

He felt a pale blue irritation rise. Why couldn't she be more supportive? He said, 'Have you started taking those pills again?'

'Occasionally. Why not?' She stood up, went over to the toaster and dropped in a couple of pieces of bread. Softening, she said, 'How was yesterday?'

'Fine,' he said, sulkily. Acting out, Janette would have called it. He didn't care.

'They know you're taking Saturday off?' she said, blithely unaware of his darkening mood.

'Yeah. I'm not on rota. It's been in the shared calendar for weeks. Which you'd have seen if you'd bothered to look.'

She yawned again and said, 'I ordered the stuff for the party.'

'Oh,' he said, without enthusiasm, standing and taking his cereal bowl to the dishwasher. 'Do I need to go and pick it up?'

'No, I bought everything except the booze from the village shop.'

His ears were hot. So here they were again. With her not respecting the fact that he was working his arse off supporting them both. But there was no point in re-visiting that grievance. Instead, he added, 'Why would you do that when you know it'll be much cheaper at the supermarket? I'll have to drive into Ashford anyway to pick up the drink. Unless of course, you want to drive?'

'Marc, we've been through this. It's as much as I can do to get into a car, let alone drive.'

He closed his eyes and did his best to calm himself. He'd imagined that he'd feel more settled once they moved. Instead, he felt lonely and exhausted by the commute. What did he care about housewarming? He was never bloody here.

He heard Meg say, 'Why are you trying to pick a fight?' and felt something inside him collapse.

'I'm not, I just...' How could he say what he really felt? That he was afraid she might be losing it, hearing sounds and going back to the pills, because she had lost it, once, not long after Lily's death.

'I asked Janette if she'd like to stay a bit longer, not just weekends,' she said.

'I know, she told me on the way to the station on Monday,' he said. He'd conveniently forgotten this on Tuesday morning and Meg hadn't brought it up.

'I think it would help us.'

He nodded and moments later, wary of any further conflict, he left the room feeling oddly devastated. Was a live-in therapist really the only solution to saving their marriage? Couldn't they fix this themselves? He pulled on his boots, picked up the bag containing his penguin suit and within minutes he was in the car driving through the woods on his way to the station.

A couple of hours later found Marc leaning against the wall at the front of Pete Starr's gorgeous Georgian villa in St John's Wood wishing he'd bought some Marlboro Lights in the newsagents by the tube station. He'd quit smoking about the same time as his last audition for session work but if he went back to the shop now he'd risk being late. He needed this gig. While Meg wasn't working and they were having to spend money on the cottage, things were uncomfortably tight. His plan was to ask Pete to make an introduction to someone who could help his songwriting along. One great song brought to the attention of the right person at the right time would be all it would take to solve his financial problems. But here he was, getting ahead of himself again. First things first. Bag the gig. It was by no means a sure thing. He hadn't been a session guy for so long that no one on the scene really remembered him and he'd had to lean heavily on Pete Starr's affection for Jimmy to secure an audition. The two old rockers had bonded over their mutual love of the Fender Starcaster. Pete had played on a couple of Jimmy's failed post-Cascade singer-songwriter albums and Jimmy had returned the compliment on a couple of Pete's much, *much* more commercially successful outputs. Jimmy was a better player than Pete but he, Marc, wasn't going there. He'd told Marc at Jimmy's funeral that he felt bad for the old man, had wanted to do more to try to revive his career but that, for whatever reason, Jimmy hadn't come up with the goods. As for Pete, he'd continued long after what the record bosses considered to be his sell-by date, grinding out albums designed to slot into the popular, commercial middle ground. His later work was horribly received by the critics but there was the odd low-level hit. He bottomed out in the late Nineties but had been much cannier than Jimmy about his back catalogue and used the royalties to fund a songwriting career. It paid off and now, on account of his business acumen and string of songwriting credits, Pete Starr had money. One look at the house told you that. Marc ran an eye along the immaculate gravel driveway, bypassing a Lexus and a Lotus to the broad front door with its gleaming brasswork, the double-fronted facade, the expensive matt paint of the frames offset by the original Georgian glass, its ripples shimmering in the sun.

For a long time, a life like Pete's would have been the dream for Marc. A big-hitting career in a band followed by some collabs with rising stars, some songwriting hits and then into production. Marc knew he was a bloody good musician, though in the music business that only got you so far. He also knew that he'd never had the stomach for being in a band. Too much of a basic introvert. Plus everything had become so hard. The industry, online streaming, Marc himself. Now he felt lucky to be just another washed-up chump eking out an anonymous living in the orchestra pit. You had to deserve success, especially when the industry was geared to depriving you of it, and Marc didn't deserve anything. Not after what he'd done. Sometimes, in his gloomier moments, Marc felt almost like he didn't deserve to be alive.

He checked his watch and thought about the row with Meg, how when he played it back in his mind, he'd sounded deranged, how Meg's face had betrayed a new wariness. He was afraid of himself sometimes. What he'd done, where he'd been, why he'd forgotten to pick up Lily so Meg had had to do it, at no notice, leaving the parent-teacher meeting at her own school and rushing over to meet their daughter. If she knew she'd never speak to him again. No one would ever speak to him again. That was why it was so important to make a success of their new life in Coldwater. No one there knew about what he'd done.

A voice called his name. He turned his head in the direction of the sound and saw a young woman in the doorway of Pete's place.

'Dad saw you standing outside.'

He smiled and went over, hoping Pete hadn't seen him talking to himself like a loon.

'So you must be…' His mind went blank. The young woman came to the rescue.

'Debby, yeah. Come in.'

Following Debby down an elegant hallway of chequerboard tiles, he found himself in a large sunlit living room. Pete was leaning back in a Charles Eames office chair with his feet on his desk, a cigarette burning between his lips.

'Hey, man. Been a while,' he said, in the languid, trans-atlantic/mockney mash-up favoured by ageing rockers.

'Yeah, Dad's memorial, but we hardly got a chance to speak.' He tried to put his mind to working out how long it had been since Pete had been a regular fixture in his life. Jimmy had left London more than a decade and a half ago and with the exception of the brief exchange at Jimmy's funeral, he and Pete hadn't met since then.

'So what you been up to, friend?' Pete said now.

'Oh you know, man, paying my way until my ship comes in,' Marc said. This wasn't the way Marc usually spoke but, hey, whatever it took. 'Got a few irons in the fire right now in fact. Beyoncé's people.' As he said this he felt a sharp pull. It was an absolute lie that he hadn't even known he was going to say until it came out of his mouth.

'That right? Cool,' Pete said in a disappointingly unimpressed voice. He leaned forward and dropped his cigarette into an ashtray on the desk. 'You know I woulda done anything for your old man.'

'Yeah,' Marc said.

'Soo…' Marc saw Pete's eyes flick to his watch. 'You wanna play me something?' He gestured to a custom Steinway sitting in one corner of the room. Marc got up and went over to it, settled himself on the stool and stared at the keyboard. *Worth more than my house.* He blinked away the thought. Not helpful.

'What you wanna play?'

'The Beyoncé song?' The instant Marc said this he regretted it, obviously, since no such song existed.

'How about one of the old man's tunes?'

'Oh, yeah, right.' On the one hand, relief. On the other, how much longer was he going to have to act as Jimmy's stand-in?

He thought about the money, blinked himself calm, took a breath and began to play 'Twilight'. Across the room Pete nodded and beat out some air drums.

When he'd finished, Pete said, 'Okay, man, I'm seeing some other villain in a little while but I'll let you know pretty soon.'

He left feeling tense. Pete hadn't mentioned he was seeing anyone else. On the corner of the street he stopped to check his messages. Just one, a text from Meg asking about the audition. He replied with a thumbs-up then walked back to the tube, not stopping at the newsagent, his urge for a smoke having dissipated. He took the Jubilee line, changed at Baker Street and got off at Oxford Circus. He lunched at a cheap Italian place in Soho and made it to the theatre in good time for the two o'clock matinee.

The audience, which was spartan, consisted of a couple of coachloads of pensioners and some confused-looking tourists who'd swallowed the cut-price ticket booth salesperson's schtick. During the break between the end of the matinee and the start of the evening performance, Marc found a quiet corner backstage to familiarize himself with Pete Starr's last solo album, a lacklustre rehash of some of his earlier, more successful work, then tagged along with some of the other members of the orchestra for a quick drink at The French House. There was much gossip about one of the strings players, Patty Leary, who had left without warning directly before last night's performance. After that everyone paraded back to the theatre in time for a staff meeting to run through schedules and rotas and to discover who management had been able to hire at such short notice to replace Patty. The conductor, Tan Rable, made a big play of keeping them in suspense. Eventually, with all the other business out of the way, he said, 'I know you're going to be excited to welcome back an old member to the string section.' They looked at one another. Rable disappeared momentarily backstage and there was a collective holding of breath before he reappeared. Following on shortly behind came Patty Leary's replacement.

The moment Marc saw that angelic face, the long muscular legs, the lithe, cat-like walk, he felt his balls shrink and the breath leave his body.

Daisy Godwin. Bloody Daisy Godwin. BDG.

He became conscious that Fabian Tucker, the oboist-cum-sax player standing beside him, had begun to clap. The entire orchestra, in fact, was applauding.

Everyone except Marc who was thinking *crap, crap and double crap*. He'd hoped never to see Bloody Daisy Godwin again.

Rable showed Daisy to the front of the stage. She took her place in among the strings. Their eyes met only once and only briefly. Marc felt his skin flame but to his relief BDG turned away. Rable called for a moment's quiet then they tuned their instruments and the performance began. Twice Marc caught himself hitting a wrong note, his fingertips clammy on the keys and during one mistimed bar he grew conscious of Rable's disapproving eyes upon him and it took everything he had to force himself to focus. The moment the performance ended, feeling very out of sorts, he took off and made his way as fast as he could to the artists' entrance to avoid bumping into Daisy. The theatre crowd was dispersing along Shaftesbury Avenue to catch their tubes at Leicester Square and Piccadilly Circus. Ducking into the nearest newsagent, he bought a pack of Marlboro Lights and settled himself on a bench beside the winos in St Ann's churchyard, smoking four cigarettes in rapid succession. Feeling a bit calmer now, he switched on his phone and saw a missed call from Pete. He punched callback.

'Hey, man.' Pete's voice, sounding cheerful. Marc held his breath, waiting for the good news. 'So I saw the other villain who was *mad crazy talented*. But I feel like I owe old Jimmy one, you know? The gig's yours if you want it.' Marc let out his breath. There was a pause while Pete cleared his throat. Something told Marc that Pete was about to launch the big *but*. 'Sooo, I told you it would be, like, on a deferred fee basis, right?'

Marc thought, *No, actually, no you fucking didn't*. What he said was, 'Oh.'

'Yeah, so nothing up front as such. Truth is, I'm doing this off my own bat. You know how it is.'

Marc's stomach sank into the pavement. 'To be honest, man, that's a little disappointing,' he said. An understatement. He was sick and livid all at once. He'd seen Pete's gorgeous house, sat in his expensive modular furniture, played at his £250,000 custom Steinway, walked by his late-model Lotus.

'I get that. Look, if you don't want to take it, I get that too. The other guy...' Pete tailed off. The words went through him and came out the other side untouched. No need to finish the sentence.

This kind of shitty bad-faith dealing was happening more and more often in his world, the session musician equivalent of zero hours. It wasn't fair. He could complain to the Musicians' Union, but then he'd lose the gig with Pete and most likely be labelled a troublemaker and never get another job. It stank, but the alternative stank worse. There was always a minute chance that Pete's solo album would go big and even if it didn't, Marc might make some useful contacts. He reminded himself that he was in it for the long game.

He took a deep breath and did his best to sound pleased. 'Okay, man. Let's do this.'

He finished the call and stood to leave. On his way out he stopped at a waste bin and drew back his foot. Time to give something a bloody good kicking.

THIRTEEN

It took Meg a while to shake off that morning's fight which brought back everything Janette had said about Marc, there was something wrong with him, a loose screw, which might cause him to blow. Still, that seemed less important to her now, somehow. Maybe he'd sensed that her preoccupations were no longer directed just towards him, but also to whatever or whoever it was that was trying to communicate with her from another realm.

It was a clear and mild November day and she spent a few hours in the garden, in the company of the robin, digging and planting. She came indoors to have a light lunch and then, as she put away her dishes decided not to return to the garden. Instead, she climbed into the attic. Once more the atmosphere was thick and she was met with a feeling of being watched, though in the thin light of the single bulb she could see that there was no one but herself. On an impulse, she opened Lily's trunk and took out each object in turn, awash in memories of a time that had already begun to recede and take on the quality of a story. When that was done, she heaved up the trunk and checked underneath it and replacing it carefully back on the floorboards, repacked it with Lily's things. Then, driven by some impulse she could not articulate, she began to hunt, though for what she could not say, bending her body to peer behind every joist and deep into the eaves, even inside an old water tank. She was about to give up when it occurred to her that the one place she hadn't looked was perhaps the most obvious. The attic was mostly boarded but in one corner the thick layer of insulating foam was still visible. She plucked at it gingerly, lifting one corner then gently peeling it back. And it was there that she found it. Musty, moth-holed and dull with age, a single pink child's sock embroidered with red polka dots, the design worn by the little girl in the old photograph now in the drawer of her bedside cabinet. How had it got there, wedged as it was under the insulation beneath a loose floorboard? Nothing moved or pulsed or thrummed. She felt dizzy and sick as if she was no longer in charge of her own body. Random thoughts marched across her brain. Bewildering, nonsensical thoughts, snippets of the tunes she used to sing to Lily to get her off to sleep. *Hush, little baby, don't say a word.* The animal sounds Marc would play on his keyboard to make her laugh. The songs he would extemporise from nothing. Such beautiful songs.

Silence poured into the attic like water gushing from a breached dam. She closed her eyes and a great grey tower rose behind them and there it was, the blue Vauxhall or maybe Peugeot hurtling towards her little girl. There she stood, powerless, having lost her grip on Lily's hand only a second ago so that she could read a text, thinking it must be from Marc… she, Meg, in a rage at him for dragging her out of her PTA meeting in order to rush to Lily's school to pick her up, and now running uselessly after her daughter and screaming her name. Her mind so fuzzy with the details, remembering red somehow, the first primary colour a baby sees, the red of broken flesh, of blood. Her whole body was in the eye of a tornado, legs fixed in place as if some centrifugal force was holding them down. Her phone was downstairs and she realized that if she called out no one would hear her. Around her the air whipped and spun, the creaks and sounds so loud she could no longer hear herself think. The dead were speaking. They were shouting.

As suddenly as it arrived it stopped, Meg left thinking, *was all that in my head?* Another pill might help. Feeling calmer she went in for a closer look at the sock and noticed that it had a maker's stamp on the sole. If she tilted her head in a particular way she could just make out the writing without having to touch the sock. Made in Great Britain. Size 2.

Perhaps she should call Marc? Or the police? But what would she say? A girl's sock. How was that news? They'd think she was crazy. She rolled back the insulation until the sock was no longer visible, unsure what to do next, then clambered down the ladder to the landing.

She was alone, suddenly, with her anxiety and her terrible need to know. Gathering a notebook and her phone, she went into the mudroom, found a warm jacket and walked the mile or so through the wooded lane from Covert Cottage to the station. There she hopped on the first train to Ashford and found herself, before too long, in the local history archives at the library. The archivist pointed her to several dusty files marked Coldwater and to an old-fashioned filing cabinet labelled 'Education'. Parish records and the electoral roll had been digitised and were available to search. The local paper from the time of Cecily's disappearance was on microfiche. She began with the Coldwater files, old photographs mostly, though most could have been taken at any time in the last fifty years since almost nothing seemed to have changed, except, perhaps, the numbers of St Cecilia roses clearly visible in the more recent images. There was a photograph dated October 1992, only a few weeks before Cecily disappeared, of the village green under an early, unseasonable blanket of snow. There was even a photograph of Covert Cottage taken not long after Cecily went missing, with a kind of mist hanging over it which, when she asked, the archivist told her was down to the poor quality of the print, though Meg wondered if it wasn't something more than that, so spectral did the milkiness appear. There was nothing of use though and Meg soon moved on to the electoral registers from the Nineties.

She saw Terri's name and a couple of others she recognized, but not really knowing what she was looking for, took a photo with her phone so she could come back to the names on the list another time. Next she checked the local paper, *The Courier*, long since defunct, and found the edition in which Cecily was mentioned for the first time, dated Thursday, 26 November, under the headline *Concern grows for missing girl. Police appeal for help in case of missing girl.* The missing girl's last name was Banner, a fact that was new to Meg, and her parents were named as Joseph and Elizabeth. The aunt and uncle with whom they had been staying were Linda and George Truelove, and from that name Meg inferred that it was Linda who was the blood relative of either Joseph or Elizabeth, which tied in with what Sandy had told her. Cecily was described as three foot ten, weighing about three stone, six pounds, with light brown curly hair, hazel eyes and of fair complexion. She had a mole on her face, just above her upper lip on the right side, and at the time of her disappearance had been wearing a blue dress and blue leggings, with a pink cardigan and a grey anorak. On her feet was a pair of Kickers Mary-Jane shoes in navy. The colour of her socks was not described. There was a portrait picture of her with a sweet smile and a glittery clip in her hair, the eyes older than her years somehow, and a certain fragile determination in the jawline.

It made Meg cry to see her like that. The dearness of the little face. But she did not wish to allow herself the indulgence of tears and so she took a breath and gathered herself, wiping the back of her hand across her face. It wasn't seemly to cry, somehow, when she knew that at least some of her tears would be for Lily. She would let herself grieve for Cecily once she had solved the mystery of her disappearance. Until then, she would not trouble the girl's spirit with her muddled lamentations.

The circumstances of Cecily's disappearance were sketched out in no more detail than was already familiar to Meg. Steven Savage was referred to only as Meg's fourteen-year-old companion on the walk across the fields, presumably for legal reasons. The occupiers of Covert Cottage and, indeed the cottage itself, were also not named. A sentence was given to the continuing search of Covert Wood. The coincidence in Cecily disappearing on St Cecilia's day was not remarked upon which did not surprise Meg, since Cecily and Cecilia were sufficiently different for the similarity between them not to jump out immediately, and the saints' days were not widely known as they might be in a country more Catholic than England. That connection had evidently been made, but later, since the nursery who had donated the roses on the ten-year anniversary of Cecily's death had known it. At the bottom of the article was a police appeal for information with a telephone number. And that was that. Meg scrolled forward to the next edition of the newspaper, which reported on a police press conference given by Detective Inspector Dave Carelli, appealing for information and encouraging any witnesses who had not yet come forward to do so. He noted that the police were keeping an open mind and doing all they could, statements Meg recognised as the familiar blandishments issued by an investigation that had already run into the weeds, just as that into Lily's death had done. So much had changed in the years between and yet, it seemed, so little too. Children were killed and life moved on.

She checked in the education file and found St Joseph's. She soon discovered that schools kept their own records of attendance but since St Joseph's had been closed down, most if not all of its records would likely have gone directly to the council archives. The records of individual primary school children went with them to secondary school. If you knew the name of a child in a particular class, the archivist suggested, you might be able to find out who else was in the same class by looking for alumni on social media. Steven Savage had a sparse presence on Facebook. Meg checked his very small list of friends, wrote down a few names. As she was finishing up, the archivist came over and said that she'd found another file on Coldwater which had been put in the wrong place. Would Meg like to see it? Meg, nodding, said she would, very much, and not waiting till the archivist had left, opened the file and let out a gasp.

'Are you okay?'

'Yes, yes,' she said, plucking the first photograph from the pile. It was an image of children playing on the village green. A late summer's day, the leaves deep green and weary, their colours somewhat faded but still distinguishable. Her eye had immediately sought out Cecily, who was standing on the outskirts of the group, watching and smiling, a hair clip in her brown curls, and wearing a dress of purple stripes. On her feet she wore pink ankle socks on which polka dots were visible.

When she got home, Meg went directly up the stairs meaning to compare the sock to the one in the photograph which she had snapped on her phone, but she had only got as far as the landing when she heard Janette's voice. She went downstairs and found Janette in the kitchen. They'd given her a key to the cottage but Meg hadn't been expecting her till the weekend.

'Hello, sweetheart!' she said, opening her arms and moving in for an embrace.

Janette smelled of some expensive but contemporary perfume. Meg allowed herself to be held for a moment then pulled away. She was pleased to see her friend but wished also in that moment to be alone with the results of her research.

'I brought cake!' Janette said, pointing to a plate of brownies on the table. She'd evidently been there a while.

'Why didn't you call me to say you were coming?' Meg asked.

Janette looked momentarily affronted. 'It was supposed to be a surprise. I thought you'd be pleased to see me.'

'Oh, it's... I just didn't expect you, is all. Honestly, it's brilliant that you're here.'

Janette said, 'Did you find anything?'

Meg was still carrying her rucksack and a supermarket

carrier bag. For a moment she thought that Janette must have read her mind somehow, that she knew what she'd been doing in Ashford, then she realized that no, it was just that the carrier bag was new and evidently not from the local shop.

'A chicken, for tonight.' She felt bad, suddenly, at having been so startled to see her friend. It was she who had told her she'd be welcome to come not just at weekends.

'That sounds wonderful,' Janette said. 'But please don't go to any trouble.'

Meg went over to the table where a jug of water and two glasses sat beside the brownies. She poured herself a drink, took a long slug, and coming up for air said, 'Have you been here long?'

'A little while. I missed the peace and quiet. But I can go straight back to London if it isn't convenient.'

'Don't be silly,' she said. The research would wait after all. In a voice full of teasing with which she hoped to put Janette at ease, she said, 'Marc won't be back till after midnight and *someone* needs to help me eat up that chicken.'

'Right,' Janette said, a broad smile spreading across her face. 'In that case I'd better work up an appetite. Don't suppose you fancy a walk in Covert Wood?'

They took the back route, through the mended gate and across the field towards the dark fringe where the trees began, talking in bright, upbeat tones about Meg's plans for the garden, how the spring bulbs would need planting soon and the perennials dug up and divided, Meg glad of the distraction from her more sombre activity.

'Have you had a chance to think more about Marc, his state of mind?' Janette asked as they moved into the dappled light between the trees. This was, after all, why Meg had invited her to stay in the studio, so that she could keep an eye on Marc, so that Meg would have an ally.

'We appear to be missing one another, like before, only he seems angrier somehow.'

Beneath their feet the needle bed gave off a resinous aroma. Janette stood beside her, calm, enigmatic, but oddly comforting. Meg wondered if she should mention the sock but decided not to. Maybe once she'd found out more about the girl. Until then she didn't want to give Janette the impression that she had some unhealthy fixation. They carried on past the pines into a dank hollow lined with beech trees. The path narrowed and Janette hung back. From somewhere above them the bird sounded an alarm before lifting itself into the air. Meg became aware of a presence close behind. Thinking that Janette had caught up with her, she turned and started. Standing behind her, so close that she could feel his breath grazing her cheeks, was Steve. He was dressed in camo and carrying a shotgun in one hand. From the other, a dead rabbit swung, blood oozing from its eyes.

'Boo!' Steve said, grinning.

Her gaze travelled over his shoulder. To her relief she could see Janette catching her up.

'Where did you come from?'

Steve swinging his head to indicate the path that ran perpendicular to where they were standing.

'Little bird tells me you're having a housewarming party. Not cheap, all that booze.'

Steve swung the rabbit which fell back onto his thigh with a thunk. It made Meg sick to see it. How could Sandy think this guy was harmless, a good egg?

She said, 'I'd rather you didn't...'

'You could have bought some beer off me. I'd have done you a deal.' Steve touched his cap at Janette. 'Who's this then?'

Janette introduced herself as a friend of Meg and Marc from London. Steve nodded as if he'd been waiting for this moment, then wiping his hand on his trousers, took Janette's outstretched hand and just as quickly dropped it. His eyes flicked to hers then spun off. It was as if he was disconcerted by her, as if he sensed she saw something in him that he didn't want seen.

'Well, some of us have work to do.' The dead rabbit swayed a little, as if it had only ever been napping and had now woken up. Blood pooled in its half open eye. They watched him stride off along the path towards the pines.

'Sorry about that,' Meg said. 'He's creepy, isn't he?'

'Wounded,' Janette said. 'A holder of terrible secrets.'

Meg, surprised by this, put her hands on her hips and cocked her head. 'Why do you say that?'

'I'm trained to look out for those things. Something in the eyes and the way the jaw is set. The way he won't let you in.'

The thought that Janette could penetrate the soul of someone she had only just met was both impressive and a little scary. If she could tell that from a momentary encounter, what was she seeing in Meg that Meg herself didn't even know about?

They carried on walking. Meg held back the brambles for Janette to pass but Janette did not move and in the dappled light that fell on her face Meg saw something stir as though she'd looked through a window and seen a stranger. They had climbed out of the hollow now and were making their way along the banks of a steep valley through which ran the clean, cold waters of Covert Brook. Meg, eager to put some distance between her and Savage, pointed to what looked like a crude tepee fashioned from branches on the near bank. She'd overheard someone in the village shop saying there was talk of reintroducing beavers.

'Shall we check it out?'

Together the two women began a slow descent towards the stream. As it grew nearer, they could see that the arrangement of branches stretched four or five feet from the soil – too tall for beavers surely – and that the ends had been cut with a saw.

'It's a hideout, for hunting maybe,' Janette said.

Meg moved closer and peered through a gap, her eyes taking a moment to adjust to the darkness inside. She blinked and peered again, then heard herself cry out and felt her body fall back into the leaf mould.

'Meg? My God! Are you all right? What is it?' Janette said urgently, crouching beside her. 'What happened?'

Meg was shaking now. She tried to speak but no words came.

Janette came over and pulling her mobile from her pocket, shone its torch into the interior. She went round the side where it seemed there was a rudimentary entrance and bending low pushed her arms in among the branches. She emerged seconds later clutching something.

'It's nothing, just some clothing,' she said, holding up a small pink cardigan. To judge from the leaf mould and damp it had been lying on the forest floor some time.

Meg swung her body around to facing Janette and choked up the words. 'No, no, that's…'

Meg felt her body drop onto the soft pine needles. She held

her face in her hands and sobbed. She felt separate from herself now, as if she were somewhere else watching her own image on a screen, the hand pressed her shoulder, Janette's hand, imperceptible. She took a few deep breaths and eventually, mustering all her resources, managed to hiss, 'That's *Lily's* cardigan.' There was a pause. What was happening? Had time stopped? Meg became aware that she was looking at Janette's frozen face.

Rallying herself, Janette said, 'You mean it's *similar*? Because...' She left the final part of the sentence hanging.

'Yes, no, I don't know,' Meg said, confused, squeezing her hands together to stop herself shaking. Was it Lily's cardigan or Cecily's? Was she confusing the two girls now, haunted by both and muddling one for the other? There was another, more likely, possibility, which was that the cardigan didn't belong to either girl. She did her best to hang on to that.

Janette said, 'Let's go back to the house.'

Meg nodded. She allowed Janette to lead her by the arm for a few paces before pulling away. She felt foolish now and uncertain, but she knew that she couldn't go back, couldn't look again and couldn't ask Janette because if it was true, if the cardigan had belonged to Lily or to Cecily, she had no idea what she would do next.

She brushed the dirt from her, took a shaky step forward, then another. 'So silly, I'm sorry. I don't know what came over me.'

They walked back through the beeches and pines until the path narrowed and Janette moved ahead, just beyond the point where two paths crossed. A bird was singing in a high branch. Her heart was still pounding and it was taking all her effort to keep walking. *Shall I go back?* No, no, there was no going back. Lily was dead. Cecily was dead. They carried on down the path in silence until they reached the stile at the edge of Covert Wood then made their way across the field. As they squeezed through the gate, Meg said, 'I just need a lie down.'

'Maybe take one of your pills?' Janette said, adding, 'And Meg, I really wouldn't mention this to Marc. He'll only worry.'

Meg nodded. She left Janette at the studio and made her way through the newly planted rose beds to the house and going directly up the stairs, climbed the rickety ladder to the attic and switched on the light. Steeling herself she lifted the lid of the trunk and peered inside. The little pink cardigan, Lily's cardigan, was lying neatly folded beside her doll, exactly as she'd left it, not two metres from the sock buried under the floorboards.

She left the attic, went into her bedroom and took a pill then lay on her bed and wished herself to sleep.

FOURTEEN

Marc needed a smoke. Artists weren't allowed to leave the theatre in the interval but during Thursday night's performance he decided he couldn't wait any longer. The reappearance of Bloody Daisy Godwin was putting him off his game. If anyone saw he'd say he'd a family emergency to deal with and had had to make an urgent call. He ran through the backstage and swung open the artists' door. Instantly, a tall man with a hard-drinking, gammon-coloured face came out of the gloom of a street lamp and removing the cigar from his lips said, 'Are you responsible for this ghastly charade my wife was silly enough to drag me to?' It was as much as Marc could do not to gag at the stench of hard liquor and gingivitis.

'Sorry you've not enjoyed it.'

The man laughed. 'It's bloody *awful*.'

With a sinking feeling Marc realised there would be no ciggie break unless he was prepared to stand out in the cold being harangued by some drunk bastard with bad teeth. 'I should be getting back.'

'I've a mind to ask for a ticket refund,' the man said, enjoying himself and keen to prolong the exchange.

Marc felt his blood thicken. Why didn't the arsehole just leave him alone? 'Look, man, no one's forcing you to stay.'

'You obviously haven't met my wife.'

Oh Christ. Marc sliced his key card through the lock, stepped inside and leaning against the door closed his eyes and took some deep breaths. Why was he so bloody angry? The gimp outside, sure, but also the reappearance of Bloody Daisy Godwin. And while he was on the subject of rage, there was Pete's shittiness over pay on the session job. Maybe he was just stressed out about the commute. At the back of his mind these days, there was also his guilt about Helen and the possibility that Jimmy had left a newer will. And then there was Lily, obviously. Always that. He took a breath in. Well, the show must go on and all that. When he opened his eyes Daisy Godwin was looking intently at him.

'Hey, Marc. Are you okay?'

He felt the skin on his face blaze. 'Just some wazzock outside moaning about the production.' Gathering himself to his full height, he added, 'I didn't expect to see you back in the pit.'

'I tried to get something with more parent-friendly hours but...' She smiled and pressed her lips together in a gesture of resignation. 'Here I am again.' Then the smile faded and was replaced by the same look of sympathy. 'I really am so sorry about your daughter.'

Marc bristled. Daisy was the last person whose condolences he'd ever sought or wanted.

At that moment a stagehand appeared. 'Oh good, I've been looking for you two. Positions for second half, please.'

As the show ground on Marc felt himself drifting off and missed a couple of his cues. At the end of the performance he stood and took his bow with the rest of the crew and as the applause died down and the musicians began to file from the pit, he kept his gaze on Daisy, anxious that she did not escape into the night before he had the chance to talk to her. As he was exiting backstage, though, he spotted Rable heading purposefully in his direction. Knowing what was coming, he did his best to slide away, but Rable had him in his sights.

'What the hell was going there? Rookie errors. Is something going on I should know about?'

'Sorry, chief, it won't happen again.'

'You make damn sure of that,' Rable said disagreeably, before turning away and disappearing into one of the dressing rooms. Marc searched for Daisy, scanning the press of musicians and performers, but in the few seconds of his humiliating exchange with Rable she had vanished. He had to hope she hadn't witnessed his humiliation.

Outside the artists' entrance he reached for his pack of Marlboros only to remember that he'd left them backstage. He was about to swipe his card to get back in when the door swung open and Rable appeared. Anxious not to invite another bollocking, he slid round the side of the theatre and dived into the crowd spilling out of the front entrance, swimming against the tide until finally he found himself in the foyer.

Above the excited hum a single voice boomed out. 'I saw you, "Muso".'

Marc's heart sank. He closed his eyes and willed himself to stay calm but gammon-man, no longer fully in control of his body, was swaying unsteadily towards him like a runaway bus. At his elbow was a thin, overgroomed woman whose glassy stare suggested that she too was well into her cups.

'Look, man, whatever, just leave me alone,' Marc said. He was no longer much in the mood for politeness, even less for confrontation.

'I said I saw you.' Gammon-man's eyelids fluttered and for a moment Marc thought he might go down.

'Now you see me, now you don't,' Marc said, ducking away, impressed by a nimbleness he'd not had cause to exercise since the days he played five-a-side at the pitch in Hackney. Those days. In the before time.

Gammon's arm shot out. It seemed to hold the strength of ten men.

'Oh no you don't. I saw you ogling my wife.'

'What?' Marc was genuinely flummoxed for a moment until it dawned on him that Gammon was just looking for a fight and wasn't going to stop until he got one.

The arm did not move. In a loud and shaky voice Gammon said, 'Apologize!'

Oh God, thought Marc, *not this, not now.* 'All right. I'm sorry.' He tried in vain to shake himself free.

'Now apologize to Sandra.' He glanced at his wife who was inspecting her shoes.

'Tell you what, let me buy you a drink in the theatre bar.' The bars would, in fact, be closed by now but he just needed an opportunity to get away.

Gammon shook his head.

'Look, mate, I don't want any trouble. We both know you've had one too many. I understand that the performance was a bit disappointing. Why don't you and Sandra go home, and you'll feel better in the morning?'

The first punch hit him in the neck, the second sheared off

and landed uselessly on his shoulder. He could hear the voice in his head scream, *Don't be so bloody stupid* even as his fist went out and landed a bull's-eye on Gammon's nose. Gammon staggered back. Blood exploded in a fine spray and graffitied Marc's jacket. Sandra screamed.

He felt a tap on his shoulder and turning on his heels saw Rable glaring at him stony-faced. For a second he thought Rable was going to hit him, but the moment passed. Instead, in a cold voice, he said, 'Get out and don't come back.'

Marc felt his legs wobble. A thick fog descended on him and he seemed paralysed by it. Then he ran. Out on the street it had begun to rain and he wandered around for some while in a daze until he stumbled into a pub and ordered a double whisky. The liquor burned him back to his senses.

An hour later, as he drove from the train station through the thickening night, the thought came upon him that he might kill someone one day. Not now and not Meg, rather some perfect stranger. He would come upon them under the cover of darkness carrying a knife or perhaps a garotte, and before they were aware of what was happening the life would already be spilling from their body and it would be too late for them to defend themselves. He slowed and pulled the car onto the verge. His heart was on fire and for a moment he was seized by the desire to fling open the door and run into the dark wood and not stop running.

What the hell is happening to me?

He took a breath and blinked. However much he wanted to run, he couldn't do that to Meg. Putting the car into first gear, he pushed off the handbrake and began to roll back onto the blacktop. When he got home he saw there were lights on in the kitchen and his heart sank. He'd been hoping that Meg would already be asleep which would give him a few hours to think about what he was going to say to her about Rable firing him. But he found Meg at the kitchen table, thumbing through a brochure for what looked like expensive home security cameras. In the dim yellow light of the single bulb that hung above the kitchen table he could see the skin on her face was mottled from crying. He flopped down beside her and took her hand in his.

'What's up?'

She shook her head. Her eyes were glassy and he worried that she was taking too many pills. 'It would take too long to explain. I hope you had a better day.'

It was too humiliating to tell her the whole story of gammon-man and Rable, and of course the whole thing with Daisy which he'd never told her and never intended to. Somewhere outside a night bird cried. He knew how much they needed the money and how devastated she'd be about the job, so he just said he'd messed up a few of his cues. He suddenly felt utterly drained, hardly able to muster the energy to move or speak.

'You fancy joining me?' She took a glass from the draining board, brought over a half-empty bottle of rioja and let him pour his own. He filled the glass to the rim. Not classy but right now he didn't give a shit.

'Janette's back, but she's retired to the studio for the night,' Meg said. 'She's going to spend more time here, like we suggested.'

'Oh,' he said. That happened rather quickly. 'Did you spend the day together?'

'Just a walk in Covert Wood, supper afterwards,' Meg said.

Something in her voice suggested to him that there was more to say about that. He waited for her to go on which she did. 'Steve's got a kind of hut down by the stream there.'

'A hunting blind?'

'I suppose.'

A stab of something ran through him. Jealousy? He wasn't sure. If it was, then who was he jealous of...Janette for the time she had spent with Meg or Meg for having passed the hours with Janette? He was struck by an uncomfortable thought that he might need Janette as much as Meg, that he might even come to resent Meg for being able to spend more time with their former therapist who was – what now? – their lodger? Or their friend and counsel. Perhaps both.

'Well, here's to Janette,' he said, glad Meg had just handed him a good excuse to drink.

'To Janette,' Meg replied and as she raised her glass he could see her eyes were bright discs, alight with love, though whether for him or for Janette he did not know.

FIFTEEN

The following morning, Friday, Marc told Meg he'd be back just after midnight as always and left earlier than usual to get to London in time to have lunch with Helen. He met his sister at their usual place and ordered what he usually ate. Helen ordered a glass of wine. Marc drank more than the usual number of beers. They spoke about the housewarming party, which Marc had texted about earlier in the week, and their plans for the cottage renovations. Marc mentioned that Janette had come to stay the weekend before and Meg had extended the invitation without asking him. It seemed she would be spending a lot more time in the studio at the bottom of the garden now, at least temporarily. How Meg seemed more settled but also more secretive somehow, or maybe just less available. She'd stopped going on about the noises in the attic, which was something, but she had admitted to going back on the antidepressants.

Helen listened to all of this intently and she said, 'It's not going to be like last time, is it?'

Not long after Lily's funeral, Marc had found Meg in bed unconscious, clutching their daughter's little pink cardigan, an empty bottle of amitriptyline pills by her side. She hadn't taken enough to end her life, but the incident ended with a trip to Accident and Emergency and it had spooked them both. From then on, the doctor had prescribed her the same tablets but in smaller quantities and she'd gradually phased them out. Or so Marc thought. He didn't like it that she was taking them again, but Meg seemed so much better that he had no fear of a repeat of the past.

'No, I think she's going to be okay. Especially now Janette's there.'

'She sounds amazing. I can't wait to meet her.'

Coffee came. He had intended to use this last part of their encounter to confide in his sister that he had lost his job, but in the end he couldn't face the shame. Instead he walked with her to the tube station on her way back to what was likely to be an unproductive afternoon at Broke Arts in Holborn and pretending he'd left something back at the restaurant, returned to street level, passing the remainder of the afternoon in a Costa Coffee before finding himself at the Prince Charles cinema off Leicester Square where he dozed his way through the remainder of the afternoon and evening in the warmth for the price of a single ticket.

Realising he hadn't eaten for many hours, he went into Chinatown to find a cheap meal and checking his balance at an ATM, was horrified to discover that a few days ago Meg had withdrawn a hundred pounds from their joint account. He supposed this was to pay for the nibbles and soft drinks for the housewarming party, but it seemed wildly extravagant. Hadn't they agreed to limit the food to a few olives and crisps? Booze, even from the discount supermarket, would add at least another hundred. The shock made him lose his appetite.

Instead he went to the French House and downed a couple of glasses of house red and by the time he got back to Covert Cottage, Meg was asleep, or pretending to be, and his appetite was gone.

He slept fitfully and for the first time all week he felt panicky, as though he'd let something important slip between his hands, and it was now gone forever. In the first light of the new day, he got up and went down to the kitchen, knowing he should be preparing for the party but feeling unable to settle to any task. Meg followed on an hour or so afterwards, looking dishevelled and still half-asleep, too out of it to notice that Marc was not his usual self. He made coffee and watched Meg while she came to. When he felt she was awake enough to be receptive, he mentioned the money, casually, so as not to worry her unduly. Meg seemed completely unconcerned and insisted that at least part of the amount was a deposit on the hire of glasses which was refundable and anyway, she was looking forward to the party and you couldn't put a price on being part of a community. After that little speech, Marc decided that now wasn't the best time to drop the bomb about his job. He'd do it tomorrow, in the afterglow of the party, or, if not tomorrow, then Monday or maybe Tuesday. Definitely next week or, failing that, the week after.

Janette appeared on the pathway. She let herself into the mudroom. The sound of humming. Moments later the kitchen door swung open and a burst of sharp air entered.

Meg, smiling, piped up, 'You're cheery.' She side-eyed Marc as if to say *at least someone is*. 'What was that you were humming?'

'Cherubini's *Medea*.'

'Thought it sounded familiar.' Meg was the classical music lover. Marc had always preferred rock.

Janette caught Marc's eye and said, 'Do you know it, Marc?' He blushed, quite sure that Janette could see right through him, that she knew he was pathetic and feeble, someone who couldn't control himself, who reacted to the death of his daughter with an impotent, useless rage that had got him sacked.

'Enough to know it's not a band,' he said in what he hoped sounded like a jokey tone.

Janette laughed thinly. Meg didn't laugh at all.

'It's not actually all that cheery,' Janette said. The story came from Greek myth. Janette went on to describe the plot in more detail, something about a woman killing her own children in revenge for their father's abandonment of her. At this point Marc wasn't really listening. Keen to make himself useful, he fetched her coffee and eager to change the subject, said, 'I think I'll stick to rock 'n' roll. A lot less grim.'

She took this in good part. When the laughter died down, Meg went off to take a shower. After she'd gone, Janette's mood seemed to change quite suddenly and looking at him intently, she said, 'I had a feeling you've been wanting to say something to me.'

He felt flustered and overheated. Oh God, did she know? How could she? 'Well, yes, since you ask.' She met him with a look of intense and unflappable curiosity.

'But can it be between us? I don't want to worry Meg.'

'Of course.' A faint smile played on her face. 'You and I already have secrets after all, don't we?'

A rush of relief shot through him. To be able to say what had been preoccupying him for days. He took a breath and it all came out; Daisy Godwin's reappearance in his life, the incident at the theatre, the loss of his job. He even confessed to continuing to travel up to London as if he was still working. As he spoke, he could feel the weight lifting until it was as if he were so light that he might float upwards like a balloon and disappear into the sky.

'How are you feeling now you've told me?' Janette asked. To his relief there was no judgement in her voice.

He sighed and closed his eyes. 'So much better.'

'I'm glad,' she said, reaching out to pat his hand, and at her touch he felt a charge run through his body, not of arousal so much as of the fragments of him being drawn back together and made whole.

He told her about Pete though he left out the part about the deferred fee.

'Well then, it sounds like a temporary blip,' Janette said. 'But I have a practical suggestion for you. To protect you and Meg. Just in case.'

'Oh?' he said, interested in anything Janette could offer him.

She told him what she had in mind, and it sounded eminently sensible. How marvellous she was. What a help to him, to them both, and to Helen too.

'You own the place outright, I assume? Your sister has no legal claim on it?'

'None. Jimmy left the place to me.' Marc reminded Janette of his promise to give half the value of the cottage to Helen at some point in the medium-term future and that this was still important to him, but that she was in no hurry.

'But I suppose that might change,' Janette said. Marc had mentioned to her before that his sister lived hand to mouth and he was reminded now about what Helen had told him about the threat of redundancies at Broke Arts.

'It might,' he said. Before this, directly after he'd lost his job, the thought had fleetingly crossed Marc's mind that a temporary way out of his financial troubles might be to ask Janette to contribute to the household expenses, but given the revelation now, he didn't want to take the risk that she would leave. It was the same feeling that he'd had when he'd suggested to Meg that they stop therapy, that she was becoming necessary to them, but whereas before, his dependence had felt uncomfortable, dangerous even, it now felt easy and inevitable, as if written in the stars. Not that he believed in the stars.

'And you and Meg never tied the knot legally if I remember rightly.'

She did of course. Janette remembered everything.

'We always meant to get married but we never got round to it,' he said.

'It's good that your finances are legally separate. Putting the cottage in Meg's name would be beneficial to all of you,' Janette said, and registering Marc's puzzlement, went on, 'It protects the cottage from being used to pay off any future creditors of yours. A way of keeping it in the family until such time as you choose to sell it or buy Helen out. It gives you more options.' One of her former clients had done just this, Janette said, and it had been a simple matter of paying a solicitor a nominal fee to draw up a transfer document. There was probably a boilerplate document that would form the basis of the transfer and so long as it was complete, there would be no need for any complicated deed of trust. 'If the place belonged to Meg, then if Helen did ever get it into her mind to challenge your father's will, she wouldn't be able to get her hands on the place.'

Marc hadn't considered the possibility that Helen might ask for the gift he'd agreed to give her ahead of the original timetable and it felt bad to be thinking this way. But he could see that Janette had a point and there was nothing wrong in being cautious. He meant to find the money, one way or another, to salve his conscience and because it was the right thing to do. But he didn't want to be forced to give up their new home and he didn't want to fall out with Helen either.

'I hope it won't come to any of that,' he said.

In the silence that followed Janette grew pensive and frowned as if she were pained by something. When she spoke, he thought he detected a tremor in her voice. 'I so wish I could help you both out financially, but it's not possible. Some years ago I fell prey to a con man who took everything I had. One of the reasons I left the UK for Australia. I needed a fresh start, just like you and Meg. I returned to this country when I discovered that he'd died. Even now I've only managed to save just enough for a tiny place to retire to.' She wore a soft, sad smile.

'That's terrible,' he said.

Janette raised a hand. 'I only mentioned it because I want to protect you from having to go through what I went through.'

He looked at her with humility and gratitude and felt something in him surge upwards and he was suddenly so full of affection that he couldn't hold back. He said, 'You mean so much to us, Janette, to me. I can't even describe how much.'

It seemed to him that he had just made a declaration

of love in a way, and that she hadn't pulled away or been shocked or disgusted. In fact, she was smiling.

'*Agape*, it's from the Greek, I believe.'

'Forgive me if my Greek's a little rusty.' He laughed and she joined in.

At last, when they were both quiet, she said, 'It means the kind of love that doesn't burden the beloved.'

He looked at her and saw that her eyes were shining. How clever and perceptive she was. She knew what was in his heart without him having to say it. It was neither sexual nor maternal, but of a kind he'd never experienced before, a light, liberating sort of love that swept in like a welcome breeze. She had returned it. They loved *each other* in a way that meant nothing more had to be said or done. Gladness rose like a little flower through the concrete of his current circumstances. He had no job and no money and a partner he loved beyond anything but who he was struggling to connect with, despite their fresh start, but Janette made everything better somehow. He wanted to tell her this but before he got the chance, he heard the click of the bathroom door closing which meant that Meg was out the shower.

Janette heard it too and, in a low tone so that she would not be heard beyond the kitchen, she said, 'Sooner or later you'll have to tell Meg about the job. But if you want my advice, don't do it today, before the party. She's so looking forward to it. That was why I suggested it really, to take her mind off…other things. It'll do you both some good to immerse yourself in your new home, meet some locals, start socialising. Especially after, well, the recent setback.'

He assumed at first that she was referring to the loss of

his job, but Meg didn't know about that. However, as she continued to speak it became clear that she was talking about something that had happened in Covert Wood a couple of days ago. They'd come across a discarded child's cardigan and Meg had reacted violently and had to be escorted home in a terrible state. Marc, who knew nothing of this, listened with a growing sense of shock.

'Why didn't anyone tell me?' he said.

'The story wasn't mine to tell, Marc. I'm only mentioning it now because I think you should know. If I had to guess, I'd say Meg might have held back because she was a little afraid of your reaction?'

'This is about *me*?' His shock had turned to astonishment.

'You must realize that your temper has got quite out of hand.'

Marc was stunned into silence, his tongue like a dried leaf in his mouth, the breath stuck painfully in his throat. For a moment he thought he might burst into tears. He'd told Janette the worst thing he'd ever done – something he'd never be able to confess to Meg – and she hadn't judged him. Now he felt the full weight of her disapproval, perhaps because she was no longer his therapist but his friend. It was uncomfortable to hear her say it even as he knew she was right.

'You're the only one who knows everything, the only one who can really help me.'

His hands twisted anxiously in his lap. He was in agony waiting for her reassurance that he wasn't a hopeless case and that she would help him. Instead, she finished her coffee and in a purposeful tone said, 'As I said, the best thing you can do is to be honest about losing your job and make sure Meg doesn't lose her home.' Janette turned to look at him head-on and in her eyes he saw something fierce and commanding.

'You're right. You're absolutely right.' He felt the prickly heat of shame rise from his belly. 'As soon as the party's over I'll talk to her.'

At that moment the bedroom door above them creaked.

'And get those papers drawn up,' she said. 'Now, if it's all right with you, I'm going back to the studio. Tell Meg to come and get me when she wants some help setting up for the party.'

And with that she left. A moment or two later, Meg appeared at the doorway. He went to her and took her in his arms.

'This is nice,' she said. Her hair was wet, and her body was still warm from the shower.

'I don't want you to have to worry about anything,' he said. 'I'm going to make you proud of me.'

'I *am* proud of you,' she said and gave him a puzzled look.

'*Even* prouder then,' he said. They laughed and in that short moment he felt that it was possible that everything might turn out okay.

SIXTEEN

When the doorbell rang Meg stopped what she was doing and checked the time. 4 p.m. It was too early for guests. Marc had just called from Ashford from where he was buying the alcohol, so she knew he hadn't got home early and forgotten his keys, and they weren't expecting a delivery.

Janette's voice came from the hallway where she was putting up some bunting. 'I'll get it.'

There came the sound of two sets of footsteps and Janette appeared, followed moments later by Helen. They'd invited Marc's sister for the weekend though they hadn't expected her quite this early. A green canvas overnight bag hung from her shoulder. In her denim boilersuit she looked dishevelled and world-weary, her face absent of make-up, hair jammed into an elastic band.

'I thought you might need some help,' she said.

'That's sweet.' Looking between the two women, Meg said, 'Have you introduced yourselves?'

'Yes,' Janette said and turning to Helen, added, 'I've heard a lot about you.'

'Same.' Helen put down her overnight bag.

'Good things I hope.' There was some uneasy laughter

before Janette excused herself, saying she had things to do in the studio. For a moment Meg and Helen followed her progress down the garden path through the kitchen window then Helen said, 'Marc told me she's practically living here.'

'Only until she finds somewhere more permanent.'

'Isn't that a bit weird?'

Meg decided to ignore this. 'Tea? Coffee?'

Helen had taken a seat at the kitchen table. Meg was standing at the counter, putting the kettle on. 'You'll like her. And anyway, she's not our therapist any more. She's more like an old friend.' She picked up a tea bag and the jar of coffee, turned to face Helen and was struck by her resemblance to Astrid, a woman she had only ever known from photographs, though Helen had none of her mother's radiant beauty.

Helen pointed to the tea bag. 'Where's Marc?'

'Gone to fetch the wine.'

The kettle clicked off and Meg returned to the kitchen counter.

'Is he driving the Spider these days?'

'No, it's still in the garage. I don't think he's even taken off the tarp. He's so busy with work and the commute.'

'Shame. I'd love to take it for a spin some time. Marc said I was welcome to, whenever I liked, he even told me where he kept the keys.'

Meg returned with the mugs of tea, put them down on the table and set a half-empty packet of Hobnobs beside them. 'Marc might have to tinker with it a bit to get it going.'

Helen's eyes narrowed but she took a sip of tea and seemed to settle. 'Maybe I'll wait till he gets back then.'

They lapsed into a thoughtful silence, Meg rehearsing

what she wanted to say before coming out with it. 'I was just wondering how old you were when Jimmy came down here?'

'I was at uni. Why?'

'Idle curiosity, I suppose. I came across a kid's sock in the attic and wondered if Astrid and Jimmy might have kept it for sentimental reasons.' The photograph of Cecily wearing the pink polka dot socks seemed conclusive, but Meg thought it was worth checking just in case.

'I know Mum kept some of our stuff from childhood but I'm pretty sure Dad binned it all when he came down here.'

'It was pink with red polka dots.'

'Doubt it. I wasn't into pink. Speaking of mementoes, I need to nip up into the attic. Dad said something about a couple of Ralph Steadman cartoons, but they weren't among his artworks.' She said this as a statement requiring no response. So this was why she had arrived early. To claim what was hers.

'I'm sorry the sale was so disappointing. Marc told me. I'm pretty sure I'd have come across the drawings if they were in the attic. I did a big clean-up there not long after we moved in.' The attic had become a sacred place where she could be alone with her memories of Lily. The last thing she wanted was Helen rummaging around and maybe even peering into the trunk.

'You won't mind if I pop up to the attic, just in case,' Helen said, rising and making for the hallway.

Meg followed her out and saw Janette arranging chairs on the patio through the French windows in the living room. She waved, hoping Janette would come in and help her navigate what was proving to be a sensitive situation, but the older woman did not raise her head and so Meg hurried on.

At the bottom of the stairs, Helen swung round. Her eyes, Meg noted, were like her mother's, warm and with a determined gleam, as though she were unstoppable. 'I'd rather go on my own if you don't mind. Anyway, Marc told me you think there's some kind of ghost living up there.'

Meg laughed, doing her best to hide her feeling of being affronted twice, once at Helen for the barely disguised amusement in her voice and again at Marc for breaking her confidence, and waved a hand in the air, as if to say that was all a silly joke. She had never seen Helen like this, spoiling for a fight.

'Well, whatever,' Helen said, turning and going up the stairs. 'I know this house better than either of you so...'

Meg bit back her indignation and returned to the kitchen to find Janette rooting around in the cutlery drawer.

'Bottle openers?'

'I already got them out,' Meg said. She felt doubly irritated by this new incursion on her domestic space. *This is my home, dammit!*

Sensing the tension, Janette stopped what she was doing and stretched upright. 'Are you okay?'

A familiar whoosh of guilt came up from Meg's belly. 'Sorry, it's just...Helen seems to be on the war path. Not like her at all. She's gone up to the attic to look for some drawings or other. I've already told her they're not there, but she was quite insistent. I know it sounds mean, but I just don't want her messing around up there.'

'I understand,' Janette replied and as so often when she found herself in conversation with her former therapist, Meg felt herself unclench. To be seen. To be *understood*.

At that moment the crunch of gravel in the driveway signalled Marc's return.

'I'll help bring in the wine if you want to keep an eye on Helen,' Janette said.

Meg nodded, relieved, and following Janette out of the kitchen, went upstairs and found Helen on the landing. The board that Marc had put over the newly enlarged attic hatch had been moved aside and replaced at a slight angle, exposing the hallway to the darkness above.

'Find anything?' she said, as brightly as she could muster.

At that moment Marc appeared at the top of the stairs. 'Hey, sis. Janette told me you'd arrived.'

'And here I am,' Helen said in an odd tone, as if challenging Marc to ask her to leave.

'Helen's looking for Jimmy's Steadman cartoons,' Meg said, by way of explaining the scene to Marc.

'They're not in the attic,' Helen said. 'Maybe I'll have another look in those rubbish bags I packed up in the studio. It's possible I missed them.'

An awkward silence fell for a moment and was broken by Meg. 'I'm afraid the bags have gone.'

'You threw them away?'

'The thing is, sis...' Marc began in the conciliatory tone he usually adopted with his sister. In that moment Meg's eye was drawn to the stairway just in time to catch sight of Janette's back as she quietly withdrew. '...Jimmy probably sold them. You know how the old man was.'

'Yeah, I do. Because I bothered to visit,' Helen said.

Marc visibly cringed and Meg felt both sad and faintly irritated at his hopeless inability to stand up to his sister.

Meg sighed. Not this again. 'If we come across the drawings, Helen, we'll let you know. But if you don't mind, I'd rather you didn't go in the attic again.'

Helen's eyes grew beady and there was something spiteful in the turn of her lips. 'There's nothing up there, Meg. No ghosts or spooks or scary spirits. You do realize that, don't you?'

Meg thought about the sock. Very much not imagined. But there was no point engaging with her sister-in-law in this mood.

Marc stiffened. 'Stop it, Helen.' To Meg's surprise Helen froze and looked at her feet.

'If you want to make yourself useful,' Marc went on, 'you can come downstairs and help me polish the hired glasses.'

SEVENTEEN

The siblings stood together in the living room, running linen scrims around the glassware. Outside the wind had died down and across the field the line of trees marking the start of Covert Wood ceased their dance. Marc, putting down one polished glass and picking up another as yet unpolished, said, 'That stuff about things in the attic, that was really out of order.'

Helen stopped what she was doing and scrunched up her face. 'I know, I'm sorry.'

'It's not me you need to apologize to.'

'I know, I know. I'll say sorry to Meg.'

'What got into you?'

'I suppose I'm feeling a bit shit about Dad and why he did what he did.'

'I know. I feel shit about it too,' Marc said, though he was also thinking about the conversation he'd had earlier with Janette.

'The only woman he ever really gave a damn about was Astrid.'

'I'm going to make it up to you.'

Helen looked up from her glass. 'I know, Sparky, and I'm

grateful, honestly. But I want you and Meg to be able to live in this place and make it your home.'

'There are some great songs in my head.' Marc tapped his forehead. This was what had kept him sane, the idea that he would eventually be able to announce his feelings to the world in song and that the world would hear him. They would hear all the longing and love and guilt and anguish he was feeling about Lily. And yes, they would hear the rage too. 'All I need is the time to work on them.' He put down his glass and stretched out his hand. His fingers lighted briefly on hers and for a moment their eyes met. Helen looked away.

'Why is Janette here?'

'I told you. Meg's lonely and Janette's good company.'

'You're sure that's all it is?'

Marc pulled his hand away. 'Yes, what else would it be?'

'Sandy thinks Meg's shooting herself in the foot trying to get to the bottom of what happened to the missing girl. I wondered if Janette was encouraging her. Sandy says...'

'You and Sandy seem pretty tight.'

'We're...good friends,' Helen said carefully. Marc sensed there was more to be said but it wasn't the right time or place to grill his sister about what 'good friends' really meant.

'Maybe Sandy should stop tittle-tattling,' Marc said irritably. 'In any case, Meg's moved on.' It was true. Cecily hadn't been mentioned in days.

'Showing up at Steve's door asking questions didn't go down well. Apparently he was the last known person to see the missing girl. It made his life a living hell so the last thing he wants is to have to talk about it. '

At the mention of Steve Savage, a pricky sensation began

to stir in Marc. He put down the glass he was polishing, his stomach churning now.

Helen ploughed on. 'Sandy seems convinced Steve had nothing to do with the girl going missing.'

'I don't care about Steve Savage or a missing girl from decades ago,' he said. 'And I'd rather you weren't talking about us behind our backs to the vicar of all people.'

Just then their attention was taken up by the sound of laughter in the garden. Meg and Janette had paused in the work they were doing setting up the table on the patio and were sharing a joke. Marc felt mildly envious, though of whom – Janette or Meg or both – he wasn't quite sure.

'Sandy said she saw Janette hanging around the village several times, even before she ran into Meg at the shop.'

An almost instinctive need to defend Janette rose in Marc. In any case, Sandy was mistaken. Janette had told them when Meg bumped into her that it was her first visit to the village. 'Janette was looking for properties so yeah, she was in the village.'

'Some coincidence, don't you think?'

'Hel, you're being a bit of a dick. No, it's no coincidence. Janette heard us mention Coldwater in a session and forgot about it till she got here and remembered the connection. That's how memory works. Why have you and Sandy got it in for Janette all of a sudden?'

For the next hour or so the four of them busied themselves preparing for the arrival of the guests. Helen found time to apologize to Meg, as she said she would, and Meg was her usual graceful self about it. By the time the first guest arrived at six, the cottage had not entirely lost its solemn atmosphere but was now wrapped in cheerful bunting. The rain had mercifully held off and although it was late October, the evening air still held traces of the fading summer. On the patio, strings of tiny fairy lights blinked. Above them the sky was navy blue, heading to deep grey and there was a thumbnail of a moon visible through ashy clouds. Meg was wearing an orange velvet jumpsuit and with her brown curls piled high on her head, she looked spectacular, her whole body thrumming with vitality as it had in the before time. Marc felt so proud, so newly charmed, that as he watched her greeting the newcomers, for a few moments he was able to forget the reality of his current circumstances.

Guests kept on arriving and by seven o'clock, several dozen people were milling about the ground floor of Covert Cottage and spilling onto the patio at the back. His own social circle had shrunk to nothing after Lily died, people he'd considered friends unable or unwilling to remain within the orbit of his all-consuming anguish, his rage. He didn't blame them. He'd been a nightmare, flailing about, his head barely above water, and taking whatever opportunity he could to get obnoxiously drunk. An absolute horror show of a wounded human bear. Then Janette came along, and he managed to get a hold of himself. It had been too late to save his friendships but not too late, mercifully, to save his marriage or himself. Now, in his own home, among the shifting bodies on the patio, he recognized Sandy and Lisa, the girl from the shop, but realized there was no one, apart from Helen, Janette and Meg, that he could really claim to *know*. It was a lonely, melancholy thought, made worse by the fact that, as he went around topping up drinks, his guests only really seemed to want to talk to him about Jimmy.

Eventually he wandered inside again and went to the fridge, did a quick count of the bottles of white wine then the red sitting in boxes on the kitchen table, totted up how much money the guests had already drunk away and felt something in his stomach seize. He remembered his intention to sign the cottage over to Meg and took another drink to settle himself.

The doorbell interrupted his thoughts and edging his way through two couples standing chatting in the hallway, he went to the door where, to his surprise, stood Pete Starr. He'd invited his new kind-of boss on a whim, keen to keep him onside, but hadn't for a moment expected him to schlep all the way from London. Yet here he was. Pete Starr!

Clasping the nicotine-yellow hand with its long, browning nails, Marc drew in his prize for a bro backslap. 'Dude, you came.'

The object of Marc's delight stepped into the hallway and began to remove his jacket. 'Curious to see the place old Jimbo retired to. Never did come down here when he was still with us.'

As it sunk in that, like everyone else here, Pete hadn't come for Marc at all but was looking for remnants of Jimmy, the cheerfully adrenalized version of Marc who had greeted the newcomer only a few seconds ago drained away like old dishwater. Doing his best to cover his disappointment, he took the jacket Pete held out and hung it on an old clothes rail he'd found in the garage and retrieved for the occasion. At that moment Meg appeared from the kitchen carrying a bottle of wine. Marc called her over and introduced them.

'Wow,' Pete said, folding Meg into a hug then holding her out at arm's length as though he was inspecting a book and hadn't brought his reading glasses. 'Your old man didn't tell me you were smokin' hot.'

Marc watched Meg's face fade then remake itself, though whether she was offended by Pete's obvious lasciviousness or by Marc's failure to broadcast her beauty, Marc did not know. 'I've been told to watch out for you,' she said, cracking a flirty smile. It was fake, anyone could see that, but still, when was the last time Meg had flirted with *him*? His eyes fluttered from one to the other in a kind of panic and he felt a small, smouldering thing inside him begin to give off a little more heat.

'A credit to his old man,' Pete said to Meg, indicating Marc.

'Ha ha,' Marc said, embarrassed, disappointed, angry at the impossibility of escaping from under the weight of his father's reputation.

'I'd love a tour of Jimbo's gaff,' Pete said.

'Everything's still a bit of a mess, but if you don't mind that,' Meg said.

Marc watched the pair of them disappear down the hallway and feeling frustrated went upstairs and stood alone on the landing, gathering his thoughts, until the sound of voices on the stairs drove him into the bathroom. He overheard two women talking. The voices were unfamiliar, but he clearly heard one say, 'Well, it's obvious, isn't it? *Menage-a-trois.*' The other voice said, 'But she's so much *older.*' Then the first voice said, 'They're bound to be a bit nuts after what happened.

Anyway, perhaps he has a mummy thing. Have you seen those pics of Astrid? Drop-dead gorgeous.'

He thought about bursting through the bathroom door or at least punching something. What the fuck did they know? He went to the window to catch some air. The moon sat slender among a litter of stars. Below, picked out in the garden lights, guests milled about. He saw Meg and Pete emerging onto the patio from the French windows, Meg clutching a champagne glass and Pete grasping a bottle of beer. It wasn't anything, obviously, but it bothered him a little. He went down and got between them. They made small talk for a few moments then Meg said, 'Oh, I forgot, one of the guests said there was a silver Peugeot blocking the drive. I wonder if that's Lisa's car? You wouldn't just poke your nose out the front door and check would you, darling?'

He looked at her and saw no awkwardness. Why was she sending him away? Maybe he'd imagined this. Wanting to seem obliging in front of Pete he went to the front door and immediately spotted the silver Peugeot, which was not, in fact, blocking anything. He came back in and returned to the patio, his eyes drifting across the crowd until they lighted on Helen. There was someone beside her. He blinked, peered, blinked again. Was that...my God, it *was*. Steve Savage. Who the hell invited him? He and Helen were laughing, throwing their heads back as though they'd never been in such scintillating company. His blood turned to battery acid but he couldn't take his eyes off them. Had Helen lost her mind or...another thought bobbed up into his consciousness. Could she be trying to get back at him? She wouldn't do that, would she?

A voice said, 'Hey.' He turned, startled, and was relieved to see Meg standing in the doorway. She eyed him with something like wariness; perhaps she detected in him something that he did not yet know, the way Janette did, the way all the women in his life always had.

'Savage is here. You didn't invite him, did you?'

'What do you think?'

'He seems to be getting on alarmingly well with Helen. He's also trashed. Dunno about her.'

'Maybe you should ask him to leave?' Meg said.

He pictured the confrontation, how it might go down if Savage refused to go. Make him look like a fool in front of Pete. He said, 'Best not create a scene.'

'I'm not suggesting a scene, just a discreet word.'

She wasn't going to let him duck out of it. He trudged obediently out into the garden, swiping an opened bottle of beer from the patio table to give his hands something to do. Sidling up to where Helen and Steve were continuing to amuse one another, he said, 'You two have met, I see.'

Helen gave him a puzzled look. '*Obviously*. Steve used to work for Dad. You'd know that if you'd spent any time down here.'

Something deep and red rose up in Marc then. He was sick of hearing about Jimmy, sick of being Jimmy's kid. Pretty sick of Helen and deeply, radically sick of Steve Savage.

'Did we actually invite you, Steve?' Marc said.

Steve took a drag on his cigarette and pinged the butt onto the ground.

'Marc, don't be so bloody rude,' Helen said.

'Your old man...' Steve began.

'...is dead. Jimmy is gone. This is my home now.' His eyes flashed across the patio to where a group of women had formed a circle around Pete. To ask Steve to leave early would probably be a mistake.

He glared at Helen. 'The party ends at nine. After that, everyone goes home,' he said. 'And that includes you, Steve.'

EIGHTEEN

Meg poured herself another glass of Pinot Grigio from the fridge and watched from the safety of the kitchen window as Marc headed over to Steve and Helen. She didn't quite trust Marc not to lose it with Steve and she didn't care to think what might happen if a fight broke out, but after the visit to his house she wanted nothing more to do with their neighbour. He'd been the last person to see Cecily and that had to make him a prime suspect in her disappearance, whatever Sandy thought or said. She had no idea why Helen was spending so much time with him. Meg had always got the feeling that Helen was gay, though nothing had ever been said. Bisexual maybe. Whatever the truth of that, Helen had been in a strange mood from the moment she arrived. Meg noticed that she'd drained her own glass. How was it that she'd taken up drinking again without intending to? *Need to watch that one*, she thought to herself. *A glass of wine too many on top of the pills. Must keep remembering to drink water. One for one. Not now though.* She refilled her glass and took a sip of the wine, then a bigger one, eyes fixed on the unfolding drama outside. Marc saying something, Helen snapping a response. Marc shrinking, then shrugging and walking away.

She felt her body settle, relieved and grateful that the encounter hadn't resulted in a scene, and went back into the mudroom, shaking off her high heels and slipping her feet into the clogs she left by the back door. The air was chilly and smelled of more cold to come. Marc had lit the fire pit on the edge of the patio which was now burning with a bright orange flame and reminded Meg with a sudden discomforting lurch of what Steve had said about the earlier houses on the site that had all burned down. She shook herself out of the thought and saw Lucy, the woman who had recently moved into the former school building, sitting on the wall. Beside her stood a tall well-built man in his thirties. She went over, smiling. The man clocked her first and turned awkwardly to his partner, hoping to be rescued. Lucy stood and she and Meg exchanged a kiss on the cheek.

'This is Nat, my other half.'

Nat and Meg shook hands and chatted about the view, Meg's plans for the cottage. Before long, the conversation turned to Coldwater and how it was to be a newcomer among residents who had grown up in the area. Meg, seizing her opportunity, said, 'I've decided to do a bit more local history research.'

Lucy said she thought this sounded like a good idea.

'Did you by any chance find any school records in the house? You know, registers, yearbooks, that kind of thing?'

Lucy and Nat looked at one another and shook their heads. Lucy said, 'We'll let you know if we do.' Disappointed, Meg finished up the conversation as quickly as was polite and made her way through the crowd to where Janette was standing recounting one of her stories. A little coterie had gathered round, rapt with attention, hanging on Janette's every word. She hovered on the periphery of the conversation feeling strangely out of it, as if *she* were the guest at a party at *Janette's* house.

'What a relief that nothing like that ever happens in Coldwater,' remarked the neighbour, apropos of something Janette had said.

'I suppose every village must have its share of tragedies,' Meg said, hoping to steer the conversation around to Cecily.

The neighbour frowned and said in a way that was casually authoritative, as if he was someone who was used to being heard, 'Our beloved war dead of course but nothing more recent than that.' He was thin, in his sixties, and held his body with a stiff, upright formality which suggested a former military man or maybe a police officer; old enough to remember the disappearance of Cecily Banner.

Janette introduced them. The man's name was Tim Nuttall. He'd lived in Coldwater for nearly thirty years.

'Thirty-three years in the Kent police. Retired a couple of years ago.'

There was a momentary silence which was broken by Janette. 'Tim was just delighting us with his riveting story about chalk stream trout fishing. We could both probably do with a top-up. Be a dear would you, Meg?'

In the kitchen there was a short elderly woman standing on her own who scrutinised Meg anxiously while pretending to be running her eyes over the cookery books. Meg fetched another bottle of white from the fridge then turning, held it out to her, saying, 'Do you already have a glass?'

Meg introduced herself though it was evident from her

handling of the wine who she was. The woman, in return, said her name was Alice.

'That's a pretty name,' Meg said, doing her best to replicate Janette's captivating charm, but without being able to bring to her performance the same level of conviction.

'My husband wanted to come,' Alice said. 'He's always been curious about Covert Cottage. The things they say about it.'

'What do they say?'

Alice allowed Meg to fill up her glass. 'Oh, silly stuff, I don't believe any of it, obviously, but the place does have a rather tragic history.' She took a sip of wine and scanned the room as if searching for someone and in a low voice said, 'Not that anyone will ever get to the bottom of that. Not while some people refuse to say what they know, anyway.'

Meg put down her glass. 'Like who?'

Alice, thrilled at having got the hostess's attention, said, 'Oh, I shouldn't gossip. But I will say that Sandy must know a thing or two. She did live in the house after all.'

Meg wondered why Sandy had never said. Maybe she hadn't got round to it.

At that moment Alice put down her wine glass. 'In any case, it's all water under the bridge now. I need to be getting back home, but I just wanted to say...about your daughter. I can't imagine what it must have been like to go through that. I do hope you get whatever it is you're looking for without having to stir things up. We value our peace and quiet here in Coldwater.' She extended a thin, chilly hand. 'Well goodbye.'

Meg waited until Alice had left then collected herself and re-emerged from the kitchen with the wine. She looked around for Sandy but didn't see her. Perhaps, like Alice, she had already taken herself off home. In any case, Meg thought, perhaps this wasn't the best time. In the corner Helen and Steve were still standing and talking, laughing at some shared joke. Why hadn't Marc asked him to leave? She went around making small talk and refilling glasses, trying not to seem as tense as she felt. Eventually Marc reappeared, sliding over to where she was standing alone, a hovering smile on his face as if wanting absolution.

'I know, I know, I would have asked Savage to leave but I didn't want to cause an upset in front of Pete.' His eyes scoped the garden to make sure they were not being overhead, then in a quiet voice he said, 'I'm on a mission.'

'A mission? Is it impossible?' she said. It all sounded a bit dramatic, a bit spy thrillery, very unlike Marc. In fact, Marc was being a bit strange altogether. Like watching a spinning top in the moment just before it begins to lose momentum. *That said*, Meg thought, *I've had a few and so has he, so perhaps that accounts for it.*

At that moment loud music started up from the living room. She was tiring now, her head rather dizzy from the booze and the pill she'd taken before everyone arrived. This was supposed to be drinks and nibbles, not some all-night rave.

He smiled. 'I'm going to introduce Pete to Janette, they're about the same age, they probably knew some of the same people. Remember those photos in Janette's room in London Fields? It could be the start of a wonderful friendship, romance even. Wouldn't do me any harm either. I need Pete onside.'

Meg did indeed recall the photographs, intimate backstage images of some of the greats of the mid- to late-Seventies rock world, Janette always rather coy about how she'd come about them. But there was something about Marc's desperation that alarmed her. Sensing her anxiety, he held up a reassuring hand and said, 'Don't worry, I know what I'm doing.' And with that he went off through the crowd towards Janette, who was standing in the centre of a circle of rapt guests, telling stories.

They were in a different place now. The shine had worn off the evening and all Meg really wanted to do was to go to bed. It was silly to have taken that pill and then drunk as much as she had. Right now she needed a glass of water. She stepped through the French doors into the living room and saw Pete standing by the bookshelf scrolling through the playlists on Marc's iPad. A small handful of partygoers had taken up the invitation to dance. Everyone else was bunched up on the side of the room farthest from the speakers, shouting at one another across the din or else edging their way towards the relative quiet of the hallway. She made her way through and into the kitchen, grabbed a mug from the shelf and poured herself some water, standing for a while to take it all in. This new life, the chance to do something important, to right a terrible wrong. She understood why people like Alice weren't on her side but the nearer she got to solving the case, her detractors would see it for what it was; an opportunity to heal the past rather than simply run from it. And they would come round.

She went back out and found Janette dazzling two women whose names she couldn't remember. She smiled and waited for a break in the conversation. 'Did Marc find you?'

'No.'

'He was looking for you.'

At that moment, as if on cue, Marc appeared carrying a bottle in each hand. He topped up the glasses of the two women then turning his attention to Janette he said, 'Can I borrow you for a moment? There's someone I want you to meet, a friend of Jimmy's from the old days. I think you'd get along.'

'He's here?' Janette said. She made a face at her two companions as if to say, *how could that possibly be of more interest to me than you two?*

'Name's Pete Starr. He's in the living room getting his DJ vibes on.'

'Oh.' Janette's smile faded. She raised a hand to her chest and began to cough. 'I'm so sorry, I have something stuck in my throat, please excuse me.' And with that she took a step back, then turned and disappeared into the throng of people.

Meg looked at Marc. Raising a bottle, he said, 'Darling, would you mind showing me where we put red wine?'

'Of course,' Meg said, picking up in his eyes that he needed urgently to speak to her. Turning to the two women, she said, 'Please excuse us,' and moved away through the crowd, with Marc following behind, and into the mudroom. He beckoned her into the tiny cloakroom and locked them both inside.

'I completely fucked it,' he hissed. He was wringing his hands and for one alarming moment she thought he might burst into tears. Instead he cradled his head in his hands. Her heart went out to him but really, now?

'I don't know what you mean?'

'You saw Janette, she was livid with me!'

'Darling, you're overthinking it. She got something stuck in her throat. That's all it was.'

Marc shook his head, and it was true that Meg hadn't really been paying attention. Her head was beginning to throb.

'I think I embarrassed her. She probably thought I was trying to matchmake.'

'It'll all be fine in the morning,' Meg said blandly. She needed a glass of water to stave off the headache. Patting Marc on the shoulder and doing her best to lighten the atmosphere she said, 'Why don't you go and see if you can find Helen? I haven't seen her or Steve for ages. Maybe they're having a knee-trembler round the back of the shed.'

He laughed grimly and said that he very much doubted that. Then putting himself back together he checked his watch and said, 'It's nearly ten o'clock. Why won't everyone bloody well leave?'

'Some people already have. I heard a car in the drive a while ago and I think Sandy's already gone.' She'd caught Sandy's eye a bit earlier. She'd been squeezed against the low wall enclosing the patio looking slightly trapped and had made prayer hands to signify thank you then pointed at her watch.

'Let's get you another drink and get through this and we'll talk about it after.' They left the cloakroom and went into the kitchen. Meg poured herself a glass of water and a glass of red for Marc. He settled a kiss on the top of her head and draining his glass, made a popping sound and said, 'Back to the fray then.' She watched as he slipped back through the mudroom and disappeared into the throng of people on the patio. Going back into the living room she saw Pete dancing by the bookshelf. Between his lips a rollie flashed red then faded in time with his breathing. The music was too loud to shout, but sensing her eyes on him, Pete twisted round and smiled, pointing to the rollie with one hand and raising his eyebrows in a gesture of encouragement. Maybe this was what the locals expected from a party at Covert Cottage? She could imagine Jimmy partying to the wee small hours, waking hungover and stepping over the bodies in the morning on his way to the kitchen. Pete would eventually get bored of DJing and people would run out of booze. She smiled and waved at Pete but anxious to be on her own, went back out into the hallway and up the stairs, thinking that she might feel more in the party mood if she could get rid of her headache, only to discover that someone had been lavishly sick in the bathroom toilet. The stench drove a wave of nausea through her body. If anything, the music was even louder now. The windows clattered in their frames and beside her a chair began to tremble across the floorboards. A drum and bass beat shook her feet and thudded through her body. She closed her eyes and holding her nose, pressed the flush and without waiting to see the results, went back out onto the landing where she noticed that the door to their bedroom was ajar and a light was on. Hadn't she shut it before the party started? She didn't want to encourage drunken neighbours to start stumbling around the upstairs rooms. She went over and pushing the door wider, said, 'Hello?' When no answer came, she crossed the threshold and went to turn off the light when something caught her eye. A bubble rose and burst, and she felt she was about to scream.

Under cover of the loud music, someone had been up in the attic. They'd opened the trunk, taken out Lily's doll, brought it down the steps to their bedroom and propped it up on the pillows on the bed. Who would have done such a thing? Only she and Marc even knew the doll was up there. She stood frozen to the spot, one hand over her mouth, the other clamped to her chest, feeling the frenzied beat of her heart.

In that moment the door flung open, and Marc appeared, giving her a look of incomprehension. She saw him follow her gaze and his eyes alighted on the doll. He froze. For a moment the two of them were just there, in the room, as if nothing else existed.

He said, 'What the hell?'

The figure lay there, lifeless, a Mini Me doll version of Lily.

'Tell me that wasn't you,' Meg gasped.

'Of course it wasn't me,' Marc hissed. 'Who would do that?'

The question hovered between them. They stood side by side in the black room, while downstairs a bunch of strangers drank their wine and danced to their music. Meg recalled this afternoon, Helen's insistence on going up in the attic, her strange mood. Her breath left her. Beside her Marc stiffened. They looked at one another and the same thought seemed to be passing through both their minds at the same time.

Helen.

At that moment shouts came from outside the room. A cacophony of footsteps. Meg zoomed back to the present. The door banged and she turned.

Pete was standing on the landing waving his arms. 'Fuck's sake you two, I've been looking for you all over. There's been an accident. Someone in the Spider.'

NINETEEN

One of the guests moved their car and unblocked the Fiesta and Marc leapt into the driver's seat while Pete swung into the front passenger side, leaving Meg and Janette to clamber into the back. There was no time to think about who should drive. In any case, they were all above the limit. The engine started first time, the car radio coming on full blast and Pete reaching for the knobs to turn it off. Marc glanced in the rear-view mirror, shouted, 'Hold tight' and floored the accelerator. The car lurched forward and made a crazy swing to the right out of the driveway onto The Lane.

As the vehicle careened down between moonlit trees, skating up onto the verge and landing with a bump back on the asphalt, Marc took a firmer grip on the wheel and steered it back into the central track. If someone was coming in the opposite direction, they'd better get out the way. Meg gasped and bit her lip.

From the front Marc screamed, 'Everyone just shut up, okay?'

Meg clutched Janette's hand more tightly. Janette reached out with her free hand and gripped the edge of the seat. The night poured out all around and as they turned a tight corner between the trees, they saw it: the Spider lying on its side at a crazy angle, a single headlight smoking, the bonnet crumpled like paper against the trunk of a huge oak, as if the tree had put out a twisted metal branch. The front passenger door was wide open and there was no one inside.

Marc jammed on the brakes and brought the Fiesta to a halt. Standing a few metres away a police vehicle and an ambulance sat in a yellow beam which pulsed with blue light.

'My God,' Marc cried as he leapt from the car and began to run towards the scene.

Meg felt her legs move and a rush of cold air. Two strong arms clasped her shoulders, a voice as solid as a rock saying, 'Stay back!' and she froze, the breath leaving her body and spilling in a grey plume into the darkness.

'No, no, no!' She heard a voice cry out and realized it was her own. Not this. Not again, no. Her legs gave way and the arms lifted her up, as everything shook and spun. Her shoulders struggled to get clear. She wanted to run into the woods and never come back. She wanted to be gone, gone. The sound of Janette's voice saying, 'It's okay, it's okay.'

Breathe. Just breathe. The freezing air rushing into her lungs. Her legs had disappeared now, gone, all that was left was a scream.

It was all wrong. It wasn't okay.

Marc was some distance away now, still running, silhouetted against the yellow light. A policeman striding towards him. The trees lit with blue then fading into night.

My God.

Marc shouting something, yelling at the policeman who was holding up his hands as if in surrender. Behind them the ambulance, doors open, a sickly grey light and in it another figure of a man, standing, head in his hands, rocking, rocking on his heels.

Steve Savage.

Helen's words in her head now. *I'd like to see it. Take it for a spin.*

A paramedic emerged from the back of the ambulance and went over to where Marc and the police officer were standing, her hands making shapes out of black air.

Such a confusion of lights and voices. Janette's voice in her ear. 'Did you hear that? Did you hear?'

She shook her head.

'It's Helen.'

Helen. Helen. The word mixed up somehow with an image of the doll on the bed. A sense of *déjà vu. I've been here before. I've been here. An ambulance. A police car.*

'Oh God,' she said. 'No!'

She saw Marc clamber up into the ambulance behind the paramedic.

Arms clutching at hers, digging in. She swung round to Janette's face, white in the headlights, as light as a summer breeze. Expressionless almost. In the darkness beside them, a single bicycle lamp and in its yellow-grey haze she could just make out the figure of a woman, a ring of reflected blue grey light around her neck where the moonlight reflected off her clerical collar. Then Sandy's face emerged from the darkness.

'Is anyone hurt?'

Meg, wanting to look away, wanting to run into the wood and never come back, frozen in place, unable to take her eyes from the scene, her gaze travelling to something large lying in the middle of the road. She let out a cry and felt her stomach turn over then a woman's arm was around her shoulder and Janette's velvety voice said, 'It's okay.' She shut her eyes tight. *Let this not be happening.* Janette's arms around her, saying, 'Look.'

Meg forced herself to look at the object lying in the road. A white flash on the chest and a set of antlers. A trail of blood oozing from the head, a tongue lolling lifelessly from the mouth, a single glassy eye locked in the death stare. She turned her head, trying to catch enough air to stop herself being sick, then took a step forward, clasping her hands to still the trembling, the pressure of Janette's arm on her.

'It's a deer.' The relief hitting her solar plexus with a thud.

Janette's voice saying, 'Let them get on with it.'

'No,' Meg said, struggling to get free, her legs propelling her forward past the dead animal, to where Steve was now standing with the policeman.

In a voice that surprised her with its cold rage, she said, 'What have you done to Helen?'

She felt Sandy come up beside her and rest a shaky hand on her shoulder, murmuring something, perhaps a prayer, but in that moment she did not want any consolation and shrugged her off. She was angry now, furious, the rage enormous and uncontrolled.

Steve turned, aghast, his mouth a rictus, eyes blank. She wasn't sure if he recognized her. His eyes seemed glassy and his jaw twitched. Gone was the grin, the cheeky cockiness, the arrogant disdain. She repeated herself and this time she saw his face change, his body tighten in rage.

'What have *I* done? That bloody deer came straight out of nowhere, could have killed the both of us,' he said.

The deer. Yes, but still. She could smell the alcohol on Steve's breath. 'You're drunk.' She turned to the policeman and said, 'We've seen him driving drunk before.'

The policeman held up a hand. 'Let's all stay calm now.' To Meg, 'Are you a relative?'

'She's my sister-in-law.' She glanced over at the ambulance. Marc was still inside. 'Is she okay? Please tell me she's okay?'

Without missing a beat, the police officer said, 'And your name is...?'

He scribbled something in a notebook as Meg told him her name and repeated her question, thinking, *why is no one listening?* The anger fizzing in her body.

'Ms Mair has sustained some fractured ribs, a lot of bruising, broken wrist. There may be some whiplash injury.' They were going to take her in to Ashford Hospital, run some tests.

Relief came up again, this time cool, like water from a deep well.

'If you wouldn't mind waiting over there?' The policeman gestured towards where Pete and Janette were standing.

She did mind. She minded that Steve got what was coming to him. 'You're going to arrest him, aren't you?' She sounded anxious and fretful and not altogether sober herself. 'That's my husband's vehicle in the ditch. Neither of us gave this man permission to drive it, and he's obviously drunk.'

The policeman's expression did not change.

This time Sandy's arms were around her, gentler than Janette's had been. She seemed to be weeping but she gathered herself and in a solemn voice she said, 'Let's head back.'

Meg had no choice in the matter, she knew that. So she turned and allowed Sandy to guide her back towards the others. They were walking slowly, skirting around the dead deer, when a sudden yelp came from behind her, a sound more like a war cry than a distress signal, and swivelling in the direction of the noise, in the light from the ambulance she saw Marc running towards Steve, his hands already clenching into fists. The first blow caused Steve to crumple over and as he did Marc delivered a knee full to his face. Steve cried out and reached for his nose with his hand. Blood began to pour.

Meg heard herself scream, 'Marc, Marc, stop it,' but Marc carried on the assault, kicking Steve behind the knees to bring him down like an animal. In that moment, the police officer standing nearby rushed over and grabbed at Marc's clothing, causing him to stagger backwards. The policeman unsheathed his truncheon but still Marc went at Steve, who was on the ground with his arms wrapped around his head to stave off the blows. And in that moment Meg glanced at Janette and saw on her face something like resolution, as if this were the culmination of something inevitable and foreseen. This was what she had predicted, it was what they had talked about, the event that Meg could not bring herself to believe would ever come about. But here it was. Marc's rage in all its mad frenzy. Meg's hands clamped firmly to her face. She had a good sense of what was about to happen next, and she didn't want to have to bear witness to it.

TWENTY

Nearing midnight the police told them to go home. They didn't appear to be interested in breathalysing anyone in the Fiesta except Marc. Janette, who'd had the least to drink, drove with Pete in the passenger seat and Meg in the back. In the few minutes it took them to get back to the cottage Pete fell asleep. All was quiet, everyone having abandoned the party and gone home. Together, Janette and Meg manhandled Pete through the front door. He was in no fit state to travel back to London and had in any case missed the last train so they directed him to the sofa in the living room where he blacked out, still in his clothes. Meg fetched a blanket while Janette took off his boots. Janette made coffee and the two women sat down in the kitchen to wait the arrival of the police with Marc. Just after 2 a.m. they heard tyres crackling on the gravel driveway. She turned to Janette, who gave her a faint but encouraging smile.

Janette got up but Meg waved her to sit back down. 'It's okay. I'll get this.'

'Go easy on him,' Janette said.

To Meg's surprise, a lone uniformed officer stood at the front door. Meg thought it was the copper who had been standing near the ambulance, but she wasn't sure. Where was Marc? She looked over the officer's shoulder, straining to see into the darkness. The vehicle's headlights were off, engine silent, exhaust ticking down the seconds. The officer introduced himself, but she couldn't take in his name.

'Where's Marc?' She felt Janette's presence behind her.

'If I could come in?'

Meg's pulse began to tick. They sent two coppers round if it was really bad news, didn't they? So it wasn't that. He must be at the hospital with Helen still. 'And…and how is Helen?'

The officer took a step forward and raised his eyebrows in a gesture aimed at Janette. 'Mr Mair is still at the station for now. I believe that Ms Mair is comfortable.'

Janette's hand landed gently on Meg's elbow and swept her to one side. The officer stepped into the hallway. Janette slipped past and shut the front door. In the quiet of the cottage Pete could be heard snoring on the sofa in the living room. The remnants of the party still lay around.

'Everything's a mess…' Meg said. She felt a bit helpless and stupid, too shaken to be of any use to anyone.

'I wouldn't worry about that,' the police officer said.

Janette led them into the kitchen and suggested they take a seat at the table. Meg resumed her former position. The policeman took the chair opposite. Beside Meg a pot of strong coffee was rapidly losing heat and there was a taste of metal in her mouth, either too much coffee or blood from where she'd earlier bitten her lip. Janette offered the policeman a cup of something then went over and filled the kettle. It was clear from the way that the officer looked everywhere except directly at Meg that he had decided not to speak until the refreshments were on the table and they had all sat down but Meg, unable to wait, said, 'So...so...you're just keeping Marc till the paperwork's done?'

'It's a bit more complicated than that,' the policeman said. He had removed his hat to come in and now began to move it in his hands as if it were a steering wheel.

'He can't handle his drink,' Meg said. She sounded pleading and pathetic. 'He's had a lot to deal with.'

Janette appeared at the table and put down three mugs of coffee. The policeman laid his hat on the table and took a sip.

'I've one or two questions which you might like to answer here and now, or you could come along to the station in the morning if that suits you better. It may be simpler for you if we go through things now.'

Meg shot a look at Janette on whose face there played the whisper of an encouraging smile. 'I'm not sure what I can tell you.'

'Is it correct to say that you invited Mr Savage to your housewarming party?'

'What? No, absolutely not.' Meg thought back to the conversation with Lisa in the shop. 'I mean, we didn't specifically invite him. Steve isn't really our kind of person.' As she was saying this, Meg was already regretting it. Made her sound like some sort of horrible snob. She decided the best thing to do was just to shut up; she'd seen enough cop shows to know that the less you said the better.

'Right,' the policeman said. 'And the vehicle involved in the incident...' The officer reeled off the model and registration number. 'Belongs to...?'

'Marc. It was his mother's car. His father left it to him in his will.'

'Can you take me through what happened this evening?'

Now, as she related the events of the party, it seemed as if it had happened to someone else or that she'd watched it on TV.

'I'm sorry, this is all a bit... When will Marc be home?'

The policeman continued to make notes and said, 'I should imagine they'll wait till the morning to charge him. After that he may be released on bail in which case he'll be free to come back to the house or the custody sergeant may make a decision to keep him a little while longer.'

'But this is just a silly thing. A mistake.'

The policeman picked up his hat once more. 'Mrs Mair, your husband assaulted a member of the public and resisted arrest.'

'He resisted arrest?' They'd gone home before this happened, but she couldn't quite imagine that. Marc fighting with the police?

'He was also driving while intoxicated, I believe. We take that seriously,' the officer went on. He stood and held himself fully upright. 'You'll need to get an emergency tow truck to pick up the vehicle.' He mentioned the name of a firm and suggested they call immediately.

Janette showed the man out. Outside the wind breathed heavily through the trees. Meg supposed there was nothing for it but to retire and hope things looked sunnier in the morning. She remembered the doll in the bedroom, Helen's doing she was sure, and this led her to think about the pink cardigan hanging from the branches in Covert Wood and the dear, terrible little sock sitting in its hiding place under the attic insulation. All of that seemed like a lifetime ago already. Had it even happened? From the front of the house came the sound of tyres on gravel and an engine accelerating. Janette reappeared looking tired and drawn, her age showing on her face in a way that Meg had never noticed before.

'We should get some sleep,' Janette said simply. The snoring from the living room started up again. 'Shall I stay here with you tonight?'

'Yes, please. I don't want to be alone with Pete.'

'It was Marc I was thinking about. If they release him who knows what mood he'll be in.'

'I can deal with Marc's moods,' she said, though she'd never seen anything like this before.

'I really mean his violence.'

Meg turned to Janette in shock. This again. She said, 'I've told you. Marc would never hurt me.'

Janette fixed her with a steady gaze. 'Do you really want to take that risk?'

Sighing, Meg rubbed a hand across her forehead. She was so exhausted now, so completely depleted, near to collapse. In a voice so quiet that she herself could hardly hear it, she said, 'I'll make up the sofa bed in Marc's study for you. Helen's things are in the spare room.'

While Janette went off down the garden with a torch to fetch her nightgown and toiletries from the studio, Meg went upstairs to look for clean linen which she kept in the cupboard in their bedroom. At the top of the stairs a rush of nervous anxiety leapt like a tiger into her throat, and she had to cling to the banister in order not to fall. The doll! She had momentarily forgotten it. She took a deep breath to steady herself, went over to the door to their room and cracked it open. In the darkness something thick and slow stirred. She reached for the light, her eyes blinking back the blood-red retinal shadows until the walls came into focus. Aside from the usual furniture the room was empty. No doll. She checked on the floor then under the pillows and the duvet. Had it been a dream? A misremembering? How could it have been there one minute and gone the next? She searched again and found nothing. It seemed so long ago now. An age. So much had happened. Her hand went to her head and pulled out a skein of hair. She looked at the threads in her hand in dismay. Not that again. A habit developed after Lily had died which she thought she'd got a grip on. Trichotillomania they called it. Trich for short. She went into the bathroom and flushed the hair down the toilet then took another pill. Then she went into Marc's study and the spare room and searched for the doll but did not find it. She felt so disorientated now that she wondered if she could trust herself to remember anything. What was becoming of them? She with her ticking anxiety and memory outages, Marc with his consuming rages?

When Janette appeared carrying her nightgown and robe and a small washbag, she said nothing about the doll nor its disappearance, but only goodnight and thank you, the feeling of unreality turning cartwheels inside her as she went through the motions of readying for bed. She let Janette use the bathroom first and went in after, settling at last into the pillowy cradle of her mattress. She woke sometime later to the sound of tippy-tapping from the attic, the new drumbeat of her life, her head swimming. Could she still be asleep? She reached out and turned on the bedside lamp and then she heard it again, a faint tapping, the sound of fingernails rapping overhead. Her mind began to turn but slowly, as if the contents of her psyche were a porridge being slowly stirred. The noises continued. Tap tap tap. Too steady, surely, to be the walls and floorboards of the cottage settling as Marc had suggested? Too regular to be animals. Supposing Helen was right and this too was just a product of her imagination?

She rose and steadying herself on the bedframe for a moment, went out into the hallway sure, now, that she could not spend this night alone. Laying her ear against the door to Marc's study and hearing slow, heavy breathing, she steeled herself and rapped very lightly on the door.

The breathing sounds ceased. A sleepy voice said, 'Is that you, Meg?'

'Yes, I'm sorry. I thought I heard something in the attic.'

The door creaked open and Janette's face appeared. Meg pressed one finger to her lips and pointed upwards with her other hand and Janette tilted her head towards the attic. For a long while the two women listened, their faces taut with attention.

No sound. No scratching or shifting or scraping. Nothing.

There was a crumpling feeling, a sense that something devastating had just taken place.

Meg laughed then. A thin, tinkly sound, nothing real. 'You must think I'm mad.'

'That's not what I think at all. You've had a terrible shock and when that happens, our minds can play tricks on us.'

Yes. That was it. Mind playing tricks. She closed her eyes and tried to recall through the fug of the pill she had taken what exactly had happened. She pictured the Spider crumpled and smoking, an electrical smell mingled with the warm scent of burning wood and resin where the vehicle had made contact with the oak. Beside it, in the road, lay the deer, its form only partially illuminated in the headlamps of one of the police vehicles, the tongue lolling as if it were tasting the asphalt. A short way away, the interior of the ambulance, so brightly lit you couldn't look at it the same way you couldn't look at the sun. She could see Marc racing away from her screaming.

It was true that she'd had a terrible shock.

'Did you take one of your pills?' Janette said sleepily, evidently anxious to go back to bed.

Meg nodded.

'Maybe take another. You need to get some sleep. I've a feeling that tomorrow is going to be a big day.'

TWENTY-ONE

Marc woke with a god-awful hangover, took in his cucumber green surroundings, wondered where the hell he was, remembered, then wished he hadn't. From last night he recalled only the door to the cell slamming, though some shadowy remnant of events before that hovered as if behind a door marked *No unauthorized access*. He blinked, conscious that he had been woken by a sound, and looked up to see a face peering at him through the door slot. He swung his legs over the thin mattress, into what he realized only after it was too late was a semi-dried pool of vomit and sat up. Beside the bed someone had left a bucket.

The door cranked open and a uniformed police officer appeared carrying a tray. A small chink opened in the door to Marc's memory. The hollowing sickness at the sight of Helen in the ambulance, the Spider crumpled into tin foil, a hard adrenaline spike as his fist contacted Steve's face. Two policemen wrestling him to the ground. Especially that.

Oh crap.

The uniformed officer put the tray down on the mattress beside Marc. When his eyes alighted on the vomit, the wrinkles around his nose deepened. Shame boiling inside him, Marc apologized for the mess, asked after his sister and received the news that Helen was still in hospital but wasn't thought to be in any danger.

'You might want to splash some water on your face. They'll be interviewing you this morning.'

'I've made a complete tit of myself, haven't I?' Marc said.

The officer said, 'I suggest you clean up that mess. If we get any more information about your sister, I'll let you know.'

Then the door swung shut leaving Marc alone again. In the corner by the sink, the eye of the camera watched unblinking. Much of last night was still a blank but pressing the heels of his hands into his forehead to quiet the insistent bonging, a memory came up of Meg's horrified face telling him to stop hitting Steve. He'd heard the words and a part of him, even then, knew that he'd pressed the self-destruct button on his life, but somehow he hadn't been able to stop himself. *Why am I so bloody angry?* Now *there* was a question.

Some time passed before he was alerted to the sound of voices and the door clanked open once more. As he stood up a little pile of fingernail shreds that he'd bitten off dropped to the floor. This time a woman's face appeared.

'Mr Mair?' The woman introduced herself as DC Harper and asked if he wanted to make a call, reminding him that he was entitled to a lawyer and so on. Marc didn't know any lawyers, let alone any criminal ones. As his mind formed the word 'criminal' he thought, *is that me now?* No, no. It was all a bit of a misunderstanding. He could handle it, make it go away. If he asked for a lawyer it would seem more serious than it really was.

'I'd like to call my wife,' he said. Not that Meg was his wife, officially, but it made him sound more confident, somehow, to use the word.

What felt like a long wait ensued then DC Harper reappeared and asked him to follow her. Two uniformed officers accompanied him along the corridor and through a few doors to the main foyer of the cop shop where the duty officer asked him how he was, recited some more procedure, punched in the number Marc gave him and passed the phone. Marc left a message on Meg's voicemail to say he was very sorry, and he hoped that everyone was okay and that he would let her know how he was getting on when he could. Then he told DC Harper he didn't need a lawyer and was led back to the cell. Another interminable wait followed before DC Harper came back and led him into an interview room. He sat in a metal chair and was offered another coffee. He asked after his sister and was given a repeat of the previous information. Imagining things might go better for him if he asked after Savage, he did that too, but DC Harper replied only that they'd get to that. She introduced herself for the tape and asked him for his name and in the blur of his hangover he had the strange feeling that he was someone he didn't recognise.

Marc's version of events: Pete rushing up the stairs saying there had been an accident involving the Spider. Running to the Fiesta parked in the driveway, and the four of them – him, Meg, Janette and Pete – setting off. He recalled the police sirens, the yellow bulk of the ambulance, a feeling of disintegration. And then the rage set in. After which, everything went red then black.

'You accused Mr Savage of stealing your vehicle, a 1979 Alfa Romeo Spider I believe.'

'Did I?' Marc said. It was all rather hazy. His head hurt.

'I had a right to. It's my car.' He registered DC Harper clocking his defensiveness. 'Plus,' he went on, unable to dig himself out of his groove, 'Savage has been making a nuisance of himself ever since we moved to Coldwater.'

DC Harper wrote something in her notebook.

Foolishly encouraged by this – he knew he really should just shut up – Marc began recounting the meeting on moving day, how Savage had been very off-colour with Meg. DC Harper said nothing but continued to take notes. As he spoke, the details of yesterday evening began coming back to him more clearly. The feel of his knuckles making impact with Savage's collar bone. Still he went on, with the misplaced confidence of a man still too hungover to smell the shit in the creek, let alone look for a paddle, recounting the incident at the Palterer's Arms, exaggerating only a little to make it seem that afterwards Savage had been driving at them.

'I know he must have had at least five double whiskies by the time he came at us in his car because I paid his bar tab.'

'Did you call the police on that occasion?'

Marc felt confused. 'We'd only just arrived in the village and I didn't want to make enemies.'

DC Harper looked up from behind her eyelids.

Marc felt an urgent need to add to the story. 'And, and… Meg ran into him in the woods behind our house and…' He decided on a tweaked version, '…he threatened her.'

This caught DC Harper's full attention. A small triumphant surge shot up Marc's spine. 'Threatened how?'

'He had a rifle in his hand.'

'Did he do anything with it? Point it at her for example?'

'Well, no, it was in his hand.'

'Mr Savage holds a firearms licence.' She gave him a vaguely amused look. 'It's quite common in the countryside, you know.'

Marc had a sudden, panicky feeling that he was about to sink. He took a deep breath and tried to settle himself by pushing his feet, hard, into the floor. He couldn't lose it now, not here, in front of DC Harper. 'My wife is afraid of him. Ask her, she'll tell you.'

'I see,' DC Harper said, looking up from her notebook. 'In the light of what you've just said, I'm wondering why you chose to employ Mr Savage...' She checked her notes, '...to clear out some rubbish and widen the attic hatch in your house?'

Marc thought he might choke. He had expected DC Harper to be more understanding. He reached for the coffee, trying to buy himself some time, and noticed his hand trembling. 'Yes, well, but that was...' He took a slow blink, doing his best to calm down. In his head a voice was saying, *you're drowning not waving, mate. Why the hell didn't you ask for a lawyer?* 'How it was, is, we needed a couple of handyman jobs doing and we didn't know anyone else,' Marc said. 'I don't think...'

DC Harper tilted her head and waited for him to go on.

'I'm here to establish the facts, Mr Mair. Just the facts.'

'Well, the fact is that the Spider is *my* car,' Marc repeated feebly. He had a sense of falling now, of being outwitted and outdone. A hot energy surged through his veins and he had to swallow hard to make it go away.

'According to Mr Savage, your sister claimed you invited her to take the vehicle for a spin whenever she liked. You even told her where you kept the key.'

'Well, I suppose...' He was about to concede this point, then thought better of it. Wasn't the rule not to admit to anything unless you were cornered into it? He thought back to the day a few weeks after Jimmy's death when Helen had come down to the cottage to sort out the studio and take the artwork that Jimmy had left her. Had he shown her the key then? Probably. He could only remember feeling wracked with guilt about the disparity in their legacies. He wondered whether he should say something to DC Harper about the inheritance, and the disappointment of the auction. Then again, weren't over-detailed responses supposed to be a sign of defensiveness or even guilt? His mind reeled.

'Have you spoken directly to Helen?' he said.

'Not yet. She's in theatre having her wrist pinned this morning.'

'She'll tell you who the Spider belongs to.' He sounded brittle, as if he was just about to crack. Maybe he was. 'I don't suppose I could I have another coffee?'

DC Harper met his gaze with a steady look. 'Let's finish the interview first, shall we?'

'Sorry, sorry, I mean, sorry...'

'If we could go back to last night. Did you see or hear your sister and Mr Savage leave your property in the Spider?'

'No. I was in the garden. There was music playing.'

'And you arrived at the scene of the accident when, exactly?'

It was all rather fuzzy. 'I don't know about ten o'clock?'

'You drove, I believe.'

'Well, yes, my wife...' There were literal holes in his memory. Big blank lacunae. Like a sweater knitted by someone who had no idea how to handle the needles.

DC Harper held up a hand. 'Are you aware that you were driving at more than three times the legal alcohol limit?'

Marc screwed up his face and rested his forehead on the heel of his hand. His head felt like one of those old vinyl records played at half speed. 'Uh , I was aware in the sense that I knew I'd been drinking, but I wasn't thinking straight.'

'It's a yes or no question, Mr Mair.'

Marc closed his eyes and gestured with his head.

'You're nodding,' DC Harper said, which was obvious until he realized that she was saying it for the tape.

'Yes,' he said simply.

DC Harper went on. 'When you arrived, the police were already on the scene, correct?'

'Yes.'

'So you didn't see anyone actually driving the Spider?'

Mental pictures flew across his mind like cards in a zoetrope: Helen laughing, allowing Savage to put his arm around her waist. 'Where is this going?'

A pause. Marc stopped, a realisation beginning to dawn. He sat back hard, the chair's metal frame cutting into his shoulder blades. 'Savage shouldn't even have been at the party. He gatecrashed. Isn't that trespass?'

DC Harper consulted her notes. 'Your wife told us that it was an open invitation. Did the invitation specifically say Mr Savage wasn't invited?'

'Obviously, no.'

DC Harper repeated this, leaving a gap between the words. Obviously. No. When she leaned forward, pressing the palms of her hands together on the desk, Marc noticed without connecting anything to the thought, that she wore no rings. DC Harper looked up. There was a frown on her face, not of anger or disappointment, but of confusion. 'So even though you'd extended an open invitation to everyone in the village, you weren't expecting him at the party?'

Marc moved around the boxes in his memory. Was there a way to make this better than it seemed?

'The thing is, everyone in Coldwater makes excuses for him like he was on the sharp end of something terrible and you have to make allowances for the guy, but honestly? He's a bully and they're scared of him.'

The pen between DC Harper's fingers began to rock. She stilled it between her lips for a moment then laying it on the table, began to leaf through her file. Seconds later she pulled out a collection of large-format photographs and passed them across the desk.

Marc glanced down at the images. Puffy skin, purpling at the edges, a smear of blood, an unmistakeably broken nose. A face Marc didn't recognize.

'I regret that, obviously, and I didn't intend...' he said. And he did regret it, but only because the incident meant he was now here, in the cop shop, potentially facing charges.

'If you regretted your actions then why did you resist arrest?'

Bloody good question, Marc thought, but said nothing.

'Mr Mair?'

He searched around for something to offer DC Harper that would satisfy her.

'I guess I was stupid.'

'You guess?'

'No, I mean, I was out of control.'

He watched DC Harper writing down the words. Out. Of. Control.

TWENTY-TWO

Meg woke hours later to the smell of fresh coffee drifting up the stairs, checked her watch and realized that in spite of everything, she had slept. Her phone was sitting on its charger on the bedside table. She'd left it on all night in case Marc tried to get in touch and seeing now that there was a voicemail, kicked herself for missing it. He must have called her when she was speaking to the police officer. She tapped the screen and held it to her ear. Marc sounded shaken but there was nothing in the message that she didn't already know. She rose and went to the bathroom, thought about taking a pill, then decided against it. In the warm fug of the shower cubicle she allowed the events of last night to come trickling back and realized that she felt nothing. Maybe it was a hangover from the booze and pills or maybe she'd just run out of feelings.

She found Janette in the kitchen reading on her iPad.

'I hope you don't mind, I helped myself to coffee. There's some for you too if you like. Take a seat.'

Relieved not to have been asked how she was feeling, Meg pulled out a chair, sat and wiping the sleep from her eyes said, 'Thank you…and for last night. I'm sorry I got so…' What?

She could hardly remember through the blanketing numbness. '...anxious.'

Fetching a mug from the dresser, Janette brought it and a full cafetière to the table. 'Have you heard from Marc?'

'A voicemail last night. He was still at the police station and Helen's doing okay. Nothing since then.'

Janette suggested they call Ashford police station for an update. A woman answered and put them on hold, then returned to say that Marc was still being 'processed' and advised against coming to the station because they might have a long wait.

After the call ended, Meg said, 'What does "processed" mean?' She hadn't dared ask the duty officer.

'Charged I suppose.'

'With what though? Driving over the limit? We weren't even thinking. In the circumstances, you know, Astrid having died driving that car, you'd have thought they would make allowances for Marc's state of mind.' She sounded petulant even as she ploughed on. 'Anyway, it's not like you can just book an Uber in Coldwater.' She scraped at a stain on the table which refused to come off however hard she rubbed at it.

'Meg, dear, you saw what Marc did to Steve,' Janette said steadily, a gentle admonishment in her tone which Meg herself recognized was deserved.

Janette brought over some toast and while she was buttering it, she floated the possibility that Helen had taken the Spider and crashed it as a way of sending Marc a message. An enactment, Janette called it. In the absence of being fully able to express her rage at Marc and her father, and at her mother for favouring her son, Helen had unconsciously destroyed the thing that Marc closely associated with Astrid and which also happened to be Jimmy's most prized possession. She went on to say that, psychologically speaking, you could see the incident as Helen's first experiment in revenge. A re-enactment of her mother's death. 'People like Helen need to hurt the internalised representation of the father figure and punish the favoured sibling at the same time. All unconscious, but no less real for that.'

To Meg that all seemed rather far-fetched. She reminded Janette about the deer.

Janette put down her cup and gave her an exasperated look. 'Oh Meg, dear, this is so typical you, always thinking the best in everyone but yourself.'

'I suppose I don't want to think that it could have been Helen's idea,' she said, even now remembering the doll. The coffee bubbled sourly in her stomach. Surely Helen didn't hate them enough to do something so cruel, did she? But who else could it have been?

Janette began to drum two fingers on the kitchen table. 'You want my opinion?' she said, placing a hand on her chest and continuing without waiting for a reply. 'Underneath the presentation of normality is a highly disturbed young woman. I think it unlikely she will stop until she gets relief from her rage.' The idea moved through Meg with the force of a quake. It made a grim kind of sense when you thought about it. Janette reached out and rested her hand on Meg's.

'You must see that you're being drawn into something? We therapists call it a drama triangle. Persecutor, victim, rescuer; Helen and Marc alternating wildly between persecutor and victim, leaving you in the position of rescuer. Drama triangles never fail to end badly for the rescuer. You ask me, you should seriously consider protecting yourself from the Mair siblings right now.'

'But Marc and I share everything,' she said feebly. Janette looked directly at her, one immaculately French-polished fingernail tapping softly against the stoneware mug.

'Including the fact that he's lost his job?' Janette saw the shock on Meg's face. 'I see you don't know. Marc was fired for punching a member of the audience.'

'But he was going up to London every day!' Meg said weakly. Her head sank into her hands. 'Oh, I don't know what to think about anything.'

She felt two strong arms around her and a voice whispering, 'That's why *I'm* here, darling.'

Meg didn't feel much like eating breakfast after that. Instead she went upstairs to dress and found herself in the attic. Somehow the world fell away when she was up there. The doll was still missing from the trunk though the pink sock was still under the insulation, as it had always been. Sometime later she found Janette in the garden throwing empty bottles, cigarette butts and cans into separate rubbish and recycling bags.

'I thought I'd make a start on the clearing-up before the rats get to it. You know, it might be sensible to lay down some poison over the winter before they start breeding. I'm afraid poison is the only way to deal with rats.'

'All right,' Meg said. Why were they talking about vermin with Marc banged up and Helen in hospital?

'And by the way,' Janette went on, moving over to the climbing rose at the edge of the patio and shaking the dying flowers from the bush. 'Marc told me he's intending to transfer the cottage into your name. He was about to draw up the legal papers. He may already have done it.'

Mention of their finances was jarring and seemed beside the point. 'It'll wait,' Meg said.

Janette raised a finger and placed it on her chin in an elegant expression of pensiveness. 'I wonder if it will though?' She went on to ask Meg to consider what might happen if Marc was fined for the assault. If the cottage remained in his name, he'd have to sell it to pay off his fine. All Meg had to do to ensure that wouldn't happen was to sign the papers. That way, the cottage would be safe from the courts. And who knew what Helen had planned? It was what Marc wanted anyway. All Meg would be doing was signing a document which Marc himself had had drawn up.

'Maybe you're right,' Meg said.

'And while we're on the subject of Marc, once they release him, which I assume they will, it might be good for you two to be apart for a while. You don't want to get dragged back into the drama with Helen.'

'Is that necessary? It seems a bit…drastic?'

'In my professional judgement…' Here Janette put emphasis on the word 'professional', '…it would be the best thing for both of you. Marc can go and stay with a friend. It will give him the chance to widen his support network, so that he doesn't just rely on you. And some space to think things over.' Observing Meg's uneasy expression, she added, 'If you prefer me to talk to him about it…?'

It did make sense. In the months since they'd lost Lily, Marc had allowed so many of his friendships to lapse. Meg felt that she couldn't support him alone any longer. For now there was Janette, but she would find a place of her own eventually and move on. 'No, I'll do it,' she said. He'd take it better hearing it directly from her. 'Another thing... Would you consider moving into the cottage while Marc's not here? I'm a bit nervous on my own. You'd be doing me such a favour.'

TWENTY-THREE

'I'm in a lot of trouble, aren't I?' Marc said. The details of the assault on Steve and the struggle with the two arresting officers began to beat out a rhythm in his memory. He was conscious that his body knew something and that there was a haunting and undeniable familiarity in DC Harper's descriptions of punches launched and kicks delivered. He'd attacked a man under the nose of a police officer, and he'd resisted arrest.

Why had he done it? DC Harper seemed keen that he try to answer this question.

'Your sister told the paramedic that your wife said she was worried about your outbursts. "Red mist" I think was the phrase she used.'

Marc felt himself sinking. 'No, I'm... I mean, it's not been an easy time. Moving house and before that...'

'Your former employer told us that you were dismissed for punching a member of the audience.'

Oh God, Marc thought, *here we go.* How had they got to Rable so quickly? It was Sunday morning.

'As I said...it's been a tough few months.'

DC Harper consulted her notes. 'Your daughter died in

a hit-and-run accident and the culprit was never apprehended. You lost your father not long afterwards. Is that right?'

'Yes.' How did they know all this? Had they been talking to Meg? Or Janette?

'Do you have some issue with the police, Mr Mair? Is that why you resisted arrest?'

What kind of question was that? He was drunk, the details were hazy, he had been in the grip of an adrenaline rush. It was dumb, he knew that much. But why? You ask that question of yourself enough you eventually reach a giant question mark. Why had he ever done anything?

'I don't have a criminal record if that's what you're asking.'

'We're aware of that. I was referring to the fact that we weren't able to find out who killed your daughter. These cases can be very difficult to prosecute if there's no CCTV footage, as in your case.'

Marc was conscious of a bitter taste in his mouth. At some point in the night he'd managed to bite his tongue. It was sore and throbbing, the wound reopening every time he opened his mouth to speak.

DC Harper first tapped her lip and then her hair, saying, 'We can ask a doctor to see you about...' Marc put a finger to his mouth and looked at the smear of blood. Fresh blood, nothing Savage could have done. And his right hand was hurting like hell, obviously.

'One of the paramedics on the scene looked you over. You remember that?'

Marc shook his head.

'And you refused to comply with a breath test at the scene, Mr Mair. Remember that? The duty nurse at the station took a blood sample. It'll be screened for substances and alcohol.'

Substances? He hadn't taken any *substances* since he'd become a dad. Alcohol was another matter. But who didn't drink at a party? He wondered if now was the time to say he'd been drinking rather a lot recently. Too much, probably. But he decided to take another tack instead.

'Is this because of who my dad was?' Everyone knew Jimmy had been a caner back in the day.

DC Harper cleared her throat impatiently. Evidently, she thought he was clutching at straws which, he supposed, he was.

'No, I mean…' he did his best to think back to the events of the evening, 'I guess it's possible that someone slipped something into my drink? I'll bet Savage is no stranger to the big medicine cabinet on the street.' He wouldn't put it past him to have spiked him for no other reason than to mess with him.

'Oh, so it's Mr Savage's fault that you attacked him,' DC Harper stated as if it were a truth, which only made it seem more ridiculous.

'Well, no, but in a manner of speaking.' He cringed at his own feeble attempt at self-justification. He wanted to defend himself against everything DC Harper was saying even as he knew she had him pinned and squirming. All the same, he knew that if he got the chance, he'd hit that bastard all over again. He wished, once again, that he'd opted to have a lawyer with him.

The questions continued in something of a blur. After what seemed like forever, two uniformed officers entered the room; he sensed his time in the interview was up and knew in his bones that he hadn't said anything that would make it go better for him.

The officers escorted him back to his cell. More time passed, the bolts clanged and the door opened once again.

'We're ready for you.'

He stood and followed DC Harper and the two uniformed officers from before along the corridor through the doors to the main foyer. The officers stood with him on either side of the duty officer's counter while DC Harper charged him under section 38 of the Offences against the Person Act, assault with intent to resist arrest; and under section 47 of the same Act, common assault on Steven Savage. Somewhere amid that there was also a charge of driving under the influence. The words swam before him. He took a breath and heard that he was being bailed pending a summons to appear at Ashford Magistrates' Court. The duty sergeant brought over a plastic bag containing his phone and a few of his personal effects. As he made his way into the blinding light of the day the thought occurred to him that his life as he knew it was over. The Marc Mair who dreamed of a fresh start was finished. Over. Kaput.

TWENTY-FOUR

It was Janette's suggestion that they go out for a walk. Pete had left before they were up and they were alone in the cottage. Meg wasn't much in the mood for a stroll, but there was still no news from Marc, and she was thinking she might go out of her mind waiting. If she took her phone she wouldn't miss his call when it came. And so they went down the garden path, the robin following them as far as the back gate, then along the path that crossed the field to the stile. It seemed they were least likely to meet anyone here than on any other walk. Meg wasn't ready to bump into any of the party guests. Could not face their enquiries, the brutal curiosity on their faces or worse still, their pity. The trees were now in full drop, a flaming carpet beneath their feet along with the smell of decay. Here and there were circles of fairy toadstools, fly agarics as Meg now knew them, pretty but toxic.

At the ridge of pines, Meg spotted Lisa coming towards them. Her heart sank but Lisa had already seen them and there was no way to avoid an encounter. If she was lucky Lisa hadn't yet heard the news. Then she remembered this was Coldwater. Everyone knew all the news.

'I'm so sorry to hear about the accident,' Lisa said, her voice carrying across the stream bank. 'How is Helen? We were all worried about her.'

'She'll be okay,' Meg said.

Lisa had caught up with them now and was panting a little from the effort.

'I hope you won't think I'm speaking out of turn, but I've always thought Covert Cottage was a bit jinxed. What with all the fires...'

'Centuries ago!'

'Well yes, and the other thing. Cecily.'

Janette stepped forward and said, 'This really isn't the time.'

Meg held up a hand. 'No, please. I want to know.'

Lisa, glancing down at her feet, said, 'It's just that what I was told, the bloke who lived in the cottage before your father-in-law – Christopher Griffin was it? – kept going on about how sure he was that Cecily's body was in Covert Wood, but he wouldn't say how he came by that idea, just that it was a feeling. So the cops were suspicious, see?

'He turned to drink in the end.' Lisa was enjoying herself now, in the flow. 'And his wife had some sort of nervous breakdown. They sent the daughter away to uni to get away from it all. The husband died not long after. Hanged himself in the attic. Turned out he'd got into terrible debt, hadn't told anyone. The widow had to sell up in a hurry. That's why Jimmy got the place at such a good price. People were put off. Not being funny, but that's Covert Cottage. Some places have bad energy.'

Meg took a step back, legs suddenly liquid and her tongue as dry as dust. It seemed that it was of a piece of the puzzle. Coming to Coldwater, the nightly skittering and groaning sounds on the floor above, Lily's trunk in the attic, the accident. Everything led somehow to the missing girl.

'That's enough now.' Janette was speaking to Lisa.

'It's fine, really,' Meg said.

They let Lisa pass then headed back up the path running through the field. Ahead of them the gate and beyond that the studio, the shed and the cottage itself.

'These country bumpkins,' Janette said. 'Bad energy! Honestly! I wouldn't be at all surprised if they weren't in it together. Helen, the vicar and that Lisa woman. Trying to spook you into giving up the cottage. Well, they won't succeed, will they, Meg dear?'

Meg said nothing. The idea made her head swim.

They went in by the back door and took off their boots in the mudroom. Janette went into the kitchen to put on the kettle at the same moment that Marc's ringtone went off in the pocket of Meg's jacket. For a moment she realized that she'd forgotten all about him.

'Darling! Thank God. Are you out?'

Janette appeared at the door and mouthed 'speakerphone'. Meg nodded and pressed the icon. 'Janette's here. You're on speaker.'

'Oh, okay...' Marc sounded subdued and anxious.

Meg said, 'Did they charge you?'

He listed the charges. It sounded much worse than Meg had imagined. He went on, 'Have you heard from Helen? The only thing the cops would tell me was that she's still in Ashford Hospital and she's going to be all right. I would have called but I thought she probably wouldn't want to talk to me right now.'

From the corner of her eye, she saw Janette flash her a warning to be careful what she said about her sister-in-law.

'I sent her a text, but I haven't had a reply.'

'I really don't know what to say to you,' Marc said, sounding very upset.

In spite of herself Meg felt her hackles rise. 'Sorry might be a good place to start.'

'Oh God, yes, of course, and I am, really. So, so sorry.' He paused to let this sink in. 'Listen, darling, I'm going to ask a lawyer to draft some papers transferring the cottage into your name. In case I get fined or sued or, God forbid, end up in prison. Janette knows about it already. I'll get them to courier the papers to you for signing. Or…or…I could just come home?'

Meg glanced at Janette who met her with resolve. They'd spoken about this, anticipating the request. Meg drew a breath and mustering her courage said, 'I'm not sure it's a good idea for you to be here right now.'

There was a stunned silence. 'Is this about the geographical exclusion?' He'd already said that one of the conditions of his bail was not to put himself within a half mile of Savage.

'You know how small Coldwater is and I think…' She heard him cough and feeling emboldened suddenly, said, 'I don't…' Janette's eyes flared. 'What I'm trying to say is *we* think it would be better if you found somewhere else to stay for a few days. Then there's no chance of you running into Steve.' She paused to allow him to take this in, hoping that he wouldn't push back because she didn't know if she would have the strength to say no to him twice.

'But Meg…' he began and something in his voice faltered

as if he'd suddenly seen the sense of what she was saying. 'Okay. But I'll get a lawyer, it'll be fine. I promise you, this is just a minor setback.' His voice was ragged and it broke her heart to hear him like that. 'You're not going to leave me, Meggie, are you?'

'No, of course not, sweetheart.' He sounded so pitiful now that it seemed inhuman to ask him to stay away. She suddenly wondered what she was doing, turning her own husband away from his own home? 'Maybe you could…' she began, thinking out loud, but as she opened her mouth to finish that sentence she felt Janette's hand on her arm staying her and she recalled what Janette had said earlier about this being an opportunity for Marc to reconnect with his friends, to find other sources of support. There was a heaviness, too, that Janette thought that she, Meg, might not be safe from Marc's rages. She took a breath to finish her sentence. 'Maybe you could stay with Pete for a few days.' And before Marc could persuade her out of it, she cut the call.

TWENTY-FIVE

Marc found a café, ordered a cup of coffee and tried to understand why Meg had put the phone down on him. It wasn't surprising that she was angry with him. No one was angrier than Marc himself. Still, it hurt him. But was it so bad that she would cut off contact? Had Janette told her that he'd lost his job? He winced at the thought. It was possible. He had told Janette that he was going to do it himself, after all. Perhaps that was it. He guessed she would find out some time and maybe it was the right time for her to know. He took a deep breath and tried his hardest to steady himself. Maybe this was for the best. To be well out of Savage's territory. He didn't trust Savage not to try to provoke him and they'd take him back into custody if he went anywhere near the man. Marc was damned if he was going to give Savage the chance to get him deeper into trouble. He'd find a way to get his own back. He'd find a way.

The immediate task was a practical one. Find a place to crash for a while. There were a few members of the theatre orchestra he knew well enough to ask for a spot on the sofa after a late night out, but he didn't feel he could land himself on them for more than a day or two. He couldn't face any prying questions about why he'd been sacked and needed a place to stay. Plus he had no idea if Daisy had told anyone about what had happened between them and he couldn't face the inevitable gossip.

In the circumstances he couldn't ask Helen. The police had told him she was going to be fine, but she was still in hospital. Besides which, he probably wasn't her favourite person right now. He was struck by the melancholy thought that his sister was all he had by way of family. Real, blood relations. Jimmy and Astrid had both been only children and they hadn't kept up with extended family and so nor had he. He took out his phone and scrolled through his contacts, wishing he'd done a better job of staying in touch with his old mates. After what happened, the effort of holding on and keeping his head above water hadn't left much room for friendships, even old and valued ones. He struggled for months to connect even with Meg. As for his mates, he couldn't face their questions, their sympathy, their suffocating pity. How could they possibly understand all the myriad ways in which Lily's death marked him? How he had *become* different.

Longing suddenly for a cigarette he paid for the coffee and found a corner shop where he bought a packet of Marlboro Lights and a lighter and sat on a nearby wall, chain-smoking. A drink would be good right now. He thought of going back to the shop and buying a half of Bell's but he didn't trust himself not to down the whole lot in one. And he needed to be sober when he called Pete. They didn't know each other that well but maybe that was good. It was Pete who'd stepped up last night. And he'd witnessed the event, so he knew the degree to which Savage had provoked him. He pulled out his phone, scrolled to Pete's number and hit the green icon. The phone rang and a voice said, 'Mate! How's the hangover?'

Marc noted with relief Pete's friendly tone. His right hand went to his head. 'Rough.'

'The Old Bill keep you in the tank overnight?'

'Yeah.'

'As it happens, I just got back from your place. Missed the last train so I kipped over.'

'Sorry you got sucked into this, mate, I really am.' He trundled on for a bit in this manner until it occurred to him that he was boring the arse off the guy he was about to ask for a favour. Cutting to the chase, he said, 'Thing is, I could use a place to crash for a day or two. All's good with Meg and everything, it's just the Old Bill say I can't go anywhere near that bastard Savage. Get myself a decent lawyer it'll be ironed out in no time.'

'Ah.' There was a pause, and when Pete spoke again his tone was very carefully modulated. 'That's a tricky one. Thing is, I don't vibe with guests staying in the house...' Marc felt his stomach drop until Pete added, 'But seeing you're Jimmy's kin, there's a pull-out in my little basement studio and you can crash there for a few days if you like.'

Marc checked his watch. 'Mate, you're not only a star in name.'

'Ha ha,' Pete said limply.

Marc, covered in shame – *Not only a star in name* – said, 'I could be with you in a couple of hours?'

Pete grunted his assent.

With a sense of relief Marc, still in his party clothes, brushed the ash off his trousers and hot-footed it to Ashford station. A while later he was striding across the concourse at St Pancras to the tube. He made it to Pete's door in St John's Wood in an hour and a half.

Pete's house reminded him of the place he grew up. A handsome, spacious urban villa, the kind of place people dreamed about but few ever got to live in, especially now when the price of property in London had become so insane. The same Lotus he'd noticed when he'd come for his audition sat in driveway. A wave of sadness washed him onto the shore of the past. Lost youth, the death of his parents, his own failure to live up to them. Being a loser, the unforgiveable thing on the day Lily died. All of that.

He went up the stone steps and pressed the familiar polished brass buzzer. Pete's voice greeted him and the door clicked open. He stepped inside and closed the door behind him. Pete came bowling up the hallway.

'You look like shit, mate.' Holding out his hands to receive Marc's jacket, he said, 'The old lady kick you out?' Marc joined in with Pete's laughter and felt a little sick at the shamelessness with which he colluded in his own humiliation. That was the loser in him speaking. He wasn't going to let himself think that way. Right now he needed Pete's patronage. Needed it big time.

Pointing Marc towards the living room, Pete went to fetch some coffee. A tuneful whistle came from the kitchen. Marc took a seat on an expensive modular sofa then spent the next few minutes drumming his fingers on the armrest and fiddling with his phone, hoping for some soothing message from Meg or Helen. He thought about checking social media to see if last night's events came up, then decided he couldn't face it.

Moments later Pete came in carrying two opened bottles of Stella.

'Hair of the dog.' Marc took the beer with a feeling of relief. Alcohol. Thank the Lord and all his angels.

Pete took a seat in a leather chair opposite. 'Cheers then,' he said, raising his bottle.

Marc caught sight then of a photograph he'd missed before. It was a framed image of a group of young people in a glamorously dishevelled room, perhaps in a hotel, perhaps a private house. From their clothes and hair styles Marc surmised it had been taken some time in the Seventies. It seemed late and they were evidently a bohemian crowd, the young men wiry and women mostly thin, almost everyone smoking. A few of them sat about, others were grouped around a couple of guys with guitars and among these Marc thought he recognized his father as a young man and all the weight of his failure to live up to Jimmy came at him.

Pete, sensing that Marc's attention was on the photograph, said, 'You looking at old Jimmy over there? See me there next to him?' He sighed and pulled a hand across his forehead, suddenly ambushed by his own nostalgia. 'Who knows where the time goes, man?'

They sat in silence for a while, sipping their beers. Pete reached for a packet of rolling tobacco and began fashioning a cigarette. 'So, what's the plan?'

'No biggie. Find a lawyer who can steer me through.'

Pete nodded. 'I don't mean to, like, rub it in, man, but you fucked that geezer up good. I could hear your knuckles cracking his jaw from where I was standing.'

Marc felt something in his throat drop away. His right

hand was painful and swollen and his wrist was sprained. It was coming back to him now that some evidence guy at the police station had taken photos of it when he was brought in.

Pete drew on his cigarette and leaning forward said, 'You want, I know a guy. Not cheap, but top drawer. Got me out of a couple of scrapes.'

'How not cheap?'

Pete shrugged. 'Twenty large maybe?'

Marc sucked in his breath. Twenty grand. Where was he going find that kind of money? Before last night the Spider might have fetched twenty grand at auction. Worthless now, thanks to Savage. He had no credit record to speak of and no one legit was likely to lend to some random unemployed guy. He thought about going to Rable again and begging for his job back, but the police had already spoken to his old boss so he was 99 per cent sure that Rable would tell him to sling his hook.

'I don't suppose you'd rethink that deferment of my fee for the session work?' It was awkward raising this now, especially since he was already leaning on Pete's generosity, but he felt that he had no choice.

Stubbing his roll-up in an ashtray already overflowing with stubs, the long yellow guitar player's nails making little tapping sounds on the tray, Pete waggled his lips from side to side as if considering the question, but only a fraction of a second passed before he piped up, 'Oh no, mate, no can do. Cash flow all over the place. You wanna crash in the basement studio while we're working on the album, though, I won't charge you rent.'

A coil of shame rose, like a cobra rising to the snake charmer's pipes, but he forced his lips into two upward facing crescents and sensing he had no choice but to swallow back his disappointment, his sadness and his panic, he said, 'Thanks, mate.'

'Happy to help out.' He saw Marc's eyes on his cigarette. 'Wanna smoke?'

He motioned to the packet of Old Holborn and the papers on the coffee table. Marc picked them up, made himself a rollie, lit it and breathed in the spicy smoke. There was nothing for it, he could see that now. He was going to have to sell Covert Cottage and with it, every dream, every promise of a new life. And sooner or later, he would have to break the news to Meg.

'You want another one of those?' Pete asked, giving an upward nod towards the beer in his hand.

Marc checked the bottle and saw that it was already empty. 'Why not?'

Pete grinned. 'You only live once, right?'

TWENTY-SIX

On Sunday the night-time sounds in the attic began again. Above the black bedroom, where Meg lay in bed, the rafters creaked and the wind rushed and moaned over the old Kent peg tiles. Rising from her bed, Meg went out onto the landing and checking Janette was asleep, pulled down the ladder and crept up into the attic. As she reached the top step the sounds ceased and the cottage fell back into its deep silence. The light from the bulb flickered with a soft ashy flare and threw brown shadows across the boards and the air seemed to thrum with some unheard song. The trunk was sitting where Steve had left it, a silk thread now running from its lid to the rafters, a gallows for a spider. It seemed to her that she and Marc had done their very best to keep their life on an even keel, to make it possible to go on, but that everything was falling apart now, splintering, the pieces tumbling back, back to that ordinary afternoon in early winter when on the walk home from school, a walk she and Lily had done a hundred times, she made the terrible decision to let go of her daughter's hand to check her phone, hoping that Marc had some explanation for not showing up at the school to pick Lily up – a decision that had cost their daughter her life and for which Meg would never forgive herself.

She opened the trunk and peered inside, running her hand across the soft pink cardigan, then unpacked the contents, piece by piece, searching for the doll which was no longer there. Helen *must* have taken it out and left it on their bed. Maybe Janette was right and she really was disturbed. No normal person would do such a thing, would they? And now it was gone. She packed up Lily's things, laying them one by one back in the trunk where they now belonged and saying goodnight to Lily and to Cecily, she clambered down the steps, went into the bathroom and took a pill before creeping past Marc's study where Janette was still sleeping and back, back, into the dark embrace of the black bedroom.

While she waited for the pill to do its work, her thoughts turned to Marc, how much she missed him. Perhaps they were destined to fall apart, like spilled mercury, the drops spreading before moving back together, reconfiguring themselves in some new shape that neither of them could yet discern. She had no reason not to believe that Covert Cottage would soon be hers. Marc had said that the lawyers would courier the papers over and all she had to do was to sign them. And it made sense to protect the cottage from the consequences of Marc's rage, just as it made sense that she, too, protected herself from it. She knew that she couldn't go on living in dread of his fits of ungovernable temper. He knew it. He'd punched and kicked a man before her very eyes. Next time he might do something worse. Perhaps this was the shock to the system that he needed, that they both did.

What would happen next she did not know. She supposed

he'd plead guilty and might be given community service or a fine. Worst case a suspended sentence. An anger management course. And then he would return to Covert Cottage. Things would be awkward in the village for a while but memories would fade. She'd get a job and Marc would go back to making music, maybe they'd start going to church, like Sandy suggested. This was just a hiccup, a chance for them to regroup. Then she would turn her energies to finding what happened to Cecily and some equilibrium, some life-loving energy which had gone missing at the same time as the girl, would finally return to Coldwater. People would no longer have to feel that they were treading around something terrible and unspoken and unknown. Cecily's body would be found and returned to the people she belonged to. The villagers would forget about the skirmish between Marc and Steve. It would all turn out okay.

She fell asleep feeling vaguely hopeful and woke to the sound of the doorbell. Getting up and pulling on her towelling robe she went downstairs and found Sandy on the doorstep clutching a fruit loaf in one hand.

'I hope this isn't too early.' She held out the offering at an awkward angle.

Meg glanced at her watch. 8.30. She'd overslept. The pills again. She'd have to get off them, but not now.

'I'm really glad you came,' she said.

'I thought you might need some help clearing up after the weekend. Or just someone to talk to,' Sandy said, stepping into the hallway and following Meg into the kitchen. 'I can't tell you how sorry I am about what happened. Especially after such a lovely party. It must have been so...'

Sandy stopped speaking when she saw Janette sitting at the table poring over a catalogue. The two women exchanged greetings.

'Sandy came to help clear up. And look, she's brought home-baked fruit loaf,' Meg said. Janette registered this with a slight upward movement of her eyebrows.

'Still warm from the oven,' Sandy said, as Meg laid the cake on the table.

'How lovely,' Janette said.

Sandy cleared her throat, her jaw hardening. 'I wonder if we might have a moment in private, Meg?'

For a moment nothing happened. Then Janette pushed back her chair and smiling, said, 'I need to make a few calls.' The two women watched her sweep from the room. Moments later she was making her way down the garden path, leaving Meg and Sandy alone. Knowing that Meg had an interest in the Cecily Banner case it was odd that Sandy had never mentioned that she'd lived at Covert Cottage and Meg was curious to know why.

'Coffee?' she offered.

'How's Helen? I called the hospital, but they wouldn't tell me because I'm not family, so I drove over there but she was with the physio so I'll have to go back. I'd be happy to give you a lift...'

Meg, who was still confused about Helen and hadn't yet had time to order her thoughts or feelings, thanked the vicar for her offer and said she had planned to go with Janette later.

Sandy nodded and seemed to be about to say something then held back. Nonetheless, there was some urgency in Sandy's eyes that had roused Meg's curiosity.

'I gave Steve a lift home from the hospital this morning. They'd kept him in for observation.'

'How is he?' Meg said, not caring all that much.

'Concussion, one black eye, a broken nose and a couple of cracked ribs, but otherwise, mercifully, he's fine.'

Meg poured the coffee and Sandy thanked her and clasped the mug between her hands, as if she were clinging onto something terribly precious.

'I'm sorry about what happened. That was Marc's mother's car, you know, one of the first things his father bought once he found success. She died driving it and Jimmy spent years restoring it as a sort of tribute to her, so what with that and his sister being a passenger and, well, you know, our history with car accidents...I'm afraid Marc just got carried away.'

Sandy readjusted her position but did not loosen her grip on the mug. 'Steve seems to think it was more than getting carried away. But I'm not here to get into a debate about who was right or wrong. I believe Marc's not allowed to go anywhere near Steve right now anyway.'

Meg pushed away the remains of the slice of fruit loaf she'd felt obliged to cut for herself. She was feeling oddly defiant. 'I know there's no real excuse for what Marc did but you should know that Steve has been threatening us.'

Sandy looked shocked. 'Really? That doesn't sound like Steve at all.'

As Meg began to detail the encounter outside the Palterer's Arms and then again in Covert Wood she realized that, in the telling of it, nothing that Steve had done to them really added up to much. It certainly didn't sound threatening, but you had to have been there. You had to have felt the danger in your bones.

Sandy took a few sips of her coffee and waited politely for Meg to finish and Meg got the sense that whatever she had to say wasn't going to change Sandy's mind.

'Steve had a difficult beginning and certain things happened and there's no question that he made mistakes. But he's always paid his dues. A few years back he spent six weeks fulfilling a community service order doing groundworks. He rebuilt the wall around the churchyard and when the order came to an end, he donated another two weeks of his time and labour to finish the job. A couple of years after that he had another run-in with the law. A small amount of marijuana. Back to the magistrates' court. Jimmy acted as a character witness for him. I wonder if you knew that?'

Meg shook her head. It was a touching story but it didn't get him off the hook. 'When we spoke about this before, I didn't mention that Steve had set his hopes on buying a little piece of land the other side of Covert Wood. He wanted to put a caravan on it. The owner was willing to sell it for £20,000. Your late father-in-law gave him half that and promised Steve he could work for the rest. But Jimmy died not long after. In reasonable expectation of the money, he'd already taken out a loan from some...' She coughed delicately, the muscles in her face flickering, '...less than reputable people. It didn't end well.'

'I hope you're not suggesting that we owe Steve that money?'

'No, of course not. I'm just saying that for one reason or another, people in Coldwater feel rather let down by successive owners of Covert Cottage. It's not for me to say whether that's right or not, it just is.'

'Alice told me you lived here at one time.'

Sandy blinked. 'Yes, I'd rather she hadn't. She texted me after to apologize. She thought you already knew. The truth is that I've been thinking about telling you every day since you arrived and I was going to that day we met, when I said something about Cecily, but I remembered that you'd lost your daughter and I didn't want to cause any more upset.' Sandy's eyes were gathering tears. 'I suppose there's no point hiding the fact that Cecily was on her way to see me when she disappeared.'

Very softly, almost in a whisper, Meg said, 'So you knew her.'

Sandy blew the air from her lungs. For a moment she was very still as the pictures from the past rose behind her eyes. Then she took a deep breath and began to tell her story. 'Her aunt and uncle paid me to babysit her a couple of times, so I got to know her that way. Cecily was a sweet little girl, bright but you could tell she was vulnerable. She loved stories. Winnie the Pooh was her favourite. At bedtime nothing else would do. Back then I had a pet angora rabbit and Cecily got it into her head that it was Rabbit from the Pooh books. So of course she was desperate to see him.' She stopped, overcome with emotion. Meg left her chair and came over to comfort her but Sandy was in no mood for consolation. With a cry that seemed to come from the deepest part of her, she said, 'If I hadn't told her the story, if I hadn't said I had a rabbit, she'd still be here, a woman in the prime of her life, maybe with children of her own.' She looked up and into Meg's face and pressing her fist against her chest she said, 'Somewhere in here there's a sixteen-year-old girl who still blames herself.'

'That's so sad,' Meg said blandly. There was no possible response equal to what Sandy had just confided in her.

'The whole episode caused a lot of pain. Finger pointing, even at me at one point.'

'You were just a kid.'

'A sixteen-year-old gay kid,' Sandy said.

'I'm sorry.'

Sandy stood. 'I think if it's okay with you, I'll go now. Please send my regards to Janette.'

Meg watched from the porch as Sandy cycled back up The Lane. When she returned, Janette was in the kitchen looking dark and troubled.

'That visit wasn't all about the fruit loaf, was it?'

'No.' Meg relayed the part about Steve, but not the part about Cecily. Janette had already made it clear that she considered Meg's obsession with the case to be unproductive.

'Sandy's gay, I don't think I realized.'

'You didn't? It seemed obvious to me.'

Meg smiled. 'So much that comes as a surprise to me seems to be something you've known forever.'

'But you're telling me for a reason,' Janette said.

'Yes, I'm just putting it all together in my mind. She seemed very anxious about Helen last night and Helen was the first thing she talked about this morning. I think they might be more than friends.'

Alarm flickered across Janette's face. 'Did you say anything about taking over the ownership of the cottage?'

'No, why?'

'From now on, you should assume everything you say to Sandy will get back to Helen, and given Helen's state of mind, it might be a good idea to keep the vicar at arm's length.'

TWENTY-SEVEN

Marc had expected someone flashier than the conservatively dressed figure who came from behind his desk and thanking the young male assistant who had shown Marc from reception, stretched out an elegantly manicured hand. It was 9 a.m. on Tuesday, a little more than sixty hours since the accident and Marc hadn't slept much. He'd spent last night on Pete's pull-out, a wretchedly uncomfortable tangle of mostly broken springs, wishing he could turn back time.

'Phillip Bunkin.'

Money. Public school. Lots and lots of money.

Marc took the hand and hoped Bunkin wouldn't notice how clammy his own was. He took a seat in an expensive-looking upholstered chair on the client side of the solicitor's desk. Displaying his set of perfectly veneered teeth, Bunkin offered coffee with a practised grace and when Marc accepted, buzzed through to the assistant and asked her to bring two cappuccinos. They'd had a brief phone call to set up the meeting, during which Bunkin had asked only about the specific charges and the time Marc was due to appear at Ashford Magistrates' Court tomorrow morning.

'So, a friend of Pete's,' Bunkin said, settling himself into his mid-century modern office chair.

'Sort of, more like an employee,' Marc said. Pete's breezy estimate of twenty grand's worth of fees still looming large in his mind, Marc hoped Bunkin would assume from this the two men were in different financial leagues.

'Explain?' Bunkin said and as Marc began to elaborate on his connection to Pete he was conscious of tripping over himself and talking too much. Everything about Bunkin and his set-up made him feel nervous and inadequate. Suave and poised in that pricey, understated chair, Bunkin gave the impression of listening without commenting. Halfway through his explanation, Marc's phone began to buzz. Doing his best to ignore it, he stumbled on, longing for Bunkin to jump in and rescue him.

When the buzzing continued, he said, 'Do you need to get that?'

Embarrassed by his lousy performance, his shitty, dishevelled appearance, even his crappy phone, Marc pulled the device from his jacket pocket, checked the screen, saw it was an unknown number and diverted the call to voicemail.

Bunkin gave Marc a moment to settle before continuing, 'Why don't we go from the beginning, with what led up to the events?'

Where to start? Already Marc could see that the events of last night were the culmination of a feeling that had been brewing for a long time. The lead-up was not the day or even the week or the month before. Looking back, he could see that it began at the moment nearly two years ago when he picked up his phone and heard the unearthly screams that kicked off his nightmare. And so, leaving out the most secret detail of that day, a detail which, though it plagued and haunted him, he had never admitted to anyone but Janette, he began with Lily's death and the useless, pointless police investigation that had stirred him into a frenzy of powerlessness and rage. The dark months leading up to the inquest. How hanging on by their nails to the crumbling cliff face of their marriage, he and Meg had quit London for Coldwater, hoping for a fresh start. How he tried to settle into a present which contained within it the seeds of a more hopeful future, but that things had begun to fall apart again after the loss of his regular paying job, the growing pressure he felt from himself and from Helen to put right their father's legacy, and the encounters with Steve which had spooked Meg and left him feeling vaguely menaced. How circumstances conspired to draw him backwards as though he was swimming against a rip-tide that threatened to take him under.

As he spoke he watched Bunkin's face settle into an expression of polite indifference.

'What I mean is, I was under a lot of stress,' he said.

'Got it,' Bunkin said, his features set to a lawyerly neutral. 'But I wonder if we could focus in some detail on the events leading up to your assault on Mr Savage? From the charge sheet I assume you'd been drinking? Any recreational drugs?'

'A few beers, some wine. We were in the middle of a house-warming party. No drugs, or none I know about, but I was feeling very weird and I wouldn't have put it past Savage not to have spiked my drink.'

'Any proof of that?'

'None.' Savage was a moron but he was no idiot. Marc decided to take the conversation in another direction. He explained that Savage had worked for Jimmy then launched into another narrative about the unsettling encounters with Steve outside the Palterer's Arms and in Covert Wood, how Savage had hinted that he had expected to be taken care of in Jimmy's will and was resentful and angry that Marc hadn't in one way or another provided him with a steady income. 'My mother, Astrid, died at the wheel of the Spider and Savage knew that because he'd helped my late father restore it.'

Marc rambled on, in full flow now. *If I can just represent something of the whole tangled knot of it to Bunkin, and if Bunkin can somehow convey that to the magistrates, then no court in the land would convict me. I'm the victim in all this.* He said this to himself even as he knew that he was guilty. If not of this, then of the other. If only he hadn't done what he'd done the day Lily died.

Bunkin held up an elegant hand. 'Without evidence we're unlikely to be able to bring any of this to court. Most of it is hearsay and the rest is, how to put this, not strictly relevant, by which I mean that it doesn't change the substance of the charges. The facts remain that you drove whilst over the limit, that you punched and kicked Mr Savage and then resisted arrest.'

'I was angry.'

'That much is clear, Mr Mair, but in law being angry doesn't give you the right to assault people. Have you had anger issues in the past? Because if you have, the prosecution is likely to bring that up.'

Marc's heart sank. He already knew the police had spoken to Rable.

'I've been in therapy,' he said. Janette would confirm how much progress he'd made.

'Well good. But still.'

At that moment there came a knock on the door and the young assistant brought in two cappuccinos on a tray. Bunkin gestured for Marc to take one which he did, wondering how much this, too, would cost him. When the assistant had left, Bunkin continued his barrage of questions which Marc did his best to answer.

'I assume you'll plead guilty tomorrow,' Bunkin said finally. 'That would be the more pragmatic line to take.'

'What about the situation, the threats, the fact that Savage knew how precious that car was to me?'

'We could offer your circumstances as mitigation at the sentencing stage, but the facts are pretty indisputable.'

'I was provoked. Surely the law makes allowances for that?' If he'd been willing to plead guilty he wouldn't have needed a top-notch lawyer. The way he saw it, only a not guilty verdict would satisfy both his pride and his sense of natural justice. Why should he plead guilty and endure Savage's gloating smirk whenever they bumped into one another in Coldwater? So he broke the guy's nose. Savage had managed to destroy the only precious thing that remained of his mother. Fuck him. He got exactly what was coming.

'I have advised you but you are still set on pleading not guilty?' Bunkin asked.

Marc confirmed this. Bunkin, looking resigned, rested his chin on his hand for a moment then said, 'Okay, so here's what we're going to do...'

As Marc listened, he realized why the lawyer commanded the big bucks. The man had zero morals and something way more valuable. He knew how to navigate the legal system the way a rat knows its way around a sewer. And he understood strategy. If anyone could get Marc off, it was Bunkin. And then there were forms to fill in and the matter of fees to discuss. The figures made Marc's eyes bleed. There was nothing for it. He was going to have to go back to Pete's house and beg. If he was forced to sell the cottage there would be another thing he'd never be able to forgive himself for.

With that, Bunkin pushed back his chair and stood to his full height and handing a business card to Marc, he said, 'Have a think and let me know whether you wish to proceed. Once we've received the money on account, I will send you my terms of instruction. There's an Aldi supermarket near the magistrates' court. Let's meet there at 10.30 a.m. tomorrow. It's a very short drive to the court for your hearing at 11.00. I think it's a good idea for defendant and counsel to arrive together. You never know who's looking.'

Bunkin then showed Marc out to the lift, shook his hand and said his goodbyes, leaving Marc to wonder where the hell was he going to get five grand between now and tomorrow morning. It all came back to Pete, didn't it? He was just going to have to do his best to make that work.

An hour later he found himself back at the house in St John's Wood. He'd walked, evidently, though he had no memory of the journey. He let himself into the basement studio and sat on the pull-out bed trying to get his head together. Then he went up the stairs and into the main house. From the hallway he could hear Pete humming to himself. Following the sound he found Pete sitting on one of the expensive sofas in the living room watching football. 'Hello, mate. I thought I heard the door go,' Pete said amiably, turning to greet Marc. 'Fancy joining? There's a beer in the fridge. Get me another while you're at it.'

'Great. Though if you had anything stronger?'

Pete looked at him in surprise then admiration. 'Bottle of Stolly in the freezer, mate. Shot glasses in one of the cupboards, open a few doors, you'll see.'

Marc padded into the kitchen, opened the fridge, took out two beers and found an opener. He opened a few cupboards till he found the glasses then took the vodka from the freezer and balancing the lot between his arms he went back into the living room where Pete had lit a joint. He set the drink paraphernalia on the coffee table, opened the beers and poured a couple of shots of the vodka then hung back awkwardly, screwing up his courage.

His eyes still glued to the screen, Pete reached for his beer. Then he held up the hand with the joint in the air and said, 'Want a puff?'

Marc took the joint, sucked in the smoke and felt himself grow light-headed.

'Ha, yeah, Morocco's finest,' Pete said, momentarily peeling his eyes from the game. 'Take a seat, mate, make yourself at home.'

Marc got the impression that Pete was finding the interruption irritating so he decided just to come out with it. 'I went to see your bloke, Bunkin. I'm going to need five grand. If there's any way you could advance me my fee for the session work?'

Pete froze. He reached out for the remote and muted it, then turned to look at Marc.

'Like I said, mate, it's only when the album brings in the cash. But it will, mate, it will.' He was wearing the expression of a bear who had been woken from its hibernation. He turned the sound back on.

A pause. One of the teams scored a goal. Pete roared then fell back into his seat and without so much as glancing in Marc's direction, waved a hand for his joint back.

'Aced it,' Pete said, referring to the footy.

Marc, persisting, said, 'It would only be for a few months.'

Pete barely looked up before going back to the game. Marc had lost him. Moments later, during a brief break in play, he said, 'I would if I could, mate. I know a guy, though. A contact.'

It took Marc a minute before he understood what Pete was saying. 'A loan shark?'

Pete took another deep drag on his joint. 'Bit disparaging, mate, bit disrespectful.'

'Sorry,' Marc said.

Pete nodded his acceptance. 'More of a financial paddle for blokes like you.'

'Like me?'

'Yeah. Guys up shit creek.'

TWENTY-EIGHT

After a sandwich lunch prepared by Janette, which she found herself unable to eat, Meg pulled on her boots and said she was going to the shop. In truth she didn't know where she was going. She wasn't sure whether she was more shaken by Sandy's visit or by Janette's insistence that neither she nor Helen were to be fully trusted.

'You sure you don't want company?' Janette asked.

Meg was sure.

At the bottom of the drive, instead of turning left towards the village, she found herself walking in the direction of the accident scene, imagining the Spider's final journey. Up ahead, in the sky above the treeline, a pair of buzzards circled. She walked on and not long after detected a whiff of decomposition. The weather had been cool in the hours since the accident. Even so, as she got closer the smell thickened and death announced itself in flurries of flying insects. When she reached the spot, she saw skid marks in the road. The emergency tow truck guy had cleared the wreckage of the Spider though there seemed still to be shards of glass about. The firm had called Meg that morning to say that the impact had effectively jammed the chassis into the engine and that both were irreparable. A single dark stain sat where she remembered the body of the deer lying and though the carcass had been moved it was evidently still nearby. That smell wasn't coming from anything living. Where the car had come off the road the verge was chewed up and the oak which bore the impact was gouged and seeping. Around its girth a little further down, a remnant of police tape fluttered and someone had chalked a mark on the bark there, presumably to assist the police with their investigations. On the roadside a yellow board had been set up, calling for witnesses, not to the accident, but to the incident labelled 'assault'.

Lily had not died at the scene of the hit-and-run but in the ambulance on the way to hospital. She, Meg, remembered nothing about that journey, though she had been there. The memories remained stashed in some obscure filing cabinet in her unconscious. There was so much she still did not remember and she had to rely on the accounts of bystanders and the emergency service personnel. A trauma response, Janette called it, the psyche's way of protecting itself from unbearable pain. At some time in Meg's future, Janette said, when she was strong enough to stand it, her psyche would bring the memories back out. A year, two, ten, it was impossible to predict. She could be washing her hair or digging in the garden and they would suddenly appear, bright and terrible, to lay claim to her. That anguish lay on the path ahead like some distant shadow. For now, all she could do was to go forward, day by day.

She took out her phone to call Marc, realising only then that this was what she'd come out to do. Whenever she called anyone in the house it seemed that Janette appeared. There was probably nothing to it, but still it gave Meg the unsettled feeling of being monitored and she'd taken to silencing her notifications so that Janette wouldn't ask her about them. Which was why she only now saw a text from Helen with an update on her condition, or rather, it was from Sandy, who had sent it from Helen's phone at the hospital, to say that Helen was out of theatre but still drowsy and wanting to rest. She'd rather they didn't come that afternoon. Helen would text when she felt more able to deal with their visit.

She went into 'Recents' and tapped on Marc's contact. He answered almost immediately, his voice uncertain but pleased to hear from her. 'Meggie!'

The way their last conversation ended hung heavy between them.

'I'm sorry, about before,' she said.

'It's okay. You have every right to be angry with me.'

She let this go.

'Any more from Helen? She's not answering my texts. I think I'm in the sibling doghouse.'

Meg conveyed the contents of Sandy's earlier text.

It was blustery and in a nearby tree a buzzard began calling its mate.

'Are you out somewhere?' Marc said. Evidently he'd heard the bird or maybe the wind, or both.

Meg told him she was at the scene of the accident. 'They moved the deer and the mechanic doesn't think the Spider is fixable.'

Silence fell. Clearly Marc didn't want to talk about the accident. 'I've got a lawyer. Phillip Bunkin, friend of Pete's. Really smart.' It hadn't sunk in with Meg that her husband would need a lawyer who would need to be paid.

'I have to be at Ashford Magistrates' Court for eleven tomorrow morning.'

'You want me to be there? I can be there,' she said.

'It's fine. Bunkin says it'll all be over in the time it takes to confirm my name and set a date for trial.'

'Trial?' It was her belief that you didn't go to trial unless you had pleaded not guilty. And if there was one thing she was sure of in this whole mess it was that Marc was utterly, provably guilty.

'Are you all right?' he said. 'You're not back on those pills? Your voice sounds different somehow.'

'You're pleading *not guilty*? Marc, you did it. I saw you. You hit Steve several times.'

'I was goaded, baited even. We must put a stop to Savage once and for all. Otherwise he will keep coming back for what he thinks we owe him because Jimmy may or may not have made some reckless promise at some point.'

'How is it going to help to spend a fortune on legal bills defending a case you can't win?'

'Don't worry about the money. I've got a plan.'

The word 'plan' made her heart sink.

'I don't want us to lose the cottage, Marc.'

'You won't. The papers for putting the place in your name will be with you tomorrow. All you have to do is sign and the cottage is protected.'

'But why put yourself, put us, through all the stress of a trial?'

'Because I want to fight it. Put Savage in his place. And I can win.'

Meg didn't think that those three sentences followed

logically from one another, but she could sense it would only make him angry to try to argue the point. So she brought it round to herself instead. 'I just want us to get back to our lives.'

'If I plead guilty, I'll have a criminal record. How easy do you think it is for blokes with criminal records to get jobs?'

He didn't think Janette would have told Meg that he had lost his job. In a way it didn't matter. The job was gone.

There came a sudden crack from deeper in the woods and as she turned to the direction of the sound she saw movement, an indistinct shape which quickly resolved and to her alarm, Steve came trudging along a woodland path running parallel to the road. In one hand was a rifle and in the other a large saw.

'I have to go,' she said to Marc and cut the call, turning and walking briskly away but it was too late, Steve had already spotted her.

'Well, that's not very friendly considering!'

She froze. As he came closer, she could see the black eye Marc had left on him and his nose was bandaged. She remembered what Janette had said about being careful around him, about not provoking him.

'I'm sorry about what happened,' she said, her gaze not leaving his hand. 'But given the situation, it's probably best if we don't talk to one another.'

He looked at her impassively. 'I'm not stalking you, if that's what you think.' He raised the saw, the sharp edge glowing silver in the sunshine. He was enjoying this, her utter helplessness. 'I come for that deer, keep me in venison all winter,' he said. 'Van's parked further up.' There was a layby not far away and she assumed this was what he meant. He used for a moment then he said, 'I hope your old man's not here 'cos he ain't allowed.'

'No, he's staying with a friend. Janette has moved into the cottage while he's away.' She wanted to make it clear that she was not alone.

'He owes me, what he did,' Steve said darkly.

'That's up to the courts,' she said.

'I'm talking about what old Jimmy promised me.'

The pulse began to tick in her temple. She shook her head and put her hand in her pocket, feeling for the side button on her phone. She couldn't think straight suddenly. Everything inside her head was a blank.

To leave she would have to turn her back on him.

Be careful.

It was then she heard an engine, faint but approaching. She took a step from the verge onto the asphalt, her eyes never leaving the rifle in Savage's hand, saw him cock his head, listening out too. They both felt it, the rippling of the membrane between the present and the future. She wondered then if he might hurt her. If he might take the chance while the car was still out of sight, might grab her and yank her backwards or pull her down into the undergrowth and whoever was driving past would see a still, deep stand of trees in which there was nothing moving. The worst nightmare of any woman encountering a man alone in a wood carrying a weapon.

And then it appeared, a silver Peugeot, its driver too far away to see in any detail. Meg swallowed back her fear and took another step out into the roadway. Steve did not move. The car was approaching fast, the driver familiar with the curves and turns in the road. She took another breath and stepped further out. It was bearing down on her now. Had the driver even spotted her? For a moment panic prevented her from seeing that the car was slowing, its hazard lights on.

It stopped just before it reached her. The window rolled down and Lisa leaned out.

'Everyone all right?'

Meg wanted to run up and hug her. In as steady a voice as she could muster, she said, 'Could I bother you for a lift back to Covert Cottage? I'm not feeling very well.'

Lisa leaned over and opened the passenger side door. Meg slid in, her whole body trembling.

Outside Steve grinned and began to wave.

'Was he bothering you?' Lisa said as they left the lone figure with the rifle in his hand behind.

'No, yes, a bit.'

'I heard what happened Saturday night. He's an oddball,' she said. 'But anyone would be odd, being a suspect all these years.'

And so, just like that, they were back to Cecily.

'I tried to find someone who knew him back then, an old school friend, but I couldn't.'

'You wouldn't, not here in Coldwater. I heard he wasn't at the local primary, not for long anyway. They transferred him to a school for troubled kids over Ashford way.' She changed down a gear and the car slowed around a corner. 'You'd do better talking to Tim.'

'The retired copper? Was he working on the case?' Meg had made a mental note to go back to Tim after she'd met him at the party, before other events intervened.

'He was fresh out of police training academy is what I heard.

He'd been in the military for a few years before. I'm not sure if he was actively involved, but presumably he must have known something. It was pretty high profile. He moved to Coldwater some time before Cecily disappeared.'

'Before?' It seemed important to be clear on this point.

'Yes.'

They came to the driveway of Covert Cottage and Lisa slowed the car. 'I know he can be off-putting but if you think Steve did it, you're barking up the wrong tree. He talks about her sometimes. I've heard that he puts flowers in the woods on her birthday. He's never forgiven himself for leaving her that day.'

'What else do you know, Lisa?'

Lisa shook her head. 'Really, nothing. Talk to Tim.'

Meg thanked Lisa for the ride, let herself in and called for Janette. When there was no reply, she went upstairs and into the bathroom. The box of pills was in the cabinet where she'd left it and as she swung the door closed, she caught a glimpse of her reflection. How tired she looked. How worn. She took a deep breath and splashed her face with cold water, drying it and applying some moisturiser. Popping a pill from its foil, she bent to the tap, sucked in a mouthful of water, and immediately felt calmer. Then she wandered back downstairs and out through the mudroom into the garden and down the narrow path that ran alongside the great yew tree towards the studio, the robin joining her partway.

The blinds were drawn over the windows. She knocked and when there was no response, some impulse overtaking her, she reached out and pushed on the door handle until the latch clicked open.

The studio was empty. The door to the tiny wet room was open and it was obvious Janette wasn't in there either. Meg reached for the door handle again and was about to close it when her eye was drawn to a shadow where the light hit the table beside the sofa bed. Something about the shape caught her attention. Goosebumps rose on parts of her skin that were not cold. Turning her head to make sure no one was coming up behind her, she pushed open the door and slipped inside then crept across the studio floor and stepped around the corner of the sofa bed. What she saw stopped her dead. A pair of sightless eyes stared up at her, the acrylic hair matted and oddly shiny. Her foot caught on the edge of the sofa bed and all at once she felt herself slide. Her arms flailed and in a split second she was on the floor. She blinked and felt her breath catch and for a short moment everything seemed to be suspended. Her left hand arced, made contact with something hard, then carried on its trajectory. A coldness spread into her thigh and when she looked down, she saw a darkening on the rug and realized that she'd overturned a glass of water that had been sitting on the table. A sudden urge came over her to flee.

It was Janette. Janette had taken the doll.

TWENTY-NINE

Expecting Janette to appear any minute, Meg stood up to her full height, brushed herself off and hurried out of the studio and up the garden path towards the cottage. A stray wine bottle left over from Saturday night sat on the low wall at the end of the patio. She headed towards it and without thinking, tipped the contents down her throat.

After a while Janette emerged from the French windows carrying two mugs from each of which a tiny heat haze shimmered. Her hair was wet.

'There you are. I was having a lie-down while I waited for my roots to take the colour. Must have drifted off. Was that a car in the driveway? Did someone give you a lift home?' She handed her the mug and came to sit beside Meg on the low wall.

'Yes, I...I pulled a muscle. Nothing serious. Lisa happened to be driving by.' To have spoken about the encounter with Steve would have made her feel too vulnerable somehow. She wasn't quite sure who she was speaking to any more. Finding the doll in the studio had made her question everything she thought she knew. Who was Janette Hopwood really? It hit Meg that she really had no clue.

'You're worried about something. Not Marc, something else. I can feel it.'

Once again Meg had the unsettling feeling that Janette could see right through her, into the darkest recesses of her soul and she was seized by the desire to run.

'Perhaps one of your pills would help with the pain?' Janette said.

'I took one earlier.'

'Well, another won't hurt. I'll fetch them if you like?'

Maybe it was a good idea after all. 'It's all right, I'll go.'

She made it as far as the landing but instead of going into the bathroom she went instead to the hatch into the attic and leaning the steps against it, climbed up. At the top she reached for the light switch and flipped it. The pill was beginning to kick in now. She could feel its warmth in her veins. She looked at the beams and ran her fingers along them, searching for any groove in the wood where a rope might have been strung but there was none. She dug out the pink sock from the floorboards and raised it to her face, taking in the smell of must and on impulse she went over to the trunk, opened the lid and laid the sock beside Lily's cardigan. Then she shut the lid and fell to her knees beside the trunk and let the tears come.

Some time later a voice from below said, 'You shouldn't be up there on your own.' She peered down through the hatch and saw Janette staring up at her, looking worried.

'I just...'

'Come down now,' Janette said, waving her arms. It was a command rather than a suggestion. 'And be careful.'

By the time Meg reached the landing she was distinctly

woozy and feeling like a schoolkid who'd thrown chalk at the teacher behind her back.

Janette sighed and shook her head. 'You've been in my studio.'

'I was looking for you. I spilled some water...' Meg stopped herself. There was no point in pretending. Janette would see through her. Janette always saw through her. 'I saw the doll.'

Janette looked stricken for a moment, then her face softened and resumed its usual warmth. 'Oh, I see. That was what was on your mind. I was trying to keep the doll out of sight for your sake, but since you've brought it up, I heard you cry out on the landing at the party. I saw Marc bound up the stairs and I followed him up. I saw you drop the doll. When we got back from the scene of the accident I hid it in my studio so you wouldn't have to see it. I thought after what happened you could do without that right now.'

Meg let out a sigh of relief. Of course, that was the most obvious explanation. The fact that it hadn't occurred to her spoke volumes about the scrambled condition of her brain. All the anxiety of the last few hours. The party, the accident, Marc, everything. Janette had been trying to protect her, as she always did. She felt a tear forming. How could she have so misinterpreted things? The last few days it had felt as if her thoughts were tied up in knots.

'I'm sorry,' she said. 'I'm not thinking straight at the moment.' Janette leaned in and took Meg's face softly in her cupped hand. 'Meg, dear, we'd both feel a lot safer if we got a proper security system installed. Protect the cottage front and back. I've picked out something in the catalogue. It's pricey but...'

'We can't afford...'

Janette raised an eyebrow and finished the sentence. '...not to?'

At that moment there came the sound of a motorbike engine and moments later, the doorbell rang.

Janette got up. 'Maybe best if I get that? In case it's Savage.' Meg nodded but followed Janette out into the hallway all the same. *What a puppy I am,* she thought, trailing after her.

A man in a biker's helmet stood in the porch holding out an envelope with the transfer papers to the cottage. In the madness of the accident, the doll, all of that, Meg had forgotten them. Janette took the envelope and asked the courier to step inside and wait out of the rain which had newly started. The man came in and apologized for dripping on the tiling.

'Let's just sign those now,' Janette said to Meg, and turning to the courier added, 'Would you be a lovely man and witness the signature? Then you can take them back with you. Save you a journey.'

She went into the kitchen to find a pen, leaving Meg and the courier making awkward small talk. Moments later she was back and less than a minute after that, the papers were signed and witnessed, and the courier went on his way.

'There,' Janette said, closing the front door firmly behind them and turning towards the interior of the cottage. 'Covert Cottage belongs to you now.'

THIRTY

Marc spotted Bunkin's red midlife crisis Tesla pulling into the car park of the Ashford Aldi. He'd been waiting by the supermarket entrance with an envelope of cash that Pete's 'financial advisor', a dodgy geezer named Trevor McInsey, had handed over to him in a dingy office in one of the last few Georgian houses in Soho which still reeked of the antiseptic and used condoms that are the stock-in-trade of brothels everywhere. Was he was being a fool to plead not guilty? Perhaps. If he pleaded guilty it would all be over bar the reports and the court date for sentencing. First offence, ABH, resisting arrest, drink driving. Bunkin had told him that it was very unlikely he'd get a custodial. What was more likely was a community service order and a driving ban along with a criminal record. Not too late to change his mind. On the other hand, who would employ him with a criminal record? Orchestras always asked for DBS checks. He'd never live it down. And then there was his public liability insurance. He wouldn't get that if he had a criminal record. It would mess up his credentials, his work prospects, everything. Besides which, he didn't *feel* like a criminal and he didn't want to give Savage the satisfaction of having made him one. Bunkin said he might well get away with a defence of provocation. It really depended on who was on the bench on the day. Marc sensed that pleading not guilty was partly his pride talking, but it was important for a man to stand up for himself. He felt like a guy who had done his best to protect his own. If anyone was guilty it was Savage.

The Tesla drew up alongside. Rain had started sheeting down. Marc made a dash for it but still got wet. Inside the car he shook his hair and watched Bunkin discreetly brush the raindrops from his immaculate blue silk jacket. They were due in court in half an hour.

'I've got your money,' Marc said, drawing out the envelope of cash.

Bunkin acknowledged this and suggested they deal with that after the court appearance. There were a few things to go through before they lodged a plea and time was limited.

He outlined the procedure then turned to Marc and said, 'Have you thought any more about pleading not guilty?'

Marc hadn't changed his mind. He'd cop to the drink driving and to resisting arrest but so far as he was concerned Savage had provoked him into an attack. He was not guilty of ABH.

Bunkin reached over to the dashboard and turned on the demister. He repeated his earlier advice and reminded Marc that if he did choose to plead not guilty, there was a plan. The windscreen went from opaque to clear.

'I wondered if you'd managed to speak to your sister? I had an assistant try to get in contact with her but she didn't respond to a voicemail. I believe the police are still waiting for the doctors to sign her off before she's formally interviewed.'

Marc said he hadn't spoken to Helen either. He'd called

and texted but she hadn't responded. What he knew about her he'd heard from Meg.

'Your sister might say something that undermines your case.'

'I'm not exactly her favourite person right now, but she wouldn't do that to me. Look, I'm not denying what happened. I'm just saying that I was provoked into it. Self-defence.'

Bunkin blinked. 'Well okay then. You can change your mind. Remember that. For now, though, let's get to court.'

Bunkin drove a short distance and found a nearby parking spot. Together they made their way into the magistrates' building where Marc entered his pleas and the magistrate set a date for trial. It was all surprisingly simple. Fifteen minutes later he was back out on the street. Bunkin said he'd be in touch. Marc watched him walk, unflustered, back to his vehicle. A perfectly ordinary day.

Remembering what Bunkin had said in the car, Marc took out his phone, punched in Helen's mobile number and got through to voicemail. Rather than leave a message he cut the call and googled a cab company. Some things were better done face to face.

At the reception desk at Ashford Hospital he asked for the whereabouts of Helen Mair. The receptionist, a flinty-looking woman wearing the air of someone who had learned to take no prisoners, scanned her screen and squinted, raising one finger, a blood red nail, to tell Marc to wait while she dealt with the two women who had formed a queue behind. A few minutes later she beckoned Marc over and punching in a number on her phone, asked after Helen Mair. The red fingernails tippy-tapped on her console.

'Are you a relative?'

'Yeah, I'm her brother.'

'Well, then. Ms Mair was discharged earlier this morning. A lady vicar came to pick her up.'

THIRTY-ONE

Meg checked the time. Marc would be heading to court about now. Maybe she should have ignored his protests and gone to support him. Part of her was still furious. He'd known for a long time that his anger was a problem and thanks to Janette he knew why. He felt powerless and frustrated that whoever had been driving the car that hit Lily had got away with it. She wondered why she wasn't angrier. Devastated, broken, yes, but angry no. Janette would have something to say about that, no doubt. Perhaps she already had in their sessions together. Meg found it hard to remember. She was finding it hard to remember anything. Stress, Janette said, and recommended a calming walk in nature. She also said she had made a few calls and had found a security company who were able to survey the property online. Their engineers would be arriving just after lunch and could start installing locks straight away and maybe even cameras, but Meg would be back in plenty of time for that.

Meg had wandered down to the back gate, intending to head into Covert Wood and trace the footpaths, find the entry and exit points between the trees, the stiles and fences and kissing gates, map out every possible route that whoever abducted

Cecily might have taken. But some other impulse took her over and instead of going into the woods she found herself walking across the fields towards the village. She bought a gingerbread cake in the shop and asked Lisa for the address of Tim Nuttall, the retired cop who'd been in the Kent Police at the time of Cecily's disappearance.

'I'd prefer you not to say it was me who told you,' Lisa said. She held out a hand. 'Deal?'

Meg shook the hand. 'Deal.'

'I'm trusting you,' Lisa said and then reminded her, as if she needed reminding, that most people in the village preferred to remain tight-lipped about Cecily Banner's case and it might take more than a gingerbread cake to persuade anyone to open their mouths and talk.

Meg walked past the war memorial in the opposite direction from the church and ascended a steep lane lined by banks fringed with maidenhair ferns, which led up towards a wooded ridge. Here too a pair of buzzards soared above the tree canopy and as she walked a fine cold rain began again and tapped against her cheeks.

The Starlings was a small, well-kept traditional cottage. A narrow path of uneven slabs led up to the front door. It was lined with St Cecilia roses, a few bedraggled blooms still clinging. Everywhere reminders. Moments after she knocked Tim appeared.

'Can I help you?'

'We met already. At Covert Cottage?'

He squinted. 'Of course, you're Meg. I'm sorry, my eyes aren't what they were.'

Meg asked if it would be okay to come inside for a moment

and handed over her offering of cake. He nodded and from the way he waved her in, she got the impression that he knew why she'd come. They went through to the living room where a plump dachshund greeted them with a thump of the tail.

'Solomon, but I call him Sol,' Tim said, by way of introducing the dog.

He showed her to the sofa and sat in a wingback chair to one side. In the corner of the room a rifle leaned against the wall. The house was very neat but at the same time there was something unloved about it.

'Nice party, thank you for inviting me.' He'd come with Terri from the pub, he said. He'd left before anything happened but he'd heard and he was sorry.

'Not as sorry as we are,' Meg said, doing her best to make light.

'I'm imagining you've come about Cecily. They told me you'd been asking about the investigation.' He didn't specify who the 'they' were and it seemed as if the whole village knew so Meg didn't bother to ask. 'I heard about your daughter. Maybe you don't think much of us police.'

'The Met did their best,' she said.

'It can break someone, something like that,' Tim said.

'Yes.'

They let this hang in the air for a while. Eventually Tim said, 'Why don't we start by you telling me what you already know about the Banner case?'

'Not much.' Meg relayed what little she did know. 'I was hoping you might be able to tell me something about the police investigation?'

Tim shook his head. 'Not really. We were all drafted in to

253

help with the search in the woods and whatnot and I did a few house-to-house interviews but that was about it. I'd only just joined the force, so I was on traffic, stuff like that most of the time.' He shifted in the chair and she watched his eyes move to look at something out of her view. 'Anyway, the case is still open, so I wouldn't be able to tell you anything meaningful about the investigation.'

'Do you remember if the search brought anything up?'

'Some spent cartridges. Plastic. Traced back to Robert Savage if I remember rightly.'

'Relation to Steve?'

'Uncle. He'd been shooting rabbits in Covert Wood and up at the Salisbury estate, but he had a cast-iron alibi for the time Cecily went missing. Not a suspect.'

Meg's pulse quickened. Hadn't Steve told her that he'd been shooting up at the Salisburys' farm?

Whatever had distracted Tim the first time around seemed once more to call his attention. He got up, went over to a bookshelf and with his back to Meg seemed to rearrange a couple of things, then turned and came and sat back down. She noticed then a large and elaborate crucifix hanging on the wall behind the door.

'Thought I might have saved a newspaper clipping but I didn't.' His eyes went blank, as if he'd exited the room and left behind only the shell of his body.

After a moment, Meg said, 'We were talking about Steve?'

He started. 'Yes. He said he'd left Cecily and gone down to the brook to check a snare. He was questioned several times as I recall but never charged with anything.'

'He had access to his uncle's shotgun?'

Tim shrugged. 'Maybe.'

'Did the police search the Salisbury estate?'

'Not so far as I know.'

'I found a sock that I think might have belonged to Cecily. There's a photo of her, wearing an identical pair. It was under the floorboards in the attic of Covert Cottage, as if it had been hidden.'

Tim raised an eyebrow. 'Have you reported this to the police?'

'No.'

'Why not?'

She did not have a good answer for this. Anxious not to be diverted from the reason she'd come, she said, 'Was Christopher Griffin ever officially a suspect?'

Tim sighed and rubbed his head. Either he was tired of talking about the case or else her questions were making him uncomfortable. 'He would have been looked at.'

'Did the investigation get close to something that made Griffin feel under enough pressure to take his life?'

'If it did, you're not going to get that information from the cops. There'll have been an inquest but the report is closed unless you're next of kin. From what I remember, he had an alibi. His wife said she'd seen him in the garden at the time Cecily went missing. You'd be best off talking to the vicar. She might have seen the coroner's report. What you need to understand, it was 1992.'

'Sunday, the twenty-second of November.'

'You've done your homework.'

'Do you know what time she disappeared exactly?'

He rubbed his head. 'Steve left with the girl around 3 p.m.

It was a fifteen-minute walk, a bit longer maybe with a small child in tow. Steve said when he left her Covert Cottage was well in sight.'

'So somewhere between 3 p.m. and 3.30 p.m.'

'Something like that. What I heard, Steve said he went directly up to the Salisburys' place. He and his dad shot rabbits and killed moles and did other odd jobs up there. Before long he had a change of heart as it was growing dark, and he turned back to find Cecily. When he couldn't find her anywhere on the path, he assumed she'd reached her destination. The aunt rang the Griffin house about 4 p.m. and that was when the police were called. It's possible that she was already dead. By then it was dark and raining. Villagers came out with police and dogs, helicopters, the whole thing, but there were no footprints in the field, no signs of struggle or earth disturbance, nothing. She'd just disappeared. Whoever took her could have brought her to the road and put her in a vehicle. If that happened, she could be anywhere.' Tim was in full flow now. He seemed to have forgotten his earlier reticence.

Meg said, 'Christopher Griffin always said she was in Covert Wood. I wonder if that's where he found the sock?'

'Could be, or could be that he took Cecily himself. According to Griffin he was in the garden shed when the aunt called, tidying up his garden tools. His wife backed him up. That was all investigated at the time and there was never any conclusive evidence that he was involved.'

'Are you a man of faith?' Meg said, gesturing to the cross on his wall.

She watched the ligaments in his neck tighten. He seemed ill at ease suddenly, as if moving into the territory of his beliefs was a step too far. 'I need to take Sol out for his walk.' The dog, who did not seem to be expecting this, opened a single eye at the mention of his name then went back to sleep.

'I'll just get my coat and the lead and we can leave together.'

She stood and waited for him to disappear into the hallway before hurrying over to the shelf where he had been rearranging something moments earlier. A picture frame had been laid flat onto the surface of the shelf. She took hold of the edge very gently and lifted.

It was a black-and-white photograph of a little girl, not Cecily, but another, dressed in an old-fashioned vest and pants. Something creepy about it which Tim had evidently tried to conceal from her. She let the photograph fall back onto the shelf where it landed with a tiny tap and did her best to rearrange her face back into a more settled shape.

When she looked up Tim was standing in the entrance to the living room with a cap in one hand and an old leather dog lead in the other. He was looking steadily at her but there was something dark in his eyes now. 'My niece. I'd be glad if you didn't nose about in my things.' He gestured to the gingerbread which was sitting uneaten on the coffee table. 'And you can take this back. I don't much like cake.' He threw on his cap and whistled to the dog who stretched and flapping its tail forlornly, trudged towards its owner.

'Let's go,' he said.

They made their way down the garden path. At the gate he stopped. 'I've told you all I know so I'd be grateful if you didn't trouble me again. I'd like to live out my retirement in peace.'

She set off back down the lane towards the village green.

When she looked back, Tim was still standing at the gate watching her go.

On her return to Covert Cottage, Janette was nowhere to be seen. As she walked down the garden path towards the studio a text came through from Marc. All done at magistrates. Will call later. She found Janette by the back gate looking as if she had just returned from a walk.

'I thought you were going to the wood but I couldn't find you. I was getting a bit worried,' she said, sounding unusually flustered for Janette. 'It's really not safe, Meg dear.'

' I...I just got into a conversation with someone in the village that went on for a bit longer than I'd realised and...'

Janette cut in, 'You're not still obsessing about that missing girl, are you?' Meg said nothing but there was no hiding from the Oracle. With a look of exasperation on her face, Janette said, 'Really, dear, you'll do yourself no good. Now let's go back to the cottage and have a nice cup of tea while we wait for the security people. They've been marvellous. You might feel a bit better once we've got a few proper locks on the doors.'

She set off up the path and Meg followed. The more she knew about the case the less clear it became. Maybe Janette was right, this wasn't the time. They were in the kitchen, Janette making tea, Meg fixing a sandwich, when the doorbell rang.

'Helen! I thought you were still in hospital.'

Helen was wearing a fresh plaster cast on her left wrist. There was a small cut on her face, and she had on a neck brace. Beside her stood Sandy. Helen seemed distressed and blurted, 'Did you know that Marc was going to plead not guilty this morning?'

Meg nodded. 'He seems to have got the bit between his teeth.'

'I don't know what's wrong with him! Punching people and going crazy.'

At that moment she felt the air in the hallway stir and Janette appeared.

'Hello! How lovely to see you both.' She swept forward, looking very chic, and said, 'How are you, Helen?'

Helen murmured something unintelligible and then added, 'So you know, there's no way he's going to get off, right?'

Meg stood aside to allow the visitors in but to her surprise, Janette stepped into the gap and very ostentatiously checking her watch so there could be no mistaking it, she said, 'I'm terribly sorry, but Meg seems to have forgotten, we have some people coming round any minute to install a security system.'

'This isn't about Steve, surely? He really wouldn't hurt a fly.'

'It's Marc you should be worried about. What is he *thinking* pleading not guilty? Supposing he ends up with some huge fine and has to sell the cottage? More to the point, what if he ends up in prison?' At that moment, Janette reached for the front door and in that very quietly insistent way that she had perfected said, 'I'm so sorry, ladies, it's really not the time.'

Janette waited till they were gone before turning to Meg. 'Come and have some tea.'

At the kitchen table, mugs in hands, Janette said, 'You see what they're doing to you, Meg dear.'

The whole thing felt like an ambush though Meg wasn't sure who had ambushed whom. Janette was very gentle with her now, her voice almost a whisper. 'They're doing their best to set you and Marc against one another.'

'But didn't you say...' Hadn't it been Janette who'd first suggested Marc might be having mental problems? If only Meg could think straight through the mental fug that had taken over her brain.

Janette, anticipating the remainder of that question, shook her head. 'We know what Helen wants, don't we?' Janette took her hand from Meg's face and waved it in the air. 'You heard her. She's worried about losing her share of this place. Look, I know this must be very shocking for you, sweetheart, but perhaps you don't understand is that people like Helen can't help it. Oh, she hides it well, but she can't hide it from *me*. Don't you think it was unhinged of Helen to let Savage persuade her that it was okay for him to take the Spider out for a run, particularly when he was so obviously unfit to drive? She's mad, delusional. Take it from one who knows. I tell you, that woman has a death wish. You need to protect yourself, my love.' Gone was the smoothly spoken therapist with her carefully modulated tone. The insistence in her voice was something completely new. 'That's why we've done well to get this place secured. Right now, Covert Cottage remains yours. Don't let Helen take it away from you.'

THIRTY-TWO

Damn.

Marc thanked the receptionist and walked back to the hospital entrance. As soon as he was past the revolving doors, he brought up Helen's name on his phone, pressed the call icon and this time left a message. Then he walked around the block a few times and left another. Just after three Helen called. She said, 'Marc! There was a lot going on, so…'

He'd texted her at the magistrates' court but she'd ignored it. He decided to let this slide. 'So how are you?'

'Oh you know, been better. Broken wrist, some rib fractures, bruising. Sandy told me what happened. I was in the ambulance so…they must have had me on strong painkillers because I don't remember you and Steve getting into a fight. Meg said you were okay. To be honest, Sparky, I'm kind of pissed off with you. I mean, what were you thinking?'

'I don't blame you, sis.' He explained that he was staying in London with Pete. 'It's a long story, best told face to face. I could nip round to your flat and bring a takeaway?'

'I'm staying with Sandy for a few days. They've put my wrist in plaster so I can't manage on my own. I might as well tell you, Sandy and I are, you know, a bit more than good friends.'

Marc was genuinely pleased for Helen. It had been years since she'd been involved with anyone.

Helen went on, 'Look, I might not have said this in the moment because I was off it on painkillers, but I *am* sorry about the car. I know it meant a lot to you. It meant a lot to me, too.'

There was a long pause. Marc watched as a woman in a wheelchair emerged from the revolving doors attached to an oxygen tank, anxiously gripping the unlit fag that was about to take another thirty-six seconds off her life.

'Did you really plead not guilty?'

'Yes.'

'But why?'

'It's obvious, isn't it?' Marc said, puzzled by the question. 'I was provoked. That bastard stole my car and drove it blind drunk with my sister in the passenger seat and if that wasn't bad enough, he bloody totalled it. He deserved everything he got.'

Another pause. An alarm began to tick in Marc's belly.

'It was *me* driving, Sparky. And by the way, I wasn't drunk. They tested me and I passed. It was dark and the deer came out of nowhere.'

Marc felt his stomach drop as his entire argument for pleading not guilty to the assault on Savage crumbled away.

Quickly, he said, 'Maybe you're misremembering?' Even as the question came out of his mouth he saw how absurd and insulting it was.

'Why would you even ask me that? I'll admit I was a bit, you know, upset when I arrived at the cottage. Meg made it look so beautiful. Maybe somewhere in my dark heart I thought it might piss you off to take the Spider out for a spin. It was a very childish, little-sistery way to get back at you. Steve didn't need much persuading to join me. He'd worked on the Spider with Jimmy, but he'd never ridden in it. And I'd remind you that you said I could take it out any time.'

Marc's words left him. He had no idea what to say.

On the other end of the line Helen gave a short, sorry laugh. 'In a funny way I'm glad the Spider's gone, aren't you? I always thought it was a bit weird Dad holding onto it. Macabre somehow.'

'I suppose so.' Marc was still having trouble coming to terms with the news that it was Helen behind the wheel.

'Oh God, some shrink would have a field day with us, wouldn't they?' Helen said and in a more hesitant voice, 'Which brings me to something else. I went over to the cottage. Meg seems to be getting a whole new security system put in. Did you know anything about that?'

Marc listened with alarm as Helen went on to outline the afternoon's visit. He had no clue and wondered why Meg hadn't mentioned anything to him.

'Honestly, Sparky, she seemed out of it. Wouldn't even let us in. Rather, that therapy woman wouldn't. It was all quite weird. Think you should go over there.'

Marc thought so too. He reached the queue for taxis and pushed his way to the front, grabbed the first door he could and propelled himself inside. Through the window he could see a man and a woman waving their fists at him.

'You're popular,' the taxi driver said, as he pulled away from the kerb, but Marc was way past caring.

THIRTY-THREE

The security firm installed cameras front and back and fitted the back gate and front door with combination locks before leaving for the day, saying they'd be back to complete the job tomorrow. Janette dealt with them while Meg lay down on her bed and rested, getting up only to settle the eye-watering bill. Since returning from her walk she had begun to feel extremely strange. Not long after the conversation in the kitchen she began to have flashbacks, the pink cardigan in the woods, the dead deer with its lolling tongue, the doll with its tiny, perfect clothes, the sock, the photograph of the little girl.

'I feel like I'm going mad,' she said to Janette.

'That's exactly what they want you to think,' Janette said. 'But we're not going to give in to them. Go and have a little lie down. I'll deal with the security people.'

She lay on the bed, and everything went dark. The next she knew Janette was gently shaking her awake.

'How long have I been asleep?'

'The security guys have just left. The locks have all been changed and the lights work. They're going to come back tomorrow morning to finish setting up the cameras. She sat down on the bed and held out a hot cup of tea. Meg took one sip, then another. When she was finished, Janette took the cup and patting her on the hand said, 'Dear Meg, I know you love Marc and this house and you want to protect them both and the best way to do that is to protect yourself. If Marc does get a custodial sentence, you won't have anyone at your side to look after your interests except me, so I called a solicitor in Ashford and made an emergency appointment.'

'I see,' Meg said, though she didn't, not really. Odd shapes had begun to appear in her peripheral vision. She blinked and they went away momentarily, only to reappear.

'We just need to get a few documents signed. A power of attorney.' She checked her watch. 'Can you be ready in ten minutes? I'll drive.'

'Attorney?' Meg said. Her mind seemed somewhere else entirely.

'Get yourself ready and I'll explain on the way.'

Meg stepped out onto the pavement in front of an old Victorian villa housing the offices of Truelove and Swan solicitors. She felt worse than she had before the afternoon's nap. Her eyesight was swimmy and her legs were shaky and unreasonable. Surely this was something more than just pills?

'I'm not sure I feel…I mean…'

Janette grabbed an arm and steadied her. It was still raining and the cool wet breeze hitting her face made her feel a little more awake.

'A panic attack, that's all. You'll be fine in a minute,' Janette said.

Meg heard herself say 'yes' but the voice sounded as if it were underwater.

'It's all been a bit much for you,' Janette said. 'You need

a protector, an advocate, someone you can really trust who you know will be on your side.'

Janette was right. She was always right. That was exactly what Meg needed. She needed that very badly.

They took it slowly, step by step, and made it as far as the patio of the old Victorian villa housing Truelove's offices.

'I think a little drink of water will help,' Janette said, pulling a bottle from her pocket. 'Take a few sips.'

Meg did as Janette suggested. Part of her was here now and the other part was somewhere out of reach.

'Better now?' Janette said.

She nodded and the two women went inside.

A bustling woman in her fifties met them at reception, introduced herself as Gemma Truelove and waved them into a bland meeting room. She sat them down and brought up some documentation on her screen then began to talk them through the process.

They had gone over it on the drive. Meg and Marc weren't legally married. That meant Marc's official next of kin was Helen. If Marc was sent to prison, even if only for a few days or weeks, Helen might take advantage of his incapacity to contest the will. And if something happened to Meg during that time, if, say, she became ill or, God forbid, Steve or Helen did something to hurt her, then she would have no one. 'I wouldn't say any of that to the lawyer, though,' Janette said. 'We don't want her to start *busybodying*.'

Meg kept these words in mind as Truelove checked their IDs and went through the preliminaries. When that was done, she asked Janette to step out of the room for a minute and waited until she and Meg were alone before bringing up the power of attorney documents on her laptop. Truelove was speaking but her words were floating over Meg like coastal fog. Hadn't Janette warned her that this was bound to happen? Dissociative something or other. She couldn't remember now what the official term for it was. But that was okay. All she needed to do was what Janette had coached her to do. Because it had to be done. She couldn't quite remember why. Only that it was all in her best interests.

'Has anyone pressured you into this?' Truelove asked.

'No,' she said.

'And you have no medical or psychological condition which would preclude your being able to make a free and informed decision?'

'No.'

'Can you confirm that you are acting entirely from your own free will?'

'Yes.'

Her phone lit up. It was Marc.

'Do you need to get that?' Truelove asked.

'No.' The call went to voicemail.

'Right,' Truelove said finally, pushing the papers across the desk. 'If you're sure about going ahead, you'll need to sign on the signature panes beside the sticky notes.'

Meg had to think hard. She smiled and reaching for the pen that Truelove held out, signed her name.

THIRTY-FOUR

Janette plugged in the new combi code at the front door of the house and Meg went straight upstairs and crashed out in her room. Waking later she checked the time and realized she hadn't slept for long. The air felt thick and oppressive. She moved over to the window and let in some fresh air. Above the trees in Covert Wood a full moon sat huge and low in the sky. Meg moved out into the landing, calling out for Janette. When there came no answer, she went down, through the kitchen and into the mudroom where she put on her boots and outdoor parka and stepped out. The garden was bathed in an eerie light. As she made her way down the path towards the studio, she got the skin-crawling feeling that she was being watched by something living. Turning her head to look back at the cottage she saw Janette standing by the French windows, in her hand a phone. In that moment what looked to be the lights of a car arced across the side passage. She went to investigate and found a white Citroën in the drive with the engine still running. The driver switched it off and a fit-looking man in his early thirties got out.

'Hi, are you Meg?'

Her head ached and her limbs felt shaky.

The man smiled, came forward with his hand outstretched. 'Daniel Idris. I work for *Kent Online*. I've just got a couple of quick questions.'

'About what?' She hoped this wasn't anything to do with Marc.

'The girl who went missing, Cecily Banner. I'm hoping to write a piece around the thirtieth anniversary of her disappearance.'

Ah yes. A buzzing started up somewhere in her belly. Suddenly, Idris's arms were around her. She found her feet and stood upright, shaking him off.

'I thought you were about to faint,' he said.

'I haven't eaten, that's all,' she lied.

They stood for a moment eyeing one another warily. Under his jacket there was a small gold St Christopher.

At last Idris said, 'Look, I know what happened with your husband so I'm guessing this must be a really difficult time for you. I'll come clean. A source told me that you'd found a sock that might have belonged to Cecily.'

Tim. He must have called Idris soon after she'd left him. Unless…who else had she told about the sock? Right now, she couldn't remember.

Idris went on, 'I'm trying to establish whether there's a connection between the disappearance of Cecily and that of another girl, Perpetua Idris. She was my dad's little sister. She vanished on the feast day of St Perpetua, 7 March 1985. She was eight. Cecily went missing on 22 November 1992. St Cecilia's Day.'

It took a moment for this new information to land. She felt disorientated and lost. Two lost girls. And Lily at the heart of it all, propelling her on.

Idris continued, 'The police never made the connection.'

At that moment the front door opened and Janette appeared in the porch.

'Who is this?' she said, addressing herself to Idris.

Idris introduced himself.

'Oh no, no,' Janette said. She came over and took Meg's arm in hers. 'You can't be coming to our home. Meg needs to rest.'

Idris moved to protest but Janette held up a staying hand.

'Please go and don't come back.'

THIRTY-FIVE

The taxi pulled into the driveway at Covert Cottage and Marc paid the driver and got out. The driver turned and sped off, narrowly avoiding a silver Peugeot coming the other way. Marc took a step into the shadows and waited until the two cars had gone by and the road was quiet. There were no lights on in the house, but the Fiesta was in the drive. At the front door he noticed the housing for a security camera but the camera itself was missing. He pulled out his keys and went to the door only to discover that the lock had been replaced by another requiring a combination. To be unable to enter your own home! Except that it wasn't his. Covert Cottage belonged to Meg. He tried a couple of numbers, his and Meg's birthdates, and when nothing happened, he pressed the doorbell and stood back. In that moment he heard a car engine and turned to see a silver Peugeot round the bend by the driveway before it disappeared in the direction away from the village.

He pressed the doorbell again and when no one came, took out his phone and speed-dialled Meg's number. From somewhere inside there came the faint but familiar ringtone on Meg's phone. He checked the time. 6.12. Too early, surely, for Meg and Janette to have gone to bed. He wondered if they had gone for a moonlit walk? He waited for a minute or two before it occurred to him that they might be in the studio. At the back of the house the garden path stretched out past the shed and into the gloaming but beyond the old yew he could see the glint of the studio lights. Somewhere an owl hooted. Feeling more hopeful now, he made his way down the path until he reached the shed from where he could hear scratching and banging sounds. Cupping his hands to the window, he peered in. Nothing moved, no sound. Suddenly it came, something small and frantic, hitting the same spot on the window where his hands were cupped. He almost fell backwards but stilled himself. When he pulled open the door, a smell of old wood and must hit him and in a flash whatever winged creature had been trapped inside rose and flapped past. Closing the shed door behind him, he continued along the path through the vegetable garden and past the yew to the studio. Lamplight shone through the blinds. He called out, first Meg's name then Janette's. When no reply came, he let himself in. Where was everyone? He let his eye roam along the walls till it landed on a framed black-and-white photograph of Cascade, the whole band and a bunch of followers and groupies taken in the dressing room before some pub gig, long before they made it. Jammed in together. He'd seen the image before, he realized. It was among those he'd gone through with Helen not long after Jimmy died. The Green Apple pub in Maida Vale, Jimmy trying out an early version of 'Twilight' for the first time. One of those times that had gone down in the history of the band. He and Astrid had just met or maybe they were in the early weeks of their relationship, when it was all a bit on and off, before Astrid found herself pregnant. She was in the picture somewhere. He peered closer, looking to find the familiar figure perched on the arm of one of the chairs, in a tiny dress with spaghetti straps, her enormous eyes rimmed around with kohl, but in this version of the photograph, she seemed to have disappeared. Perhaps he had misremembered this after all. He allowed his eyes to drift once more, scanning the shelves before poking his head around the door of the little wet room and was surprised to see none of the usual collections of creams and brushes and pastes. Come to think of it, the studio space seemed quite empty and he was wondering if Janette moved into the cottage when his eye alighted on a black bag sitting at the side of the sofa as if it had been forgotten. He went over to pick it up and in doing so, dislodged what lay behind. He reached out for Lily's doll, the one Meg was carrying on the night of the accident, and turned it around in his hands. The little Breton T-shirt, the blue dungarees. Setting it back down he began idly to flip through the contents of the bag until he came to a yellowing piece of newsprint. He took it out, read the date before he looked at the headline and recognized it immediately. The piece was from the *Hackney Gazette*'s site, a news item about the accident. He checked the header and saw it had been accessed the same day it was up on the site. Someone had downloaded it and printed it out. Had Janette come across it somewhere in the studio? But why keep it? He folded up the paper and put it in his jacket pocket, so there would be no chance of Meg stumbling upon it and getting upset. He checked his watch. It was so unlike Meg to go out without her phone. The fact that the car was still in the driveway suggested they hadn't gone far. Making the most of the moonlight to walk to the pub for a drink maybe. To go into the village would be violating the terms of his bail to stay outside a half-mile radius of Savage's house, but he'd come too far and was too concerned to leave without knowing what was going on. He supposed he could call Sandy and Helen but they'd most likely tell him not to be such a fool and go back to London before he was spotted. On the other hand, he reckoned that if he turned up at the vicarage unannounced and asked for their help they would hardly turn him away or, God forbid, dob him in to the cops. The back route went directly past Savage's house, but it was quicker, and he was less likely to bump into anyone else than if he went by The Lane. So long as he was careful it should be okay.

He left the studio and went to the back gate. A combination lock had been fitted here, too. He wondered briefly how much all this had cost, then putting the thought to one side, used his phone torch to give him enough light and tapped in a few notable numbers. On their anniversary date the lock gave, which reassured him somehow. Who else would have set that combination but Meg herself? He took off across the field at a pace under the moonlight and soon left the house behind. He had just reached the stile and was heading on across the next field towards the village, when his eye was drawn to movement at the edge of Covert Wood and to what he thought was a momentary flicker of light.

He stopped and squinted for a better view, calling out, 'Meg? Janette?' but whoever he'd seen had disappeared behind the cover of the trees. Savage came to mind. Was he being followed? Alarm once more began to pulse through his body. He swung himself over the stile and hid behind a hawthorn for what felt like a long time, watching the treeline at the edge of Covert Wood for resumption of the movement or another flash of light. After a while, when whoever had been passing seemed to have gone by, he went on his way, reckoning that the figure must have been a hunter or maybe someone hoping to bag a badger to bait against dogs.

He crossed another three muddy fields until finally reaching the gate that opened out onto the track, glowing bone-white in the moonlight as it led past Savage's house to the vicarage and from there along one side of the church to the village green. It was quiet now, the breeze still, the stars a tremendous, spangled cape above him. He clambered over the gate and onto the track and keeping to the hedgerow where he was less likely to be seen, made his way along the path until he reached the two semi-detached cottages, in one of which Savage lived. The curtains were drawn in the house next door. No sound or light came from Savage's house. Marc slipped further down the track where it bent in sharply towards the vicarage and the church. Lights blazed through the windows of the vicarage and, from the church came the sound of the organist gearing up.

He had no wish to make any more trouble for himself but if the conversation with Helen had been alarming, the visit to Covert Cottage seemed to confirm that something was off, and he needed to know Meg was okay, so being careful not to be spotted he pushed open the front gate to the vicarage and made his way up the path towards the door. The house was hardly the picturesque English village vicarage of endless TV dramas and even in the moonlight he could see that the place looked shabby and forlorn. Maybe Sandy didn't have time for upkeep or perhaps she didn't like the place enough.

He slipped onto the porch and rang the bell twice and stepped back into the darkness. After a few minutes, when nothing happened, he repeated the procedure. At that moment he heard footsteps and the sound of the gate swinging and turned to see Sandy heading up the garden path, dressed as if about to conduct a service. She spotted him and froze. Her eyes went to his hand, which was still bruised and swollen from hitting Savage. He wondered, perhaps, if she was afraid of him. As he stepped off the porch into the shadows, she came towards him and hissed, 'Marc! What are you doing here?' and before he could say anything she beckoned him to the back of the house where it was dark and they could not be seen from the street.

He relayed the conversation he'd had with Helen and how it had set off his alarm bells, and his visit to the cottage had left him feeling very concerned indeed. Meg hadn't answered his calls which only made him more anxious. Her phone was in the cottage and it just wasn't like her to leave it behind. He knew he shouldn't be this close to where Savage might be because of his bail conditions, but he needed to know Meg was safe.

Sandy waited for him to finish and said, 'Helen's upstairs taking a nap. I could wake her but I think it better not to. I don't want her dragged into it. She's pretty upset with you.'

'I know.' Marc didn't want to think about that now.

'Steve's at the church helping us prep. Every year around this time we have a short service starting at 8 p.m. to welcome in the season of darkness. It's a village tradition.'

Marc was glad Savage wasn't roaming the countryside at night with a gun in his hand. It made him worry less.

'About Meg...all I can think is that they've gone for a walk or they're in the Palterer's.'

'I can't leave until I know where Meg is.'

It took Sandy a moment to clock what Marc was asking of her.

'I'll quickly pop my head around the pub door if you want, but if I see her, I'm not going to tell her you're here. I'm not getting myself into trouble for you, Marc.'

Marc watched her disappear into the gloom and return what seemed like a long time later slightly out of breath. The two women weren't in the pub and no one had seen them. This wasn't what he'd hoped to hear.

'They might make an appearance at the service. I certainly invited Meg and she doesn't seem to go anywhere without the therapist. We're having a mulled wine social afterwards. I can text you if they do come.' He watched her step backwards towards the light. 'I'm sorry, Marc, but you have to go now. I won't call the police, but if they ask me, I won't lie about seeing you. We've had enough trouble in Coldwater. We're not looking for any more.'

He hurried down the garden path and onto the track. There was a light on at Savage's house now and he pressed himself against the hedge on the far side of the track to make sure he couldn't be seen from the windows. Once he was out of earshot, he took out his phone and left another voicemail for Meg, this one more urgent than the last. A bank of cloud had swept across the moon and it was dark, the going over the fields heavy. There was no sign of the hunter in the woods. He moved to the edge of the field nearest to the road where the ground was firmer. He'd been walking for a while, when a set of car headlights came into view before getting lost in the trees.

Up ahead Covert Cottage loomed dark on the ridge. He

trudged on and came finally to the back gate. No lights on in the house and the studio light switched off now, so someone had been there since he'd left. He stood for a while watching the back of the house. A light went on in the kitchen and he could see the single figure of a woman pacing behind the blinds. Then a bedside light came on in the black bedroom. A moment later Meg came to the window and closed the curtains. He pulled out his phone and sent her a text.

You OK? Worried. Sandy told me Cottage has security system fitted.

He waited for a few minutes without moving.

Where are you? All good changed locks in case jimmy let steve have a key and got cameras working. Off to thanksgiving servis in church soon.

He read the text again. The errors and the lack of punctuation in the message bothered him. A small thing, maybe, but completely unlike Meg. Also, the cameras weren't working. Whoever had installed them hadn't finished the job. Why would Meg tell him they were? And then there was what Sandy had said, about Meg not being well and Janette sending them packing. Something was going on and he meant to find out what. He checked the time again. It was nearly 7.30. He decided to wait in the hope that the two women would go out and he could slip through the gate and see if he could find a way into the cottage from the back. He grasped his phone and thumb-tapped in a message.

In London. Everything fine.

THIRTY-SIX

Meg drank the coffee Janette had brought up to her and tried to focus on picking an outfit for the church service and the mulled wine social afterwards. She still felt so spaced out and groggy and would rather have just gone back to bed. The last thing she felt like doing was fielding a bunch of questions about the accident and Marc that she didn't want to have to answer. Everyone was bound to know by now. But Janette insisted, saying it was important to show a united front, and Meg was finding it so difficult to think straight that it had become easier to go along with Janette.

She padded into the bathroom and turned on the shower, hoping that a blast of cold water might sort out the wobbliness in her limbs. A few minutes later there was a knock on the door; Janette reminding her they should leave in fifteen minutes.

'I've made another coffee if you need a little pick-me-up. I'll leave it on your bedside table.'

'All right then,' Meg said, reaching for the towel. She dried herself in the bedroom, pulled on the trousers and sweater she'd left on the bed. Her head felt as if it had left the room and gone to meet the night sky. Maybe the coffee would help. She gulped it down and went to find Janette.

They got to St Joseph's just in time for the procession down the aisle. A few heads turned and one or two who had been to the party smiled awkwardly as Meg and Janette settled themselves at the back. Meg spotted Helen in one of the front rows. They had not long been seated when the door at the back of the church swung open again and Steve appeared. He passed by without acknowledgement, swaying like a sailor in a gale. Drunk, Meg thought, or maybe high.

Sandy began the welcome and not long after, the congregation stood to sing the first hymn. Meg still felt unsteady on her feet. As hymns gave way to the sermon, she struggled to keep her eyes open. All through prayers her head spun. As the collection plate went round Steve stood and stumbled up the aisle still reeking of booze and muttering to himself. All Meg could think about was getting home and returning to bed but when the service was at last drawing to a close and Sandy invited the congregation for a glass of wine in the meeting room, Janette turned to Meg and whispered that they should go.

'One drink. Let them see we're not defeated.' Janette took her by the arm and said, 'It's all going to be fine. Let me do the talking.'

Meg nodded. There was hardly any language in her head now.

In the crowded meeting room, Janette found Meg a seat and said she would be back directly with the wine. Time felt very slow and treacly, the voices reaching her as if from underwater. When she looked over, she saw Janette speaking to Steve Savage. Then a familiar face emerged from the general blur. It was Helen.

'Meg, are you all right?'

Meg frowned. One of Helen's arms seemed to be partially encased in something white and it hung at a right angle from a piece of fabric around her shoulder. Meg thought she should know the name of the whiteness and of the fabric but somehow her brain was refusing to play ball. Helen's expression changed. A hand pressed into her shoulder. 'You're trembling!'

At that moment Janette arrived from nowhere, carrying two tumblers full of something red. She handed one to Meg.

'Hello, Janette,' Helen said, steadily. 'If you don't mind, Meg and I were just about to have a private word.'

Meg was suddenly aware of Janette's eyes on her and in some dim recess of her mind she remembered that Helen wasn't to be trusted.

She shook her head.

Helen frowned and said, 'Very well. It was just that Marc's told me he couldn't get hold of you earlier. He's worried about you.'

'We were taking a nap,' Janette said. 'People do take naps.'

Ignoring this and addressing herself to Meg, Helen continued, 'Why don't you come with me to the vicarage for a bit? Sandy can give you a lift home later, or...you could stay over with us.'

Meg opened her mouth to speak but nothing came out. Janette said, 'Meg is a little upset at seeing Steve tonight. She just needs to be in her own bed. As it happens, I'm about to drive her home.'

Meg smiled, because it seemed that this was what Janette wanted.

At the cottage Janette keyed in the code and let them in.

Declining supper, Meg went into the living room and without turning on the light, sat on the sofa and stared out of the French windows. She wanted desperately to sleep but an anxious tick-tick had started up in a deep corner of her brain, like a bomb in a locked cabinet. Time seemed to slip from under her and fall away. A sound cut through the ticking. It grew louder and seemed to be coming from somewhere in the room. The phone? Hadn't she left it in the kitchen? But there it was on the coffee table, its screen lit up. There was a text from Helen and it seemed that now Marc was calling her. She reached out a shaky hand. At that moment Janette appeared carrying a cup of herbal tea. Her eyes went to the phone and there was an instant, which in Meg's mind stretched out over what seemed like an age, in which the two women seemed to form a waxwork tableau, glassy-eyed and frozen in position as if they would be stuck this way forever. Then Janette bustled forward and placing the cup on the coffee table, scooped up the device and dropped it in her pocket.

'Marc,' Meg said. Her voice sounded like some far-off alarm. She saw Janette hesitate for a moment as if she were trying to get her head around something too big and too momentous for a single person to fathom. Then tucking in her skirt neatly behind her, Janette sat down in the armchair opposite.

'I'll answer it in a moment,' Janette said. 'I know the code. I've watched you tap in it. But I'd guess it anyway. It's Lily's birthday, isn't it?'

It was.

'You know,' Janette continued, 'you can't trust that vicar and your sister-in-law. They're up to something.'

Meg could hear the words but didn't seem to be able to get her head to make sense of anything.

Janette went on, 'They may have been trying to lure you into making Marc break his bail conditions. But you know that if you did that, he'd go to jail. Which is what they want, to isolate you, and make you doubt everyone you love.'

'I'd like...if he's trying to call.'

'We must do what's best for Marc. If we love him. And we do, Meg, so much.'

'Yes,' Meg said, though she wasn't sure if this made any sense.

'Marc's not being rational at the moment. We know that.'

She did know that.

'Here,' Janette said, 'I brought you some camomile tea, to help you sleep.'

Meg looked at the cup but was not minded to drink. Summoning her fragile mental capacities, she said, 'I'd like my phone back.'

Janette pulled the device from her pocket. Meg held out an unsteady hand, but Janette continued to clasp it in her palm.

'For your safety I think it's best that I keep it for a while. You'll understand when I tell you.' Her voice was freighted with sadness as if what she was about to say something she could no longer hold back. She sat beside Meg with one hand resting on Meg's shoulder. 'God knows I haven't wanted to say this to you, but it seems that it has become necessary.'

'About Marc?' Meg said. Somehow through the murk an alarm pulsed.

'I'm afraid so.' Meg felt herself brace almost instinctively, and had the sensation, suddenly, of falling through the air. The walls around her began their familiar, sinister thrumming, and somewhere far above them she felt a crackle of static, as though lightning had found its way into the attic. 'It's time you knew what Marc was *really* up to on the day Lily died.'

THIRTY-SEVEN

After an hour and a half of trying and failing to find a way into the cottage, Marc gave up on his plan and made his way on foot back to the station. Just beyond the place where the accident happened, a car came up behind him, slowed, and as it swept by, he saw that it was a silver Peugeot like the one he'd seen earlier in the evening. Maybe the same car. The next train to London was at 9.49 via Ashford. While waiting he called Meg, but she didn't pick up. At Ashford, he called again but left no message. He passed the journey staring at his phone screen just in case she called. He guessed she was still angry and didn't want to speak to him directly.

At St Pancras he took the tube to St John's Wood and bought a half bottle of Bell's at the corner shop. A text from Helen pinged on his phone. She'd seen Meg and Janette at the church. Meg had seemed very out of it. Janette had insisted on taking her home to bed. He was tempted to call again but decided against it. In the morning he'd call Helen and ask her to find an excuse to get Meg on her own. The sisters-in-law had always been good friends. Meg might be more frank with Helen if Janette weren't there.

He made it to Pete's place in St John's Wood not far off

midnight. As he came through the gate he set the security light off but to his relief no one came to the window. He found his way down to his digs in the basement. He was tired and confused and if anything more anxious about Meg than before. He sat down on the pull-out and deciding that a night cap might calm his nerves, pulled the Bell's from his jacket pocket. Clinging to it was the printout he'd taken from Janette's bag. He took a swig of whisky and unfolded the paper. He felt fully awake, the fatigue crowded out by a sick feeling. The fractured memories of the day of Lily's death began to come back to him. He remembered clearly sitting down for lunch at the pizza place with members of the orchestra, maybe drinking a bit too much, a bit of flirty banter with Daisy. The next memory was of Daisy shaking him and screaming about an accident and getting to the hospital. The only person he'd ever confided in about having sex with Daisy was Janette. Thinking back, he wondered if he *had* told Janette that he and Daisy had slept together that afternoon, or was that an assumption after the fact, a case of two plus two equals five.

Pulling out his phone, he brought up the number of a trumpet player from his Phoenix days and tapped out a message.

Hey. Sorry it's so late. Wondering if you had Daisy Godwin's number?

Hi mate, you OK? Pint sometime?

A moment later another text came through with Daisy's contacts. He texted his thanks but didn't say anything about the pint.

His palms were clammy and a sweat was building on his brow. He took a long swig of whisky.

Even though it was late, there was a need in him to dig down

286

through the bullshit and get to the truth of what happened on the day of his daughter's death. His own culpability. To name what had remained unnameable. He steadied himself and dialled the number. The call connected and went through to voicemail.

'Hey. It's Marc Mair. I need to talk to you about something. It's urgent.'

After what seemed like an age his screen lit up and he felt his pulse quicken.

'Hey, Marc. It's awfully late. Is something wrong?'

'Daisy, thanks for getting back so quickly. I'm sorry to ask you this, but I'm trying to recall exactly what happened the day my daughter died.'

'Oh,' Daisy said, sounding pained. 'Won't it wait?'

'No.'

A long silence. 'No, I see. You know, I've always regretted not talking to you after that day. I should have called. I was struggling to know what to say, but that's no excuse.'

'You're talking to me now. And I'm grateful. Because the thing is, there are huge holes in my memory and I think you might be able to help me understand.'

'Well, okay.' She sounded a little puzzled but willing to help.

'What I do recall is that we'd just been told the run had been extended at the Phoenix and Rable took us out to that pizza place to celebrate and I... I...'

There was a pause. Marc took himself back to his solo session with Janette, where she willed him on at this point, filling in the blanks in his memory.

'Yeah, you started to look really ill.'

'I was ill?' He remembered nothing about being ill.

'Yeah, remember?' Daisy went on. 'It was really scary. You had one hand around your throat and you were pointing to your pizza.'

'I was?'

'And your face was getting really red and swelling up and you pointed to your bag and I knew what was going on because I have a niece who is allergic to peanuts, so I got your EpiPen out of the bag and I gave you the shot. Someone had called a cab and I just remember helping you into it and telling the driver to take us to hospital and you shaking your head like no, that was the last place you wanted to go, but you were recovering by then, or at least it seemed like your breathing was getting better. You pointed at your watch but you couldn't say anything. I had no idea what to do, so I asked the cab driver to take us to my flat. Do you remember, I was living quite nearby then? So it wasn't far. And it seemed like the EpiPen injection was really working. I helped you out of the cab and into the flat and you just sort of collapsed onto the bed. And then, maybe it was like an hour later, I noticed your phone was going crazy and so I woke you up. I hope I didn't do the wrong thing?'

'Did we…?'

There was a pause. 'You mean…?'

'Yes. Did we do anything in your bed?'

A sharp intake of breath. 'No, Marc, of *course* not. Where on *earth* did you get that idea?'

Marc swallowed hard.

THIRTY-EIGHT

Pills were not enough to get Meg to sleep that night. She tossed and turned but could find no relief. Her emotional turbulence seemed to have been taken up into the savage wind, the wild creaking of the trees, the sorrowful groans from the attic. Around midnight, struck by the sense that something or someone was trying to get through to her, she rose and went over to the window. The world outside felt like a madhouse populated by nature's dark and frantic manifestations. Leaves rushed about in circles in the moonlight and twigs skittered across the lawn. The St Cecilia rose had come loose from its ties and was rapping furiously against the French windows. She slipped on her robe and went out onto the landing. As softly as she could, so as not to disturb Janette, she pulled down the attic steps and climbed up into the space. In Lily's trunk the pink sock sat where she had put it beside the little cardigan, but in all the tumult of the last hours she had forgotten to fetch the doll from where Janette had left it in the studio and put it back in its rightful place. She stood there for a while with her hand on the trunk, hoping that wherever Lily was, she did not know what Meg now knew, that on her last day in the world, her father had forgotten to pick her up from school because he was having sex with another woman.

After a while Meg went back down to the landing and on an impulse went over to the door to Marc's study and cracked it open, hoping to be reassured by the sight of Janette, asleep on the sofa bed. The curtains were only partially drawn and the sash window had been pulled down a little and to Meg's surprise, she saw that the bed was empty. Perhaps Janette too had struggled to sleep. Meg went downstairs calling softly for her friend but she was nowhere to be found. Was it possible that she had gone to the studio? Perhaps she, too, had felt the need to fetch the doll back?

Pulling on her boots and coat she went out into the garden. The wind was tremendous but had brought with it no rain and in the moonlight the trees and plants danced a frenzied jig. She went down the path towards the studio and let herself in. A creeping panic rose. Where was Janette?

She went down the path and saw that the locked gate was open which suggested that someone who knew the combination had recently been through. Yanking it wider, she went out into the field. Ahead of her Covert Wood blustered and whooped and she felt exposed and afraid. A moment later she saw something moving between the trees. Yes, for sure, a figure was heading towards the place where the path met the stile. Her pulse quickened, her heart clattering like some broken thing taken up by the wind. She wanted to run but her feet felt rooted. She thought about the girls, about Lily and Cecily and Perpetua, their deaths gone unavenged. She looked about and seeing a large flint glowing wanly in the moonlight, bent down to pick it up. The wind was heading straight for her now and she had to steady herself not to be knocked over by it. She braced herself and waited as the figure heaved itself over the stile and begin to make its way along the path through the field towards her.

A voice came through the wind, through the moonlight. No words discernible but the voice she knew. Janette. The flint clattered to the ground. The figure began to pace, blown by the wind towards her, Janette's face emerging from the darkness, eyes wild, the cheeks splattered with what looked like mud.

Janette's chest was heaving, her breath catching, her body at once solid and helpless. 'Meg? What...are...you...doing...here?'

THIRTY-NINE

They made their way back to the cottage without speaking. The cold air had energised Meg. Once inside, she helped Janette take off her coat then took off her own. They both removed their boots. Janette's were muddy and soaking wet and her trousers had dark patches over the knees as if she had been wading in water.

'Get...me...a...towel.'

Meg went upstairs to the bathroom, turned on the bath taps, grabbed her largest towel then came downstairs to find Janette sitting at the table shivering, her breath ragged. She wrapped herself in the towel and asked for a glass of whisky. Meg had never seen Janette so vulnerable and it sent a wave of panic through her.

'I'm running you a bath to warm you up. What were you doing in the wood?'

Janette was too breathless and shaken to answer. She took some whisky to calm herself and said, 'Didn't you hear the gate bang? I thought that Steve had got in so I hurried out into the garden. When I got to the gate I saw it was unlocked so whoever had unlocked it had to be someone who had guessed the combination. That couldn't have been Steve so it had to have been Marc. Then I remembered that Helen had said he'd been at the cottage. I thought he might have come for Savage so I went down into the wood to look for them. If there was going to be some kind of confrontation, I thought that I might be the best person to put a stop to it. Oh Meg, I went everywhere. Up and down. As deeply into the wood as I could before the moonlight gave out and I just couldn't see. I was calling for them, but you know what the wind's like, I have no idea if anyone could hear me. Eventually I came to my senses and turned back.'

Had Marc done something stupid? Six months ago she would have thought that impossible but she'd seen how powerless he'd seemed in the face of his own rage. One hand went to her mouth to stop herself from crying out. The kettle clicked off but she ignored it.

They sat in silence for a moment. Remembering the bath, Meg urged Janette upstairs. While Janette was in the bathroom Meg searched around for her phone and found it in the last place she'd expected, on the shelf in the basement. She had no memory of leaving it there but everything that had happened in the last few hours was so scrambled in her mind now that anything was possible. She rang Marc and when he didn't pick up, she sent a text. She thought about telling him that she knew he'd betrayed them and that she was inconsolable about it, that she would try to find a way to forgive him, but she refrained. Hadn't Janette said that this was precisely what might tip him over the edge? Instead she wrote:

Why were you in back garden tonight? What is going on?

Then another.

Please don't do anything stupid.

It was well past midnight. Either Marc was fast asleep, or her plea had come too late.

Not long afterwards Janette reappeared, skin still flushed from the hot bath. Meg saw her eyes flick to the phone on the table and away. She came over and taking Meg's hand, gave it a squeeze.

'Let me make tea. We could both do with some.'

She went over to the counter and fussed about making the drinks, then returning to the table placed a cup in front of Meg.

'Has Marc been in touch?'

Meg shook her head miserably.

'All we can do now, then, is to try to get some sleep. Tomorrow is another day.'

FORTY

The first thing she saw when she cracked open her eyes was Janette's face. She blinked. A soft blue dawn filtered into the room but she did not feel ready to wake yet. She closed her eyes and turned over in bed, realising then that she had been in the middle of a dream. The dear little cat from her childhood, Magic, was sitting with her in front of a warm fire. She felt herself reaching back until someone began to shake the sleep from her.

'Meg, you have to get up. The police are here. They need to talk to you about Marc.'

Her eyelids opened. The room swam. She tried to gather herself to say something but nothing came. Janette was lifting her into an upright position. The light was on in the hallway and there was the silhouette of a figure standing outside.

She heard Janette say, 'She takes sleeping pills among other things.'

'Is Marc all right?'

A vague memory flitted across her mind of Janette handing her a cup of tea to calm her nerves. Hadn't something terrible been said? After that everything was patchy, bits and pieces.

'He's okay. We need to get you up.' The cold air hit her as

Janette peeled off the duvet. She looked down and saw that she had on her pyjamas but could not recall putting herself to bed at all.

'What time is it?'

'Early.' Janette's hands under her arms, part lifting, part dragging.

'Where's Marc?' Janette was swinging Meg's legs off the bed.

'I want you to put your feet on the ground and try to stand.' Meg did as she was told, wondering why Janette was talking to her as if she were an invalid. In the doorway, she saw now, was a uniformed policewoman.

Janette wrapped a robe around her and took her hand. 'The police need to ask us some questions. It'll be fine. Let's go downstairs and get you some tea.' Meg blinked as the light in the hallway reached her eyes. The PC stood on one side of her, but it was Janette who had hold of her, Janette who escorted her down the stairs.

Two women, both in plain clothes, were sitting at the old pine table.

One of them introduced herself as DC Gillian Reynolds and her partner as another detective constable.

DC Reynolds said, 'We're going to need to conduct a search of the house.'

'Where's Marc?' Meg said, heart ticking but her mind still sluggish from sleep, adrift almost. She suddenly remembered what Janette had told her earlier in the evening, about Marc's affair with Daisy Godwin, her attempt to find him in Covert Wood the night before. For a moment she felt as if she might be sick.

'Mrs Mair, I explained to your...' She searched for the word and finding it uncomfortable, said, '...to Mrs...'

'Just Janette.'

'...to Janette, your husband is safe but we're going to need you to stay here.'

'They're not married,' Janette said. She glanced at DC Reynolds. Had they spoken about her while she was still sleeping? Why was she the only one who didn't know what was going on? 'I think this might all be a bit much for Meg at the moment.'

DC Reynolds repeated what she'd said, over-enunciating the words, and asking Meg if she'd understood them.

Meg nodded. It was as if she were in some dark surreal dream where her body and mind had separated from one another. Janette sat beside her calmly, every so often taking her hand and squeezing. 'Meg, dear, I know this might all seem too much.'

'Too...' She was unable to finish the sentence.

'They know about the visions you've been having and the voices you've been hearing in your head. We're just waiting for the crisis team so they can make you safe.'

Some time later a man and a woman arrived. Meg wasn't quite sure who they were. Soft-spoken but all business. They asked a lot of questions about Marc and Steve and everything that had happened since the Spider accident. Meg knew the answers to these questions but she felt so confused by the whirling in her head that she found it hard to speak. Janette seemed to do most of the talking. DC Reynolds reappeared. A whispered conversation ensued between Janette and the police. DC Reynolds broke away and came to the table. 'Meg, do you understand why we've been asking you questions and why your house is being searched?'

'Not completely.' She felt she had missed some things, that her mind had skipped over those questions, that there was a blank that needed filling in.

'Okay,' DC Reynolds went on. 'Steven Savage was found dead this morning by someone walking their dog in Covert Wood. We're investigating the death as a possible murder. We've taken your...partner, Marc, in for questioning. And that's all we can really tell you right now.'

The man and the woman stepped forward. The rest was a blurry nightmare.

FORTY-ONE

At 5.50 that morning Marc had been arrested at Pete's house and driven across London to King's Cross police station. There he was processed and charged with breaching his bail conditions.

They took him back to the airless cell. He sat on the thin, squeaky mattress which smelled horribly of disinfectant and tried to make sense of it all. There was so much in his head right now. For one, how the cops knew he'd travelled to Coldwater. Pete couldn't have told him because he had no idea where Marc had been heading. Had Sandy or Helen said something? Or the taxi driver? Unlikely. His chief worry remained Meg. Helen had texted him. She'd seen Meg and Janette at the church and noted that Meg was out of it and seemed to be going along with whatever Janette said. He wondered if she'd taken a bunch of pills? Might explain the odd punctuation in the text message she'd sent him. But why now? Had Janette told her that he'd cheated? Was that why she was avoiding him?

He put his head in his hands and wished it would all just go away. Since speaking with Daisy he'd been turning over that session with Janette. His former therapist was the Oracle. He had encouraged his feelings for her, made himself believe that of all the people in the world, only she really understood and accepted him. Why would she have used his confusion to make him think something that wasn't true, something damaging and potentially explosive, unless she wanted to control him. He let out a bitter laugh. To think he'd not so long ago imagined that he loved her. He'd never loved her. He'd *depended* on her. All the while he was wondering how he'd manage life without her, she was backing him into a corner as if he were some kid who'd done something shameful. She'd manipulated him. But why? He couldn't make sense of it.

He was still turning this over in his mind when the cell door opened, and a uniform brought in a dismal breakfast tray and a cup of weak tea and informed him that he was about to be transferred to Ashford police station. When he asked why, the officer said he'd find out soon enough. Another puzzle. The cell door slammed closed. Marc drank the tea but could not eat. After another long wait he was bundled into a sweatbox. The van lurched over a speed bump, then another, followed by a sharp turn which flung him sideways into the metal wall. A stabbing pain rose in his chest. There was a screech of brakes, Marc braced himself, but it was too late. His body pitched forward until his forehead made contact with the metal. His head began to pound. There were voices coming from outside but he couldn't catch what they were saying.

Finally the door opened and two uniformed officers appeared, behind them a car park lined with patrol cars which looked remarkably like the police station he thought he'd just left. A blank-faced operative clambered into the van and instructed Marc to place his hands through the cuff slots.

On the tarmac two uniformed policemen waited. A man in

plain clothes approached, squinting in the early morning sun. One of the policemen advanced a little.

Marc felt a little panicked now, the fear swelling in his throat, cutting off his breath.

'Stay calm, mate, all right?' the policeman who was closest said.

Stay *calm*?

The officer who was closest was watching the arrival of the plainclothes copper, a pudgy dude in his early fifties, about the right age to have been a teen fan of Cascade. 'Marc Mair?'

Marc confirmed his name and the Covert Cottage address.

None of what happened next felt real. It was like someone had put his brain into a blender. He had to quell the urge to laugh because it seemed so completely absurd. He, Marc, was being questioned under caution for the murder of Steven Savage. A voice in his head screamed, *What the hell is happening?*

Obviously there had been a mistake. Some terrible misunderstanding. The sort of thing you came across in documentary strands from streaming services. *Banged Up and Innocent! Doing the Time When There's No Crime!* A whole subgenre. If that wasn't darkly comical then what was? Standing at the custody desk, he felt himself oscillating wildly between terror and bewilderment, as if he were at the movies, watching a horror movie with an unfathomable plot. *They're coming to get you.* What? Ugh! Nooo. Rinse and repeat.

Can I call my lawyer?

The custody sergeant made the call. Bunkin seemed as surprised as Marc and said he would call Meg and let her know then be on his way. He'd be with Marc as soon as he could.

The custody sergeant: 'I'll put you in the same cell you were in before.'

Thanks for nothing.

The blank walls, dank smelling toilet, the mattress reeking and a thousand terrors. The long wait for Bunkin. He didn't want to think about the cost. All the money he already owed McInsey. Bunkin would make them see that this was a case of mistaken identity. Bunkin would find a way of getting him off the hook. Because, bottom line, he hadn't done anything. He was an innocent man.

And so he waited, thoughts churning, for what seemed like days, chewing on his fingernails to keep himself busy. Eventually two uniformed officers came and led him to a windowless, cucumber-green box that passed for a meeting room. Bunkin was already in place, head deep in some papers. He looked up briefly and nodded a greeting. Doing his best to ignore the pain in his forehead, Marc pulled up the only other chair and gathered himself.

He waited until he and Bunkin were alone. 'Does Meg know?'

'Let's focus on you for now,' Bunkin said ominously.

Marc put his head in his hands. 'I honestly have no idea what this is all about.' A voice in his head said, *It's about the murder of Steven Savage.*

Bunkin looked at Marc from over his reading glasses as if he, Bunkin, were a kindly boss and Marc his eager intern. Irritating. This wasn't a bloody day at the office. This was his life. The body of Steven Savage had been found lying in Covert Brook at dawn by a man out hunting rabbits with his dog. It was the dog who had alerted the hunter to the body. The exact cause of death had not yet been established but there was a large wound to the skull. The police were working on the likelihood that Savage died either of blunt force trauma or drowning.

'I didn't have anything to do with that.' He made direct eye contact, trying to impress on the lawyer the craziness of the accusation.

'They haven't charged you yet and they may not.'

'So I'll get bail?' He explained that he was worried about Meg and needed to see her urgently. 'There's something happening at the cottage.' Marc tried to convey the depth of his worry and the reason for it.

Bunkin raised an eyebrow. 'What have they told you?'

Marc felt the breath leave him. 'Tell me Meg's okay.'

Bunkin blinked and continued, 'She's safe. But she's been taken to a psychiatric unit for evaluation. It seems that she may have had some sort of breakdown.'

Marc lurched backwards, nearly falling off his chair as he repeated the word 'breakdown'. What was Bunkin talking about? He knew Meg. She wasn't...his mind moved back to the weeks after Lily's death. She'd been mentally unwell then for sure, but wouldn't anyone have struggled in the circumstances?

'How did this happen? And when?'

'According to the police, this morning.'

'Why didn't they tell me?'

Bunkin sucked his teeth and shook his head. 'I can't answer that but Meg's safe and there's nothing we can do about it now so I suggest we focus on what we can do.' On Marc's nod he said, 'The police have twenty-four hours to charge you unless they apply for an extension. But they're not going to release you while they're continuing their investigations. There's the magnitude of the offence for one thing. And they're entitled to hold you for breaching bail on the assault charge, which, frankly, was…' Bunkin searched for some moderate-sounding phrase, '…ill-advised.'

'We'll have to wait for the interview before we know what they've got on you. The forensics won't be completed yet but the speed at which you were arrested suggests there are images of you on CCTV and maybe even witnesses.'

He thought about the cameras at the cottage. Presumably they'd searched the place. This was a comfort somehow because it suggested that Sandy hadn't dobbed him in. 'I'm not denying I was in Coldwater but I don't know anything about any murder. I did see someone down by the wood, though, who looked, I don't know, suspicious.'

'Would you be able to identify this person?' Bunkin said, interested.

Marc closed his eyes and did his best to take himself back to the scene. Savage was a big guy and on second thoughts the figure didn't seem to have been tall enough. The way they moved. The thought occurred to him that the figure could have been a woman. Too tall to be Meg. And whoever it was had been carrying something, hadn't they? It was all a little fuzzy. He shook his head.

Bunkin was drumming two fingers ever so slightly on the table. 'It's not going to help you to try to deflect this onto someone else, Marc, unless you have evidence. I'm not sure you realize the trouble you're in. You have motive and a track record of assaulting the victim.'

Marc felt himself shrink. 'I didn't do this,' he said feebly.

Bunkin made a note which Marc very much hoped reflected his innocence, then gave a small cough. 'For now, I strongly suggest you give a no comment interview. And for heaven's sake, don't throw out any accusations about anyone else. They'll eat you alive.' He'd seen all this a hundred times. Or maybe he hadn't. Marc suddenly felt that maybe Bunkin wasn't the right lawyer. It occurred to him that he might have to spend the rest of his life in prison because he'd backed the wrong horse.

Bunkin rose from his chair. 'Remember, whatever they ask, you say...' Marc knew what was coming. He'd seen it, or a version of it, in the TV shows. And that's how it felt in a way. He was in a prank show and any moment now an invisible director would shout, 'Cut.'

He took a breath. 'No comment.'

'Good man,' Bunkin said, clearing his throat and staring at his hands. 'And Marc, I...' He took a breath. 'There's something else...perhaps you already know? I asked my associate to do a little digging around so I could report back to you. Obviously they wouldn't let my associate speak to her but she did find out something slightly peculiar. The day before Meg's breakdown, she signed an LPA.'

Marc leaned in. An LPA? What was that? Bunkin, picking up on his confusion, explained, 'Lasting power of attorney. It gives the appointed person the right to act on the signatory's behalf in financial and medical matters.'

Marc sat back puzzled. He thought about Helen and the cottage. Could she have made some moves to claim her portion of the place? That didn't sound like Helen.

He said, 'I suppose, maybe, because I'm in this legal mess. We're not officially married.'

'So you didn't know anything about it?'

'No, but…'

'I see, well…' This time Bunkin visibly gathered himself, as if what he was about to say came uneasily to him. 'The thing is, Meg appointed a woman called Janette Hopwood as her attorney.' He paused. 'I assume you know her?'

Marc swallowed hard. For a moment he found it impossible to muster any words. What was Meg thinking to do such a thing? As for Janette, he was acquainted with her, sure, but as to whether he *knew* her? He was beginning to think that he didn't. Not at all.

FORTY-TWO

Meg was sitting in an annexe room in the Oak Unit at Walton Hospital waiting for a visitor. The clock on the wall ticked. 10.27. Beside it hung a bland print of a country scene which recalled, in a very general way, the woods and fields around Covert Cottage. On the table beside her sat a mug of herbal tea. She drew it to her, smelled the contents, then pushed it away. How had she come to be here of all places? Somewhere through the mist in her head she could remember returning from the evening church service, feeling groggy and going to bed. She'd drunk a cup of something hot that Janette had given her. All she could remember after that was that she was in the kitchen and there were police. She'd had a terrible shock, she remembered that, though when she searched her mind she couldn't find it. This morning was an almost complete blank. She remembered being asked about the drugs she had taken and feeling confused. Something about hearing sounds that weren't there, seeing things that did not exist. They'd given her something at the cottage to steady her nerves but whatever it was had left her feeling jittery and disorientated. Was that what got her here? There was something about Marc, too, but her mind wouldn't give up any details. The cops were searching for something. She remembered now. Something to do with Cecily? The brain fog was so frustrating.

She checked the clock again, shifted and stretched, wishing for coffee. She'd asked and been told that caffeinated drinks were not allowed. No matter, any minute now Janette would come and tell the doctors there was nothing wrong with her. They'd listen to Janette. At 10.30 precisely, there was a knock on the door and a moment later Janette entered, smiling. She came over to the table and taking a seat, in her beautiful smooth voice, she said, 'Meg, how are you doing?'

'You have no idea how glad I am to see you.'

'Perhaps I do,' Janette said.

Meg heard herself let out a brief tinny laugh that didn't sound at all like her. 'Well of course, you know everything.'

'If only that were true.'

It was an odd exchange, the meaning of which Meg couldn't, in her brain-fogged state, quite grasp. In the back of her mind came some faint stirring of alarm, some small remembrance of the events of the night or the early morning perhaps, but whatever it was left as quickly as it had come.

One of the nurses, in pink scrubs, walked along the corridor, appeared then disappeared then reappeared again as she passed along the series of windows doing her best not to peer in. Everything and everyone was under some kind of constant scrutiny. The only privacy to be found was in the tiny shower room attached to her bedroom. The door lock worked only from the outside.

'You've slept and eaten?' Janette said.

On her arrival at the unit Meg had fallen into a drugged slumber, only to be woken by Paula, the nurse in pink scrubs, carrying a breakfast tray a couple of hours later. She was told to dress quickly because Mr Trethorn would be visiting her on his ward round and he didn't like to wait. She could take up any questions with him. After Paula had left Meg got up and took a shower. Some of her clothes were hanging in the cupboard though she had no recollection of putting them there. She pulled on a pair of joggers and a sweater, ate half a stale breakfast roll and sat on the bed in a state of puzzlement to await the arrival of the doctor. An hour or so later he appeared, dressed in chinos and a button-down shirt, and in a kind but distracted manner bombarded her with so many questions she was left feeling dazed. He appeared to think that the voices she was hearing were the result of psychosis. He wasn't sure enough to make a diagnosis yet but it was best for Meg that she remain in the unit.

'For how long?' Meg asked.

'It's hard to say.'

It seemed pointless to try to explain that the dead did speak, that their voices arose from inside her like an autumn mist coming up from the ground, hazy but no less tangible. Besides which, she had other, more pressing things on her mind. She asked to see Marc. He'd cheated on her but right now that seemed of less importance than her need to touch him, to speak to him.

Trethorn consulted his notes and awkwardly cleared his throat. 'What exactly do you remember about, um, recent events?'

It was only then that it came back to her that Steve Savage had been found dead in Covert Wood. The police had searched the cottage, had wanted to ask her questions about Marc and she'd told them that he was in London. She remembered asking what they were looking for and the police saying they were unable to provide any details there and then. There had been a man and a woman, nurses perhaps, medics of some kind, who had driven her here to the unit.

Trethorn listened patiently and then pronounced his opinion. It would be best, he said, if Meg stayed at the unit for a few days. During that period, she would be allowed approved visitors if she wished, but she would not be allowed to leave. The approved visitors did not include Marc. The team thought it best for her mental health that she remain calm and avoid any potentially stressful encounters.

In an annexe room Meg relayed this conversation to Janette. 'Obviously, I had a bit of a shock, but there's nothing actually *wrong* with me. You'll talk some sense into them, won't you, Janette? They'll listen to a psychotherapist.'

Janette regarded her with a beady eye. 'Oh Meg, you really have no idea, have you?'

Meg felt words bulging in her throat. The table, four chairs, the clock ticking. At one end, by the windows, orderlies walked up and down and a camera blinked. A woman who'd been babbling in a made-up language passed by. If only any of this made more sense.

'Marc breached his bail conditions. He was spotted in Coldwater around the same time Steve disappeared. They've arrested him in connection with Steve's death.'

Meg suddenly felt as if she were dreaming. Somewhere buried she suspected she already knew this, but couldn't recall any of the details.

'I'm afraid you've been in denial, Meg. I told Mr Trethorn,

I said, she's been building up to this.' Janette sighed theatrically and a sickly smile appeared that Meg had never seen before. 'It's all been too much for you, hasn't it? That fantasy about the trunk, the noises in the attic, the imaginary pink cardigan in the woods, the doll. All that talk about a missing girl. I understand how real all that felt to you, but it wasn't *actually* real. Can you understand that? You've been living in an unreal world. And now you're here, which *is* real and the best place for you.' Janette's face seemed to go in and out of focus. They had given her something with breakfast, she remembered now, made her open her mouth to show that she had swallowed it.

'It's the drugs.'

'The drugs are there to help you.'

What Janette was saying was all wrong. Everything about the last few months, the doll, the cardigan, the sock, the noises in the attic and Cecily... That had all happened, not just in her head, but in the real world. 'I want to speak to Marc.' Meg stood up, a crawling, itching pulse moving through her like a beetle.

'Sit down!' Janette's face was craggy, almost hostile.

For a moment the churn in Meg's head stopped. She held her breath. In her chest the robin, its breast ablaze, fluttered. She could feel its fire inside her and felt stronger and less alone.

'Please, take a seat,' Janette said, smiling now.

Meg, continuing to stand, said, 'I demand to speak to Marc.'

She watched Janette's smile fade out and her eyes turn cold and brittle.

'You don't get to demand *anything*.' Meg looked at the face of the woman she had trusted and was shocked to see no softness there, no pity, no regard. 'You gave me power of attorney, Meg. So now *I* make all the decisions.'

Everything in Meg told her to run but they were in a locked unit and there was nowhere to go. Besides which, it was true. She had given up her freedom. Her head swirled. How could she have been so stupid? At the time, it had seemed like a sensible course of action. Given that...perhaps she was a bit nuts after all? And yet, was it really so mad, so reckless, to trust your therapist? Wasn't that what therapists were for?

'Don't look so shocked,' Janette said, pushing the mug towards her. 'Have some tea. You'll feel better.'

Tea. How often had she heard those words over the past few weeks? Janette pressing it upon her. Meg eyed the mug. She could feel herself beneath the drugs now. It was as if the bird inside her had flown about, popping the clouds with its sharp little beak, leaving her gazing into a clear sky. She shook her head.

Janette leaned in, her eyes fixed on Meg, her face close enough that Meg could feel the breath on her cheek.

'Don't be like that. Not now, not when everything is finally slotting into place.'

Meg kept looking upwards to the clear sky in her mind. That sour breath, hissing now. 'Don't forget, Meg, they'll listen to me. They already have. I *am* a mental health professional after all.'

Meg shook her head in disbelief. It suddenly seemed so obvious. Janette had engineered this. She had encouraged Marc to hand over the cottage to her, and then pushed Meg into signing over her independence, her freedom. Janette had persuaded her to stop trusting Marc and even Helen. Janette had waited patiently until the moment had come to pounce.

'Is this about the cottage?'

Janette gave a bleak, momentary laugh but said nothing and in this moment Meg understood she was helpless. Nobody would believe her. Not now.

She stood up and spinning on her heels, made a beeline for the door. As she reached for the handle, it opened and Paula appeared and looking over Meg's shoulder she said, 'You called?'

'Yes, I'm afraid Meg is rather distressed,' Janette said. Her hand was on a panic button.

In a last bid Meg pointed at Janette and said, 'That woman tricked me. She is trying to control me.'

Janette smiled and her tiny shake of the head was taken up by Paula.

'Maybe you've had enough for today,' Paula said to Meg.

Janette's hand came out and attached itself to Meg's elbow. Meg looked at it, the fingers clutching so tight that they left little white pressure points on her skin.

A smile appeared on Paula's face. Its mildness infuriated her. Janette, her enemy as she could now see, was physically restraining her, assaulting her almost, and both Paula and Janette were pretending that it was a kindness. 'Why don't we have a nap?' Paula said.

'I want to leave,' Meg said, shaking Janette's hand off her.

Taking a step back so it seemed as if the separation were her idea, Janette said, 'Speaking as Meg's therapist as well as her attorney, I think it might be an idea for Mr Trethorn to increase the sedation?'

Meg shook her head and in a voice in which there was a hint of panic, said, 'No, no, that won't be necessary. I was being silly. I'm all right now.'

'Okay then,' Paula said, one foot still in the door. 'Shall we go back to your room, Meg?'

Meg nodded meekly though inside her body seethed. All she could do was to hope to fend off the unit's drug regimen long enough to keep her mind clear and plan her freedom. For Marc's sake.

FORTY-THREE

Marc found himself at a desk in an interview room looking, once more, into the eyes of DC Harper. Beside her sat another detective who introduced himself though Marc couldn't hear clearly over the insistent drumming of his heart. A beep signalled that the tape was rolling and DC Harper launched in, asking him if he was responsible for the murder of Steven Savage, or knew who was. It was nearly 11 p.m., almost sixteen hours since his arrest.

Marc glanced at Bunkin who looked up briefly from the papers on his knee and said, 'No comment.' He saw Bunkin's shoulders relax. *Good boy.*

It turned out that the police had cooked up a detailed timeline of their version of the events of the previous evening. They had spoken to the taxi driver who dropped Marc off at Covert Cottage at approximately 6.10 p.m.. He knew this because he called dispatch to let them know he'd completed the job and was allocated another. The cameras at the cottage had not yet been fully installed but at 6.12 p.m. he called Meg from the vicinity of the cottage. They knew he had let himself out of the gate because the combination lock had been opened and left unlocked. At 6.45 p.m., he was seen on the

CCTV camera at St Joseph's church. Police had spoken to the vicar there who had confirmed that Marc had come to the vicarage looking for Meg. Sandy had confirmed that he was aware that he was breaking the terms of his bail and that she'd informed him that Savage was in the church helping to set up the service to welcome the season of darkness. He'd waited for Sandy to return from the Palterer's and left the vicinity at 6.58 p.m. heading in the direction of Steven Savage's house. The next time he was caught on camera was at Coldwater station, where he arrived at 9.33 p.m., having just missed the train. He waited on the platform and boarded the 9.49 p.m. to Ashford. CCTV cameras at Ashford station captured him getting on the 10.18 p.m. train to London.

Because of her mental incapacity, the police hadn't yet been able to speak with Meg, but Janette had confirmed that at that time of Marc's arrival she and Meg were both having a nap prior to going to the evening thanksgiving service at the church. This explained why neither of them had heard him ringing on the doorbell or calling Meg's phone and also why there were no lights on in the cottage.

The police had also constructed a timeline for Savage's movements on what would turn out to be the last evening of his life. They would say only that he had been drinking before attending the church service. Afterwards, he'd returned home, picked up some more beer and his sleeping bag and headed off to spend the night in his hide in Covert Wood. Various neighbours had confirmed that this was something he did from time to time. The preliminary intelligence suggested that he died sometime between 8 p.m. and midnight but forensics would likely be able to narrow that window. Savage had been viciously attacked with a blunt instrument with a single blow to the head. A hunter out before dawn had spotted his body facedown in Covert Brook. The fact that there seemed to be no other blows and no defence injuries suggested that Savage had not been struggling at the time of his death. Police had not yet confirmed whether he'd died from the blow or from drowning. They would know more later.

This was all shocking enough but Marc had no knowledge of any of it, nor of the story that the police had put together about his actions. DC Harper seemed to be suggesting that he had left Ashford with the intent to hurt or even kill Savage in order to get back at him for totalling the car. They knew, too, that Savage felt he had some entitlement to a bequest from Jimmy's estate and that he'd made as much clear to them and they were saying now that Marc wanted Savage out of the way because he was being put under pressure to pay up. They seemed to think that Meg, too, had joined in Marc's campaign against Savage, raising the spectre of the disappearance of Cecily Banner when they knew that this would unsettle and even destabilise Savage. They weren't suggesting that Meg had any hand in or knowledge of Savage's murder, only that the couple had it in for their handyman and wanted to put him in his place. They already knew from the prior charges that Marc was quite capable of violence towards Savage. What they were surmising now was an escalation in that dispute. Marc had perhaps intended to threaten Savage which was why he'd taken the mallet from the shed. The victim's blood and hair had been found on it and the wound seemed consistent with a blow from just such a mallet. They anticipated that the pathologist would confirm this. Perhaps Marc had first gone to Savage's cottage – they had evidence to suggest he was in the vicinity – and not finding him there, had called on the vicar with the excuse of looking for Meg, hoping to get some more information about Savage's whereabouts. The vicar had confirmed that, although Marc had not asked specifically about Savage, he didn't have to, as she had told Marc that Savage was in church at that time helping to set up the service and was planning to attend.

Marc listened, answering 'no comment' to whatever question was put to him, but with a sinking feeling that while it was nothing like the truth, it all sounded very plausible.

He had motive and he had opportunity and he had the means.

The interview ended just before 1 a.m. Marc was led back to a cell in the custody suite and asked Bunkin to request that the custody sergeant keep him up to date with Meg's condition whatever the time of day or night. He'd only received the flimsiest of reports that Meg had had a 'psychotic breakdown', that she was in the process of being assessed and would likely be in the psych unit for some days, even weeks. What had precipitated it? He thought about her obsession with Cecily, the noises she'd been hearing in the attic. Was it possible that all these weeks she'd been losing her mind? Possible, but he couldn't see it. Sure, Meg had been in a deep depression after Lily died and had taken an overdose but she'd never been delusional. Had news of his arrest shocked Meg into breaking down? Who could have called the mental health team? The only possible candidate seemed to be Janette. Could it have been Janette who'd also called the cops on him? His thoughts turned to the odd text he'd received from Meg's phone. Who had sent that? His mind went back to when they first knew Janette, after she had approached Meg in the park. He'd been sceptical about that at the time. It seemed to cross a line somehow, not something an ethical therapist would do. But he had allowed Janette's skill to soften his concerns. He'd never met anyone who understood human nature better. His nature. His grief. She'd wormed her way into his heart through a tear in the muscle, planted inside a seed of shame and tended to it till it grew into something ugly and unspeakable. If he hadn't felt so ashamed of himself, so savagely broken, he might have been able to refrain from punching the theatregoer and thereby kept his job. He might have been a better support to Meg. He might even have stopped himself laying into Steve the night of the accident. But none of that happened. Instead, the feeling of being a cheat, a betrayer, a man who failed to pick up his daughter from school on what would turn out to be the day of her death because he was having sex with Daisy Godwin had twisted in his gut. A part of him felt that he deserved whatever happened to him. Another part fumed at Janette's deception and longed for revenge.

And then there was Meg, the blameless victim of his mess. How would she live as the partner of a convicted murderer? To lose him when she'd already lost so much. There was no way he could do that to her. The thought of it lent him a new kind of energy. He knew he had nothing to do with Savage's death. And since there was nothing to do in the cell but wait, he went through the events of that fateful evening in his mind again. Janette. He'd seen the light go on in the black bedroom and then go off again. Hadn't Sandy told him that there was going to be a social event after the service?

Maybe Savage had declared his intention to spend the night in Covert Wood? Someone else might have known where he'd be? Hadn't the police said that Savage had been drinking? Bottles of his homemade brew had been found at the site. What if Savage was passed out drunk? Whoever had killed him might have delivered the fatal blow while he slept. They could have incapacitated him then dragged him to the brook. If the blow hadn't killed him, he might have drowned without ever gaining consciousness.

It was all supposition but it had the feeling of the truth. The way that when you hit on anything true it settles down into your body like it's always been there. He thought about the figure he passed on his way to the vicarage. Might they have been the killer? He was sure that whoever it was had been carrying something large and heavy, the kind of weapon that could later be used to deliver the blows to Savage. What was missing was motivation. The Big Why.

FORTY-FOUR

Paula escorted Meg back to her room and she did not see Janette again that day. That night she dreamed that she was in the black bedroom at Covert Cottage looking out of the window. The wind had come up and the tips of the trees at Covert Wood rippled against the skyline. A bird was singing in the garden and when she looked down she saw Lily standing on the path beside the old yew. In the dream she could hear the scratching in the attic. She took her gaze from the window and when she looked back, Lily was gone. She woke, shaken, and with the conviction that her daughter had been trying to communicate with her from the moment the noises had begun in the attic. If only she knew what.

The following morning she took breakfast in the communal room with Judy, who referred to herself as Mary Magdalene, and Michaela, who wouldn't – or couldn't – speak, and gathered from snippets of conversation between the orderlies and the nurses that there had been a psychiatric emergency on another unit, as a result of which Trethorn's usual morning ward round had been postponed. What was she doing here? She knew in her heart that she wasn't crazy, so why did everyone seem to think she was? There was nothing she could do here, imprisoned in this ward with the mentally ill. She needed to get everything clear in her mind and find a way to persuade Trethorn that it would be okay to release her.

When Paula arrived with the drug cart and handed her a small plastic cup containing pills and a glass of water, she pressed the pills into the back of her lower teeth so that when Paula required her to open her mouth to ensure that she'd swallowed, there was nothing to be seen. She waited a few minutes so as not to arouse suspicion then went into the bathroom and extracted what remained of the pills with her finger, splashing her face with water. No control. Not anymore. Not from Janette and not from the drugs. She needed to seem well because she was well. It was the only way she would escape. At nine or thereabouts, one of the junior psychs arrived, introduced herself and asked her a few questions about the doll, the sounds in the attic and the missing girl and after scribbling some notes, left her alone. Not long after that there came a knock and a familiar voice called her name. She opened the door to see Sandy, dressed in her dog collar and with a delicate gold cross shining from her black sweater.

'Hi, I was doing the rounds and they told me you were here. They're letting me make a pastoral visit, as your parish priest.' She checked the corridor briefly. 'Can I come in?'

Meg held open the door and as Sandy entered her room, Paula appeared and hovered just outside. Turning to face her, Sandy said, 'A few minutes of private prayer.'

Paula nodded. 'Of course, I'll leave you to it.'

The instant the door clicked shut Sandy put a finger to her lips and in a low voice, she said, 'I'm here to help.' She gestured to the bed. Meg went over and sat down as Sandy pulled the chair around at an angle to the door, able to see at a glance if anyone peered in through the privacy window. She drew out a Bible and rested it on one thigh.

'Have they told you why the police are holding Marc?'

'Janette told me. I don't believe it, Sandy. I can't believe it.'

Sandy reached for her hand and squeezed it very tightly. 'You know I loved Steve. I was all he had. Me and Jimmy. It upset him dreadfully, you bringing all the pain of Cecily's disappearance back. But I don't for one moment think Marc killed him. Nor does Helen. Marc's lawyer called Helen after he'd been arrested. He said they'd tried to get hold of you, but the police told him you'd been sectioned. What happened? When I saw you at the social it seemed you were really out of it. Helen said the same. I knew something was wrong.'

Meg told her how she'd been feeling confused. The tea Janette had kept pressing on her. How in the days before she'd been feeling fuzzy, almost as if she'd been drugged. How Janette had suggested they visit the lawyer because Helen might try to take possession of the cottage. How even then the idea had seemed outlandish but she'd lost the ability to protest. She'd gone along with it knowing there was something very wrong but she hadn't been able to think straight.

Sandy listened intently then she said, 'Helen would never have done that.'

Meg nodded. 'I know that now. I think it was Janette. She wanted the cottage and now she's got it. I effectively gave it to her when I signed that power of attorney.' She covered her face with her hands. 'I can't believe that I didn't see it.'

'You seem pretty clear-headed now.'

Paula's face appeared at the privacy window. There was a light knock, and the door was inched open.

'How are we doing?'

Sandy, smiling, said, 'Another five minutes?'

Paula checked her watch and nodded. The door clicked shut behind her.

'Can you remember exactly what happened that night?'

Meg thought back. It was still all such a blur. She closed her eyes and allowed images to form. The words, what was said and by whom, all that was still very vague but she'd seen things. The tea and Janette's face as Meg had turned back and caught sight of her in the French windows, clutching Meg's phone in her hand. The journalist. More tea. How everything at the evening church service felt distant and unreal. The black bedroom. After that nothing until Janette shook her awake.

'I think Janette played you,' Sandy said. 'She's been playing you for a while.'

'Yes.' In some strange fashion Meg already knew this. 'I think you're right. She gradually cut me off from Marc. She said that he was a danger to me, that he might do something silly. She told me Marc forgot to pick Lily up from school the day she died because he was...' her stomach lurched, '...he was having sex with another woman. So I had to rush out of work to pick her up and I was flustered and instead of holding my daughter's hand so firmly that she couldn't wriggle away, I didn't. And she did.' There were tears in her eyes now.

Sandy looked shocked and said, simply, 'We don't know why God allows these things to happen. But right now, we need to focus on Steve. Marc's lawyer told Helen what the police are saying. Marc wanted Helen to know.'

Sandy passed on what Helen had learned of the case against him. When it came to finding Marc's DNA in Steve's shed, Meg took a long breath out.

'Oh God, no. That was *me*. I went to see Steve. I sat in his brewhouse. It was cold and I mislaid my hat so I put on Marc's red beanie.'

'Did you tell anyone about that?'

'No, I had no idea it would be relevant.' She pressed her hands into the bed. 'Who's going to believe me now?'

'Listen,' Sandy said. 'They haven't charged Marc yet, so the police must have their doubts. There's hope, Meg, let's focus on the hope.'

'I had a dream last night. About Lily. I think she was trying to tell me something. Does that sound crazy?'

Sandy shook her head. 'People say the dead are silent witnesses but I think they're wrong about that. The dead speak to us all the time. If only we'd listen.'

Relieved, Meg said, 'I wonder if she was trying to warn me all along about Janette,' and told Sandy about Janette approaching her in the park and then appearing in Coldwater, then how Janette had first suggested staying in the studio. 'She knew so much about us. How to work our vulnerabilities. I'm pretty sure it must have been Janette who called the psych team. Who else would have done it? I was so out of it that I didn't ask the question. She wanted me out of the way.'

She propped herself up on her elbows, her look intense, wanting Sandy to understand the urgency of the thing. 'I need you to help get me out of here. Tell them that Cecily isn't someone I made up in my head. Tell them what you told me about the dead.'

At that moment the door opened and Paula's face appeared. 'That's probably enough for now.'

Sandy nodded and stood to leave. At the door she turned and whispered back to Meg.

'I'm on your team.'

FORTY-FIVE

Marc worried about Meg but figured that so long as she remained in the psych unit, she was at least safe from Janette's manipulations. The most pressing task was to come up with some way to prove his innocence in the death of Savage. The police had been granted another thirty-six hours to investigate the case before coming to a charging decision and so he passed another night in the custody cell going over and over the events of his last night of freedom, drawing maps in his mind and making timelines, rehearsing each moment, minute by minute, only to come back to the same dismal conclusion, that he had been set up by a mind sharper and more ruthless than his own.

When morning came, he was driven the short distance from the police station to Ashford Magistrates' Court, where on Bunkin's advice he pleaded guilty to breaching his bail conditions and was remanded in custody. There followed an interminable, airless ride in the sweatbox to HMP Elmley on the Isle of Sheppey, where he was processed and placed in a grim cell in the induction wing with a cellmate called Luke Stoddard who had a habit of constant, tuneless whistling. He did his best to ignore the symphony and Stoddard himself, and as soon as he was allowed, he called Bunkin.

'There's some more information,' said Bunkin. 'They're now pretty sure that Savage was dragged into the water alive. Cause of death, drowning. He'd drunk a hell of a lot. The alcohol levels in his blood would have been enough to kill a less heavy drinker. It's looking likely that he was already unconscious when he was dragged from the hide into the brook. The wind was high and blew the topsoil and leaf mould from the drag path, so forensics can't be sure whether he resisted or not but they seem to think, on balance, not. There are no defence wounds and the various minor scratches and lesions seem to have happened peri or post mortem. The wound to his head was apparently inflicted post-mortem. The force of the mallet pressed some water weed into the flesh but there was no bleeding. Whoever did this was keen to make it seem as if Savage was attacked.'

'I've told you who I think did it,' Marc said.

'Have you had a think as to how your DNA was found in Savage's shed?' He'd broken this news the day before. Marc had spent some wakeful hours trying and failing to come up with some solid rationale for why his DNA should be there, given it was a place he'd never been anywhere near.

'Savage could have picked up my DNA at the cottage.'

'Right,' Bunkin said. 'And that's perfectly possible, of course, though depending on exactly what they've got, that might present us with some difficulties if we get to a jury trial. In my experience, juries favour concrete explanations.'

'I really think the police should be looking at Janette Hopwood. She could easily have found out that I was in Coldwater that night. Maybe the vicar told Meg or...maybe she figured it out. I think she might be trying to frame me.'

'What's the motivation?' Bunkin said.

Marc let out a long sigh and shook his head. 'Maybe she's trying to get her hands on the cottage.'

'Pretty extreme, don't you think?'

'Why don't they interview her?'

'They have, I believe. Listen, Marc, without proof that's just a hypothesis. One of dozens, maybe hundreds.'

'Did the police come back to you with a more accurate time of death?'

'There's no update on that yet.'

''Cos I arrived at the station at around 9.30, right? And if Savage died somewhere between 9 p.m. and 11 p.m. how would I have had the time? It would have taken me half an hour to walk from Covert Wood to the station.'

'They've already said those are approximate timings. In any case, an adult human being can drown within a minute.'

'Whose side are you on anyway?' Marc said moodily.

'I have to look at all sides in order to be on yours,' Bunkin said.

It would be hard to get a jury to convict on what the police had so far, he went on. But who knew what else they might turn up? A witness, another piece of the forensic puzzle.

And juries were unpredictable.

Marc went back to his cell, clambered onto his bed on the top bunk and awaited his fate. He woke to the sounds of Luke whistling tunelessly to himself again. The thin grey light from the window and the clanking of doors announced the start of another day. He rose and climbed down from his bunk. Luke, watching him with a quizzical expression, said, 'Hey man, you ever write songs like your old man?'

Marc shrugged. That seemed like another life now. One he'd never get back. He went over to the sink and splashed his face. Luke, who was evidently not done with him, sat on his bunk and waited. As Marc was drying himself, Luke said, 'It's my little girl's eleventh birthday. She's my world. I was gonna ring her and sing happy birthday and all that...she loves a sing-song...but what kid would want to hear from her dad in prison on her birthday? It's not like I have a present for her or anything.'

Marc thought of Lily then, how he had sung his own songs to her, the memories stuck in his throat. He wondered if he'd ever write or play or sing again. Not for Lily. But perhaps to help out his cellie who, like him, was missing his kid. That he could do.

He said, 'What if you gave your girl a song, written just for her?'

Luke seemed surprised and then delighted. 'Would you do that for me?'

'I'll have a go. What's her name?'

'Lisa.'

'Leave it with me then.' He repeated the name in his head. *Lisa, Lisa, Lisa.*

Luke rose and patted him on the shoulder. 'Thanks, mate. She'll be right made up.'

When the cell door opened for breakfast and morning association Marc took himself out into the yard to think. At lunchtime he went back to the cell and found Luke lying on his bunk with a newspaper tented across his belly. His eyes were closed and he appeared to be having a nap. Marc was about to head up to the top bunk when a sub-headline on the front page of the paper grabbed his attention. He moved closer and craned his neck, at that moment inadvertently alerting Luke who instantly sat bolt upright, eyes wide with alarm. The newspaper fell to the floor.

'What you doing?'

'Sorry,' Marc said. He bent down to pick up the paper. The words that had caught his attention stared back at him. His eyes flicked up to the headline.

30 years on, no leads on missing Coldwater girl

'Ain't that where you're from?' Luke said, following his gaze. 'You should read it then,' he added, pushing his way past Marc to the kettle. 'Fancy a tea?'

Marc held the paper and ran his eyes over the page. Hadn't Meg told him that Savage was the last known person to see Cecily alive? Had he witnessed her abduction and never spoken about it? Was it possible that Cecily's killer had come back to silence him for good?

Luke put a mug in front of him and came to sit in the chair beside the tiny table.

'Sad, innit?' he said then, more brightly, 'You got a kid?'

Marc felt himself hover above his body for a moment as he always seemed to whenever the topic of Lily came up. 'A daughter. She died.'

'That's rough,' Luke said, shaking his head.

They fell silent. Luke picked up his mug of tea and began to sip noisily from it.

'I got you a first draft of a song,' Marc said eventually,

glad to be able to change the subject. He took a breath and began to hum the fragments of the tune that, in his head anyway, he had written long ago, the one he'd always hoped to sell to Beyoncé's people. That was all gone now. He closed his eyes and held up a hand to signal to Luke to wait while the fragments began to come together. Soon enough Luke began to sing along. 'Lovely Lisa, Lisa my love.'

'We're far away...' Marc began.

'...on your birthday,' Luke added.

They continued to build it line by line and by the time the cell door opened for evening association, Luke had it down and went off to make the phone call. He stayed in the cell for a while after Luke had left, focusing on the timeline of events on the night of Steve's murder, trying over and over in his mind to find something, anything, that might sow doubt in a jury's mind. He went down to the bank of phones and joined the queue, intending to call Helen. Luke was still there too, near the front of another line.

Lisa. Lovely Lisa. Lisa my love.

A thought bubbled up about the silver Peugeot that had narrowly avoided the taxi driver at Covert Cottage. It was a silver Peugeot that had passed him in the road on his way to the station. Someone had seen him. It suddenly hit him that he'd seen a silver Peugeot at the party, when Meg had asked him to check on the cars in the drive. It belonged to Lisa, the girl from the shop. Pretty common, silver Peugeots, sure, but what if it had been Lisa at the wheel that night? Maybe she'd got a clear view of him in the headlights. If he'd made his way directly to the station from murdering Steve in Covert Wood then he'd have taken

bail but I googled around and I think they'd struggle not to release him.'

Meg heard herself cry out. The relief!

'How are you getting on? I told Trethorn about Cecily...'

'Thank you. I told Trethorn I'd taken some drugs to help me sleep. I didn't mention Janette obviously, but Trethorn said that what happened might have been a drug-induced episode of psychosis. He's going to think about letting me have some supervised time outside the unit prior to release. I think he's looking for an excuse to let me go. The ward is stretched to capacity.'

'There have been other developments I think you should know. Helen checked out the various professional bodies for psychotherapy. There is no one called Janette Hopwood registered as an accredited psychotherapist.'

Meg felt herself choking. Sandy patted her on the back and waited till she'd had a chance to settle.

'Turns out psychotherapy is a completely unregulated profession. You or I could set up as a therapist tomorrow. But it says something.' As Meg opened her mouth to speak Sandy raised a hand. 'There's more. A guy called Daniel Idris called me. I've come across him before. Local journo. Nice guy. He says you know him.'

'Yeah, he'd heard from Tim that I was interested in Cecily's case.'

'That's what he told me. I mentioned Janette to him and he did a bit of research as a favour. It's not a very common name and he didn't come up with anything significant. But there *was* a Jean Hopwood living in Adavale in 2010. It's a small town in Queensland.'

Meg blinked. 'Janette told us she'd been in Australia.'

'She mentioned that to me at your party. It could just be a coincidence, but it could also be that Janette Hopwood and Jean Hopwood are one and the same person. I asked Daniel to see what else he could dig up.'

'And?'

'A Jean Hopwood filed for bankruptcy in the UK in 2008.'

'Who *is* this woman?'

'I'm not finished.' Sandy checked the viewing window in the door. 'Daniel called in a couple of favours himself. He's waiting to hear back but our man's got the bit between his teeth. In return I had to agree to an interview about the Cecily Banner case for the anniversary.' She pressed her lips together and took a deep breath. 'What I didn't tell you was my dad became one of the suspects.' Sandy gazed at her hands for a moment and her face grew solemn. 'He didn't do it, obviously, but living in the shadow of that got too much for him. He'd got into debt too, which didn't help. Any case, on the second anniversary of Cecily's disappearance, he killed himself. From then on, people in the village assumed it was the act of a guilty man.'

'I'm so sorry.'

'It's about time I started talking about that stuff. I've been quiet about it for too long. We all have. Everyone in Coldwater. It was after Dad died that I found God. I guess that being the parish priest was some sort of atonement. But it's time for us all to reconcile with the past. That's the only way we're ever going to have a future.' She gave a smile clouded with the pain of the years. 'My priority is to find a way to get you out of here but if they discharge you now, Janette would still have the right to make decisions about your future.'

'So we need to be strategic.'

'Exactly. That's why Helen and I did a bit more digging around about the power of attorney. If Helen raised a legitimate challenge to it the Court of Protection would have to look into it. You and Marc aren't married which means that Helen's not officially family but the court might be prepared to overlook that. The grounds are very limited but the most compelling one is bankruptcy.'

The two women paused for a moment in their deliberations. Something about the night of Steve's death was forming in Meg's mind. Ever since the drugs had begun to leave her system, she'd sensed that she'd been witness to something that even in her doped-up state she knew to be off. It was about Janette's face when she'd confronted her in the garden. The wild look in her eyes. As if she'd seen something so shocking that it had ruffled even someone of Janette's composure.

'I think she might have seen something in the wood the night Steve died.' Meg carried on tentatively at first as the memories came back, then in a rush as if a dam had burst, 'There was mud on her face. She told me she'd heard the back gate banging and thought Marc might somehow be planning some mischief against Steve, but her trousers were soaked as if they'd been immersed in water.' As she spoke she grew more confident in the idea that Janette had witnessed Steve's death and that perhaps she'd even been a part of it.

'What about the mallet? They found it in the shed. It had been in the brook and the head had Steve's DNA on it. But there were no prints on the handle.'

'She wasn't carrying it when I saw her, but she saw me before I saw her, so she might have dropped it and gone back for it later.'

'No guarantees but that might be possible. I was thinking something else though. Let me tell you what.'

FORTY-SEVEN

Marc met Bunkin in a tiny damp-smelling room at Elmley, the lawyer looking more like he was off to the opera than visiting a remand prison on a windy patch of nowhere in North Kent. Marc imagined the gawking as the red Tesla purred into the car park. To think about the money he must owe by now. Or not to think about it. Either way, he was sure Bunkin would have long since burned through the five grand Pete's man had fronted him. Marc was surprised, in fact, that Bunkin hadn't bailed already. He'd signed up for assault, couldn't have anticipated that his new client would wind up arrested for murder. Decent of him to stay loyal.

Bunkin had, in fact, come directly from the police station in Ashford, a drive of maybe an hour, to pass on to Marc the intel on the police interview with Lisa. She'd given a formal statement now, to say that she'd had to swerve to avoid a taxi exiting the driveway at Covert Cottage around ten past six. She'd caught a glimpse of a figure standing in the house lights but hadn't got a good look at whoever it was. She'd gone to the church service and to the social afterwards and on her drive back home she'd passed another man in the road walking away from the village. When she checked in the rear-view mirror she saw it was Marc. She didn't know the exact time but she did recall that 'Imagine' had just finished playing on the radio. From Lisa's account, police had been able to pinpoint the moment at 9.16 p.m. Bunkin and his assistant had walked the two possible routes from Covert Cottage to the station, Bunkin taking the road, the assistant tromping across the fields. The journey had taken Bunkin thirty-three minutes. His assistant had completed it in twenty-eight. On the evening of Savage's death, the full moon had bathed everything in yellow light but the going could not have been as fast as it would have been in broad daylight. The station CCTV had Marc arriving at 9.33 p.m. and he remained on the platform until the train, at 9.49 p.m.

'They're narrowing the window of time to after ten. Wind stress on the temperature of the water in the brook had skewed the initial findings. And a hunter had come forward to say he'd seen someone moving on the path by the stile just after eleven.'

'So it *couldn't* have been me,' Marc said.

Bunkin sighed and raised a finger. 'They're not giving up on you, Marc. You're all they've got right now. And they can still hold you for breaching bail conditions on the assault charge but given that the victim is now dead and there's no chance that you'll be likely to assault him again, I'm going to apply to have that lifted. It's unusual to remand someone in custody for breaching bail on a common assault charge if they have no previous and they didn't contact the victim. Even with the extension, I don't think they can justify holding you now unless they charge you with murder. Which, right now, they haven't got sufficient evidence to do.'

'What does that mean for me?'

'It means that tomorrow, first thing, I'm going to apply to have you released on licence. That means they can still rearrest you but so long as you behave they're unlikely to do that unless they're going to charge you with the murder.' He looked up over his expensive glasses. 'Which they could still do.'

'But it's looking unlikely.'

'Correct. By tomorrow afternoon you could be a free man.'

*

The hours felt like feathers dragged through treacle. Marc called Helen who was thrilled by the news and relayed what Meg had said to Sandy. 'While Meg's still on a section it's going to be hard to argue that she doesn't need an attorney. We'll have to find a way to show that the original application for power of attorney was bogus or that Meg really wasn't fit enough to sign it. There'll be legal fees. It could all get very costly. And it could potentially take months. If they let you out today or tomorrow, just keep a low profile. Don't do anything to alert Hopwood to the fact that you're out.'

'Got it.'

'And Sparky, we'll find a way through this, okay?'

Back in his cell, Marc found it hard to keep in check his feelings about the woman who had tricked him but he knew that to display his rage now would backfire. Instead, he kept his head down and looked forward to lights out so that he wouldn't have to look at the peeling paint on the walls. A new day dawned. After what seemed like a lifetime, a couple of screws came by the cell and announced that he would be leaving that afternoon. He didn't have lunch. When it was time, they gave him fifteen minutes to pack his things, not that there was anything to pack. He gave what little he had to Luke. When the screws returned, he turned his back to allow them to handcuff him and Luke said, 'All right then, Twilight, you tosser, I ain't gonna miss your boring-arse face. Straight up. But I owe you one, mate, and I always pay my debts. Remember that and look out for yourself, all right?'

'Noted,' Marc said.

Behind him he heard Luke begin to whistle Lisa's song and as he made his way between the two screws down the long walkway the inmates in the next cell picked up the melody and by the time Marc reached the exit, a chorus of male voices was belting out, 'Lovely Lisa, Lisa my love.'

Then the locks clicked open and Marc got in the van and was taken back to Ashford police station where he reacquainted himself with the rank mattress until such time as the door swung open and he was marshalled to the desk then released on licence pending further investigation.

For the longest time he stood on the pavement and let the rain fall on him. Lisa at the shop had come through. This virtual stranger had stood up because she believed in the truth. He found a chain coffee place, ordered a cappuccino and plugged his phone into a charging socket. As soon as he had enough juice he called the number for the Coldwater village shop. It went through to voicemail. He waited for the beep and left a message of thanks. Once his phone was fully charged, he left the coffee place and walked across town, shivering in his twill jacket, past a string of feeble Christmas lights and through the shopping centre, past the supermarket and the train station until he reached Walton Hospital. He pushed through a swing door, walked up to reception and told the woman sitting there that he had come to see Meg. The woman checked her screen and made a couple of phone calls before informing him that he was not on the visitor list for the patient and would not be admitted. If he wanted to see Meg the first step would be to contact her attorney. He persisted politely until she grew exasperated and threatened to call security. He was a marked man now. One wrong move and he'd be back in Elmley.

As he walked back to the station, he allowed himself to feel a little more of his anger. At the entrance he passed some pigeons pecking at a pile of vomit. He flapped at them with his hands and watched while they took flight, then went into the station and took the first train to London and from there the tube to St John's Wood. When he got to Pete's house he rang the doorbell and waited in the porch.

Eventually the door opened and a blast of warm, dope-filled air hit him and when it cleared there was Pete, dressed in his habitual band T-shirt and jeans, peering at him.

'Hey, man. Cops let you go?'

'Can I come in?' Marc said.

Pete shuffled awkwardly on his feet. 'Look, man, no offence, but I don't really want police at my door.'

'No cops. Plus I've got something you're gonna want.' He waited for Pete's face to soften and took a step closer.

'Well, okay then.'

Marc stepped inside the tiled hallway, followed Pete through to the living room and didn't wait to be invited to sit. A football game was on the TV. Pete grabbed the remote and muted the sound then came over and hovered by the coffee table, the long, lean fingers of his right hand playing with his hair. 'I figured you'd reappear eventually. And here you are. As a matter of fact I was just thinking about your dad. Something from the past. You want a beer? You look like you need one.'

Marc said he did. Pete got up and disappeared.

Marc took a few breaths to steady himself then looked around and saw immediately the photograph of the party.

Pete returned in short order carrying two bottles of Stella.

'Hungry?'

'No, thanks,' Marc said, though he hadn't eaten since the day before, he had no appetite.

Pete took in a breath then reached out and began rolling another joint. 'So, you said you had something for me.'

'Yeah, a song, the best thing I've ever written.'

Pete's eyebrows raised. He leaned across the space between them with the joint. Marc took it and looked at it for a moment before taking a deep toke. He said, 'It's still a bit sketchy but I can bang it out on the piano, if you like.'

Pete took the joint back from Marc and closed his eyes while the dope went into his system. Then he pointed to the piano in the corner. 'Be my guest then, mate. No promises mind.'

Marc got up and went over.

Silence fell. A full silence, the kind that was so often a prelude to a kind of panic for Marc. Not this time though. This time he took a breath and let the air out slowly, scanning the chords in his mind. He began the opening bars. He was playing it for both the Lisas; for the girl who missed her father and the neighbour in her silver Peugeot who came through for him. Maybe even for Lily. It meant something – a few bars that spoke to him, some tiny piece of phrasing that settled his being, a bridge that stirred his heart. From the corner of his eye he watched Pete close his eyes, the fingers of his right hand tapping against his thigh. For the first time in a long time the music he was making meant something.

'Promising,' Pete said when he was done. He came over to the piano with his hand outstretched. 'You wanna make a deal on it?' He scratched his chin. 'The song *and* the publishing rights. I'll get my people to get in touch with yours, iron out the business side.'

Marc's mobile buzzed. A text from Helen. He'd look at it later.

'Okay,' Marc said. The two men shook hands.

Marc stood and let Pete sit at the piano. 'You said you were thinking about Jimmy,' he said, remembering.

'It'll keep,' Pete said, trying out the first chords of Lisa's song. 'Like this?'

Marc nodded.

Pete closed his eyes and began to hum the first line.

FORTY-EIGHT

'We're meeting Marc in an hour,' Sandy said. Meg opened the back door of Sandy's car and took a seat. Helen, her arm still in the sling but the cuts on her face almost healed, turned to her and said, 'How are you?' She held out a paper cup of coffee. The bitter liquid slid down Meg's throat, the first caffeine she'd had in days. Almost immediately her pulse began to quicken. After all the soothing blandness of the unit it felt good. Sharp.

Sandy keyed the engine and began to manoeuvre the car out from the parking bay.

'I've been better but I've been much, much worse. Big picture, I've managed to avoid taking whatever it is they're giving me, but sooner or later they'll take bloods and find out I've been faking it.'

'We'll have you out by then.'

'How?'

'Still working on that part.'

'You're here now, though. We're lucky. We weren't sure Trethorn would grant you day release.'

'Psych ward refuses patient permission to attend memorial service for missing girl. Not a good look.'

Sandy let out a grunt. 'We don't have to get you back until late tonight. So we've got plenty of time. All else fails, what you said about Janette, the mud on her face, her soaked trousers, and what Daniel found out about her declaring bankruptcy, changing her name...'

'She's not even a real therapist,' Helen said. 'We could go to the police?'

Meg closed her eyes and tried to get her thoughts in order. 'And say what? We've got a mad woman in the back who's got some conspiracy theories she'd like to pass by you? It's not illegal to be bankrupt, or to change your name. It's not even illegal to be a bogus therapist. It should be, but it isn't.'

'We'll figure it out.'

They pulled into another car park.

'There's a decent café in the precinct,' Sandy said, as they got out of the car. 'We thought you might like to have a proper breakfast.'

They went in and took seats by the door. Meg felt anxious, perhaps too on edge to eat. On the other hand, it had been days since she'd eaten anything decent. The food in the unit was sub-school mush.

'There's still no why to any of this,' Meg said, taking a sip of her coffee.

'The cottage?' Sandy offered.

Helen tucked into a stack of pancakes. 'She must know we can appeal the POA. There are easier ways to swindle someone out of a house.'

'Something tells me it's more complicated than that,' Meg said.

'I'd like to know why she filed for bankruptcy then fled the country,' Sandy said. 'What was she up to back then?'

'Stiffing some other poor mark probably,' Helen said.

Sandy began to load marmalade onto her toast. 'I know you had your issues with Steve, but...'

'Everyone has a right to justice,' Meg said.

Sandy looked relieved and sat back and said, 'Yes, just that.'

Helen piped up then. When she'd spoken to Marc he'd told her that he thought he'd left the back gate open. 'So anyone could have come in and taken the mallet.'

'If they knew it was there. Which so far as I know only four people did,' Meg said. 'Me, Marc, Steve and Janette. And from what Bunkin told you, the police think the injuries to Steve were caused peri or post mortem.' The language of criminal investigation wasn't entirely new to her. The investigation into Lily's death, cursory though it had seemed, had been full of unfamiliar terms she had hoped never to hear again outside TV dramas. 'Why use it on a dead man unless you want to make it seem that whoever had access to the shed killed Steve?'

Since stopping the drugs, Meg had begun to be able to dredge up memories from the night of the murder. She remembered now that Janette had told her she'd gone into the wood that night looking for Marc. She'd heard the gate bang and was worried Marc had broken in through the back gate and gone to the shed to get a weapon, and that he was intending to do Steve harm. 'What if Janette had come upon Steve's body and thought she could frame Marc for the killing?'

'But why did she think Steve was likely to be in Covert Wood and not at home?'

Sandy stopped eating and sighed and looking up, said, 'I saw Janette talking to Steve over by the drinks table.'

'She would have known he was drunk and he might have

told her he'd decided to camp out in the wood so...' Helen tailed off.

'And then Meg finds her covered in mud and soaked to the skin,' Helen said.

An idea hit Meg with the force of a runaway train. 'What if Janette killed Steve hoping to pin it on Marc?'

'What do they say in all those TV crime dramas? Opportunity, motivation, means,' Sandy said.

Helen put down her fork. 'We don't know why.'

'We don't have to.' The final denouement was close. Meg could feel it on her bones. A chance to see through the murk of lies and deception into the clear air beyond.

'We don't?' Helen said.

'Not if we get her to confess.'

'How are we going to do that? The woman's not stupid.'

'I think she's playing a psychological game,' Meg said.

Sandy pushed away her food. 'If she is it's a very dangerous one.'

A part of Meg that she'd thought had gone forever had in that moment resurfaced. A vivid, vital part. You could call it a survival instinct. You could call it what the hell you liked. She smiled to herself. 'She nearly won. But only nearly.'

'What do you mean?' Sandy said.

'I know her, remember? I spent weeks being groomed by her. Somewhere in her heart Janette wants to get caught. She's just waiting for us to play the winning move.'

FORTY-NINE

As they worked on it overnight and into the early hours, Lisa's song, which had been a sweet ballad when Marc first penned it, began to morph into something deeper and more poignant. As dawn broke, a stirring in their bones told them it was done. They had a smash on their hands.

'We should go in to the record company ASAP,' Pete said. 'Like today.'

Marc wanted to, he really did, but not now. Today, he had bigger things on his mind. 'I got plans. You go and if there's a deal, cut me in.'

Pete smiled and gave Marc a slap on the back. 'Jimmy would've been proud of his boy.'

'I hope so,' Marc said. But that mattered less, somehow he thought, than being proud of himself.

There came a knock on the door and Debby came in carrying a tray on which sat a large pot of coffee and some mugs. She had flung a robe over her pyjamas. It looked like she hadn't been out of bed long. 'Hey, Dad, Marc. I thought I heard you guys down here.'

'You're up early,' Pete said.

Debby put the tray down on the table by the mixing desk.

'Yeah. Exam later, remember? Thought I'd do some last-minute cramming.' She thumbed back towards the door. 'I should get to it.'

They thanked her for the coffee. When she was gone, Pete said, 'Astro-bloody-physics! You'd have asked me thirty years ago, what I would have wanted in a kid, I'd have said a son to, you know, jam around with. But that girl means more to me than all the rest of it put together.'

Marc felt himself falter. What would Lily have become if she'd lived to adulthood?

Pete, sensing he was steering into choppy waters, said, 'Sorry, man. Bit insensitive. But that reminds me what I meant to tell you last night.'

'Oh?' Marc said, helping himself to the coffee.

'Yeah, the strangest thing. That photo you mentioned the other day? The one with...'

'I remember,' Marc said. It was the image of Jimmy and Pete in the old days, jamming together in a hotel suite somewhere, surrounded by hangers-on. The one in the living room that someone, he presumed Pete, had taken down but had then made a reappearance.

'It came back to me. Jimmy's old girlfriend, the one with her back to the snapper? I think that was the evening he got together with your mum. But his old lady was there then too. What a piece she turned out to be.'

Marc, sensing a shaggy dog story about to come, surreptitiously checked his watch. Just after half seven. Plenty of time to hear Pete out and get to the station in time for the train to Ashford.

'They'd been together since before he made it. Old Jimbo

got her up the duff. Twisted her arm into getting an abortion, then left her for your mum. Can't blame him in a way. Astrid was…well, you know. That woman was like the Milky Way. The light just shone from her. The other one had no chance.' He reached for his tobacco, started pressing a generous pinch into a paper. 'His old lady took the break-up really badly. Started pestering him, calling at all hours, hanging around outside the house. Stalking I guess you'd call it. Old Jimbo wouldn't do anything about it. I guess he felt bad about the pregnancy, talking her out of it. Went on for months. In the end, your mum took things into her own hands, called the cops. Astrid would have been pregnant with you by then. The ex was charged with harassment. It was all pretty ugly.' He stopped to light his rollie and took a long toke, reached for his coffee. 'Your parents ever tell you any of this?'

Marc shook his head. He was wondering where this story was going.

'After your mum died there was an inquest, right? This was years later. Anyway, I went along to support Jimmy and I remember coming out of the coroner's office and there she was, the ex I mean, just standing there on the other side of the street. Jimmy was still inside, so I went over to her and said, "Look, lady, I don't know what your beef with old Jimmy is, but this really isn't the time."'

A ticking had started up in Marc's brain. The coffee or something else? 'Did she go away?'

'Yeah, she did. But it was weird, you know? Like she'd been watching your folks all this time. Like she *knew* something.' He finished his cigarette, dropped the stub into his empty mug.

'And?' Marc said. Somewhere in his head the gears were grinding.

'She was there, at your party.' Marc stopped breathing as Pete went on. 'Jimmy's old lady. She went by a different name in the old days, Jean I think it was, but it was definitely her. The psychotherapist. She was your dad's old squeeze.'

There was a shattering sound as the coffee mug left Marc's hands and fell to the studio floor.

FIFTY

Marc arrived at St Pancras station without knowing quite how he'd got there. His mind was still reeling. He still had no proof but there was now a possible motive for Janette or Jean to have been involved in Steve's murder. If she'd never forgiven Jimmy for pressing her into an abortion then leaving her, wouldn't she have longed for revenge? Maybe she'd held out a hope that she and Jimmy would get back together until she discovered that Jimmy and Astrid were getting married and, if that wasn't bad enough, that Astrid was pregnant with him, Marc. Looking back, it made sense. The way she'd inserted herself into their lives, had persuaded them to reveal their most intimate secrets, her appearance in Coldwater, the way she'd already exploited his guilt and Meg's vulnerability. Her desire to destroy him by framing him for Steve's murder. Wouldn't that be the ultimate revenge?

He decided to say nothing to Helen when he called her from the station and finalized the arrangements. Then he bought his ticket and boarded the fast train from St Pancras. He got out at Ashford and left the station alone. Under the terms of his release, he was barred from contacting anyone involved in the case but together, he and Helen had devised a plan that would ensure he was unlikely to be caught. He took a cab and asked the driver to take him to Cravenfold, eight miles outside Ashford. In only a few moments they were on the outskirts of town and heading into deep countryside. His phone rang, a number he didn't recognize. He picked up the call.

A voice said, 'Hello? Is that Mr Mair?'

'Yes, who is this?'

'It's Jared, from the body shop. We towed your car. The Spider? We've been trying to get hold of your wife but she's not been picking up.'

'How did you get this number?'

'Your wife gave us both numbers. You're the registered owner of the vehicle, correct?'

'Yes,' he said. His eyes flicked to the window where the Kent countryside was opening up under a weak wintry sun.

'I told your wife that the car's basically a write-off.' He knew this already and was wondering why the man had chosen to call him. At that moment Jared went on, 'When we looked at the vehicle more closely there was something a bit troubling. I'm mentioning it because it might impact the insurance claim. There seems to have been a leak in the brake fluid. It's possible that it happened on impact but it might have been a pre-existing fault.'

'Meaning?'

'Well, if the leak was there beforehand, it's possible that the Spider's brakes might not have worked as well as they should have done.'

He took this in. Then he said, 'But how would you know?'

'I don't,' Jared said. 'But if you kept it in a garage, there might be some evidence of the leakage before the car was driven; a greasy patch on the floor, something like that.'

Marc felt his stomach contract. 'You mean it was tampered with?'

A silence followed. 'I wouldn't know about that.'

'But it's possible?'

'Yes, it's possible.'

Marc ended the call. He was struggling for breath now. The taxi driver, making eye contact in the rear-view mirror, said, 'Are you all right, mate?'

'I'm fine,' he lied. He put a hand on his chest to steady himself and looking down, noticed his knees beginning to shake.

A few miles further on they came to a bridge over the Sour. Gathering himself, Marc asked the driver to drop him on the other side. The half-mile walk to the tiny Norman church of St Mary's brought some life back to his limbs. As he reached the gate into the churchyard, the bits and pieces of the puzzle were beginning to gather in his mind. Sandy had suggested meeting here. The church was one of three in her priestly rotation and by far the smallest and most remote. There was no CCTV and the doors were usually locked. The congregation was small and skewed to an elderly population living in cottages scattered about. Unlikely to come by unexpectedly. Sandy had been by early that morning and opened up before driving to the unit to pick up Meg.

He was feeling anxious, a tic pulsing in one eye, the knees no less shaky. The cool calm of the church helped a little. As he sat and waited, he saw the Spider on the night of the accident, the metal twisted and pushed into the tree. An age passed. And then – to his relief – the door swung open again and he saw Sandy and Helen entering, followed shortly behind by Meg. He got up from the pew and ran to meet them. It occurred to him that he had never been gladder to see Meg than at this moment. She seemed frailer and thinner than when he'd last seen her, but there was a solidity there, as if she had been on a long journey and finally returned to herself. They embraced for a long time which seemed not nearly long enough.

As they sat in the church, a watery sun began to shine through the stained-glass window. Bit by bit they slotted in the pieces.

Finally, Sandy chipped in, 'It's sad,' and chastened by Marc's raised eyebrow, added, 'I only mean, no one is beyond the reach of God's mercy.'

'She needs this to end as badly as we do,' Meg said.

'So what do we do?' Helen asked. She was still wearing a sling and her face bore the last remnants of the bruising from the accident. Which, as they now knew, maybe wasn't an accident at all.

They fell silent for a moment.

'We could just take what we know to the police?' Sandy offered.

Marc shook his head. 'What evidence do we have?'

Meg said, 'They took some blood from me when I was admitted. The nurse told me they'd found ketamine in my blood, wanted to know if I was using. No wonder I felt so out of it.'

Sandy said, 'She went over to Steve at the social and put a glass of wine in his hand.'

Marc frowned. 'I'm guessing Steve was no stranger to

class As. We don't have any proof that Janette spiked his drink or drugged you, Meg. We can't even prove that Janette and Jean are one and the same person. And even if we could, all we really know is that Jean filed for bankruptcy and took off to Australia and she's not accredited as a psychotherapist, which you don't have to be to practise.' There was a hint of frustration in his voice.

'I've an idea,' Helen said. She outlined her plan.

Marc hesitated a moment then nodded. 'I'm in.'

'Me too,' Meg said.

They went over it again and agreed on the details. Then Sandy rummaged in her bag for her phone and dialled the number for Daniel Idris.

FIFTY-ONE

On their way back to Coldwater they stopped off at a DIY store. Meg, Marc and Sandy waited in the car while Helen bought a bolt cutter and an electric saw. They drove through the open country of the Weald in silence. As they approached Coldwater, the dark mass of Covert Wood loomed. The buzzards were out, scanning the fields with their razor eyes, looking for something to eat.

'I can take the back route so we don't have to pass Covert Cottage,' Sandy said as they neared.

Meg said, 'Please don't. I want to see it.'

In the rear-view mirror she noticed Sandy side-eye Helen then clear her throat. She said, 'She's made a few changes, even in the time you've been at the unit. It might come as a shock.' Meg steeled herself as Sandy elaborated, 'As you know, Steve made enemies as easily as friends. He owed money all over and to some pretty shady characters. Plus, he'd made suicide attempts before now. And there's something it's only fair to tell you. Janette has been around the village drumming up support, telling people that Marc has been charged with murdering Steve and the stress of all has driven you mad. I don't know if anyone really believes it, but you know how charming she can

359

be. And…' another glance at Helen, '…Daniel Idris is asking questions about Steve's death.'

Marc let out a moan. More press attention. All he needed.

Helen swung round. 'He spoke to Tim Nuttall, the retired copper. Nuttall got some stick over the police's failure to catch Cecily's killer and it seems he's seized the opportunity to redeem himself by pointing the finger at you. It's pure opportunism if you ask me. I never liked the guy. Something creepy about him. But Daniel is obviously going to take what he says seriously.'

In the mirror Sandy's pained face looked back at them. They were passing the scene of the accident now. An image came into Meg's mind of Savage tromping through the woods with an axe in his hand, he'd said to dismember the dead deer. She'd pre-judged him, just as some of the villagers were now doing to her and Marc. Steve was never a danger to her, she saw now, he was just a troubled man who had lived through something terrible when he was a kid and never recovered. The real enemy was in her own home.

Janette.

'I'm not sure but I think Tim might have been Daniel's mole inside the Kent police for a while now. Tim recently retired but he may well have his ear to the ground still. I saw them having a pint together in a pub in Ashford a month or so ago,' Sandy said.

Marc groaned again.

Sandy brought the car to a halt at the place where the road turned and led to the driveway to Covert Cottage.

'Are you sure about this?' she said.

Meg and Marc both nodded. Meg squeezed Marc's hand.

He pulled his collar up and plucked a beanie from his jacket pocket. Meg slunk low in the back seat. The car moved forward and Covert Cottage came into view through the trees. Meg blinked and gasped.

Three strands of barbed wire sat above the highest slat, making the gate impossible to climb. A heavy chain hung from the latch picket to which was attached a shiny new padlock the size of a fist and the house nameplate had been replaced by an ugly metal sign reading, *Private Property. Trespassers will be prosecuted.* At every window were new shutters and an iron gate guarded the front door from where a camera still blinked. Meg remembered the trunk containing Lily's pink cardigan, the blanket she carried around, her pale yellow party dress, the little sock she'd found that might once have belonged to Cecily.

'So, from what I heard, she's saying that the security was your idea, Meg, because you're afraid of what Marc might do.'

Meg put her head in her hands and the car moved on until Covert Cottage was no longer in view.

FIFTY-TWO

Sandy parked outside the vicarage and they made their way inside, checking to make sure they had not been spotted. Meg's legs felt wobbly and her heart pounded as if it were desperate for someone to open a door out of her chest and into the world, but she had had long hours at the unit to think about exactly this moment and she was ready for it. A short way away, inside the Palterer's Arms, Daniel Idris sat waiting, a half pint of something at his side. He'd agreed to meet them on the promise of new information about the death of Steven Savage. Marc would make his way to the vicarage and await Helen's instructions. It was best if he stayed out of view. So far it seemed Idris had been ready to believe that Marc was responsible, but Helen and Sandy seemed to think he'd be open to hearing the alternate view. They'd share with him what they knew about the case and outline their suspicions about Janette. He'd told Sandy that he hadn't spoken to Janette directly, but once they'd told him what they knew, he'd surely want her side of the story. Whether she accepted his invitation to meet or not, it was a win-win for Idris. They'd given him new information on the case which he could pursue if he chose to.

The first part of the plan worked like a dream. Idris listened attentively and could hardly wait for them to finish speaking before he was picking up his phone and tapping in Janette's number as Meg dictated it to him. Idris switched to speakerphone and held a finger to his lips to signal for Sandy, Helen and Meg to be silent. They waited.

Soon Janette's unmistakable, velvety voice said, 'Who is this?'

Idris introduced himself.

'What do you want?'

Idris outlined his idea of an interview, adding that of all the people in Coldwater, other than Meg, Janette knew Marc best.

'With your expertise, you might be able to shed some light on his psychological state.'

Janette seemed to hesitate before gathering herself. 'Who do you think killed Steven Savage?'

It was a test but Idris was too good a journalist to take it on. Instead he said simply, 'I'm interested in your view.'

'I see. Well, in my professional opinion, Marc's homicidal tendencies were evident. It was only a question of time.'

Meg clamped a hand over her mouth and swallowed a gasp.

Idris's gaze flicked to her before he gathered himself and in a calm voice full of flattery he said, 'Fascinating. I would be so interested to hear more, Ms Hopwood. But this is probably a conversation best had face to face. I'd only need you for an hour. I'm actually at the Palterer's right now. Would you allow me to buy you a drink in, say, fifteen minutes?'

There was a pause on the line. Meg caught Helen's eye. She gave a tight smile. Finally the voice said, 'Well, I suppose. But I don't want to be named. Professional boundaries. I'm sure you understand.'

'Absolutely,' Idris said and ended the call.

Meg, Helen and Sandy hurried from the pub and settled themselves in the kitchen at the vicarage with Marc. Then they waited while Sandy retrieved the bolt cutter and saw. After ten minutes she left and went to the church from where she would be able to see Janette's arrival. Seven minutes later she was back.

'She's there.'

Marc and Meg threw on their outerwear, hiding the bolt cutter and saw under their coats and on Helen's signalling the all-clear, hurried up the track, past Savage's house, to the gate and onto the path through the fields. The wind was up, the trees in Covert Wood a frenzied Mexican wave as if anticipating some darkly thrilling event. A bullfight perhaps or a show trial. Above the fringe of branches, buzzards banked like drones. Meg stopped for a moment, stirred by the spectacle. To her the wood had never seemed more hectic nor more sinister. Shivers chased along her torso, and she had to hurry to catch up with Marc.

On they hurried until finally they arrived at the back gate to Covert Cottage. A large bunch of St Cecilia roses lay on the ground, tattered and frost-burned. Meg bent down and gently moved them to one side. Over the weeks she had come no closer to discovering who left the flowers and why, but it was way past their season now, so someone had to be growing them in a glasshouse, only to leave them out here to die. Even now, in the midst of so much else, she felt a pang of sadness at the thought.

They had no other plan than to let themselves into the house in the hope of finding something – documents, police records, interview transcripts, letters, photographs or objects – either in the few remaining boxes of Jimmy's effects or hidden somewhere among Janette's – Jean's – things which might add weight to the idea that Jean Hopwood had pursued a vendetta against Jimmy, and by extension Marc, for decades. If what Pete had said was to be believed – and there was no reason not to believe him – she'd resorted to stalking, deception, threatening and identity fraud to try to win Jimmy back. From the Australian records that Idris had unearthed it seemed that she had gone over there to start a new life, only returning to London some time shortly after Lily's death to wreak havoc on the life of his son. They were in no doubt that the woman they were dealing with was dangerous. So far there was reason to believe she'd tampered with a vehicle, drugged and effectively kidnapped Meg, interfered with a police investigation and even, possibly, murdered a man and tried to get Marc arrested for the killing. She must have known when she ran into him that there was a possibility Pete might recognize her. Maybe she'd imagined that she was living on borrowed time and needed to get Marc and Meg firmly out of the way before Pete came to his senses. There was no doubt in Meg's mind that Jean Hopwood was very, very dangerous.

She punched in the code to the back gate. Nothing. Damn. Jean had changed the combination. They tried her birthday, then Jimmy's birthday and Marc's, plus a few other generically obvious combinations but nothing worked. Jean was too smart for that.

Time was moving on. It had already taken twelve minutes to reach the cottage. Meg felt the flutter of a creeping panic. The camera seemed to have been installed but unless Jean happened to be looking at the feed right then she would be unlikely to see them. They could, of course, saw through the door or maybe even cut through the bolt but she would know they were on to her.

'It won't be any date we could guess,' Meg said, finally.

They stood in the wind for a moment scratching their heads.

'Something to do with her pregnancy,' Meg said finally. 'Or maybe Jimmy.'

Without wasting a moment Marc was on the phone to Pete.

'All the dates you can remember,' he said, having explained briefly what he needed. 'First date, anniversary, whatever you've got.'

Pete had to scan back over the years. He drew a blank on Jimmy and Jean's first date but he did remember the date that Jean had her abortion because Jimmy had met him in the pub afterwards to watch the FA Cup final. Everton vs Man United. He wasn't sure of the year.

Marc googled and shouted over the wind to Meg to enter some combination of 18.05.85 and mouthed the word 'abortion'. As Meg plugged in the numbers she considered that 18 May 1985 may have represented more than the termination of a pregnancy to Jean. Perhaps it was the day hope died and in its place revenge had begun to stir.

The lock clicked open. She pushed the gate and stepping onto the path, made her way past the studio and the old yew, with Marc following on behind. At the back door she entered the same code and once again, the lock gave way. Had Jean been truly in her right mind, she might have anticipated this and used a different number but it was obvious now that for decades Jean Hopwood had been driven by a single maddening obsession, to get back at Jimmy for his desertion. When that proved impossible she became bent on destroying Marc. And now, finally so close to succeeding, she'd begun to slip up.

They let themselves into the mudroom and were surprised to see it almost empty. A faint pulse seemed to reverberate from somewhere beneath them.

Meg whispering: 'What's that?'

Marc moved over to the door to the basement and flung it open. The thrum grew ever so slightly louder. He flipped on the light switch and slowly descended the steps. Moments later he re-emerged and switched off the light. She waited while he brushed some dust from his hands and shook himself. 'Definitely something weird down there. An atmosphere.'

Meg thought about what Steve had said previously, about the cottage sitting on the site of a portal. But it wasn't helpful to remember that. Not now.

They moved into the kitchen. Here, too, all their personal effects had been removed. Family pictures, an apron digitally printed with Marc's face that Meg had given him as a Christmas present, the metronome Meg had brought Marc, all gone. Meg and Marc exchanged looks. Meg glanced at the kitchen clock. No time for discussion. 'You check down here, I'll look upstairs and in the attic.'

'What are we looking for?'

Meg shrugged. 'I don't know exactly. Evidence.'

Marc nodded and headed back into the mudroom while Meg went into the hallway. From the living room came the smell of burning wood. It seemed Jean had left a fire smouldering in the grate which suggested she wasn't intending to stay out long. Gathering herself, Meg hurried along the hallway and took the stairs two by two until she reached the upstairs landing. She took a breath to calm her nerves and went over to the hatch leading into the attic. Her hand reached for the pole in the corner and with it she pulled down the steps, locked them into place and began her ascent. The atmosphere in the attic space seemed alive and brimming as if the dead were gathered here. Her thoughts went immediately to Lily, then to Cecily and on to Christopher Griffin. To Jimmy and Astrid, back and back, through the thicket of time to the generations of dead, unknown to her by name, who had made Covert Cottage their home. Unable to free herself from their presence she went over to the trunk and opened the lid. There sat the yellow party dress and the books and plush toys that had once seemed such a familiar part of her everyday life but even now had taken on the fragile, timeless feel of old mementoes. She took out the pink cardigan and the little pink sock and stuffing them inside the pocket of her jacket, closed the trunk, stood up and brushed the dust from her jeans. Full of grim purpose now, she cast her eyes around the remainder of the space looking for anything that might throw light on Jean's current intentions or act as evidence of her past misdemeanours but the trunk aside, the attic was more or less empty. She made her way back down the steps to the landing where Marc was standing with his hands on his thighs, doing his best to catch his breath. The blood raced to her head and made her spin.

'There's a…' he was panting, falling over his words, '… slick of brake fluid…in the garage. Makes me wonder if this is the first time she tampered with the Spider. The coroner at Astrid's inquest only said that the probability was that the brakes had failed but the car was so badly damaged that there was no way to know for sure. Dad had to rebuild it virtually from scratch.'

Meg froze, struggling to take this in. It wasn't proof of anything in the way that you could bring it to a courtroom, but it was significant and they both knew it.

'I wanted to take a picture but I think my phone must have dropped out of my pocket on the way over here.'

Meg drew out hers from her jacket. It had been handed to her on the way out of the unit but it hadn't been charged and the battery was now in the red zone. Marc took it and dashed back down the stairs, leaving Meg to head for the spare bedroom where Jean Hopwood's bags sat unopened in one corner. Meg unzipped a tan leather holdall and began to turn over the contents. Underneath a pile of neatly folded cashmere she came upon a small zipped pouch in green velvet, of the kind that women generally kept for their jewellery. Instead of a dress watch or pair of earrings, there sat inside a single glass phial.

Marc was hovering in the doorway. She held up the phial and read out the label. 'Ketalar 50mg ketamine. That explains why I felt so out of it.'

'You poor darling. Why didn't the police find it when they searched the place?' Marc said. He sounded angry.

'They weren't looking in Janette's things.'

'If I'd had the slightest inkling...' She laid a hand on his chest to stop him. There was no time for guilt or regret now.

'There's no way to prove she actually gave it to me,' Meg said.

Marc shook his head. 'She's always one step ahead.'

'She's had decades to think about it.'

They resumed their search, unpacking clothes, feeling

in the pockets, unzipping pouches, rifling through bundled documents, each working their way through a different case, hopeful that they would find the small chink that Janette had left open. And when they did, they were finally going to expose it to the light.

FIFTY-THREE

Marc stood frozen to the spot while his head boiled and all around him a dark aura was gathering. He sensed that any moment Meg would look up and see what he saw and then she too would know what he knew now. He wished he could stop time, distil their lives into just this moment. He could protect her then, could return to his search and pretend he hadn't found anything but then the truth would never be uncovered. He would have to take it to his grave. Where would that leave him? Where would that leave Meg? Of all people didn't she have the right to know? He felt hemmed in with questions that had no obvious answers. He loved her and he loved Lily and that was about as much as he had right now. The months of uncertainty, the night-time hours of terrible grief, all that seemed to have receded in his mind now. He was back in the before time. How he wished he could stay there. Just him, Meg and Lily. Oh to be able to stop the clock, to hold on to time, to be able to buy Meg just one more second of innocence. But that was nothing more than a fantasy. He had come to a crossroads and whichever path he chose now he knew that he would always remember this moment as the one when the final piece of the jigsaw slotted into place.

Sensing something was wrong, Meg turned. One more second of innocence. One more tiny moment of stillness. But it was not to be. He watched as her eyes went first to his eyes then travelled for what seemed like an age down his body until they alighted on the red baseball hat he was holding in his right hand. Then her face seemed to grow huge and there was a wildness in it he'd never seen before and sensed that he might never again. Her skin turned ashen, as if all the blood had drained from her body. The eloquence of her silent fury terrified him. In that moment, it seemed to him she might be capable of anything.

'This might not be what we think it is,' Marc said. In that moment he would have said anything for the evidence in his hand to be indicative of anything other than what it patently was. He knew, as Meg must, that given what they knew now, how unlikely it was that the driver in the red cap who had killed their daughter was anyone other than Jean Hopwood. Which meant that the cap in his hand was a memento, a souvenir, of the worst thing that could ever happen to a parent. To witness your child murdered in a vendetta, a blood feud you had no idea even existed.

Without missing a beat, Meg said, 'I swear I will bury Jean Hopwood.'

He moved closer, desperate to hold on to her, to clutch her tight, to make the agony of the realisation easier. As she rose and ran from the room, he felt the cap fall from his fingers. He did not follow her. There was nothing she wanted from him now.

His body folded and he found himself slumped on the floor with the red cap beside him. In all this time he had not cried, had not been able to bring himself to shed a tear for fear that the tears would never stop. From the bathroom he could hear the sound of Meg being violently and repeatedly sick. His eyes burned but he choked back his feelings. He told himself there would be time for that.

Moments later Meg reappeared, wiping the back of her hand across her mouth. There was an unboundedness to her, an unbroachable energy. Her eyes were hard and dazzling. He had seen her like this once before, just after Lily was born. It was as if she had finally come back to herself. Slowly she opened her mouth to speak and, in a calm, resolute voice, she said, 'No more creeping around as if we have something to hide. I'm staying here, in *our* house.'

They went back down the stairs, Meg first, Marc following on, and into the living room to wait. Whatever it was that they could hear in the basement seemed to have made its way here now and it felt as if the walls were alive and moving in on them.

Time passed. They continued to wait. Outside, the light had begun to fade into a winter gloom. From time to time one of them spoke to comfort the other. Marc threw another log on the fire. The wood cracked and spat. There seemed to be voices other than their own in the room now, though Marc could not say for sure that he could hear them, only that he sensed their presence somehow. Was this what Meg had meant all these weeks when she'd said that the cottage groaned and creaked with the restless dead? He didn't know and in a sense it didn't matter. He was concerned with the living now. He saw how tense Meg seemed. Was it foolish just to sit here and wait for Jean to return? Shouldn't they be doing something?

And then it was too late. The purr of an engine and the faint crunch of the car tyres on the gravel. Meg's eyes blazed. She darted a look at him. He raced to the door, pulled it closed and stood with his back to it. Moments later they heard the click of the combination lock. Marc's heart thrummed in his chest. The sound of a footstep, then silence, as if she was sensing the air and wondering if something had changed. A sweeping sound as she removed her coat followed by a faint click of the hanging chain on the hook. One step, then another. She was halfway down the hallway. The sound of her footsteps turning to go into the kitchen. He blinked. At that moment a loud crack came from behind them. Marc's eyes turned to the grate. An ember had flown out and landed on the rug. It began to smoulder. The footsteps stopped. The adrenaline was like hot oil pouring through his arteries. Protect Meg. He was ready. The door handle turned. The pressure on his back as Jean tried to push it open, gently at first, and then with more force. There was silence.

A soft sound, almost a laugh. Then the unmistakeable voice said, 'Open the door.'

Marc hesitated. He saw Meg pull out her phone. She tapped on the screen and turned it towards him so he could see that the device was now recording. Then she put it in her pocket, went over to the fireplace and plucked the poker from the stand. On her nod he stood back from the door. A moment or two later, Jean Hopwood entered. She saw Marc first and if she was surprised, she did not show it. Her eyes flared when she saw Meg. Clearly, she hadn't expected them both. Marc saw her gaze land on the poker.

'Meg, dear.'

Meg shook her head. 'Don't you dare.'

Jean's eyebrows raised and her forehead wrinkled.

Meg went on, 'We found the red baseball hat you wore when you murdered our daughter.'

There was a moment, less than a moment, a millisecond perhaps, when Marc thought that Jean was about to crack. Stumbling over her words, she said, 'I... I don't...' He watched her collect herself, '...you think I had something to do with that?'

'This is not one of your games, *Jean*,' he said, using her real name.

She blinked, a savage composure on her face. What he would have given then to put his hands around her neck and squeeze the life from her.

'I see you've done some research,' she said. The glassiness had returned to her eyes and a thin half smile began to play on her lips. 'Very flattering of course, but what does a baseball cap and a name change prove?'

Marc began. 'You remember Pete? He was at our party here only a few weeks ago. He has a photograph of you the night Jimmy met Astrid. Not much of a grand night out for you, I'm guessing. Not even able to drink your sorrows away. Were you still pregnant at that point, or had you had the abortion by then?'

She let out a yelp which sounded more like the cry of a wounded animal than anything human.

'We know it was you who tampered with the Spider. Twice.'

A laugh now. But he could see her chest heave and there was a faint tremble in her hands. They'd rattled her.

'Meg, dear, you're not going to let him control you like this, are you? Because it won't stop, you know?'

Meg stood frozen to the spot. For a second he thought she was considering what Jean was saying until he saw that she was actually fishing in her pocket. Using a tissue to pull out the phial of ketamine, she said, 'This will have your fingerprints on it.'

Her face twitched and suddenly, in a voice as sharp as a steak knife, Jean said, 'What makes you think anyone is going to believe either of you?'

And then, just as suddenly, she began to cry.

Meg looked at him, unsure what to think. Marc took a step towards her and as he moved, the red cap fell from his pocket.

For a moment they froze. Marc bent to retrieve the cap and as he stood Jean, taking advantage of the instant, rushed him and with both arms on his shoulders, pushed him backwards with tremendous, almost super-human force. He felt himself stumble, nothing he could do to stop the fall. As his feet slipped from under him he saw Jean dart forwards and grab the poker from Meg's hands. He hit the ground and felt something in his shoulder pop as it slammed into the floor. For a moment the shock took away all the pain. He felt dazed and bewildered. Above him Jean loomed, the poker raised above her head. He scrambled to get up and as he did so a searing pain surged through his shoulder and back. No power there whatsoever. He cried out and repeated the move, without his right arm this time, his eyes glued to Jean's. There was no pity in her.

He heard a clanking sound of metal hitting flesh. For an instant he thought, *I'm done for.* But at the same time his mind was telling him something different. He struggled to fit the two versions of himself together but when he looked up at Jean he saw at once that her expression had changed to one of astonishment. Marc stared transfixed as Jean began to buckle. There was a terrible shriek as she went down, as the poker clattered onto the floor. Marc scrambled to his feet, his right arm hanging uselessly at his side. He heard himself cry out, his shoulder a flaming sail whipped up into a rage by a pitiless wind. His eyes screwed shut as he braced against the physical agony.

Meg seemed frozen with the shock of the moment, the coal shovel she had rammed against Jean's back held firm in her hand. Jean lay a couple of metres away. She was moving and groaning but she was conscious. He looked at his right shoulder. He could see where the humerus was pushed forward out of its socket.

Meg said, 'I'm calling an ambulance.'

'No!' He went over to her and in as calm a voice as he could muster, said, 'The ambulance comes, all hell will break loose. We're never going to get this chance again, Meggie.'

Meg blinked and swallowed and he shot her an encouraging look. On the floor beside him Jean was groaning, not badly injured but not getting up any time soon either. And so it was the two of them now, just the two of them, together. He'd been on a course to prevent musculoskeletal injuries in musicians way back when. He knew how it could be done. He gave her a steady look. 'I want you to put my shoulder back. I can give you instructions. Please, Meggie, do this for us.'

He saw her take a deep breath. Nodding grimly Meg followed him as he went over to the sofa and lay down, his useless right arm hanging limp and already beginning to swell. He told her to sit on the floor and brace her legs against the sofa, then to grip his hand and to place her other hand on his lower arm. As she took hold of him it felt as if a fierce, sharp spear had penetrated the bone. He swallowed back a scream.

'The ketamine,' she said. 'For the pain.'

He shook his head. He needed his mind to be sharp, telling Meg to pull his arm firmly and evenly and hard. 'If I cry out, don't stop.' All pain, he realized, as he felt the tug, was the same. Psychological or physical. There was no essential difference between the two. He'd already endured the worst pain that could be visited on a person. Compared to the pain of losing Lily, this? This was nothing. 'Harder,' he said. Beside him, Meg redoubled her efforts. He felt the humerus slide under the shoulder blade and back into place. His shoulder burned like hell but he didn't care.

He stood up and shook his legs and felt himself arrive back in his body. Beside him, Meg looked on, either shocked into silence or thinking something through, he wasn't sure which.

Meg, anxious, saying, 'What do we do now?'

Marc felt oddly calm, as if nothing much mattered though he knew, in fact, that nothing had ever mattered more. He looked at the figure lying on the carpet and remembered the time, not so long ago, when he loved her.

But that was then.

'We want a confession. Lily, Astrid, Steve. Then maybe we'll call for help.'

Jean remained on the floor, one hand clenched into a fist, the other nursing her back. She pressed her lips together and shook her head. There was an odd glassiness in her expression. Pain perhaps? Or something else?

Marc went to the French doors into the garden, checked they were locked and took out the key. No exit that way. He moved to the entrance into the hallway and waited for Meg to follow him then he closed the heavy door behind them and went into the kitchen, returning moments later with one of the kitchen chairs which he jammed up against the handle of the door into the living room, checking that it held firm.

When he returned to the kitchen Meg was waiting for him with a glass of water and a couple of pills. 'Just paracetamol.' He took them. His shoulder was no longer agonising, but he was clammy and shaky and the pain remained intense and it would take a while before the swelling began to subside and he would be able to use his arm properly.

In a low voice, Meg said, 'Now what?'

'We wait.'

FIFTY-FOUR

It would have been easier on Meg if she'd lost her humanity. But it didn't happen. An hour or so after they'd locked Jean in the living room, she moved the chair from the door and went in carrying a glass of water and a couple of painkillers.

Jean was lying on the sofa. As Meg put the glass of water and the pills on the table beside her, she blinked and twisted her head ever so slightly so that she was looking up at Meg. Her eyes burned.

'Marc is right outside the door in case you're thinking about doing anything silly.'

Jean shook her head. 'What are you going to do to me?'

'I don't know,' Meg said.

The light was low now through the French windows, the sunset not far off, and in its golden glow Jean's face seemed as soft and welcoming as it had the first day they had met, in London Fields, all those months ago.

'Maybe we can only ever expect to be loved for a while,' Jean said.

'Maybe,' Meg said. A part of her wanted to get up and go, so that she would never have to see this woman or to listen to that velvety voice again, but there was another, more insistent part, that could not bring herself to do it. She wanted to understand. She owed that to Lily. And maybe if she could understand this woman who had taken Lily from her, then perhaps, in some way, she would discover something about herself which would help her to live in the aftermath of her daughter's death. And maybe she owed that to Marc and to herself.

She gestured to the sofa. Jean looked taken aback for a moment before nodding. And so Meg sat down next to her daughter's killer. For a long time there was silence between them, which was broken only by the odd crack and creak of the fire in the grate. There was something terrible about their predicament, the unbreakable bond they now shared. But there was something almost beautiful about it too, something elemental which Meg understood that she would not get back again.

Eventually Jean said, 'I wrote a letter explaining things. In case something like this happened. I slid it down the back of the radiator in the studio.' She turned her head towards the garden and then back to Meg. If Meg wondered, even for an instant, whether this was some new trick, another means by which Jean worked her dark magic, then the look on the woman's face made her think again.

'Why don't you get it?' Jean said, simply.

Getting up from the sofa, Meg went through the living room door, replacing the chair. Marc was waiting for her. She told him what Jean had said.

'I'll come with you,' Marc said, immediately. 'There's no way she can get out of the living room and I wouldn't put it past her to have laid some trap for us.

'I don't think so, not this time,' Meg said. There was

something about the way Jean had told her that sounded final somehow. Still, there was no point in taking the risk of going alone. They let themselves out of the back door down the path by the climbing rose, past the raised beds of what was to become the vegetable patch, brushing the leathery leaves of the old yew, and found themselves at last by the studio. To the west in the sky above Covert Wood the setting sun blazed red. Meg made for the front door but Marc stopped her.

'I'm doing this,' he said. He opened the door, switched on the light, then stepped inside. A minute later he was back, holding in his hand a large plain Manilla envelope which he handed to Meg. 'Open it.'

The envelope had been sealed. She hooked her right thumb under the edge of the flap but before she began to tear something stopped her. A strange flickering at the edge of her vision. Instinctively she looked up and as she did her nose flared with the unmistakeable odour of burning. As they sprinted up the path the smoke was already billowing from the French windows. Two columns of fire shot up on either side as the curtains caught light. There was a loud whump and the glass of the French windows cracked, sending glass shards scattering across the patio. Meg and Marc looked at one another. Meg felt her insides melt. She thought about Jean but there was no way they could approach the living room from the exterior. It would be too dangerous.

'I'm going in.' She felt Marc's left hand on her arm and he tried to hold her back but she shook him off. As she raced towards the back door he was following behind. In the kitchen the smell of smoke hit her but it was by no means overwhelming, which meant that there must still be some time. Meg, grabbed tea towels, held them under the tap, then handing one to Marc wrapped another around her face and the third around her right hand. She turned to see Marc struggling to fit his, his right arm still weak and swollen. She pulled out her phone to call for help only to find that the battery had died.

The keys to the Fiesta were lying on the surface. She grabbed them and held them out to Marc.

'You can drive with one hand. Get help.'

Marc put the keys in his pocket. 'I'm not leaving you.'

'Just go.'

He shook his head. No time to argue. Together they ran to the hallway, Meg screaming Jean's name.

Smoke was snaking out from under the door to the living room. Meg pulled the chair away and reached out for the handle with her bandaged hand. A voice behind the door shouted. She couldn't make out the words over the growling flames but she knew that voice and she knew too that there was no panic in it, no alarm, no fear even.

The handle refused to move.

'Jean!' Meg dropped to the floor and peered through the gap between the bottom of the door and the floorboards. The smoke hit her nostrils. Acrid now. She held her breath and blinked, saw what looked like a chair leg. Beyond that the faintest intimations of movement. She got up.

'She's dragged furniture to the door and blocked herself in.'

The fire alarm in the kitchen was sounding now and the security alarm had begun blaring. Marc, skin already reddening from the heat, was shouting, 'Get out by the front door. I've got this.'

Meg had no intention of leaving him, instead standing by

while he took a short run and kicked the door hard with his right foot. When nothing moved he repeated the action. Then rushed forward again, this time using his good shoulder as a battering ram. Still the door did not move. He was taking in more smoke, yelping as his shoulder slammed into the door and then reeled back, choking.

On the fifth attempt Meg put a stop to it. 'No more. We have to leave before it's too late.'

The heat was intense and beginning to bubble the paint on the hall side of the door. Smoke billowed from beneath, obscuring the entrance to the kitchen. It was too dangerous to go back that way. Their best hope was through the front door. They hurried along the hallway, keeping one eye on the door behind them, Meg sensing that there would only be one chance. Once the front door was opened a backdraft would cause the flames to leap forward into the hallway. For some reason the day of the hit-and-run came back to her. Lily's hand slipping from hers. The blue or, some said, silver car with the driver in the red baseball cap. And in that instant something odd happened. For the first time since before Lily died Meg felt completely calm. She took Marc's one good hand.

'Ready?'

At his nod she threw the door open and they burst onto the driveway. There came a tremendous roar as the flames curled around the living room door then shot through the hallway. For an instant they stood in the driveway frozen to the spot. Then the moment passed and they were running towards the old Fiesta. As she popped the lock they heard a roaring sound and a gaping hole opened up in the roof, tiles collapsing into it. She saw smoke then flames emerge and she felt something leave her body and float on the thermals and she was light, suddenly, almost as light as air.

Marc was cradling his bad arm. 'You'll have to drive.'

She pressed her lips and blinked. She was calm now, all her fear of getting behind the wheel gone. They clambered inside. As she pushed the key into the ignition ash pattered on the roof. She took off the handbrake and lifted her gaze to the padlocked gate. Of course. She'd forgotten.

Marc, reading her mind, said, 'Just floor it.'

She took a deep breath and slammed her foot on the accelerator.

The car jumped and bolted. There was a snapping sound of metal on metal as it slowed and ground into the chain around the gate. Then it sprang open and they were out. There came a furious roar then, as though the cottage had fallen in on itself.

'Don't look back,' Marc said.

She didn't.

FIFTY-FIVE

They drove straight to the vicarage. Helen let them in and reported the fire to the emergency services. She wanted to call an ambulance because of Marc's arm but he brushed her off. Neither he nor Meg felt like talking much. Their faces were greasy, hair coated in ash. Helen brought them towels and each took a shower while Sandy dug out some fresh clothes from donations she had washed in preparation for an upcoming church jumble sale. While they were dressing, they heard the distant sound of sirens. Not long after, Sandy's phone began to chime with the news of the fire and she went to join the villagers who were already gathering in The Lane by Covert Cottage. While they waited for news, Meg and Marc sat in the living room. Marc, staring at the fireplace, saying nothing, feeling nothing but the adrenalin draining from his system. The tremble of Meg's limbs beside him. When he looked at her next, her cheeks were wet with silent tears. He held her as well as he could.

They heard the sound of ice cubes clinking and Helen appeared carrying coffee and whisky.

'Sandy just texted. The police have cordoned off the area around the cottage. She's going to stay just in case someone from the emergency services is willing to give them an update.'

They each picked up their glasses and took a few sips.

'I wanted to look into her eyes when she admitted to killing our daughter.' Meg rubbed away her tears with the back of her hand, more angry than sad suddenly.

Helen said, 'It's possible that the firefighters might have found her alive.'

Meg was shaking her head. 'She wanted to go. She was ready. The only person who ever made Jean do something she didn't want to was Jimmy.'

Marc, remembering Jean's letter, said, 'The envelope?'

Meg rose to fetch it and came back with an anxious look on her face. She thumbed the remainder of the seal and pulled out the contents, three sheets of paper neatly folded over so that only the blank side of the topmost sheet showed. She steadied herself, then, with her right hand, slowly opened the fold. Marc waited, holding his breath. Beside him, Meg hastily shuffled the pieces of paper then held them up, turning each so that Helen and Marc could see what was written there.

Nothing.

'*What?*'

'Maybe I just...' Meg went back to the envelope and checked inside, turning it upside down and shaking it hard. She held up the pieces of paper to the light.

'Invisible ink?' offered Helen.

Meg turned down her lips and shook her head. 'Not Jean's style.'

'We could try at least,' Helen went on. She got up and returned a moment later carrying half a lemon.

Meg, handing her a sheet, thanked Helen for taking the trouble. Marc, on the other hand, felt irritated by his sister, though he knew she was only trying to help. So here it was, the final petty act of revenge. To deprive them of a confession. How Jean would have enjoyed their confusion. It was as if she were laughing at them even now. Who was Jean Hopwood? What drove her? Questions they'd almost certainly never know the answers to. It felt to him then that her death was as much a performance as her life had been.

'Well,' Helen said, giving up on the lemon idea, 'it was worth a go.' She sat back and took a small sip of her whisky.

Even now, knowing what he knew about Jean, hating her as he did, it was odd to find himself still, in some way, under her spell. He supposed that hate and love were bedfellows of a sort.

Just then the sound of Meg's mobile came from the kitchen where she'd plugged it in to Helen's charger. She got up and went out to fetch it and came back a moment later clasping it to her ear.

'If you could bring it to the vicarage that would be wonderful.'

She finished the call. 'That was Tim, the ex-copper. He found your mobile while he was walking his dog and ICEd it. He says he's going to drop it off here.'

'Shit,' Marc said. Hadn't Sandy told her Tim was fingering Marc for the Savage murder? He could make a lot of trouble if he thought Marc had been around Coldwater.

In a flash Helen said, 'I'll tell him you gave me the phone and I haven't been able to work out how to change the ICE. Don't worry, I know Tim; he'll be so thrilled to mansplain it to me that he won't suspect a thing.'

Marc and Meg went upstairs and waited in the bedroom

where they wouldn't be seen. Not ten minutes later the doorbell sounded. They heard Helen and Tim talking. The door closed and there came the sound of footsteps.

'I had the feeling he was trying to trip me up,' Helen said when she came to release them from their temporary prison. 'So, what happens now?'

'We stay as far away from Covert Cottage as we can.'

*

They drank strong coffee until they felt clear enough to sketch out a plan. Marc's phone would remain at the vicarage. Helen would drive them both to Ashford, where Marc would buy a burner and let Helen and Meg have the number. He'd board a train to London. In the unlikely event that the police checked the station cameras they'd see only that he'd gone to Ashford. Meanwhile Helen would drop off Meg at the psych unit. If asked she would say that Sandy had been preoccupied with the fire and that they'd wanted to get Meg back to the unit where she would feel safe and supported.

It was a long goodbye and a difficult parting. Marc passed the train journey from Ashford in a state of numb exhaustion. From St Pancras he took the tube to St John's Wood. Using the burner phone, he called Helen from outside the tube station. Put the cops off the scent if ever they traced the call. His sister told him that firefighters were still at the cottage but the roof had caved in and there was unlikely to be much left of the building.

'I see,' he said, as though he'd already known this. Sadness bloomed inside him but he knew somehow that it was better this way. 'Does Meg know?'

'Yes, we got a message to her at the unit.'

'How did she take it?'

'She seemed, I don't know, relieved almost.'

Something heavy rolled away as if Marc had pushed it. 'And how are you?'

'I don't feel anything, really. Except for you.'

They finished up the call. Marc found a bench, sat down and called Bunkin's personal mobile.

'Marc! You've changed your phone number. Is that a sign of something?'

'Fraternal love. I gave my old one to Helen.'

'I see,' Bunkin said in a measured tone. He wasn't about to ask for details. Less said and all that. 'Are you in London?'

'Of course.'

Sounding relieved, Bunkin went on, 'I was going to call you anyway. I suppose you've heard about the cottage? I saw something about it on my news feed. Rock star's former home and all that.'

'Yes, Helen called me.'

'I'm so terribly sorry.'

'Don't be,' he said. The words came easily now, as if they'd always been waiting to be said. 'It didn't bring us much luck, did it?'

'No, I suppose not. If one can think of a house that way.'

There was a pause while Marc waited for Bunkin to say something about the discovery of a body. Instead he went on, 'Well that's good then. The police might pay you a visit at your friend's house in…St John's Wood, is it? They might be prepared to escort you down to Coldwater tomorrow but don't be tempted to go on your own, will you? It's all about not making contact with anyone involved in the investigation into Savage's death. Potential witnesses and so forth. Ashford magistrates will probably go ahead with sentencing you for the assault, but in the circumstances, it's likely to be community service or a fine.'

'That's a relief.' Marc didn't like the idea of being held in suspended animation awaiting the outcome of the investigation. He supposed that the killing of Steve Savage was unlikely to be solved now that Jean was dead too, but there was no way to seek reassurance from Bunkin on this without revealing his hand, which he was not prepared to do, not even to his lawyer.

'Another thing. Man called Luke Stoddard contacted the office. Name ring any bells?'

'My cellie at Elmsley.'

'He's out now and wants you to call him. He didn't want to share the reason with my assistant, so your guess is as good as mine. I'll text you the number.'

They finished the call. The sky was now a bruisy purplish black. While waiting for Bunkin's text, Marc went to the nearest kiosk, bought some cigarettes and sat on a low wall outside the station for a smoke. He considered putting off the call to Luke then decided what the hell. He keyed in the number.

The two men caught up briefly. Luke had been let go after the case against him collapsed. But he got to the point quickly. 'I got a story for you, mate. Think you might like to hear it.'

'Oh yeah?' A tic started up in Marc's eye. Was this some attempt at blackmail?

'It's like I said, I owe you one.'

Marc felt himself relax. He couldn't think of a thing he would want from Luke, but he appreciated the gesture and didn't want to seem ungrateful or worse, antagonistic. Blokes like that could quickly turn nasty.

'About this geezer, Tim Nuttall, lives in Coldwater.'

The tic started up again.

Luke went on, 'Nutter, we used to call him. Private Tim Nutter.'

FIFTY-SIX

Luke met Nuttall in the Royal Artillery Logistic Corps, garrisoned at Shorncliffe near Folkestone in the Nineties. Remembered him because 'he was a bloody Bible-basher, did all that crossing himself, praying'. Luke went on, 'The rest of us squaddies, we all thought he was twisted, like. Anyway, I was out on a pass and Nutter came into the same pub. He was drunk, like, and he wanted me to keep him company. So we both got bladdered and we had to walk back to the barracks, just me and Nutter, and that was when he told me.'

Marc had had no idea where this was going, but Luke had drawn him in and he was anxious to see how the story unfolded.

'Well, I remember you said your wife was interested in that little girl what went missing.'

'Yes, Cecily Banner.'

'Well, see, I was plastered after Nutter told me, I thought maybe I'd dreamed it, but then it sort of came back to me over the years in dribs and drabs like.'

Marc cleared his throat. The pulse thumped in his neck.

'I thought about it a lot. But Nutter definitely told me he took her. He said he done two or three. Picked them out. They was all named after saints. He'd find them on the registry.

I don't know what registry, but he'd find them, and then he'd wait till it was, like, a particular saint's day, and then he'd take the one called after that saint. One of them had an unusual name, don't remember what he said exactly but it was something like Purple? He was specially proud of himself for that one. Took him a long time to find a girl with the right name.'

Marc waited for the skin-crawling feeling to subside, but it didn't and it was hopeless to expect that it would.

'Luke, you need to tell the police.' A passer-by stopped in her tracks as he said this, gave him a curious look and walked on.

He could sense Luke withdrawing. There was a silence and he said, 'Nah, man. Anyway, what I heard Nutter was one of them, so they weren't going to do nothing, were they? I didn't think much of it till I saw it in the paper.'

Marc felt his mouth dry. He swallowed hard and said, 'If I gave your number to a journalist, would you speak to him?'

There was a pause. In the background a girl could be heard singing Lisa's song. 'Uh, I dunno, mate,' Luke said. He sounded as if he'd said as much as he was willing to and was anxious to wind up the call. But Marc sensed that there was more and he wanted to make sure Luke told someone who could use the information. Someone like Daniel Idris.

Thinking on his feet he said, 'That Lisa?'

'Yeah, my angel.' Luke's voice warmed as he said this.

'They're all someone's angels, aren't they?'

Silence. Marc held his breath. The pulse in his neck was a drum roll now. At that moment a man sat beside him on the wall and he swivelled away. He didn't want Luke to know he was in a public space. Might make him nervous.

Time ticked by. Eventually with a dry laugh, Luke said,

'Look, mate, so long as I don't have to give my name, I'll talk to your geezer, all right? Give me his number.'

'Thank you.'

Marc texted him Idris's number and the two men finished the call. Marc pulled out the pack of cigarettes, lit one and took a long drag. The purplish sky had faded to a deep city grey but he didn't feel like moving. The day had drained him and if there had been anything left to give, anything left to feel, then the news about Nuttall had used it all up. He finished his cigarette and slumped on the bench, lit another and smoked that and the hours went past, buses arriving at their stops, people going to and fro, a shift change of buskers outside the organic food store. Every so often he checked social media for news of the fire. He and Helen exchanged messages. Twice they had a brief phone call.

He felt vaguely hungry but did nothing about it. The smokes helped quell his appetite. As the evening drew on, he began to feel the cold creep into his bones. The discomfort sharpened his thoughts. Meg had told him that Nuttall had arrived not long before Cecily's disappearance. A newly minted constable, he would have been perfectly positioned to keep the investigation close without having to take much, if any, responsibility for solving the case. Maybe Steve had seen Nuttall take Cecily that day and Nuttall held his position over Steve to keep him quiet and remained in the village to make sure he stayed that way. He was a local, so he could plausibly have suggested that the police look into Christopher Griffin. What if it had been Nuttall leaving the roses outside Covert Cottage? You heard about that on the TV shows, the killer memorialising the killing.

When the wind began to chill his bones, he checked the time

on his phone. 9.15 p.m. Rush hour long gone. He should get up, take himself back to Pete's place. He thought of Meg at the unit, most likely in bed, lights out, and wondered if she would finally sleep peacefully. For himself, he knew he would not. He thought of Jean, how much he hated her and how he wished she were still alive. Unfinished business. Standing, he shook out the stiffness in his limbs and made his way towards Pete's place.

The grand Georgian house was quiet; Pete and Debby were either out or had gone to bed early. The fancy cars in the driveway. He let himself in by the basement door and sat down on the pull-out bed, all at once wired and ready to drop. His shoulder ached and the rest of his body was beginning to join in. Stupid to have sat in the cold for so long. He wondered vaguely if he was trying to punish himself. He laid his phone on the floor and swung his legs up onto the bed. His eyelids began to droop. The phone lit up and began to buzz. He reached down and saw that Daniel Idris was calling.

'Hi.'

'I'm sorry to call you so late, Marc,' Daniel began. 'But I was hoping we might have a talk. Presumably, you've heard about...' his voice dimmed and grew solemn '...the cottage?'

'Yeah.' Marc sat up and swung his legs across the bed.

'The police have cordoned off the whole area. There's talk in the village that Jean's missing.'

Marc thought of the trees waving madly at the buzzards flying overhead.

'I feel I got roped into something. Look, I'm not accusing you of anything but I know you and Meg were there.'

'What did Jean say to you at the Palterer's?'

'We talked about Steve. She was very keen to drop you in it.'

'But you didn't believe her?'

'She can be very charming and persuasive. But no. I still want to know the truth and I think you can help me.'

'I already have.'

A pause. 'If you're talking about your mysterious friend, yes, he called me. Quite the story.'

'You believe him?'

There was a pause. 'It's going to be hard to stand up. The police don't like to implicate one of their own.'

'I know something about you, Daniel. Nuttall was your source in the Kent Police.'

A pause. 'I get it, Marc. You think I'm some wide-eyed rookie who got played.'

Marc rubbed his eyes and then his shoulder. He suddenly felt raggedy and exhausted. And old. So *old*.

'We all get played.'

'So now you know, what are you going to do about it?'

'First tell me about the fire.'

'It was already set. That's all there is to say.'

At that moment the garden security light came on and when Marc turned he saw that a fox had come right up to the French windows and was peering in. He moved towards it but the creature stood its ground and cocking its head to one side, blinked at him.

'Has Jean Hopwood had the last word?' Daniel asked.

Marc shook himself out of his reverie. 'Never,' he said, simply.

FIFTY-SEVEN

Marc appeared, carrying a bottle of beer and a mai tai with a little blue umbrella balanced on the glass. He put Meg's drink down on the table between their sun loungers.

'When in Hawaii...'

Meg picked up the cocktail and they clinked glasses and each took a sip of their drink.

'This is more like it,' Marc said, lowering himself back down onto the lounger.

'It'll do. Though I miss the psych unit.'

'As much as I miss HMP Elmsley?'

Meg took another sip of her drink and pretended to consider this. 'No, probably not that much.'

They'd flown in to Keāhole airport from LA where Marc, Pete and his crew had just finished wrapping up a three-week session recording 'Lisa' and a dozen other tracks for Pete's revival album, *The Grass Grows Greener and Other Lies*. Before that, they'd been back in East London where Marc had been painting a youth centre as part of his community service, and helping some at-risk kids to make the most of their musical talents. He was intending to return once 'Lisa' was out. The hope was that he'd earn enough royalties to set up a more permanent music programme there.

Covert Cottage was gone. What little of it remained untouched by the fire had been razed by bulldozers. Loss adjusters were in the process of determining an insurance payout. Helen had told them that someone had left a bouquet of St Cecilia roses on the site. Human remains had been found among the ashes. Jean Hopwood had been identified from her dental records and a scrap of skin on which was tattooed the words *Stat sua cuique dies*. Everyone has their day.

There was no desire to return to Coldwater. In time they would sell the land. Whoever bought it would doubtless build another house and, full of hope, step over the threshold to begin a new life in the shadow of Covert Wood. Meg would think of them every so often and hope they were okay.

They'd agreed that the insurance payout would go directly to Helen. She and Sandy had decided to stay put in Coldwater. There was a lot of mending to be done. As for Meg and Marc, who knew what their future might hold? For now they were just allowing themselves the luxury of feeling that they had one.

'Look,' Meg said. The sun's dimming had made the glow of tiny phosphorescent creatures buffeted by the waves more visible. She took in the wondrousness of it all, closed her eyes and sighed. As she opened them again Marc's phone began to buzz. It was Helen. He slid over to Meg's lounger so they could both be on the call. Helen's face appeared on the screen.

'Hey, Sparky, Meg. How's Hawaii?'

Marc held out the phone, waved it around to give Helen a view of the beach, the sun low over the sea and the painted sky, the phosphorescence of the sea.

'Oh my, you poor things,' Helen said once Marc and Meg were back in the frame. Sandy appeared beside her, waved briefly and said hi, then disappeared. 'Tell me all about it later. There's someone here who wants to see you both,' Helen said. The image wobbled and Daniel Idris appeared.

Marc glanced at the time. Wasn't Coldwater ten hours behind?

'We've been having breakfast together,' Helen said.

'I wanted to be at the vicarage when my piece about the missing girls went live,' Daniel explained.

Meg took a breath. She'd known the piece was likely to be published while they were away but *Kent Online,* which was breaking the story, hadn't given Daniel any firm date.

'Call us back when you've read it?' Helen said.

Marc said he would and finished the call. Turning to Meg, he said, 'You want to do this now? It all seems so far away.'

But Meg did. Very much. The Saint's Day case, as the disappearances of Cecily Banner, Perpetua Abdullahi and two other children had come to be known, had crept into her DNA. And at this moment, her DNA was in Hawaii.

Marc clicked onto the piece on his phone and side-hugged her close.

Former policeman arrested in Saint's Day case

Police have arrested a 65-year-old man, after a tip-off in the case of 6-year-old Cecily Banner who went missing more than thirty years ago. The alleged suspect, who is believed to be a former Kent police officer, is reported to be linked to a series of other cases of missing children, including the 1985 disappearance of 8-year-old Perpetua Abdullahi.

According to several sources, police have sealed off Covert Wood near the village of Coldwater and cadaver dogs are searching for remains. The families of Banner and Abdullahi have been informed.

Cecily Banner disappeared on 22 November 1992 while making her way to a friend's house. Two previous suspects in the case, Christopher Griffin, a local man, and Steven Savage, who was only 14 at the time and was the last to have seen her, have both since died. Griffin died by suicide in 1997 and police are still investigating the suspicious death of Savage whose body was found in Covert Wood on 22 November last year.

Perpetua Abdullahi went missing on 7 March 1985 after leaving mass at St Mary's Catholic church in Fordham, Kent, where the family had gone to celebrate the feast of St Perpetua. After extensive searches at the time, police drew a blank but the case into Abdullahi's disappearance remained open. Abdullahi's sister, Adebi Idris, told Kent Online, *'Not a day goes by when we don't think about Perpetua and we won't rest until we know her whereabouts.' Cecily Banner's family declined to comment.*

A tear dripped from Meg's chin onto the sun lounger, then another. Marc, squeezing her, said simply, 'At last.'

Meg nodded. A sob rose up and caught in her throat. Sad-happy. She did not feel like talking. She took the mai tai and drank half of it down in one. Then she replaced it on the little table beside the lounger and gave Marc the signal to go ahead.

Marc pulled up Helen's number in his recents. An instant later his sister reappeared.

'It's good news even though it's bad news,' Helen said.

Daniel materialised on screen.

'Congratulations,' Marc said. Meg gave a thumbs-up.

After the fire at Covert Cottage they'd handed in the pink sock to the police, who tested it and determined that there were skin fragments belonging to Cecily Banner trapped in the fibres. Someone, probably Sandy's father, Chris or her mother Charlotte, must have come across the sock in Covert Wood and picked it up and, perhaps understanding its significance, pressed it between the floorboards in the attic. Why they hadn't reported it no one knew. Maybe Chris didn't wish to attract more police attention. Maybe Nuttall had said something or even threatened them. In any case, another identical sock had been found during a search of Nuttall's property. Nuttall's DNA was found in both socks, along with skin fragments belonging to Cecily Banner and a single micro droplet of her blood.

'There's more,' Daniel said.

Meg looked at Marc. They waited. Meg picked up her drink again. It was turning out to be the kind of evening that called for it.

'I haven't yet come up with anything definitive about how Steve died but I've got one or two ideas...' There followed another, maddening, silence broken at last by Marc who said with less patience than he probably intended, 'And so...?'

'The BBC wants me to make a podcast about the case. I'd like to interview you.' He outlined his ideas for the show and promised them that they could decide how much of the Jean story they were willing to talk about. 'What do you say?'

Marc turned his gaze to Meg and raised an eyebrow.

'Give us a few days to think about it,' she said.

'When you get back, then?' Daniel said, persisting.

'Maybe.' Marc continued to search her face and as she held his gaze there came a realisation that for the first time since Lily's death there was nothing in his expression she wanted to turn away from. No crease or muscular tic, no bleakness in the eyes that had spoken only of his pain. For so many months they had been wandering in the dark, wintry forest of their grief, each lost to one another and to their truer selves. They could never leave the forest behind completely. Over and over across the years they would journey back to where there was some soft, sorry comfort that only they could understand. But here in Hawaii they had stumbled upon a clearing and in its dappled light a vista had opened up. It was nothing like the future she'd dreamed about and planned for, but here on what felt like the fringes of the world there was space to rest and gather themselves to go forward once more.

She was aware of the sound of her own voice. 'We're not sure we're coming back.'

From the corner of her eye Meg saw Marc press his lips together in an approving smile and turning away for a moment, she allowed her eyes to wander along the beach to the dimming sun and the deep and spangled sea.

Acknowledgements

Thanks to my supportive agent, Georgia Garrett, and to my hard-working editor Emily Kitchin, who both helped shape this book and supported me to write it. Cari Rosen and Eldes Tran did a great job of copyedityng and profing, and Seema Mitra and Clare Gordon made sure everything happened as it needed to. Any errors are entirely my responsibility. My gratitude goes to Lisa Milton and the team for keeping your promise. I've always felt at home at HQ. Dear friends Lynn Keane, Marina Benjamin, Ana DeJuan, Liz Vater and Laura Wilson helped see me through the ups and downs. Thank you. How lucky I am to know you. Though he will never read this, I want to express my gratitude to my sweet and eccentric dog Milo who daily accompanies me on the path. As always, very greatest thanks go to Simon Booker. You *are* jolly nice, as you are fond of telling me, but also tremendous, which you sometimes overlook.

Turn the page for an exclusive extract from *Two Wrongs*, a gripping and shocking psychological thriller from bestselling author Mel McGrath . . .

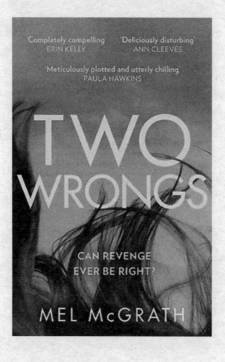

Prologue

The lights on the Clifton Suspension Bridge are dazzling in the thin Bristolian rain. The woman walks across it all the time on her way to and from her shift cleaning at the Royal Infirmary and even though it is a notorious suicide spot she has never yet seen anyone fall. But there is a first time for everything and as she spots a young woman clutching the railings of the suicide fence, the thought zips through her mind: this might be the time.

She hears herself call out reflexively – Hey! The young woman clutching the fence looks her way and for an instant hope surges in the woman who has just come off shift until the younger woman, turning back to face the gorge, reaches out and begins to climb the fence. There is a terrible purpose in the way she moves. The woman who has just come off shift knows that whatever she does now could make the difference between life and death, and knowing that, sensing it, makes the hairs on her skin lift and her heart hammer and her legs surge forward.

Still the young woman clambers upwards.

'Hey!' The woman who has just come off shift feels her breath quit. She is so tired. It was a long day at work and she cleans the A&E department and there is always so much blood and grease and body fluids and so many cups and snack wrappers to clear up. She is accustomed to seeing bodies and knows what that three-second flight from the bridge through the air and into the water can do to flesh and bones.

The young woman lifts one arm and shouts, 'Go away!'

The woman who has just come off shift stops in her tracks, three or four metres from the figure making her way up the fence. It is all in this moment. Life, death. She hears her own voice bark back, 'Please, stop!' The young woman freezes and shouts down.

'Stay where you are,' the young woman screams. 'I don't want your help!'

'OK, OK,' the tired woman replies, holding up her hands as if in surrender. 'But talk to me!' She has no idea what she is going to say but she knows that she must find a way to connect. The tiredness has drained from her. Her mind is razor sharp. If I let this happen, she thinks, what will I tell my kids? How will I live knowing I have let a woman die?

She wonders how the young woman can think of leaving this city that she loves so much, this wonderful, stone city with its dark history, its independent, almost feral people and its brilliant, hopeful bridge? She wonders if the young woman knows that this bridge was first conceived of by a woman with six children who drew up the plans and gave them to a man and refused to take any credit because women 'shouldn't be boastful'. Women are always building bridges, linking things, people, moving between worlds not made for them, always thinking up new ways to reach across the darkness, to connect.

She wants to ask the young woman why she is doing this,

how can anything be this bad, but she knows enough not to. Instead she shouts out, 'I'm Sondra, what's your name?'

The young woman turns her head. 'Satnam.'

'We've all felt like you're feeling now, Satnam,' the tired woman says. 'I'm older than you, so I know. But the feeling passes. It always passes.' They are more than strangers to each other now. Each has made her way indelibly into the other's experience, their history, the story of their lives.

Satnam shakes her head. 'I can't, I just can't.'

Her words are slurred. She's not in her right mind, Sondra thinks. 'Please, Satnam, come down from the fence. If we stand here any longer, we'll both be wet through. I live just the other side of the bridge. We can go and have a cup of tea. I've got chocolate chip Hobnobs! We can talk.'

Sondra reaches for her mobile phone to call the emergency services but, guessing at her purpose, Satnam shouts, 'No, no police!'

'OK,' Sondra says. 'No police. But let me call the Samaritans. You don't have to speak to them. You can just let me do the talking.' She'd love to call the Samaritans right now. They would know what to do and the tired woman has absolutely no idea.

Satnam's head is bobbing. She's mumbling, trying hard to remain conscious and on the fence. The wind is up, the bridge swaying minutely underfoot. Bristol is such a blowy city. The tired woman loves that about it. Every day is a bad hair day in Bristol. You can't be a Bristolian and be fussy about your blow-dry. What odd thoughts come unbidden when you're up against it. Sondra scopes around in her head for some better ones. 'I don't need to call the Samaritans. I can call anyone,' she says. 'Just give me a number.'

Satnam is looking at her now. She is so young and beautiful, with delicate, even features and long, black, unruly hair. 'I don't know any numbers. My phone...' She's losing focus, slurring her words. Sondra can't tell if this is a good thing or not. She takes a step closer. It's the wrong move. Satnam resumes her grip on the fence and climbs higher, balancing herself by bracing on the upright.

'OK, OK, I won't move. Is your phone here?'

Satnam nods. She's pointing away, towards the bridge tower. 'You left it over by the tower?' Satnam moans in response. Sondra says, 'Promise to stay there and I'll get your phone.' She walks backwards towards the tower, slowly, one step at a time. In a minute she's reached the spot where Satnam was pointing. One eye scouts about under the lights, the other remains on Satnam. It's hard to see. The rain is on her glasses and so much is in shadow. She wants to ask, What does it look like? What colour is it? But those questions will be wasting time and there is no time to waste. Besides, the young woman is growing more and more incoherent. Soon, she thinks, Satnam won't be able to say anything at all. Sondra's eyes sweep the paving on the walkway. Just as she is beginning to feel desperate, her foot makes contact with something. She bends and gropes at the pavement and there it is. An iPhone. Oh, what a relief! She has found it and it's an iPhone. Sondra also has an iPhone so she knows how they work.

'You need to tell me the passcode.' She thinks she hears one oh four oh but it's so slurred that might not be it. Hurriedly, she plugs in the numbers. And thank God, thank God, the homescreen appears.

Satnam says, 'Call Nevis.'

Nevis? Is that a last name or a first? Will Sondra find it in the contacts? Maybe, but it'll take too long. Another better idea bubbles up. She pushes the menu button and waits for the tone then speaks into the phone as clearly as she can. 'Siri, call Nevis.'

The phone speaks. 'Calling Nevis.'

At that moment the eye that is on the young woman registers movement. Sondra turns her head and sees that the young woman has jumped down onto the walkway and is dragging herself towards the gap in the fence where the suspension wire attaches to the bridge.

Oh God, thinks Sondra. I shouldn't have walked away. I shouldn't have left her. She's going to go and I'm not going to be able to pull her back. She feels herself take a leap forward and closes her eyes.

Chapter 1

Nevis

Nevis Smith, student mathematician, bird lover, and keeper of secrets, is lying on her bed in the flat she shares with Satnam Mann trying to finish a tricky piece of coursework on deep vent modelling when her phone bleeps with Satnam's ringtone.

'Hey, I thought you'd gone to bed already.' The door to Satnam's room was shut and the light was out when Nevis came in late from the library.

An unfamiliar voice replies. 'My name is Sondra. I'm with your friend Satnam on the Clifton Suspension Bridge. She wants you to come *straight away*. Please come, right now.'

Nevis says, 'Is she hurt?'

'Not yet, not yet, but she's in a bad way. Oh please. Don't call the emergency services. She's says that if she sees a blue light she'll jump. Please, I don't know what else to say to her, just *come*.'

The words hum and hiss and swirl around in Nevis's head. Is this some kind of joke? Or a scam? Someone playing a sick prank. What would Satnam be doing on the bridge past midnight? Why would this woman be calling? In any case what Sondra is saying is impossible because it's after midnight and Satnam is asleep in her bed.

And yet the urgency of the voice is unmistakeable. Nevis rushes into the hallway and throws open the door to Satnam's room. In the murky light she picks out the shape of an empty bed. There is something rancid in the air which she has never noticed before. Is she imagining things? She can hear her head drumming or is it her heart? What is happening? Nevis, who prides herself on thinking straight, can hardly think at all.

She reaches for the light switch and flips it on as if that might illuminate the inside of her head. But no. The bed remains empty. She walks around it and opens the wardrobe. She calls, 'Satnam?' and hears traffic outside and the clamour of her pulse. What is going on? As she turns to leave, her eye catches a bottle of vodka on the bedside table. How could she have missed it? She hurries over, picks it up, shakes the few remaining drops inside the bottle, puts it back down and feels the moving parts of her brain clicking into place at last.

Is this *The Moment*? she thinks. Has it come?

Honor always told her that in every life there is The Moment. It might be very small, like holding out a hand to stop a child stepping over a pavement, or very big, like giving the go-ahead for a doctor to flick the switch on a life-support machine. It may be saying yes or saying no. It might be as simple as making or taking a phone call. The Moment can steal up on you and arrive in the most unexpected minute of the most unexpected hour. It may hit hard or be so soft-footed that you may not hear it coming. Your life can be defined by it. It can be your making or your ruin.

Satnam is on the Clifton Suspension Bridge with Sondra. Satnam is... oh it's too horrible to think about but Nevis must steel herself. Satnam is in deep, deep trouble. This is my

Moment, she thinks. This is my time. Whatever decisions she makes, whatever action she takes now will be etched on her soul. She cannot escape this; she can only move towards it.

Nevis's hand is trembling so hard now that she can hardly hold the phone. 'Let me speak to her.' She can feel her adolescence receding. So distant now. Adulthood coming at her like a rocket.

'She won't let me approach. Please just come,' Sondra says.

Nevis thinks. Can I do this? Do I have a choice? She takes a deep breath. You always have a choice, Nevis. The right thing or the easy thing. Step up. Stop asking questions. Control yourself. Take a breath and quiet your heart. This is The Moment.

'Tell Satnam I will be there in fifteen minutes.' Her voice sounds weirdly distant, Nevis thinks, as if it belongs to someone else. She grabs her phone to summon an Uber and throws on clothes. A different person from moments ago. A crisis will do that. In seconds she's rushing down the stairs and into the street, one eye on her screen to follow the progress of the taxi, willing the driver to go faster. Farok in the black Prius, *come on*. Three minutes, two, one. The longest one hundred and eighty seconds in history. There's a moment, maybe a second or two, when she loses heart and thinks, how can I do this? But how can she not? Satnam is her best friend, her only friend. Nevis owes her this.

The Prius has barely come to a stop at the side of the pavement before Nevis is throwing open the door and hurling her body inside. Farok whips his head round, meets the expression on her face with a look of alarm.

'Nevis, Clifton Bridge?'

'Yes. It's not what you think. Or it is what you think, but it's not me, it's my friend.'

Farok hesitates for a second as if trying to decide whether this ride is way above his pay grade. He turns back to the dashboard and glances at her in the rear-view mirror and – miracle – a look of resolution is on his face. He's decided this one is worth doing.

'OK,' he says. 'We'll go very fast.'

As they speed up the hill towards Clifton she calls Satnam's number again, but the device goes to voicemail. What if it's too late? Oh God, please no. This is like solving an equation, Nevis tells herself, perhaps the most complicated, challenging equation you have ever been asked to solve. There will be a point where you can take one of several different pathways. Only one of these pathways will lead to the correct solution. You have to think it through. You have to get it right.

But how? She does not have all the parameters. This isn't the Satnam that she knows. This is not the friend who sits on her bed and watches crap telly or the friend who called out the wanker who thought it was funny to spray-paint 'Mentalist' on Nevis's daypack. This isn't the friend who dreams of becoming a medical researcher, the girl who is determined to marry for love whatever her parents might think. It's not the girl who jogs even when it's raining and is always happy to share her chips. But perhaps the Satnam on the bridge is the same Satnam who says she's going to the library but never seems to be there, the friend who has lost weight recently but says she hasn't, the one who cries in her bedroom and once – recently – threatened to leave Avon University. Perhaps this Satnam has secrets.

People are complicated. Satnam is complicated. If only people were as simple as mathematics.

'I don't know what to do,' Nevis says, to no one in particular.

The person she would normally ask in a situation like this is Satnam. Because Satnam has everyday, ordinary, practical smarts. Nevis has maths smarts as well as knowing a great deal about river birds. But Nevis has no people smarts. I am useless, she thinks.

Farok doesn't answer. He doesn't know either. Of course he doesn't. He has no idea. In any case, he's doing what he can, which is driving really very fast across the northern edges of the city towards Clifton. Farok is looking at Nevis in the rear-view mirror. He also seems terribly concerned.

I can't speak, Nevis thinks, the words have gone. There is just wire wool in my throat where sentences should be. Who can I text to help me?

She pulls out her phone. There are so few numbers in her contacts. There is Honor of course but they haven't really spoken in months, not since Nevis found the letter.

ONE PLACE. MANY STORIES

Bold, innovative and
empowering publishing.

FOLLOW US ON:

@HQStories